Hunting

by Andrea K Höst

Hunting
© 2013 Andrea K Höst. All rights reserved.
ISBN: 978-0-9872651-0-4
EBook ISBN: 978-0-9872651-1-1
www.andreakhost.com
Cover art: Julie Dillon

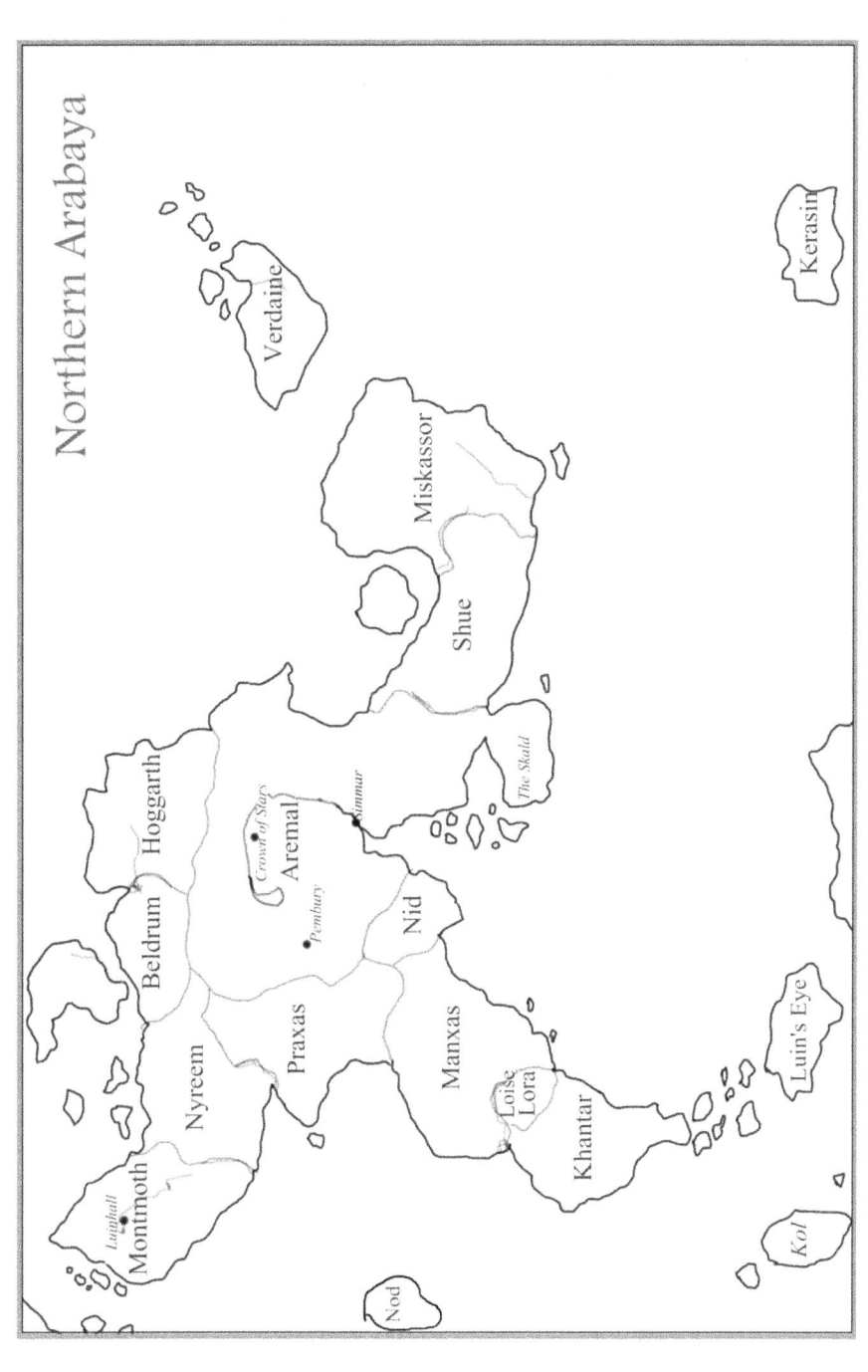

Northern Arabaya

Kerasin

Verdaine

Miskassor

Shue

Hoggarth

Beldrum

Crown of Stars
Aremal
Simmur

Pembury

The Skald

Nid

Nyreem

Praxas

Manxas

Montmoth

Laughall

Loise
Lora

Khantar

Luin's Eye

Nod

Kol

PROLOGUE

A barefoot, smoke-scented girl sat above the River Milk. Deep night transformed the river into a murmuring blackness, and its glacier-fed waters exhaled cold as they split around Luin's Island. In the dual light of the moons, the girl studied the single statue that filled the island, tracing the winding cloth that hid Luin's breasts but revealed the angular, more masculine planes of the stomach.

An accented voice interrupted her reverie. "Thinking of jumping?"

Sitting between the stanchions that separated road from river, the girl had expected the gloom to conceal her. But she kept her response calm, simply glancing over her shoulder at a lush-figured, curly-haired shape standing silhouetted against one of the hanging streetlights.

"Thinking of climbing."

The woman laughed. "Because it's there?"

"Because if I tied a ribbon in its hair, everyone would see it." The girl shrugged. "But I need a bigger ribbon, and I maybe need to be taller to get from the robe folds to the arms."

"A ribbon? As a boast? Or...a message? Well, I agree that you need a few more inches to attempt Luin, but I'm sure we can find you something else notable to adorn. Save Luin for later?"

The woman's quick understanding startled the girl, but the offer of assistance she dismissed with a shake of her head. "I'm not short of ideas."

"Just a place to sleep?"

Not inclined to tolerate interfering do-gooders, the girl decided it was time to leave, and stood. "I'm fine."

"Also short of shoes, I see," the woman added. "How were you planning to get to the island?"

"The Kylo ferry's just upstream. If you let it down by the guide ropes, it's only a short jump."

"Huh. What about Astenar's Mask above the Bowl? That's in shadow at the moment. I could lower you down by the ankles. You'd get wet, of course, but it's the second-most visible thing in the city. And the wash might make you smell a little less like bacon."

The girl gasped, and then laughed.

"You want to dangle me in the Milk? I'd end up a block of ice."

"I've night passes to Rithmay's Bathhouse, just a street away," the woman said. "And I've spare shoes. And a place to sleep. Most of all, no price, no conditions attached. Though I would like to see a ribbon in Luin's hair one day."

The girl, who had had no intention of trusting helpful strangers, looked back up at the statue, which almost all of the world would have told her she was mad to consider climbing. And the wound spring that had driven her since sunset suddenly relaxed.

"I'll take that bargain. One day, a ribbon for Luin's hair. Because it's there."

"Do you have a name, then?" the woman asked, turning upriver. "I'm Genevieve."

There was a limit to trust.

"Ash," the girl said, and followed.

CHAPTER ONE

Ash Lenthard struggled to hide her rage.

Strangers were walking through Genevieve's house. Tramping into the still-room in their heavy boots, fumbling through the small shelf of books, crushing the plants lined in orderly rows in the huge garden. Uncaring outsiders in Genevieve's bedroom, standing over unmoving flesh, ignorant of all that had been wonderful about the woman whose home they invaded. Just another in a series of unexplained deaths.

But Ash's fury was for herself, not the city's Watch. In the last two months, six people had been murdered in Luinhall. The one link they shared was their knowledge of remedies, of medicines and herbs. It had seemed only logical to Ash for her herb-wise guardian to leave the city until the killer had been caught, but Genevieve, who had so much to risk in an early death, had refused. They had quarrelled about it not two days ago, Ash searching for the right argument while Genevieve, calmly immovable despite all that she'd told Ash about her past, had refused to abandon clients who relied on her skills.

Too little effort too late. Now Ash, a sun-browned young woman dressed as a boy, huddled in the big chair in the kitchen, bereft of all her usual self-command. She could not move past the fact of death. It had been beyond any nightmare Cuinefaer had brought her, to walk into her guardian's bedroom that morning and find...all that blood.

Everything smelled so wrong! All the old scents were there: sharp rosemary mingled with sweet marjoram, thyme, heartsease, pennyroyal, countless other herbs. But they had become thin, weak notes against a heavy, underlying iron.

A butter-soft voice cut through red thoughts.

"The condition is much better than I expected. A day or two of work and we can put it to use."

Disbelieving, Ash turned to see a plump, sweet-faced woman, smoothing her carefully coiled white hair and surveying the room as if she owned it. Which, Ash hated to admit, she did. Something glittered in the woman's eyes as they found Ash's, but her expression held nothing but cloying sympathy.

"Poor child. A terrible thing to have happened. But perhaps not unexpected. Didn't I say just yesterday, Morton, that Sera Haiden took a dreadful risk remaining in Luinhall?"

"Yes, my love," said Morton, a towering bulk in the background. He wore a long-barrelled pistol tucked in his belt, and gripped a heavy, silver-topped cane that could easily be used as a cudgel if the chancy flintlock failed him.

"Allow the lad to remain and recover himself while the cleaning crew works," the woman continued. "So long as he does not get in their way, I do not see the harm of it. Though remind the crew that both house and contents are my property."

Ash rose to her feet, hands curling into fists. How could she? Genevieve wasn't even out of the house and this creature was already flourishing her triumph? Gloating beneath her show of sympathy.

The woman's sweetly complacent smile widened a fraction, a deliberate goad. Ordinarily Ash would have no difficulty controlling herself, but the temptation to take the bait filled her, until that smug expression at least wavered. She was no bravo, no mound of muscle, not even the boy she pretended to be, but to have this excuse for a person in the house that had become a refuge...

A quick step behind, then a strong hand closed over Ash's shoulder. "Don't be a fool, boy. She'd see you hanged," said a voice too low for the other occupants of the room to hear. Then, louder: "Can I assist you, Landhold Dunn?"

The woman became brisk. "I could hope that the Watch would find some level of competence and prevent further tragedies. As it is, I expect that you at least exercise your duty toward my property and ensure that nothing is taken from it."

"You'll see no harm," said Captain Garton, voice flat. Garton, kind beneath his gruff demeanour, had been a firm friend of Genevieve's and certainly no ally of 'Charity' Dunn. But opposing the wealthiest Smallholder in the Commons would do him no good.

"Well now, I wish I could believe that, Captain." Landhold Dunn gave a tiny, regretful shake of her head. "But the Watch has done so little to inspire confidence these past weeks."

The exchange brought Ash back to a more usual frame of mind, and she slipped out of Captain Garton's hold, heading for her bedroom. Charity Dunn was a triviality, nothing which would distract her from a newly absolute imperative: finding Genevieve's killer.

The pocket-sized bedroom held a host of memories, but few belongings. Genevieve had not been wealthy, always giving away any excess – buying redemption, she would say – so a single bag was enough to take care of most of Ash's belongings. Two items could not be so easily managed.

From the gap between mattress and wall she removed a heavy roll of leather, which she wrapped in her spare breast-band. Briefly cracking the shutters, she dropped the bundle into the lavender growing outside her window. Something to collect later. The book of tales and Genevieve's Herbal were too fragile to stash outside and too large to conceal in the bag, so she simply wrapped them in a shirt and carried them in her arms.

It did not surprise Ash in the least when Landhold Dunn made a diffident noise at her return. The woman had spent years wishing Genevieve gone, and this performance was simply some late-served revenge.

"Such a discomforting thing," Landhold Dunn said. "You understand, of course, Captain, that the boy's bag will need to be checked. That will clear any shadow of doubt."

"Surely there's no–" Captain Garton began, but Ash forestalled any further argument by putting the books on the table and upending her bag beside them. Sturdy, serviceable cloth, a few useful ointments, and a purse holding a scattering of coins.

"Morton, if you would..."

Ash supposed she was meant to be humiliated, or protest the injustice. The salves in the stillroom and the potential held in the garden had not insignificant value. But sorting through the house and establishing exactly what belonged to Landhold Dunn would only be time wasted. Ash felt nothing but impatience, her mind already on options once she had left this house behind her.

The colourless man who was Landhold Dunn's husband moved forward, sorting delicately, and then unfolding the shirt to reveal the two books.

"I recall there was a small library," Landhold Dunn said. Her eyes were bright, summoning a small flare of spite from Ash, wishing the Smallholder would finally accrue enough land to stand before Luin and be tested for her worth as guardian. Though from what Ash had seen of the world, Luin would probably accept her. Charity Dunn would not be the first truly awful person to gain the privileges of the Luinsel.

And now was not the moment to care. "The books are written in Khanteck," Ash said, forcing a note of indifferent confidence. "These were Genevieve's and she gave them to me."

"Well now, it's not that I don't wish I could take your word on that—"

"What is going on back here? Captain, can't you keep these people out?"

It was the Investigator, bringing with her an air of effortless authority, despite the fact that she was, of all unlikely things, a woman in the Rhoi's Guard. She came into the kitchen, wiping her hands on a rag, and Ash stared at the red stains on that greying cloth, forgetting Landhold Dunn in favour of the tragedy that had destroyed her happiness. Genevieve was dead, her throat slit neatly from side to side, face robbed of its serenity by a permanent expression of surprise.

"Who is this?" the Investigator asked Garton.

"Landhold Dunn, Sera. She, uh, this is her house."

"Oh? The herbalist did not own it?"

"I fear Sera Haiden was far from being in such a position," Landhold Dunn said, her treacle-tone thinning just a fraction.

"Have you information for us? If not, I'll have to ask you to vacate the area until the initial investigations are done. The Captain here will send you word."

Charity Dunn clearly resented the crisp dismissal, but her Smallholder's rights naturally gave way to palace authority.

"There is just a question of ownership of some valuable books," the Landhold murmured. "I simply can't permit anything to leave the premises until some evidence of ownership has been produced."

"Books in the language of Khantar," Captain Garton murmured.

"The herbalist's homeland?" The Investigator's clear grey eyes assessed Charity Dunn. "Well, if you can offer some proof that you own such, Holder, I'm certain they can be returned to you. Perhaps you have some form of inventory? If you oblige us by providing it, the Captain here will be able to ensure nothing listed is removed."

The Investigator turned away, clearly dismissing the Landhold from her thoughts. Unlike Garton, the woman was not a low paid Watch Captain responsible for a small part of the city's general safety, but a member of the Rhoi's Guard, trained to deal with tricky problems troubling Luinhall and ensure the Rhoi's safety. The rod of authority awarded her could not be taken by any but the Rhoi.

Stymied, Charity Dunn took her leave with carefully maintained dignity, and a smile for Ash that would chill a lesser girl's heart.

"What was that about?" the Investigator asked Garton, flipping open the cover of one of the books.

"Landhold Dunn's father left this house to Sera Haiden for the term of her life. Gave him back the use of his hands, she did. Landhold Dunn always...resented the bequest." Garton's eyes flickered over the five men and women standing in the room, obviously wondering if word of what he said could possibly get back to Charity Dunn.

"And this is Khanteck?" the Investigator asked, flicking a page of one precious book. "You can read this, boy?"

Ash, who had been barely responsive during the Investigator's previous attempt to question her, nodded and tried to suppress her desire for action. This woman should be regarded as a useful source of information, or at least another hurdle to Ash's speedy departure.

The Investigator passed the books to a man who had watched the exchange without comment. This was some form of foreign Landhold, his black hair and bronzed skin suggesting a Firuvari heritage, though the closely tailored thigh-length robe of heavy cream cloth decorated with near-invisible geometrical embroidery was an Aremish style. Ash only half restrained her frown. Ghoul. What was he doing here, prying into Genevieve's death?

"You have relatives you can go to, boy?" the Investigator asked.

"He's an orphan," Captain Garton answered before Ash could glibly invent a half-dozen other aunts. "Sera Haiden was his only living relation." Ash glared at him and the Captain shook his head. "Genevieve would haunt me if I let you run off to join that street gang you get around with, Ash. You'll come home with me for now."

"I'm not going to push your brood out of what little space they have, Captain. Besides, you live in one of Charity Dunn's shoeboxes and she'll treble your rent the instant she hears I'm there. I've places to go, thanks all the same."

"Did your aunt teach you her trade, boy?" the foreign Landhold asked, his voice only lightly accented. He closed the book he had been flipping through: Genevieve's herbal reference, her most precious possession, which she'd bestowed on Ash with more formality than Ash had ever seen from her. As he asked this question, the Landhold shook his head, ever so slightly. A barely detectable order.

"No," Ash said, since that was what she had been planning to say anyway. Admitting you had herbal knowledge had recently become a dangerous thing. But this man must suspect otherwise, since he'd been looking at the Herbal as if he could read it, or at least could make a simple deduction from the detailed illustrations. "She taught a girl named Jenna a bit, though." Ash had regular employment exercising animals at a nearby stable. Only a few people knew that she'd made any shift to learn what Genevieve could teach her.

"I'll take charge of him, Verel," the Landhold said, to Ash's complete surprise. "I'm told I need a seruilis."

Ash stared and even the Investigator looked a little unsure, but shrugged. "As you wish," she said. "At least I'll know where to find him, if he's with you.

The man nodded. "Tell me if you find anything unusual," he said, picking up the other book from the table and glancing at the frontispiece. It was a book of heroic tales, and Ash resented him handling it almost as much as his calm assumption that he could command her into service as a seruilis, if that was what he truly intended. It was a period of training-by-observation usually reserved for Kinsel, family of Luinsel who wanted to learn more about maintaining Luin's Laws of Balance.

She studied the stranger warily: a commanding figure with a thin sword at his side, undecorated and serviceable. The tight tailoring of the robe showed him to be athletic and he was handsome enough, with a faintly aquiline nose and high cut cheekbones, his hair short at the nape, but the bangs worn longer and swept back. Glossy black wings.

Ash checked his hands and saw none of the roughness that spoke of heavy labour. Long, thin fingers, the nails not manicured, but not ragged with continual work, either. His boots were more than fine. If he wanted a seruilis, did that mean he was Luinsel?

Not that it mattered. She had no intention of playing servant-apprentice. Biding her time, Ash scooped her clothing back into its bag.

"I'll send word about the funeral arrangements," Captain Garton said

Ash blocked her mind from thoughts of what that funeral would mean and nodded, then let the stranger lead her outside.

CHAPTER TWO

A curious, watchful crowd had gathered. Nervous strangers, and a few familiar faces, made distant by fear. Luinhall was dealing not only with murder, but also a spate of disappearances. Nerves were on edge, and if Ash tried to abandon the Landhold here, there was a fair chance that they'd catch and hold her.

Fortunately, the Landhold led her down the side alley to speak to yet another Watchman, this one in charge of a collection of horses. If she went over the wall into Renus' garden...

"Can I have my books back, please?" she asked as he returned, and then was distracted by the animal he led.

The equipage was plain and serviceable, but the horse itself was the finest she'd ever seen. Black with one white sock, more than eighteen hands high and close to perfect in form. A stallion, which was chancy for a riding animal, but this beauty looked to have been trained out of any immediate displays of temperament. Ash found herself rechecking his points in the hope of spotting some narrowness of the shoulders or splaying of hooves. As if aware of the inspection, the stallion curved his fine, muscular neck, stepping smartly.

The Rhoi's mount probably didn't show better than this, and Ash reached out involuntarily to offer her hand. The stallion condescended to whuffle at her skin, ears pricking back and forth, obviously excited by the too-near presence of the crowd.

The Landhold unbuckled a saddlebag, and slid her wrapped books inside instead of returning them as asked. "Much as Arth here would like a run, I've no wish to spend what's left of the morning chasing you down."

It had been too much to hope that he was stupid, but maybe he could be talked out of this impulse.

"I'm not going with you," Ash said, bluntly, and followed his glance to the Watchman, who wasn't quite close enough to hear what they were saying, but was gazing at them in obvious interest. "Find yourself another seruilis."

"I don't recall offering you a choice," the Landhold said pleasantly. He mounted, splits in his robe's skirt showing it was designed for riding, and held a hand down to her, bronzed fingers parted. His bangs flopped into his eyes, spoiling the authority of the gesture.

Looking at the outstretched hand, Ash made a face. Well, she'd just have to run off later rather than sooner. After she'd ridden this extremely magnificent piece of horseflesh and stolen her books back.

Wishing she had her knives, Ash handed the man her bag, gripped the saddle and sprang up behind him. He passed her bag back, waited till she'd taken a light hold of his robe, and then nudged the stallion into motion.

The black had an easy gait, but giving in never did Ash's temper a great deal of good, and she spent her energy on glowering at the Landhold's back and being annoyed at his height as he negotiated the press of people, skirted a nightsoil wagon, and oriented on the towering statue of Luin which rose out of the River Milk. But by the time they joined the flow of morning traffic on the Great River Road Ash had recovered her equilibrium, turning her mind seriously to the possibility of making use of the man, or giving up on her books and running.

She made a quick survey – from the side valleys and heavily planted slopes of Westgard to the abrupt, fern-bedecked rise of Eastwall – seeing nothing unusual in the city packed between the two mountains. Luin's stone face, carved with careful ambiguity to match a god's dual aspect, offered no guidance.

"Where are you taking me?"

The Landhold turned his head, but didn't slacken the stallion's swift walk. "To the palace."

"Why?"

"I told you. I need a seruilis."

"And I told you, I'm not going to be your seruilis. I've better things to do with my time." Ash wasn't in the mood to mince words.

"There are some who might consider it an honour to serve me in that capacity." He sounded amused, not offended.

"Well, why don't you go give them the opportunity? And stop lying to me, while you're at it. Seruilisi, in case someone never explained the concept to you, are supposed to be the children of Luinsel learning the duties of their parents. Why are you really taking me with you?"

"I've thrashed men, in my time, for calling me a liar," he said, still in the same pleasant tone.

"Then that should give you some idea of just how tiresome a seruilis I'd be," Ash said reasonably. "Think of the energy you'd save if you had a seruilis happy to let you fib all day just to avoid being beaten up by someone twice his size." Part of this response was her grief and anger resurfacing, but only part. Most of the rest was calculated risk, with a fraction of enjoyment at saying outrageous things. "Anyway, I'm going to run off the first opportunity I get," she informed him.

"Why?" He wasn't the slightest bit perturbed, guiding the stallion expertly through the bustle of the city's busiest road.

"The Landsmeet's a viper pit. And as I said, I've better things to do with my time than playing your servant."

"Revenging your aunt?"

She supposed that was a natural conclusion. "Yes."

"From what the Captain said of her, she didn't strike me as the kind of person who would wish her nephew to burden himself with the cost of vengeance."

Ash didn't reply immediately, not wanting the tears in her eyes to be obvious in her voice. He was wrong, besides. Genevieve had had a highly complicated attitude toward the question of taking life. For all that her guardian had never believed that she could balance the debts of her past, she had refused to be paralysed by the fear of damnation. It was Ash who would hesitate at the thought of killing, no matter how necessary it felt.

"Genevieve would expect me to not charge in headlong, but do my best to prevent further murders. Which is beside the point. If you need a seruilis, go commandeer someone suitable for the role from the Kinsel."

"But none of the Kinsel I've encountered were raised by a herbalist," he said, matching her earlier tone of implacable reason. "Nor would a book of herbalist lore be their first choice of objects to take with them when being precipitately evicted."

"So you want a herbalist, not a seruilis."

"I want an ally whose skill with herbs is not generally known, and who has every reason to not align himself with the killer. Someone with no connection to the Landsmeet."

That had the tang of truth, which made it harder to simply reject the idea. "You think the person behind the killings is among the Luinsel?"

"Perhaps. It seems clumsy and obvious, but this could be a precursor to an attack on a much-scrutinised target. A friend asked me to aid the Guard in their investigation because I have Estarrel blood which, if nothing else, allows me to confirm that the same person brought about all the deaths. Consider me a source of information, and an opportunity to hunt for the motive for all this."

It was true that Ash had few immediate routes of investigation, though there would be many eager to aid her in finding Genevieve's murderer. Estarrel blood was a surprise – he meant he was related to the family of the Aremish Rhoi, descendents of the Sun and the World.

"If I stick around, do I have to bow and scrape to you?"

"What a burden that would be. In public. For the sake of verisimilitude, if nothing else."

If he had hoped to stump her with the word, he was in for a disappointment. It was one that Genevieve had used often when Ash had first come to her. And there was the rub. This new deception may well compromise the old, and the Landsmeet was not the safest place for Ash to be.

"What would being your seruilis involve?"

"Running my errands, attending to my equipage, serving me at table, doing whatever else I require of you. Attending the Mern and listening for anything useful."

"I'm not likely to be very good at it," she said cautiously, summoning up vague childhood memories of harried seruilisi running to and fro and enjoying themselves very little indeed. "They'll think you strange to have a seruilis like me."

"You will learn to be good at it," he said, in an uncompromising tone of voice. "And 'they' seem to think anyone not born to this Rhoimarch strange."

"Is there someone you suspect?"

"Nothing beyond complete guesswork. You?"

"Not yet. If you hit me I will hit you back."

"I doubt it. I do have limits to my patience. And I am, as you pointed out, somewhat larger than you. No, you will act as my seruilis and you will do your job well in order to increase your chance for revenge. If you please me, I will teach you swordplay, though you are late come to the art."

The man obviously considered that a high treat, and Ash wondered whether to tell him she couldn't be less interested. Knives were her weapons.

"Are you any good?"

Her exaggeratedly dubious tone only made him laugh. "Stop trying to provoke me, boy. What's your full name?"

"Ash Lenthard. What's yours?"

"Rion Thornaster, Visel of Pembury."

Visel meant he was the lowest rank of the Luinsel, with just enough property to drink from the Well of the Heart and be judged on his worth as a steward of the land, one of the Luinsel who strove to keep a Balance between the needs of Luin's children and Luin's own health. But it was the man's name that gave Ash pause. Thornaster, one of the foreigners behind the Rhoi's review of Montmoth's laws, and focus of far too much attention to be comfortable.

They had reached the mid-section of the river, where water tinted white by powdered rock thundered down from the ridge called Luin's Table. Since the bridges around the Bowl – the circular pool at the fall's base – were the busiest part of the city, Ash kept her silence as Thornaster crossed the Milk and headed beneath the natural stone arch which guarded the climb to the Deirhoi District. The stallion briefly shifted from a walk to a trot, and Ash firmed her grip on the man's robe, thinking through the complications of deception. She had changed a great deal, but her pretence would be put to the greatest test if she stayed with this man.

"Where did you live before you came to your aunt?" Thornaster asked, oblivious to the hurdles she faced.

"Khantar."

"Which part, Ash Lenthard? Don't be obtuse."

"I lived in the third house from the west end of the main street of the village of Cadoken in the shire of Meeps in north-west Khantar. It rained every second day and we saw the sun for a good ten hours every year. It smelled of mud and rot." Ash had never been out of the Rhoimarch of Montmoth in her life, but Genevieve had brought Cadoken to life for her. Ash had long since cherished a heartfelt desire never to go there. "I was only nine when I left," she added.

"How old are you now?"

"Seventeen. Almost." Twenty-one in a few weeks, but no one would ever believe that to look at her. Not without beginning to wonder at her beardless cheeks and slight build. "Where's Pembury?"

"Southwest of Crown of Stars."

Crown of Stars was the capital of Aremal, a sprawling Rhoimarch on the far side of Montmoth's neighbour's neighbour. When pieces of the shattered moon, Yurefaer, had rained down on Luin, it had been at Crown of Stars that two of the gods – Luin and the new Sun, Astenar – had manifested to still the trembling in Luin's depths and clear the skies. When the worst had passed, the two gods had lingered to leave behind three children who had become the rulers of the great Rhoimarches – Aremal, Firuvar and, on the far side of Luin, Araslea. The Estarrel line descended from the child Astenar had born to Luin.

Montmoth – like Ash – had issues with the god who had become the Sun, but the link to Astenar had certainly benefited Aremal, which remained the most powerful and stable Rhoimarch of the region. Montmoth's old Rhoi had sent the current one there for some form of advanced schooling, and he'd stayed away for almost two years, until his father had died unexpectedly at the end of autumn.

Arun Nemator had returned in time to be judged, however, and brought this Thornaster back with him. Someone who would be the focus of a lot of attention among the pale grey towers of the palace in the centre of the sheltered Deirhoi Valley. It would be a gamble for Ash to show her face there, but not truly a great one, surely. Eight years had passed, and there were few who had actually known her.

"What's Pembury like?" she asked, needing to distract herself.

"Hilly."

"You're a real wordsmith. You should consider a career as a player."

"And you would make a remarkable diplomat, Ash. I shall recommend you. Now close your mouth and, if you cannot master your tongue, say nothing."

Ash snorted, but kept quiet as they followed the hedge-lined side road to the Inner Stables. The stallion came to a restless halt and Ash hopped lightly to the ground, watching Thornaster as he dismounted. This was the second time someone new had arrived just as her world had turned sideways. But Ash was no longer a child and did not feel any need to confide in this foreign Landhold. He was not Genevieve. He plainly saw her as a potential spy, with useful herbal knowledge, but if he led her to Genevieve's killer she would owe him her thanks. Until then, she would play the part he had assigned her, would even make a game of it.

And consider her own opinions on vengeance.

CHAPTER THREE

The Inner Stables, which housed the most important Luinsels' horses, was all bustle and dash with an underlay of dust and dung. The foreign Visel took her books out of the saddlebag, handed the reins to the nearest stableboy and, with barely a glance to see if Ash was following, headed into the palace.

For a short time Ash tried to imitate the easy glide of his walk, but couldn't quite manage it. Genevieve had coached her on how to walk, talk, look at people, hold her hands, eat and laugh and do a host of things which subtly led people to see her as male, but she had not been able to alter her bone structure. Giving up the attempt, Ash's attention was caught by the group of the people they were passing.

An angular, bony man in lead pretended to flick some speck of dirt from the sleeve of his dusky purple coat, then raised stony eyes at the last moment and greeted Thornaster with the merest fraction of a nod as he swept past, a half-dozen followers and attendants trailing in his wake all taking their cue from their master.

Schooling her face not to reveal her sudden interest, Ash took in the surreptitious glances over shoulders, the guardsman whose mouth turned down suddenly, the woman who checked at the sight of Thornaster and developed a sudden interest in her hands, while her companion blushed and preened. Fascinating. Thornaster was certainly not popular among the Landsmeet, few reacting with pleasure at the sight of him striding along. Not terribly surprising, given all the rumours of his influence over the Rhoi, and their plans to remake Montmoth in Aremal's image, but she hadn't expected people to show their feelings so openly.

Preoccupied, it was possible the Visel didn't even notice.

Thornaster opened their way, finally, into an equally surprising apartment. Unless there was a considerable space shortage, these small rooms were an insult to a man of his rank, let alone a good friend of the Rhoi. A desk and brazier barely fit in the first. The other contained only a couple of chests, a pair of narrow side tables, and a bed that lacked even bed curtains to cover the ceiling-scraping frame. Her own room, in Genevieve's house, hadn't been much smaller.

A cloth covered the wall at the foot of the bed, and the Visel tied this back to reveal an alcove about three feet deep and a little less than a body-length long. A couple of leather bags were piled down one end. These he lifted out and replaced with three blankets from one of the chests.

"Do all seruilisi sleep on the floor?" Ash asked, eyeing these arrangements dubiously.

"Seruilisi sleep wherever is convenient to their masters," Thornaster replied. He picked up one of the bed's two pillows and dropped it on the blankets, then added one of Ash's books to the pile. "You don't have a Khanteck accent."

"I can do one, if you really want me to," she retorted, with her best imitation of Genevieve's slightly lilting turn of phrase. "I've not forgotten how to speak. Genevieve liked to use Khanteck about the house." It was becoming slightly easier to say her benefactress' name. There was still a catch in her throat each time she formed the word, but not as noticeable. "How do you know the tongue?"

"It helps to be conversant when you're in my position," he replied absently, turning through the pages of her book of tales.

His position as Visel, or as a relative of the Rhoi of Aremal? The Rhoimarches of Northern Arabaya had once shared a common language, which had evolved into distinct dialects, but Khantar was not part of that group, or a neighbour of Aremal. Perhaps because it lay on the major land route to Firuvar, and sent out so many traders?

"This is a very valuable book," Thornaster told her, looking up from an illustration of a makki cat. "Extremely old, in remarkable condition. A teaching text in the Old Tongue and Khanteck both."

"I know," Ash replied, shortly. Genevieve had brought it from Khantar, like the Herbal. Turning away to hide the tears once again springing to her eyes, she headed for the single, rather poky window. The little table before it was dusty. "Don't you have any servants?" she asked crossly. "You're a funny sort of Luinsel."

"I'm travelling light," the man replied, neither angry nor amused now. A little wry, perhaps.

"You've been in Luinhall for months. That's not travelling. No wonder they don't want to greet you." The tears were being obstinate, threatening to spill no matter how she worked to keep them back.

"Greet me?" Thornaster echoed, understandably a little lost.

"The people in the corridor. Wondering if they should be polite or snub you, not knowing if you're even really a Visel. You should collect two or three retainers to impress people with your importance."

"Well, you could say I've made a start. For now, stay here while I go speak with Arun."

He moved to the door, but didn't leave. Ash could feel him looking at her stiff, unhappy figure, but for the moment couldn't summon a stalwart display.

"There's no shame in mourning, lad," he added. "Honour your dead."

Ash waited till the door in the next room had opened and closed, then, with a choking gasp, dropped to her knees and, for the second time that day, wept till she was ill and empty, numb beyond action. She was not given to tears, but she had failed Genevieve, who had most particular reasons to postpone death as long as possible.

Thornaster's prolonged absence gave Ash the space to recover, and then to search his belongings. Two rapiers, two sabres, and the weapon he'd been wearing, which seemed to be some compromise between rapier and sabre. Two long daggers, and some smaller blades, but no revelations, though there was a locked box, heavy and flat, which might give her more information if she could find the key. That done, she leaned against one post of his bed and decided whether or not to be there when he came back.

What chance that anyone would look at a wiry and sun-browned boy and recognise a sallow slip of a girl thought to have died eight years ago? Cutting off her unsatisfactory braids had made an enormous difference, with her short brown hair lifting in a near-curl, but the pointed shape of her face had not changed. Still, her features were not particularly unusual, and Genevieve had taught her to school the individuality from her expression.

With her father dead, and her mother remarried and living in the Folding Valley, only Kiri posed any real risk. Childhood neighbour and friend, she had known Ash's former self best, and was the only person who Ash had given any hint that she lived. Once, Ash would have been completely certain Kiri would not betray her, but it had been years.

Surely Genevieve was worth the risk?

By the time Thornaster returned Ash had herself in hand, and was weighing different plans of action. The Visel looked at her sharply as he came in, and seemed to nod to himself.

"Very well. Your duties here are to keep my rooms clean, to ensure that there is always water available for my use, to receive callers, lay out my gear, assist me in dressing, and do anything that looks like it needs doing, all of which should be performed without calling attention to yourself or disturbing me in any way. Is that clear?"

Ash supposed that by remaining in the room she had made some sort of implicit agreement to act as this man's servant. She hadn't even thought of his departure as a test, but there had been nothing to stop her leaving.

"Who helped you get dressed up till now?"

"No one," the man replied, his expression flickering. Ash realised that, whatever his motives had started as, part of the reason the Visel was doing this was because he found Ash entertaining.

"Then why do you need me to help you do it now?"

"I don't, boy. But it is part of the duties of first seruilis when there is not a servant specifically employed for wardrobe, so you will do so."

"First seruilis?"

"In a group of seruilisi, the oldest or best-skilled is usually first seruilis, unless another is promoted over him. That, however, is an extreme punishment."

"Oh. Are you going on a recruiting drive then? I don't think you'll fit many more seruilisi in here."

"You'll do for now. I wouldn't want to impress people too greatly with the number of my retainers."

Ash couldn't restrain an amused twitch of her lips, but allowed the comment to pass. "You said my duties here. What are my duties elsewhere? Do I get to look after that horse?"

"Perhaps. If I judge you able and if he accepts you. Arth is very particular in his choice of attendants." His eyes, a dark brown-black, narrowed. "I trust you aren't quite fool enough to try to ride him. You haven't the strength to control him and I would take any damage to him out of your hide."

Ash, who had a great deal of confidence in her ability to ride anything vaguely resembling a horse, experienced an instant desire to prove him wrong, but she had to admit that she had never attempted an animal as sheerly powerful as Thornaster's black. Not that that was any reason not to try. She would consider the question again if an opportunity presented itself.

From Thornaster's expression, she'd allowed the progress of her thoughts to show too clearly on her face, but he refrained from comment. "I'll detail any other specific duties at another time," he said. "You will attend the Mern with your fellow seruilisi. As a rule, your afternoons will be spent with them, though you will not join them at swordplay. I have already given instructions on that point. Master Humboldt is expecting you in the Mern in a ten-measure. He will outfit you in my colours." He pulled a key from his pocket, and handed it to Ash. "This is a spare. Don't lose it."

She glanced at it. "What are your colours?"

"Pembury is dark grey and blue. When you wear those colours you represent Pembury and you will do nothing to bring shame upon it. Any transgressions of conduct you make beyond this room will merit disciplinary action by the Master of the Mern."

"And if I don't...polish your boots and stuff like that here?"

"Then I will make you wish that you had."

"I'll bet. Were you ever a seruilis?"

"Yes."

"What was it like?"

He looked thoughtful, obviously choosing how to answer.

"That bad?"

"Not really. I had a little trouble with my fellows, who thought me overproud. I earned myself friends and enemies in the usual fashion. It did not help that I was insufferably sure that my way was correct."

Ash looked for exactly the right reply to this, and decided he didn't need to be told how little he'd changed. "Remind me never to become a seruilis for real," she said. "Where's the Mern?"

"It's not far from the stables. Ask your way." He let her head for the door. "And Ash?" She looked back. "You are a seruilis for real. Don't mistake that."

He thought he was rescuing her. Giving the orphaned boy she seemed to be the colours and the protection of his House. A fatally flawed plan, if so.

"There are some," she said, trying to catch the exact tone of his voice, light, with an undernote of seriousness, "who might consider it an honour to serve you in that capacity."

She bowed low, a courtesy suitable for someone of far higher rank than a Visel. A bow to a Rhoi. Then, seeing that open amusement was the only reaction, she shrugged, and left.

CHAPTER FOUR

Ash lied habitually, but was not nearly so blithe-tongued as she had been working to appear. Out of Thornaster's sight she fought weary hurt. How had she managed to play games with words on the day Genevieve had died? The same morning? Was it a betrayal to be able to keep the anger and loss inside?

She couldn't let that matter. There was business to attend to before she could revisit grief, and she would restrain her sorrow for the sake of stopping further deaths. And the hunt would help her not think of the horror that would be Genevieve's funeral.

Finding the stone halls and yards of the Mern with time to spare, Ash considered her approach to her fellow seruilisi. She needed to ensure they didn't interfere with her investigations, but accepted her enough for palace gossip to come her way.

It would not be the first time she had inserted herself into a group. The most interesting people in Genevieve's neighbourhood had been a year or two younger than Ash, children of shop keeps and crafters. They had thought her a child of nine and regarded her as too young for their games. Instead of tagging along behind she'd led the way onto the roofs, her climbing gaining her acceptance, until she'd become one of those who shaped what was now The Huntsmen.

This new group of peers, drilling with slim wooden swords in a sand-strewn, sun-baked practice yard, were a more complicated proposition. The wider spread of ages created some issues, but the vagaries of rank would be the major difficulty. Theoretically she had nearly as much or little as this mixed bunch of boys and near-adults, who lived in the uncertain state of the children of Luinsel: only the first choice to stand before Luin rather than guaranteed heir. Even the Rhoi's younger brother and only near relative, the Veirhoi, could not become Rhoi unless Luin accepted him.

But rejection was not common. The Mern taught both matters of command, and of care for the land, ensuring the Kinsel were well versed in proper stewardship before they risked losing their land to Luin's judgment.

Ash crossed the sand toward a heavily muscled man who stood in the shade of one of the pale grey walls. Aware of many glances, she stopped a short distance from the man who could only be the Master of the Mern, waited a moment, and then began her new role as Thornaster's seruilis. Polite, she had decided. Respectful and obliging. Not without resource, but clearly marked by recent loss. They would not accept an impertinent imp.

"Your pardon for any intrusion, Ser. My name is Ash Lenthard. Visel Thornaster told me to report to you."

The Master's head turned slowly, and faded eyes studied Ash minutely, the man's face impassive beneath thick grey brows. "So," he said, a short exhalation of air two steps up from a grunt. Then he turned on his heel, walked away. "Follow," drifted back to her.

Obediently Ash followed, leaving the bright sun and clatter of wood on wood for a tangle of dim corridors leading to a room where a creamy-skinned woman directed a dozen underlings among bolts of every kind of cloth imaginable. Clothing cut, assembled or repaired: all very neat and orderly and efficient. Master Humboldt spoke to the woman in his brief, ponderous way, and she looked Ash over. Almost immediately Ash was provided with dark grey trousers and two shirts that, after a brief retreat behind a curtain hanging across a corner, proved to fit remarkably well. A search provided a second outfit of the same shade, but of a sturdier fabric.

Then the woman gestured forward a blonde-haired girl, who measured Ash across the shoulders and around the chest. After the measurements were done, she cut sections of heavy cloth, dark blue and grey, and pieced them together around Ash, fastening the forming tabard with pins. This was handed off to be sewn, while a second was cut.

Fascinated by the speed with which everything was being accomplished, Ash watched until Master Humboldt returned and began to circle her, studying the fit of her clothing, nudging one scuffed boot with a tip of his own. He was a man of considerable presence, breadth making up for a certain lack of height.

"Polish up," he mused, presumably to himself. "And another." Then he bent, fingered the side of her left boot, where the soft leather crossed and was over-laced. "Knife fighter?"

Ash was startled by his comprehension of the distortion, a gaping caused over time by a currently absent knife. "Yes, Ser," she said, a fraction late.

"Throwing or close quarters?"

"Throwing, Ser."

"You'll not carry them without permission. Other weapons?"

"Very basic staff work, Ser."

"Hit me," he ordered, holding his arms wide in invitation.

Ash blinked, then curled her hand into a fist and put her shoulder into a blow to his stomach, her arm jolting with the force of the impact. But the Master had set his feet and did not even rock with the blow.

"Do you dance?" he asked, face still wholly impassive.

Ash was beginning to find his measure now. He was watching her carefully, taking stock of her character through her reactions. She wondered how many new seruilisi he brought here to test. Judging from the unperturbed interest of the still-working seamstresses, more than one. "No, Ser," she replied, still respectful, a little more cautious. A dangerous man, this Master of the Mern. Between the Investigator, Thornaster and now Master Humboldt, she had had her fill of over-perceptive people that day. She did know many of the dance forms, but she had learned them from the female point of view.

"Swim?"

"No, Ser."

"Ride?"

"Yes, Ser."

"Cook?"

"Yes, Ser."

"Are you diseased?"

She didn't quite manage to maintain her rapid rate of reply, but the hesitation was only minor. "Not that I know of, Ser." That was a question one would ask a soldier, not one of the Mern, in training to lead. Is that what he considered her? A foot soldier thrust among his betters?

"Can you count?"

"Yes, Ser."

"Read? Write?"

"Yes, Ser."

"In Khanteck and the Old Tongue both?"

"Yes, Ser. Firuven, also, Ser, just a little."

He grunted. "Wait for the tabard. Then report to the first seruilis." He turned and walked out of the room without another word. Ash watched him leave, thoughtful. Had she passed, then?

The tabard was not a complex garment, but it required a lot of hemming, and two girls worked on it together while Ash watched their flying fingers. A few cautious questions showed her they were well aware of her link to the household of the latest murdered herbalist, and were inclined to treat her with wary sympathy. They thought the murders meant someone was going to poison the Rhoi.

Gossip. Ash had been sifting city rumours for weeks. Time to see if the palace had anything new.

CHAPTER FIVE

Freshly turned out in Thornaster's colours, Ash found the Mern's training ground deserted, but lucked upon a boy leaving as she arrived. He wore a dark blue shirt and black trousers, the uniform of Mern attendees who served no Luinsel as seruilis. When asked where to find the first seruilis he looked her over with considerable curiosity and behind his brief response Ash caught the wistful regret of one who knew he was going to miss out on a juicy scene. The new seruilis was obviously expected to be the source of some entertainment.

The boy's directions led to a room of raised voices. Ash paused out of sight of the open doorway and, keeping an eye on the corridor, listened.

"...out and out insult. We can't possibly allow a guttersnipe among us! Thornaster has run mad!" The voice was forceful, self-assured and genuinely angry.

"And the Master as well, it seems, since he has given his leave," pointed out another voice.

"Do you think he makes a deliberate comment?" asked a third voice, soft and serious. "That those among the Kinsel of Montmoth do not meet the Aremish standards of service to Luin?"

First Voice snorted. "More likely he chooses one who is unable to see how base-born the man is himself."

Ash smiled faintly. The divide between an ordinary person and a Landhold was simply ownership of land, but the Luinsel, Landholders accepted by Luin as guardians, were able to draw on Luin's strength in a limited fashion, to purify water or encourage growth. While the laws of Luin were very clear – anyone could be put forward to be judged worthy stewards of the land – it was still common for Kinsel to consider themselves born of superior stock, spiritually linked to Luin's self. Genevieve said – had said – that Montmoth was particularly bad in this respect. Among other things.

First Voice continued to hold forth: "I, for one, will not stand for it. He cannot foist this creature on us. Intentionally or not, it will be the worst parody imaginable, a gape-toothed yokel aping his betters. He'll tarnish us with his very presence."

A new voice broke in, laughing. "Can you see him at table?" The voice dropped into an unlikely accent, more South Valleys than city. "'Lumme! Nain't yer gointa eat t'rest o' thet there 'am 'ock? Luin firgive ye f'r bein' sich a wastral! 'Ere, lit me finish it orf f'r ye.'"

Laughter, ranging from giggles to deeper chuckles, gave Ash a chance to estimate the number of people in the room: perhaps seven or eight. This was not all the seruilisi then.

"Laugh as much as you want," First Voice said. "Wait till the laughter's directed at you, when he makes the entire Mern the butt of the city's jokes."

"Are you proposing a plan of action, Marriston, or just blowing hot air?" Second Voice asked.

"Mind your tongue, Vendarri!" the one called Marriston said, brusquely. "But yes, I am."

There was an expectant pause.

"It's quite simple, really," Marriston said. "A campaign, if you will, designed to teach the little ragamuffin how truly out of place he is. He won't last the week."

"You'll do no harm to a fellow seruilis, Marriston," said a new voice, its quiet authority making clear who held rank of first seruilis. From the sudden hush the words brought, the speaker must have entered the room through a second door.

"I'm not talking harm," Marriston replied, the faintest hint of deference in his voice confirming Ash's conclusion. "Just making things unpleasant for the scut, nothing that would even leave a bruise he didn't deserve. And it's not, you must admit, as if he could ever be a true seruilis."

"You'll treat him as any newcomer," the first seruilis said firmly. "If he errs, correct him and he will learn. More, you will remember that he is alone in an unfamiliar place, with no family to support him."

Ash debated changing her approach, seeing whether a little humour would break the tension, but decided against a parody of this gutter seruilis they feared. Arranging her face to be clear of anything resembling arrogance, she stepped into the doorway.

Five out of nine boys were facing her. One, facing away from the door, hadn't yet registered their changes of expression.

"Correct him? When he like as not cannot even read? His failings will reflect on all of us. How shall we correct him when he trips flat on his face serving at table?"

"I'll do my best not to, Ser," Ash said, and could not resist adding self-deprecatingly: "Not even if there's ham hocks."

That brought a titter of laughter, and a startled glare from the speaker. Ignoring his reaction, Ash walked calmly across the room to place herself before the one she marked as first seruilis. He had been one of the older boys instructing at swordplay and was one of two who wore the Rhoi's shield embroidered in gold on the breast of his otherwise stark black clothing. More than good-looking, with dark, faintly waving auburn hair and vivid hazel eyes, he was oddly familiar, though Ash could not place the resemblance.

"Ser," Ash began, hitting the exact note of unassuming obedience she'd hoped for, "my name is Ash Lenthard. Master Humboldt ordered me to report to you." Her voice held the faintest hint of a Khanteck accent, but otherwise fit well with their own.

The young man nodded, showing no flicker of surprise at her changed accent, then indicated a boy sitting at his left. "Vendarri."

Vendarri, with a spark of laughter in his eyes, nodded. He was wearing sky blue and silver, and was darkly handsome.

"Vicardie."

Freckles, large nose, pale blue eyes and shaggy blond hair. Tall as a stork and gawky in his green on green uniform. He grinned at her.

"Kittahar."

A narrow-chested boy, perhaps eighteen, whose features would forever be condemned with a description of 'average', wearing red and mid-blue, glancing at Ash and then anxiously at his neighbour.

"Marriston."

White-blond, handsome features marred by a smouldering glare. Ash judged him to be a eighteen or nineteen, and recognised his colours, rich blue and dark purple, as being those of Decsel Enderhay, a most respected man. The name Marriston was also the family name of the Setsel of Strathaden.

"Lirindar."

A boy with warm brown skin, his hard expression and position by Marriston's side proclaiming his loyalty. Yellow and red did not quite suit him.

"Pelandis."

Only child of Decsel Pelandis, he wore black and white, along with a jittery, permanently miserable look.

"Gibrace."

Slightly shortsighted, she would guess, from the way he peered at her. A washed-out sort of boy, mousy and mild, but he reminded her of one of her Huntsmen, Melar, who they used as bait when it was necessary. He looked a complete pushover, but was deadly with a close-quarters knife. She wouldn't be surprised to find that Gibrace, in dark green and red-brown, was much the same.

"Nemator."

The Veirhoi. Like the first seruilis he wore stark black embroidered with gold in the shield of his brother, the only device she would see among the seruilisi's garb. Gold-topped, violet-eyed, and the youngest boy in the room, his eyes were both serious and cautious, but he looked at her without any hostility. Ash thought about bowing, but all seruilisi were, theoretically, equal, so she just smiled slightly, as she had for the others and turned back to the first seruilis.

"Carlyon."

Ash recoiled. Almost comically, just managing to control herself so that a leap backward became no more than an exaggerated flinch. It was such a disproportionate response that for a moment they simply goggled at her.

Then Marriston said: "Looks like he's mistaken you for your father, Carlyon," and laughed as the other seruilisi murmured in disapproval at the comment and Ash both.

The first seruilis did not respond immediately, then, the neutrality gone from his eyes, said: "I am told you will not be instructed in sword with us. Why is that?"

The mood of the room now entirely against her, Ash slapped herself mentally, told herself that this was *not* the Decsel, not Eward Carlyon. But it was hard to ignore the resemblance, so obvious now, despite the first seruilis' slim youth and undissipated vitality. And she did not know quite how to be, because this was her stepson.

"I've never held a sword, Ser." Unable to apologise, she would simply speak as if her misstep hadn't happened.

"You have no weapons at all?"

"I've never been instructed, Ser," she replied, cursing the damnable irony of his identity and hers, retaining an air of quiet obedience through sheer force of will, and refusing to let any more of her true emotions skip haphazard across her face.

Someone whispered behind her, probably Marriston and his cronies. Damn, she was losing. It wasn't critical to make any friends in the Mern – the Kinsel were far from the only source of palace gossip – but she had no desire to endure a campaign of persecution. Beyond tedious, and it would hinder her investigation.

"Listening at doors is poor behaviour on the part of a seruilis," Carlyon commented, placing the worst possible light on her entrance. "It breaches our code of conduct. Breaches of the Code of the Mern are punishable by five strokes of the switch."

Beginning to dislike him heartily, Ash kept her features under control. He might set a precedent to make her into the group's whipping boy, but she would not give them further reason.

"Come now, Carlyon," interrupted Vicardie, and she recognised his voice as the one who had been parodying the gutter seruilis. "Can you breach the Code if you don't know it? And, before you make the obvious answer, he's hardly had a chance to learn it."

The pair must be friends, because the stony chill in Carlyon's eyes faded. "Well, Frog, you may spend the rest of the afternoon ensuring that he knows its every sub rule."

There was a disappointed murmur behind her, but Vicardie took charge of Ash and led her from the room without incident.

"Thank you, Ser," she said, as they passed beyond the range of the others' hearing. "That was kindly done."

"Oh, call me Frog," he said, shrugging off her thanks. "Everyone does. And you're Ash?"

"Yes."

"Did Visel Thornaster truly find you covered in blood? I've heard a hundred different rumours today, none of them particularly likely."

"No. Just...without a place to be."

"And so Thornaster has dropped you in the Mern? On the same day as your – as you lost someone? Harsh. Do you want to postpone this lesson? I could meet you tomorrow morning, when you've had a little more time to adjust."

"I–" She blinked. "I guess I'd rather think about this than my aunt right now anyway."

"Well, if you're sure. Here we go." He veered into a small room filled with an oddment of things like cups, books and banners. Questing through a pile of books, he pulled out a slim volume with a cry of satisfaction.

"Right!" said Frog, striking a proclamatory pose. "Rule number one!"

"I can read, you know," Ash said, mildly.

"Can you? That'll make things easier. But if Carlyon said I was to teach you, then it means I'm to teach you and be certain you can recite the entire thing back to me before we're done. So you just hush. Now, where was I? Ah, yes! Rule number one..."

Since there were no chairs Ash sat down on the floor and watched as Frog strode dramatically about the room, making a game of reading an unsurprising list of prohibitions. The rule against carrying weapons without the Master's leave was an irritant, but she could improvise something in a pinch.

When he'd finally exhausted the book, Frog dropped it on one of the piles, and gave her a sympathetic grin. "Got all that?"

Ash obligingly began to recount everything he had read her, earning a look of open admiration.

"Wonderful! You're one of those people who don't forget, are you? Well, you're certainly nothing like the fumble-footed street urchin we'd been expecting. I suppose we'll have you medicking us all within a week, and wonder what we ever did without you."

"Medicking? Oh, no – unless it was to do with horses, I didn't pay much attention to my aunt's trade. I've been earning my keep as a stable hand."

"I guess that means you can at least ride, which will save a lot of lessons. No chance you're a deadly master of the sword, I suppose? That really would set the cat among the pigeons."

"There's not much call for deadly masters of the sword in the Commons. Can I ask why you're called Frog?" He did look just a little like one, with his skinny arms and legs, but not so much it deserved a nickname.

"Frog-shaped birthmark," he said briefly, and Ash wondered if, despite his apparent acceptance of it, he disliked the name.

"What are the unofficial rules?"

"What unofficial rules?" Frog asked, folding his long-limbed body down onto the floor beside her.

"There are always unofficial rules. The ones that change from year to year along with people, the ones which are constant but not things which are written down."

"I guess it would help if you avoided a few things. Let's see, there's standard stuff, like never gossiping about what you hear in the Mern with your kin. '*The Mern is not a breeding ground for espionage*'," he added, in a deepened voice.

"No tattle-tales," Ash said, nodding.

"Always pass on messages, no matter what personal reasons you may have for not doing so. Don't, for your life's sake, go disturbing the Master in his office for anything other than official business or an emergency. Don't start fights. That's an important one. If we're caught scrapping, there's hell to pay."

"Have I offended Carlyon very badly?" she asked.

"Well, acting like he was the Black Carlyon himself wasn't the best start I've seen. But you needn't worry. Lauren isn't one to put grudges over duty. He won't be granting you any favours, I'd suspect, but you'll not find yourself on scrub duty for no reason at all."

"Lauren," Ash said, mostly to herself. She looked down at her hands. Lauren Carlyon was Eward Carlyon's youngest son.

"Ash, do you have some particular problem with the Carlyon family? If you do, don't even think of pursuing it. You won't achieve anything more than getting yourself banned from the Mern." There was more than a hint of steel in Frog's voice. It sounded so out-of-place she blinked up at him. He could look remarkably severe, this clownish Kinsel. Vicardie was the family name of the Setsel of Bychester. She wondered which of his sons Frog was.

"Ash?"

Which particular should she start with? The forced marriage? Astenar's inexplicable failure to reject the bond? Or her hastily staged suicide? The whole tale of how she'd run away from herself and become someone she liked better?

"No," Ash said, decisively. "I don't have any problems with the Carlyons. The name caught me off-guard."

"Well, you'd do well to get over it, then. Whatever Lauren's family might be, he's solid, and you'd get nowhere in a war with him."

"Believe me, Frog," she said, standing up. "I have no wish to start any wars. The only person I hold any grudge toward is the one who brought about my eviction, and I don't think that was a Carlyon." She hoped it wasn't a Carlyon.

A bell sounded, deep and hollow.

"That's the signal to return to our respective Luinsel," Frog told her, scrambling to his feet. "Be back in the common room a decem after noon tomorrow, when Carlyon gives us the day's tasks. Don't be late, and remember what I said."

Ash detoured to the kitchens on the way back, frowning as she realised how difficult the distinctive clothing of a seruilis were going to make wandering about. And how easy it would be to identify her by her colours. That held her back from simply wandering into the kitchens, as she might have done if she had not her new "master's" name to worry about. Instead she took hold of a harassed-looking boy, greasy and well fed. "Do you know a woman by the name of Mirramar?" she asked.

The boy nodded.

"Good. Go find her and tell her that Ash is here and would like to speak to her."

The boy pulled free and disappeared inside the kitchens without responding, and Ash loitered, hoping he would do as she asked, her stomach pinching her painfully.

"It *is* you!" A woman some years Ash's senior had appeared, wiping floury hands on her apron. Pleasant features and tight blonde braids wound close to a round skull. "Stars, look at how you're dressed! You...Ash, are *you* Thornaster's gutter seruilis?"

"I see I've become notorious."

"Ash, you little wretch, what's happened? How did you come here?" Mirramar, who had treated Ash with exasperated indulgence since Ash had befriended her brother Larkin, gave her an admonitory shake. "However did you get involved with Visel Thornaster?"

"Genevieve's dead, Mimms," Ash said, and looked away to avoid witnessing Mirramar's shock. She had cried enough. "I'm going to find her killer. Thornaster will be useful to me, because he's involved in the investigation. I need you to get a message to Lark. Just tell him to 'look up'. He'll know what I want him to do. I can't myself. I think I'll be stuck hopping to Thornaster's tune a while yet."

The cook's head rose, eyes fierce, and she nodded. "Save a piece of the scut for me and I'll do anything you want, Ash. Genevieve, murdered! How could Astenar allow such a thing? It goes against all justice!"

Ash had never found much justice with the gods. She preferred to rely on careful planning.

"Mirramar, you might consider pretending you don't know me that well. I'll be winning a few enemies along the path I'm taking."

"You will if you try to train Luinsel and Kinsel to your rein like you did my Lark and his friends," Mirramar said. "They won't be quite so simple to twist around."

"People are basically the same, whatever their rank," Ash replied, shrugging. "Do you have any food in the pockets of that apron?" she added, hopefully. Mirramar's one weakness was people she judged underfed. "I haven't had a chance to eat since yesterday and I'm not sure of the protocol for seruilisi and supper yet."

Mirramar narrowed her eyes, but only said: "Wait here," and returned with a bowl of sliced meat and roasted root vegetables. The smell of it made Ash's stomach pinch, and she ate with grim concentration.

"The idea of you as a seruilis!" Mirramar said. "You'll have them baying for your blood before the week's out, or I don't know you. You'd best not try any of your silly jokes on Visel Thornaster!"

"Tell me about Thornaster," Ash said. "He seems a strange sort."

"Strange! He is everything that's–!" Mirramar's mouth closed with a snap, and Ash made sure not to look too entertained. Well, it was probably a good thing that her new Luinsel wasn't universally unpopular.

"What's the story behind his quarters?" she asked, ignoring the flush that touched Mirramar's cheeks. "Does a Visel only rate a cupboard? And it looks like the palace servants don't ever venture near."

"When Rhoi Arun returned with his two friends, they brought no servants or guards with them, and Visel Thornaster was dressed very plainly. The Seneschal thought he *was* a servant, belonging to Setsel Hawkmarten. No-one had any idea that he was Luinsel until after the rooms had been allocated and he'd been given what the Seneschal thought very generous indeed for a guardsman. He'd almost given him a bunk in the barracks, which would have been disastrous."

Ash snorted. "One look at that stallion of his and they would have known better. But why didn't they move him? Once the mistake was discovered?"

"Oh, well, old Marail would have to take offence at his own error – Simeel said that it was as if he thought Visel Thornaster had dressed so quiet deliberately, just so Marail could mistake his rank. He vowed not to move the Visel unless Thornaster or the Rhoi actually requested the move. And neither of them has. Not including the rooms on the cleaning roster is just spite. They say he cleans them himself."

"I'd say he doesn't clean them at all. I wonder what game the man's playing? Has he lost the Rhoi's favour?" Ash wiped her bowl with a last chunk of sweet potato.

"Now, how would I know? There are no rumours that he and the Rhoi are anything but the firmest of friends. They spend a deal of time together, with Setsel Hawkmarten, but it's not as if I eavesdrop on their conversation."

"I suppose I'd better go fix the room situation," Ash told her, handing the bowl back. "If you'll point me in the direction of cleaning gear I'm allowed to use. This seruilis business isn't going to be much fun. Tell Larkin not to worry, Mimms?"

"I will. You take care, Ash Lenthard."

Thornaster hadn't returned when Ash let herself into his rooms, so she filled the last of the afternoon with cleaning, an unformidable matter of ridding the place of dust, then mopping the floor thoroughly.

The palace had been built over one of Montmoth's many hot springs, so there was plenty of warm, if oddly-smelling water to be had for the asking. And after all was clean except Ash, there were privies just a short way down the hall, and a sluicing room which could be used for washing, once a fresh bucket of hot water had been carried up and the door secured with the mop. The steam-filled luxuries of the central baths were something she could not risk, but she preferred to be clean.

All that was left to do was remember to fill the water jug, and arrange a newly-obtained bedroll on the floor of her cupboard, which would keep the stone floor's chill out of her bones far better than a couple of blankets.

Sunset, and still no capricious Visel. Ash did not want to sit in this room and let herself think. Not about Genevieve, and certainly not about Lauren Carlyon and the moment of recognition before she'd learned his name. She would suffer enough for that later, when the nightmares came.

The sky had faded enough to see the brightest of the gods. Both moons were rising: dull, shattered Yurefaer, a blot of purple hidden by spirals of rock and dust; bright Cuinefaer, bringer of visions. Cruel Comfort. Ash had never been able to tell which of her dreams were guidance given by the pale moon: hers were all equally bad.

Lighting the lamps, Ash set about looking for more to do. Thornaster's boots proved better for polish, but most of his gear was in good order. She decided not to risk trying to break into his lockbox – the velvety feel of the lock suggested there was more to the thing than a simple mechanism, and she had no idea when he would show up. Eventually she began to read through the Herbal. Her studies had always been more dutiful than devoted, and she could hardly claim to know the whole of it by heart.

But Ash's mind would not stay on the dry recitation of ills and ailments, of plants and their uses, and the book's ingrained scent kept reminding her of blood, pulling her thoughts toward the unbearable prospect of Genevieve's funeral. So Ash turned to the storybook and read her favourites, though she could recount every one of these tales without effort. They were all from the time of the Shattering, when Karaelsur's jealousy of the burning moon had nearly led to the destruction of both Yurefaer and Luin, and the most powerful of the far gods had stripped Karaelsur of sunhood, and raised Astenar up instead.

Still the Visel did not come.

Ash was accustomed to unbinding her breasts when she slept, but while her new tabards were usefully unrevealing, it would be odd of her to sleep in one. She'd just have to put up with the discomfort of wearing the chest band beneath her nightshirt.

Thornaster represented the greatest danger to her masquerade. Presuming he had no inclination to attack the boy he thought she was, living in close quarters still offered too many chances for discovery. But right now there were older enemies to fear.

Climbing beneath her blankets, Ash closed her eyes and grimly waited for sleep.

CHAPTER SIX

The same nightmare, over and again. Past and present troubles linked so that Ash dreamed of being bound in a darkness that stank of blood and rot, aware of someone standing over her. She broke out of every dream, shuddering in the shadowed alcove, and lay moving hands and feet to prove they were free. Was that what it would be like to be damned? Thornaster was lucky that she was not inclined to wake screaming.

Finally an edge of light crept around the heavy tapestry curtain. Dawn. Bare feet flinching from the cold stone floor, she stepped out of her alcove and discovered Thornaster tangled in blankets down one side of the bed, an arm tossed above his head. She took another step forward and his eyes opened, not even looking mazed.

"Let me guess," she said, irritated. "You sleep like a cat and wake the instant anyone moves about."

"Something like that," Thornaster replied, and sat up. He looked appealingly boyish for a moment; his hair tumbled over his eyes. Then he flicked it back, a habitual, unconscious gesture, and turned into someone older, with a face made for arrogance.

"I should have known. I'm glad I decided not to murder you in your sleep."

"Do you suppose you could?"

"Anything's possible."

He laughed. "Unlikely, boy! And, I might point out, you have no weapon."

"You've a round dozen lying about."

"But you didn't take any of them."

"You checked!" Nice to know he wasn't quite as confident as he pretended.

"How could I not, when at least four people warned me that you would rob and kill me at the first opportunity?"

"I've bigger game in mind," she said, remembering her purpose. Would Genevieve still live if she slept lighter? If Ash had taken better care? "Tell me everything you know about the murders."

"Mph. After you've fetched me breakfast." He swung his legs over the side of the bed and stood up.

Naked. Very naked.

"How exactly am I supposed to help you dress?" Ash asked, while he stretched long limbs, unperturbed by her presence. Odd how he looked even taller without clothing. Lean without being skinny, muscle sliding cleanly beneath a smooth surface.

"Just hand me clothes." He turned around, looking out the window. There was an interesting scar down the back of one of his thighs, a long jagged depression that only a very deep wound would have left. It stood out pale against his light brown skin, but the rest of him was unmarred, the only variation a burnished copper tint wherever he had been kissed by the sun.

Dress this? Look at this? Every morning?

"Which clothes, then?"

"Use your initiative."

Ash made a face at his back and opened one of the chests. Having already picked through them, she knew there was little variation from what he'd been wearing when they'd met. Thin shirts, loose trousers, short tunics and creamy robes decorated with near-invisible embroidery.

"You really need me to do this? Every day?"

"I don't need you to do this, Ash. But you will do it all the same."

She handed him a shirt. "You want me to cut your meat up into little pieces too?"

"I want you to be quiet for now. I have some matters to think over."

She lapsed into silence, passing over boots and socks before heading behind her curtain to get dressed herself, warily listening to him move about the other room. Perhaps the rumours were true and he really wasn't a Visel. He was as self-assured as any Luinsel, true, but so tolerant of her insults and jibes that she was uncertain of his authority.

Emerging from her niche, she watched him pour water from the jug into a bowl. "Do you want anything in particular for breakfast?" she asked.

"Something hot," he replied, picking up a fine blade honed for shaving.

Ash left, wondering why he used a blade. Luinsels – anyone with a bit of money – could afford murmitti to take care of excess hair. He was oddly contradictory, this Visel Thornaster.

And annoying. When she returned he was frowning over a letter, and said: "I won't need you for the rest of the day," without glancing up.

It was possible Thornaster was testing her ability to be quiet on direct command, but there were limits to Ash's willingness to play servant. If he wasn't going to provide her with information, he wasn't going to be much use. Another postponement and she would have to conclude that he didn't intend to tell her anything of worth.

Vaguely disappointed in the man, Ash spent the rest of the morning making a thorough exploration of the palace, and trying to work around the hurdle to gossip posed by her newfound infamy. By the time she presented herself at the Mern, she had set a definite limit to how many days she would invest into searching out motives in the palace.

Having no wish to enhance her reputation as a sneak, she didn't linger by the door, despite the wall of cold shoulders that greeted her. Frog was absent, a minor blow to Ash's hopes for the day. If she tried to start a conversation with anyone here, they would snub her.

Not willing to give up entirely, but resigned to a slow campaign, she seated herself to one side. Carlyon came in just as the distant palace bell marked the end of the first full-measure of the afternoon. The first seruilis looked around at them all, the only one to meet her eyes even momentarily.

"Frog's out for the day," he announced. "Vendarri, you can take seniors in Balance. Marriston, you'll be doing signal drill with the younger group. The second session will be mock combat. Go. Not you, Lenthard."

The seruilisi clattered out, leaving her to face a youth who needed only forty years, fifty pounds and a river of alcohol to make him the image of her nightmares.

Carlyon walked out, so she ran her fingers through her short hair, and had herself well in hand before he returned. No more missteps.

"Read," he said, dropping a square of vellum into her lap. For a moment she just sat blankly, and her good intentions suffered a setback when she looked up to see his expression. So he thought she had lied, did he? Thought her illiterate and stupidly boastful. She folded out the animal skin, saw that it was the common tongue, and read:

"On this day, twenty-third of the month of Tempere in the fourth year of Malaster's reign, came into the world Arun Ridel, child of Malaster and Lisenna. Long may he live, by the grace of the Star and the World." An old proclamation. She handed it back to him, as expressionless as he.

A book written in Khanteck was next, a history of one of the great heroes, Jacian. Ash was delighted, having encountered more than a few tales of the Star-bearer. This seemed to be an account of his entire life and she happily began to translate it. Perhaps the less easily found accounts of Halide's life would be included with those of her lover's.

"That's enough," he said, before she'd hardly started, removing the book from her hands and replacing it with another. A treaty written in formal Firuven, the immensely complex language of most of Southern Arabaya. She stumbled through an attempt, managing the gist if not the detail. He took it away from her soon after she'd begun.

"You are a reader," he said, having apparently set aside his prejudices in favour of a very searching study of her face. "What have you read?"

That was a difficult question. A wildly mixed hotch-potch of work. "History," she began, a little doubtfully. "Mainly from Montmoth. Travel accounts. Poetry. Anything I was given." Genevieve had swapped and traded to supply Ash with material, and required a certain amount of reading each day, no matter Ash's desire to spend time at the stables or in the Shambles.

"Any strategy? Animal husbandry? Water management? Heraldry? The Balance?"

"No, Ser."

He strode out again, returning with two books, which he set on the long table where she sat. "Vendarri will take you in the second half. Read these until then. Return them when you're done. They are your responsibility."

She was alone before she had a chance to speak. Another shining start to the day in the Mern.

CHAPTER SEVEN

One copy of Luin and Astenar's laws, and one treatise on the Balance, the fundamentals of managing the land by Luin's Grace. Whatever Carlyon's opinion of a gutter seruilis who flinched at the sight of him, he'd apparently decided to train her in the basics of guardianship. A very correct response, since anyone might come to own land, just as it was possible, if unlikely, for anyone to be put forward to be Rhoi.

Ash fingered the leather covers, then postponed tedium for a brief exploration of the currently empty rooms, but was dutifully bent over the books when a bell heralded the return of the seruilisi. The seniors she'd met, as well as the juniors who made up most of the Mern's population, streamed in. Marriston came in last, followed by Carlyon.

"You know the rules," Carlyon said without preamble. The room hushed immediately. Ash watched the faces of the seruilisi and realised that whoever his father might be, Carlyon had won himself a great deal of respect. The younger brother of the current Decsel, likely to manage part of the family's lands unless an opportunity rose to stand before Luin.

"Three teams, three rounds." Marriston was making his way through the room, tapping each boy in turn on the shoulder, saying "one, two, three" over and over. The groups divided up while Carlyon waited. Then the first seruilis, seemingly at random, appointed a 'Captain' for each army. The Captains, looking variously delighted and horrified, led the teams from the room, followed by Carlyon.

Ash remained behind with Vendarri, who said impatiently: "Come along, Lenthard. I've been given the honour of catching you up in archery. Don't make it any more of a bore than it has to be."

During the irritated lecture that followed – on the construction of bows, their maintenance, the way of stringing them – Ash began the slow task of making up ground. Gravely quiet, she followed Vendarri's instructions with solemn attention, and concentrated on the task at hand, which was a good deal harder than it looked. She could get arrows to fly in the general direction of the target, but placing them exactly was a different matter. She responded with dogged determination, patiently trotting back and forth to the target to fetch her arrows, pulling the bow out till her shoulders ached and her fingers stung. Vendarri strung another bow and showed her up completely, leaving her determined to at least consistently hit the target before the next bell sounded. She didn't quite succeed.

"A slight improvement," Vendarri said grudgingly as she unstrung the bow. She'd given him nothing to complain about, which was the most she could aim for at this point.

They walked back to return the bows against the tide of departing boys, everyone ripe with sweat and vigour. There were a few bruises, Ash noticed, and a split lip, so she silently thanked Thornaster for sparing her general swordplay. It set her apart even more, but let her avoid a lot of physical punishment. Vendarri met up with Carlyon and they departed without a word to her, so she shrugged, and went to fetch the books. They were gone, of course.

"Sometimes," she said, to the empty bench, "I wish things weren't so Sun-damned predictable."

So what to do now? She couldn't raise a fuss. Accuse Kinsel of stealing? Not likely. Besides, Carlyon had charged her with the care of the books and it didn't matter how they had disappeared, simply that they were gone.

Would the first seruilis have stood by while whoever walked off with two large books? No. Whatever his family, he took his position seriously. So, assuming that the thief could not have removed them, they must still be in the Mern. Quickly she checked all the seats, and tried the door to the inner room, but found it locked. The winding stair that led to the Master's office was empty.

Hesitating, Ash debated the risk of trying to search the Master's office, and then stared at the stair's arrow-slit window. She couldn't quite fit her head through, but could angle to see out and down. And there they were, tumbled on the roof of a round building below.

"Scuts."

Lips pressed together, Ash studied the area, mapping a course to it from the Mern's entrance. She left the Mern and worked her way through the palace. The roof belonged to the Gods' Hall, which brought a shiver of memory, but at least wasn't likely to be full of people. The outer walls were sheer and unadorned, but she circled to the section of building set against the base of the Mern, where the two walls together looked scaleable. A long drop, and the books unwieldy to bring down. If there was something she could...

Leaving the hall, she headed toward the Water Yard, the junction between the bathhouses, laundry and kitchens, searching the slow cross-stream of foot traffic for a likely target. A girl came into view, perhaps eighteen, with a hint of Firuvari ancestry in the warmth of her skin. It was the wide basket of dirty linen she was lugging which caught Ash's attention.

"Can I ask a favour, Sera?"

"What is it, Ser?" The girl's wary interest showed Ash's tabard was doing its job of announcing the gutter seruilis' identity.

"I need you to catch something. It won't take a moment. Can I help to carry the basket?" At the girl's hesitation Ash produced her best three-pointed grin and added: "It's not a flirtation, I promise you. I'm mostly harmless, and only charm pretty girls on my days off."

The girl snorted. "You're a few years ahead of yourself if that's how you think you go about catching 'something'."

"If you're tremendously busy, could I borrow the basket if I give my word to bring it right back?"

Curiosity overcame caution, and by the time they'd reached the Gods' Hall they'd established that the girl was Cassia and Ash was indeed Visel Thornaster's gutter seruilis.

"Though why 'gutter seruilis' I don't really understand," Ash said, leading the girl around the curve of the Hall. "It's not like the Commons are the Shambles, and even in the worst part of the city I've never seen anyone spending much time in the gutters. Too much horse doings."

"There's nothing here," Cassia said, suspicion returning as Ash handed back the basket.

"On the roof," Ash said, and lifted her tabard over her head. "Can you hold this as well?"

Turning, Ash ground her shoes on the stony paving, and then swarmed up the junction of the two walls, combining slight handholds with speed to get her within hands-reach of a stony drain. The roofs of Luinhall had been the playground of her adolescence, and she resisted an urge to let loose with a Huntsman's cry as she flipped herself neatly up.

In plain view of a number of windows, she wasted no time collecting the tumbled books. One had come close to splitting at the spine, the pages loosened and stained. Ash scowled and cursed whoever had thrown them from the window, then returned to the edge of the roof.

The laundress stared up at her, then suddenly flicked tumbled brown curls out of her eyes and smiled. "You're making me want to see what you're like on your days off."

"Not so harmless," Ash said. She dropped to her knees, and then hung over the side of the roof with one of the books in her hand. "Hold up the basket."

The books quickly delivered, Ash looked about her, considering the possibilities of the palace roofs for exploration, but the stone, wood and tile landscape was too disconnected. Shrugging, she slid over the edge, hung for a moment and dropped lightly to the ground. The Huntsmen called her "Ash Cat" when they were on patrol. Now she even wore colours to match the name.

"Thank you, Cassia," she said, accepting back her tabard. "I believe I owe you a favour."

"I'd settle for an explanation," Cassia said, taking one handle of the book-heavy basket and waiting until Ash lifted the other.

"Oh, nothing too complicated. I was charged with the care of these books. They walked out a window. They'll know better in future."

"I see," said Cassia, in a voice that showed that she did. "Is it very hard, Ash?"

Ash blinked. "It...could be going better," she said, slowly. "But I am hoping for a turn in my fortunes. You won't speak of this?"

"Of course not! What do you take me for?"

Smiling, Ash paused near the double entrance to the Gods' Hall, glancing into the spangled depths. "Strange," she said. "No, not you. Look at the Sun."

Cassia followed her gaze into the Gods' Hall, where black walls, ceiling and floor glittered with specks of white, and a great golden ball hung from the ceiling, surrounded by far smaller globes, cleverly suspended.

The glass and metal Sun gave out a warm, steady glow, thanks to a special inner lantern maintained by the Godskeeps, who would visit every decem to adjust the positions of the globes to reflect the gods' movements. The strangeness Ash had spotted was a dark stain veiling the inside of the glassy Sun, as if the Godskeeps had used cheap tallow candles instead of the expensive enchanted stone.

"Smuts?" Cassia said. "Should we fetch a Godskeeps?"

"Maybe." Ash put down the basket and approached, looking for the hatch in the Sun's metal framework that would give access to the inside.

A chill lifted her skin to goose bumps and she shivered, unable to avoid remembering the first and last time she'd been in the Gods' Hall. Unlike the sons of Luinsel, daughters did not attend the Mern – at least not in Montmoth. Instead they were tutored at home, in matters considered suitable to the type of woman Montmothians considered ideal, and had little to do with the palace until they were old enough to attend official functions.

Ash's first visit had been for a garden party, and she and her friend Kiri had wandered off and discovered the Gods' Hall. They'd been amusing themselves trying to name all the near gods, down to the tiniest moon circling Delkrio, when a boy a year or two older had begun to bother them, and Ash had had to knock him down to stop him from being offensive to Kiri. And then Eward Carlyon had emerged from the rear of the Hall and escorted them back to the party, a thing Ash had thought so little of at the time, beyond being glad he didn't suffocate Kiri with ponderously elaborate compliments, the way too many of the old men did.

"It's so cold in here!" Cassia said, bringing Ash back to a present when Eward Carlyon was years dead. "Look, my breath is misting."

Montmoth, with its glacier-fed rivers and multitude of high mountain valleys, was far from the warmest of Rhoimarches, but in late spring the room's biting chill was a definite oddity. Frowning, Ash puzzled out the mechanism to open the figure of the Sun, and saw only a warmly glowing stone in the central mount – nothing that would discolour the glass. Weirdly, the inside of the Sun didn't even look shadowed.

"The smudge is gone," Cassia informed her. "Maybe there was some kind of smoke?"

"I didn't see anything." Ash closed the Sun figure and frowned around at the room. Other than the model of the near gods, the room held nothing but walls painted with the constellations of far gods. There was an exit in the rear, a deceptive intersection of two curving walls that gave an illusion of a solid barrier, but there was no hint of smoke. "We'd better get out of here."

Back in the Water Yard, she parted from Cassia with thanks, and detoured to the kitchens to collect an early meal and a delivery from Larkin via Mirramar. A tiny cloth bag.

"Lark said to say: 'He found them'," Mirramar added, frowning. "What are you up to, Ash Lenthard?"

Rolling the bag between her fingers, Ash dodged Mirramar's questions, picked at her meal and left.

Chapter Eight

Thornaster was still absent, which suited Ash. She checked over the condition of the books, fetched out the Visel's tack repair kit, and restitched the one with loose pages before polishing the leather up on both. Her stitching work wasn't perfect, but it would hold and, except for the stained pages and a slight crack down one spine, there was little sign of the volume's misadventures.

Making a mental note to reserve some soft bread to blot the pages, Ash replaced Thornaster's kit and tidied the room. Rubbing some salve on the fingers of her right hand to ease their continuing stinging, she thought up a few neat revenges to repay the books, but dismissed them. Her hunt came first.

The Visel returned much earlier this evening, while she was reading in her nook. He smelled of horse, and looked strained and abstracted.

"I hope you're not planning on turning this into a library," he said, picking up one of her new acquisitions and flipping through it.

"They're a loan," she said. "Today's lesson." In more ways than one. She should have taken them with her to the archery ground, whatever Vendarri thought of her carrying them about. It was no use anticipating trouble and then not doing enough to avoid it.

"And how have you been accepted?"

"They haven't killed me yet. Always a good sign. How go the investigations?"

Thornaster sat down on the foot of the bed. "Seruilisi aid in the removal of boots," he said, holding one leather-shod limb toward her.

Ash considered the scarred sole, traces of mud clinging to the sides, then studied his expectantly amused face.

"Can't get dressed, can't get undressed." She managed to drag off one of the high boots and started on the other. "Or, rather, you can but you'd just prefer someone else did it. Next you'll be wanting me to comb your hair and give you baths." The other boot came off in a hurry and she fell backwards.

"I think I can manage those," Thornaster said, mouth quirking. "The boots need cleaning, however." He wriggled toes at her through knitted socks, watching her face. "While you do so, I'll tell you what I know about the murders."

"Have you had a seruilis before?" she asked, fishing among his gear for cleaning implements. "Did you make him do any of this?"

Glancing back, Ash caught a look of concerned evaluation, which the man swiftly hid beneath a smile. "Some. But my last seruilis was entirely too proper to make it entertaining. He had none of your talent for incredulity."

Ash lifted her eyebrows, then collected cloth and a jar of yellow goo from his belongings, and sat on the floor just outside her niche, with one aromatic boot in her lap. So he thought to distract her from grief by teasing her? It wasn't an unkind gesture, but she had too much to think of to play the game this evening.

"Talk," she said.

Thornaster took off his socks and dropped them beside her, flexing long, narrow feet, but apparently deciding to take the command seriously. With a sigh he lay back on the bed, so her view of him was limited to knees and toes.

"Sera McCready," the Visel began. "A full five weeks past. Only the Watch investigated her death, since the Rhoi's Guard at that time were not involved. A swift blade across the throat. She'd been taken unawares from behind, sitting at the single table in a disreputable pile of lumber mistakenly called a building. It seemed possible that she had been killed by an acquaintance, someone she had allowed into her home. How else had this person positioned himself behind her without alarming her? A great deal of guff was mooted about because she was thought to be a blood-draw, but I could find nothing to hint of that. I didn't visit the scene 'til long after, though, when most traces of magery would have faded.

"Sera Murchison, five days later. Almost the exact same scene, but in a different part of the city. A different Watch House involved, and they didn't make the connection."

The Kinriddys had, though, bustling around to Genevieve's to gossip and exclaim. It was a specialised profession, and the herbalists all knew each other, bargaining hard for traded plants. Two of their number dying in rapid succession in the same manner had brought Ash's adoptive aunt three worried visitors in the space of the same morning.

"Then came Ser Bertram, the palace apothecary. A man who had access to the Rhoi. He died in exactly the same way, six days after Dame Murchison. Alone in a room of his apartments, dead from a single knife stroke which opened the throat. The Rhoi's Guard took charge, of course, and swiftly learned of the other two deaths. Arun asked me to lend any aid that I could." There was a long silence. "Magic had been used to accomplish the killing," Thornaster said, surprising Ash into pausing in her methodical polishing. "That was kept quiet, of course, but I could sense the draw, thick in the air over the body. Investigator Verel, who has a small ability with magery, confirmed my suspicions, though we had no detail.

"We questioned Bertram's apprentice, a singularly tongue-tied boy, and learned only that the man was in the habit of working late into the night, but always with the door locked, especially recently. Either the victim had admitted his murderer into his workroom or magic was used to gain entry. No-one was seen near his rooms."

"Are you a mage, or can you tell about the magic because you're Luinsel?" Ash asked.

"I only have the benefits of being Luinsel while on my own lands. I can sense the draw because of my Estarrel blood, not any mage talent. There's an interesting lack of mages in this Rhoimarch. Verel is one of only a few dozen, and most of them aren't strong enough to sense more than the most recent working of power." The man hooked one leg over the other and swung his foot back and forth, sighing. "Next were Seras Loua and Mae Kinriddy. A number of those skilled in the herbal arts had left Luinhall in the eight days following Bertram's death. The Kinriddys were preparing to depart."

Ash had helped them pack, two tall, willowy women with soft, soft voices that never fell quiet. Biting her lower lip, she switched boots.

"Again there were traces of draw, even stronger than that I sensed at Bertram's. These deaths were different, in that one of the women faced her attacker."

"She would have woken when her twin died," Ash said, as softly as Mae or Loua had always spoken. "They were tied that way. They felt each other's pain."

"The second victim's screams could be heard to the end of their street," Thornaster continued, after a pause. "They slept in separate rooms. It took the killer long seconds to reach her and this death was not as clean. She fought him. She died. No one saw anything. No fleeing bloodstained madman. Nothing. Neighbours surrounded the house quickly, but somehow the killer had slipped past them. There were, however, two imprints of the heel of a foot on the floor where the second of the Kinriddys died. Not a shoe, but not bare feet. An odd, hazy shape."

Much had been made of the killer's escape, in Ash's neighbourhood. All sorts of stories, of invisible monsters, or soul-stealers, or creatures who could turn themselves to mist.

"Next a man named Ezah Johans. The owner of a tap house, and a cook well known for his use of unusual herbs. No problems with this death. No interruptions.

"Nor with the next. Your Genevieve, who died despite a house thoroughly shuttered, with an interesting array of noise-making traps strung about. Again there was a residue of magic. I have discovered that residue at all the death sites I've attended and have no reason to doubt that it was also present at the two previous murders."

Ash didn't say anything, trying to make a decision.

"Lacking physical clues, we have been examining motive," Thornaster continued. "Why kill herbalists, of all folk? Most were valued and respected, not easily replaced. Several possibilities come to mind, but they all verge on the fantastic. A competitor clearing the market? Would it not, eventually, become suspicious when one practitioner alone survives? Someone who had taken harm, intentionally or not, at the hands of a herbalist – out to revenge himself or herself? But that would not explain the cook. The common link seems to be not only herbs, but also an expert knowledge of them, whatever use they are put to. So, discounting the ruthless competitor, there is an obvious possibility behind killing those with herbal knowledge."

"Poison," Ash murmured.

"A substance normally undetectable, which only the most expert might identify."

"You think they're going to kill the Rhoi?" Ash asked, since that was the conclusion the entire city had come to.

"If so, this is a strange and clumsy way to go about it, raising suspicion in advance. And the murder of a Rhoi is one crime not lightly forgiven during Astenar and Luin's judgment. This Rhoimarch – there is more going on here than... Do not repeat what I tell you now."

Curious, Ash made a tiny noise of assent, wishing he would sit up so she could see his face.

"In late autumn Arun received a letter from his father recalling him to Montmoth. If we hadn't already started out in response to it, I'm not sure we would have made it through the passes which block this place off so effectively in winter."

"Did Rhoi Malaster say why he wanted Rhoi Arun to return?"

"He instructed Arun to ask my Rhoi for an advisor on matters of Balance. Which is me, and I don't even need to see you to know you've screwed your eyebrows up into those doubtful arches. It's the Estarrel blood – it means I'm sensitive to Balance thanks to Luin, just as I am to magery because of Astenar. Rhoi Malaster didn't explain why he needed an advisor – it's an unusual request, since most Rhois would do anything rather than admit to a failure of Balance."

"Is there—?"

"There's certainly something wrong here, although I don't think it's with the Balance. Luin's laws are kept well enough, but many of Astenar's are skirted around, some almost openly flouted. This book is a good example." He held up the volume Ash had repaired. "Instead of recording the gods' instructions, it interprets them. And very few of Astenar's are discussed. Even if the full volumes of the Edicts are available somewhere in this benighted place, they're rarely directly *taught*. At any rate, Arun has not discovered whatever specific issue was behind the summons. Nor have I."

Finished with the boots, Ash lined them at the foot of the bed and eyed the Aremish Visel as he sat up.

"Was Rhoi Malaster murdered?" she asked, bluntly.

"I don't know. A fall down a stair could be anything. The Guard found nothing definitive." He handed her back the book. "Arun is taking what care he can. His brother – well, it is possible that someone works to enthrone him without his collusion. But there was an incident, a blocked chimney in the Rhoi's quarters, producing suffocating smoke. It was a near thing, and kept quiet. The Veirhoi nearly died."

"Why are you telling me this?"

Dark eyes assessed her. "As I said, I know where you stand. You want, most fervently, to destroy the killer. Since spreading that tale around will only hinder any investigation, you will not do so. And I want you to know this because I have placed a street-wise boy, with some herbal knowledge, in the Mern with the Veirhoi. You will do well as Heran's bodyguard."

Ash digested this. She'd not intended to stay long in the Mern, but this was a complexity to overset hasty plans.

"Do you know anything about magic?"

"A little. I can't use it, but I know the basic theory of its practice."

"Do witches or mages or whatever, do they ever use a kind of coarse grey powder? To do spells with?"

Thornaster's eyes narrowed. "Yes."

"What for?"

"Why?"

She drew the little bag out of her pocket and handed it to him, watching as he pulled loose the drawstrings and tipped out a minute sample of the powder.

"Emanite," Thornaster said, carefully pouring the dust back into its container. "Where did you get this?"

"What do you use emanite for?"

"A number of different things. You didn't have this when I brought you here yesterday."

"No. I asked someone to look for me." She sighed, disliking the steadiness of his gaze. Was it a mistake to tell? "When Genevieve wouldn't leave the city, I checked the other murder sites, as much as I could. I found this dust on the roofs – at least, on the Johans' and the Kinriddy twins'. I don't know if there was any above the others."

"Indeed."

"I set some traps – trip-wires and bear-jaws – on our roof. In case the dust wasn't a coincidence. The killer spotted them."

Thornaster's expression shifted from surprise to a combination of amusement and dismay. "You didn't trust me enough to share this?"

Ash shrugged. "Why would I?"

He laughed, a startled cough, and shook his head. "Why would you indeed? There's a lesson for me. Get some rest – I'll arrange with the Investigator to look at these traps of yours, tomorrow." Pulling on a new pair of boots, he left.

Had her delay been the mistake? Ash thought it all over, trying to fit Thornaster's information into the puzzle. The Veirhoi was Rhoi Arun's nominated heir, as well as taking first precedence as closest of his kin. After that, though, anyone could in theory be chosen by the Landsmeet to drink from the Well of the Heart and be judged. Any conspiracy could do no more than create an opportunity. Luin and Astenar would be final arbiters, and weighed those who would be Rhoi on a stern scale. History was full of attempts to become Rhoi that had fallen at this final hurdle.

Who would the Landsmeet choose as a candidate, if both Nemators were dead? Decsel Enderhay had a reputation for being a fine judge of Balance, and was favoured by those who were strongly traditional. Decsel Donderry was more progressive, with many ideas to improve Montmoth's fortunes, which might be why he was considered faddish and easily led. The Carlyons offered a middle ground so deeply shadowed by their father's damnation that it seemed unlikely any would back Eman Carlyon as a candidate. Decsel Pelandis had been bedridden for years. A carriage accident had left him without his health or the use of his legs. His two brothers conducted his affairs, and Ash had heard Ryle Pelandis spoken of in glowing terms. Since there was no requirement to choose from Montmoth's Decsels, or someone bound as Luinsel, there were countless possibilities. The most she could narrow it down was that it seemed unlikely the Landsmeet would look outside the Kinsel.

Which was no news at all.

CHAPTER NINE

Arth snuffled at her offering, and then accepted the withered apple with an enthused chomp. Juice foamed and dripped from his mouth and Ash scratched the stallion's muscular neck. The black had already lost most of his winter coat, but hair still came free beneath her nails and Arth half-closed his eyes blissfully, leaning into the motion of her hand.

"If you've quite finished seducing my wayward steed," said Thornaster, coming in from where he had been talking to the Investigator, "perhaps you would consider doing as I asked and saddling him?"

The stallion snorted in recognition, ears pricking eagerly towards his master. When Thornaster walked into range, Arth almost buffeted him from his feet, smearing apple slime generously down his front.

"Itchy, are you?" the Visel asked. He scratched vigorously while Ash tossed a blanket over the horse's back and fastened the light saddle into position. Despite Thornaster's warnings, Arth was perfectly behaved, not crowding her into the side of the stall or trying to crush her feet beneath shifting hooves.

"He likes you," Thornaster commented, watching critically as she exchanged halter for bridle.

"I've never met a horse who didn't like me," Ash replied, tickling the whiskers on Arth's chin. He was a lovely animal.

"Well, the stable hands will be eternally grateful to hear that. He does tend to forget himself and mistake them for roaches a little too often for their comfort. Caring for him when I don't have the time will be part of your duties from now on."

"*Always* a pleasure to serve," Ash said. This was an even better redeeming factor for being a seruilis than Thornaster's morning display.

He grinned and ruffled her hair, which Ash immediately added to the negative side of seruilisi-dom. She followed him out of the earth, manure and sweet hay scents of the stable to find the Investigator and a single accompanying Guard waiting. The Investigator had given no sign of holding Ash's silence on the matter of emanite against her, and simply nodded as they mounted.

"Captain Garton sent word that your aunt's funeral will be tomorrow morning, lad," she said. "The Blue Valley at third bell."

"Thank you," Ash said, and spent the ride down the long linked valleys to the middle of the Commons fighting her dread of the Sun's judgment of Genevieve. Would all the good Genevieve had done balance her past? Would Ash's hunt for – not revenge, but some kind of justice – involve taking a life, putting herself on the same path which had left Genevieve so imbalanced?

She found her fingers were digging into Thornaster's robe and forced herself to relax them, to breathe and be focused on a task and not memories.

"The house is still sealed," Investigator Verel said, as they came into sight of it. "Pending further examination."

Was that a faint smile in the woman's voice? Charity Dunn must be fuming. Still, Ash did not want to go inside. The place could only ever be a shell without Genevieve. Instead, she led the three from the palace into the same alley where they'd kept their horses the first time. An upended water barrel, a foot on the fence, and then she was on the roof.

It was a place of angles and varying levels, less familiar to her than many of her neighbours'. But it was solid and well kept, the tiles firm, not in danger of caving beneath her feet as one had a couple of years ago. What a leap that had been, an instinctive, frantic thrust for safety!

As Thornaster and the Investigator joined her, Ash moved away. No matter how sturdy the roof, there was no need to test it with their combined weight.

Crossing to the point that would be above Genevieve's bedroom, Ash glanced at the sprung bear trap she had placed in the middle of the logical route, at a point that would be cloaked in shadows at night. A piece of wood, half a foot in length, was clenched upright between metal teeth. The trips – thin, dark cord stretched at the right height to snag passing feet and cause warning clatters – had all been neatly cut through.

Only the faintest trace of the grey powder remained. As the other two joined her, Ash bent to touch it, then dusted her fingers clean.

"A considerable oversight," Investigator Verel said, annoyance surfacing briefly through her customary lack of expression.

"It explains why there was no result when you tried divining entry points," said Thornaster. "Is it too late to get some residuals?"

"Even a decem after is too late, really. But I should be able to pick something up. The slightest hint would be more than we have now."

She knelt, and began to draw on the roof with a piece of chalk. It was all very interesting, recognisably magical, but Ash was distracted by the street below. They were not far from the front of the house, and people had noticed and were gathering to watch. Among them, leaning casually against the wall of the cobbler's opposite, was a blond girl in a blue smock. She was tossing a ball into the air and catching it, but when Ash came into sight she closed her hand over the toy and deliberately placed it behind her back. After a moment more, she turned and walked down the street. The girl was called Bitty, and Ash puzzled over what had to be a deliberate signal. Back or behind?

"What is she doing?" Ash asked Thornaster, as the Investigator seated herself in the middle of the pattern of symbols she had marked on the roof. "Residual whats?"

The Visel glanced at her briefly. "It seemed most likely that our killer gained entry with a translocation spell. A powerful piece of magic. Not only that, but also one set to return him to the point of departure. Verel, having found the place the spell was cast, may be able to catch a glimpse of the caster's identity. Now be silent. This requires concentration."

Ash lingered a short measure more, then wandered off, giving the impression of too much energy and too short a span of attention. She crossed the roof, looked down at the Guardsman left with their horses, walked to the back of the house and leapt down into the garden, landing in a crouch. Weeds were growing. She frowned, itching to continue the endless fight against them, but knowing there was no point. Still, she felt guilty, as if the weeds were some sort of betrayal of Genevieve.

Glancing around, Ash crossed to the lavender beneath her bedroom window and retrieved the hidden bundle. The breast cloth she tucked inside her trousers, to keep company with the artistically sewn and stuffed bit of leather she and Genevieve had laughed so much over. From the roll of knives she selected two – dully gleaming pieces of metal without decoration or binding – and slipped one into each boot.

Then she walked down to the mimmerberry bush squatting in the farthest corner and began to search the mottled pink and white berries for ones almost ripe enough to be edible.

"Do you need an out?" whispered the bush.

"Hello, Lark," she replied, unsurprised. "And, no, not as yet."

"Why'd you tell 'em?" asked Larkin. He would be, she knew, leaning casually against the back fence, looking for all the world as if he had just stopped for a rest – a tall, moderately handsome boy, probably with flour dashed carelessly through his blond hair. His was a baker family.

"Because they knew what that dust was. Something called emanite. Because I will use any means necessary to discover Genevieve's killer, including the Guard."

"I'm sorry, Ash."

"So am I. I should have made her leave. Any news?"

"Nothing. No-one saw anything at all."

"Anybody else left town?"

"Old Pokeface. And Caspersonn's packing up. Soon there won't be anyone left."

Ash stopped herself from nodding, which was a pointless, give away gesture. "Four remain who really know herbs," she said, putting a berry in her mouth. "That I know of." She started to make a suggestion, then stopped, narrowing her eyes. No, she would try the official investigation first. "I'd better go. Keep the rest from getting too ahead of themselves, Lark. And take care of this." After a glance at the roof she slid the roll of knives through a gap beneath the palings.

"Call me if you need anything, Ash Cat."

Walking back through the neat rows of herbs, Ash stopped to harvest a cluster of sanac pods. She could brew a tea from them that would stop her monthlies for a while. It would make her ill if she took it too long, but would remove one complication from her close quarters with Thornaster. After cleaning her hands with a sprig of mint, she climbed back onto the roof, avoiding looking at the back door to her old home. The Investigator was still sitting motionless in her mess of chalk. Ash waited, thinking magic a particularly undramatic way of investigating matters.

Finally the woman opened her eyes, raising a hand to her forehead.

"What?" Thornaster asked.

"The barest glimpse. I could only tell one thing, but I suppose it will narrow down our search somewhat." She raised hard brown eyes to Thornaster's. "Our killer is a woman."

ooOoo

Ash was so preoccupied by the thought of a woman killing Genevieve that she did not notice for some time the route Thornaster took after leaving the Investigator. When she did look up to see they were not heading for the palace she asked: "Where are we going?"

"Patience, boy. It is a virtue you would do well to cultivate."

"Funny," she said, after a pause. "I thought I was being very patient with you."

"Then let this be a lesson to you on how perceptions differ."

"Uh-huh." She looked around. They were following the Milk south. "There are only four people really knowledgeable about herbs left in town. Do you think the killer will use the roofs again, after our performance today? If the Guard posted a watch on the neighbouring roofs, they might have a chance of spotting him. Her."

"So Verel suggested last night," Thornaster replied, an odd note to his voice. "We had the houses watched before this, but not the roofs." Ash wondered if he was thinking along the same lines as her – that if the Guard had known of the emanite earlier, they may have been able to catch the killer before she had murdered Genevieve. Was Ash guilty of causing Genevieve's death because she had held back her findings?

Following the southern slope of Westgard, Thornaster left the wide main road for a drive Ash had peered down many times when exercising the city hacks. Screening hedges of dagger-thorned morrion bushes hid most of the property, but along the drive it was possible to glimpse the horses kept in the outer paddocks. Luinhall's premier stud, belonging to Setsel Ormsley.

"Visel Thornaster!" A burly man emerged from the nearest of the several rows of stables as they rode up. "A pleasure to see you again. But I said I'd send word when Alki was ready. Unless you'd care to renegotiate."

"Arth is not my reason for coming today, Bendress," Thornaster replied. "I need a mount for my seruilis here. Can you set up a selection for me?"

"Of course, Ser Visel," the man said, turning away and calling for a couple of hands to come help him.

"I don't think I want to be in debt to you to the tune of a horse," Ash said, after they'd dismounted.

"Now that's not the right reaction at all," Thornaster replied, dividing his attention between Ash and Arth, who was tossing his head, calling a greeting and being answered severally. "You're supposed to be overwhelmed and near speechlessly grateful. Something on the lines of 'Oh my, Visel Thornaster, thank you! For this I will serve you with eternal and unswerving loyalty, even to the point of being polite to you unprompted.'"

"Would you want loyalty given in return for a bribe?" Ash asked, curious.

"Hm – not when it's termed that way. But don't worry yourself about debt. This is for my convenience, not yours. It will make our arrival at your aunt's funeral a little more dignified, and I'm certainly not having you dragging me out of the saddle during the upcoming hunt. Consider it a loan, for the duration of your...well, we'll call it service, for want of a better word."

"Better pick a horse I don't like then," she said, uncomfortably. "Or you'll find it mysteriously disappearing the same time that I do. And I *don't* drag you out of the saddle."

"Child, you are a leaden weight. Where are you going to mysteriously disappear to?"

"If I told, it wouldn't be a very effective disappearance," she replied, watching horses making a game of avoiding their pursuers. A particularly nicely formed bay being led out caught her eye, and she looked it over semi-approvingly, then watched a grey mare standing tall and aloof in the middle of the pen. The grey knew the stable hands weren't chasing her, so didn't bother to run.

Five horses were presented. All nicely made, neat little animals. She wondered which Thornaster would pick, and studied the expression in the bay's long-lashed eyes.

"Display your acuity, boy," the Visel said, eventually. "Which animal here draws you? Do *not* say Arth."

Ash, pleased for the choice, turned to the stable's manager. "Isn't the grey for sale?" she asked, nodding towards the mare still standing at the centre of the holding pen. Now if she could get Thornaster to buy her that one, she'd be quite cheerful about being a seruilis.

"Cloud Cat? Oh, yes. But she's no animal to learn on."

Ash just smiled. "Why's she called Cloud Cat?"

"'Coz she clim's trees," chortled one of the hands.

"Now that would be a sight," murmured Thornaster. "If true."

"Well, Visel, in a way it is. Back when that one was only a few weeks old, we had her in a paddock with a big old lean-over tree." Bendress held an arm up to demonstrate the angle. "One day we went down and there she was up the wrong end of it! Caused a great set-to, with us trying to figure how to get to her without spooking her into a fall, and the mother fussing around the base of the trunk and going all leery-eyed. But, after watching us arguing it out long enough to get hot-tempered, down the foal trots, sweet as you please. She'd never manage it now, of course."

"Really?" Ash was delighted with the tale. Ignoring the animals selected for her, she leaned across the fence and held out a hand in invitation. The mare was a smoked grey, a tall animal with black socks, tail and mane, and a coat the colour of a thunder-cloud elsewhere. Cloud Cat looked at her intently, snorted, and trotted up to Ash to lip delicately at her fingers.

"You've not shown me this one before, Bendress," Thornaster said, behind her.

"Ah, we've not bred her yet, and we'd want to see if she dropped clean before we wasted your Arth on her."

"She's trained to the saddle?"

"Oh, yes. A very nice piece all round, but high-spirited and strong."

"Too much for you, Ash?"

"Of course not," Ash replied, scornfully. Except in price, no doubt. This was definitely not a gutter seruilis' horse.

"Saddle her," Thornaster ordered. "We'll see if my seruilis is more of a rider than he looks, or merely boastful."

"As you say, Ser Visel," the stable master replied. A swift order, and Cloud Cat was saddled. The cushioning blanket was dark blue and Ash smiled at Thornaster as she climbed up onto the fence.

"No choice at all," she said. "In your colours and everything. You can't not want her."

"Perhaps. But if you split your skull reaching beyond your abilities, you won't find me sympathetic."

Ash transferred herself from fence to horse, and felt the mare tremble with anticipation beneath her. Cloud Cat, hmm? A horse on which to *fly*.

She waited as they adjusted the height of the stirrups, then touched the grey's neck, and nodded at the boy holding the bridle. "Let her go."

There was no dramatic take-off. Reins held lightly, she sent the mare around the holding pen for a single circuit. Cloud Cat had the sweetest gait imaginable, and responded to the slightest touch. She tossed her head and sidled a little, wanting to *run*, but obeyed readily when called to hand. Finding herself grinning, Ash looked over at her audience, and considered the height of the outer fence. Nothing spectacular – it was sized for easy viewing of the display ring.

"You're a jumper, aren't you?" she whispered to the horse. "You'd better be, or I'm going to make an utter fool of myself."

Making another circuit, she judged the distance, then set the mare at the fence, heard a belated cry from the stable manager, but was concentrating on encouraging Cloud Cat with every fibre of her being. And there was no balk. Ears firmly forward, the mare cleared the fence easily, landing without a stumble. Ash brought her around in a neat circle, watching the other horses straining and shifting in response. Arth called, a deep stallion's cry.

"She's a bit fresh!" Ash said. "I'll just take her for a run!" And off she went, down the drive towards the gap in the morrion fence. Cloud Cat flowed like water. What a beauty! What an absolute beauty!

CHAPTER TEN

The exultant gallop took Ash south, away from Luinhall and murderers, irritating seruilisi, and the prospect of Genevieve's funeral. On her return she found Thornaster and Arth waiting patiently by the morrion hedge. His expression was benign, so she didn't rein back her enthusiasm as she brought Cloud Cat dancing up to him. The mare was scarcely winded, a fine sheen of sweat slicking her coat.

"She's perfect!" Ash said, glowing. "Smooth as silk. I've never ridden better."

"A good choice," he allowed. "Bendress even threw the tack in with the price, so, all colours correct, we may head back to the city."

They started off without another word, the two horses exchanging greetings. "She's really too fine for a seruilis," Ash said, eventually, and the corner of his mouth lifted.

"Some might see it that way. She is certainly more impressive than most of the horseflesh I've seen in these parts. I will, I think, put Arth to her when she is in season and present the foal to my sister."

High spirits damped by the recollection that Cloud Cat wasn't hers to keep, Ash seized the chance to change the subject. "You have a sister?"

"A brother also," the Visel replied. "And you?"

"No," Ash said, wiping a hand over her hair and turning the conversation a second time. "Does being descended from Luin and Astenar allow you to do anything special? Other than feel when magic's been used recently?"

"Do? It varies on the time of the year."

"What can you do now then? You can heat water, right?"

"You noticed that did you?"

Ash shrugged. The water he'd used to shave that first morning had been warm when she cleared it away, though he'd taken it from the jug of cold water. So she'd watched closely the second time and seen that he'd stared at the bowl for a moment of intense concentration before he'd wet and lathered his face. "How much water can you heat at a time?"

"It depends on how much of a headache I want to give myself. At this time of year, a few barrels full in exchange for a mild migraine."

"You get a headache every time you do that? Sun, I'll bring you heated water if you want it so very much!"

The Visel laughed. "A bowl of water won't tax me. I'm at my strongest at Midsummer, and can manage, oh, dozens of barrels without much pain."

"Midsummer? It would make more sense to be able to heat things in winter."

"Most thoughtless of the gods not to have considered that," Thornaster agreed, eyes dancing.

Ash nodded absently, thinking over the various things she'd heard about Aremish rulers and their bloodline. "Can the Rhoi of Aremal really call lightning from the sky?"

"No. Though it does seem so to any watchers. What the Rhoi does is the same as what I do, but many times magnified by the Rhoi's formal bindings to Luin and Astenar. I can make things burst into flame, with effort. He can make them so hot they explode."

"That's what Parclivvy meant about only attacking Aremal in winter," Ash said, in tones of revelation. She had never understood that brief chapter in one of the history texts.

"Yes. Once it was a great secret, this fluctuation of the power. Then Aremal's weakness was discovered, became well-known, and is now just a factor to be taken into account."

"Do your Rhoi's eyes really glow? Is his immediate family much more powerful than you? Could you make things explode if you were Rhoi?"

Laughing, Thornaster held up a hand. "Slow down. I'm not sure I'll dare let you out riding again if this is how you respond to it."

Resisting an immediate recommendation that he speed up, Ash held her tongue, only wrinkling her nose at him.

"Rhoi Vorlan's eyes don't glow," Thornaster went on. "All Rhois have a certain intensity about their gaze, which is a product of the bond to both Sun and World. The combination of the Estarrel blood and that bond produces a particularly strong effect, and it can be difficult to meet his eyes, but there's no actual radiance. As for comparative strength – the Estarrel blood tends to weaken away from the Rhoi's immediate family. My mother is the Rhoi's second cousin, still close enough that there's no significant variation in strength. I've never sat down with Aremal's Veirhoi and tried to compare exact strength, but I should say we are similar."

"So could you make things explode if you were Rhoi?" Ash asked.

"I expect so. Does that satisfy your bloodthirsty heart, stripling? The thought that I could boil a lake or blast towns to rubble, if only I were Rhoi? I assure you that it's not an event I anticipate occurring. My Rhoi expects a long life and I would not be offered first chance to stand before the gods, even if we lost him."

"I don't imagine it would be much fun."

"Being Rhoi? A lot of hard work, from my observation."

"No, being able to burn things just by glaring at them. I mean, I suppose it would be handy, being able to crisp your enemies and things like that, but I bet every time there was a fire, when lightning burnt down a house or something, everybody'd be whispering about how whoever owned the house had offended the Rhoi. And just imagine how the Landsmeet must act around him. Does he have a temper?"

"A well-controlled one," Thornaster replied, face more solemn now.

"And the ambassadors and probably other people as well, knowing of his power, all flinch when he says something even slightly grumpy." Like Ash had done with Carlyon, just because he was related to someone who frightened her. "That on top of all the horrible things about being Rhoi. I feel sorry for him. Unless, of course, he likes it. Does he?"

"I don't think so," the Visel said, slowly. "I don't believe I've ever asked him. He can be very autocratic at times, and the strengthened link with the gods is, I am told, a great joy. But like it?" He shook his head. "What damnable things you say, boy. I quite dread the thought of bringing you in contact with Arun in case you should ask him to describe 'all the horrible things about being Rhoi'."

"I've better manners," Ash said, wondering if he truly thought her such a numb-wit.

"Not that I've seen."

"If the Rhoi gave me leave to speak to him plainly, I might ask him something like that, unless I thought him likely to get offended. But I'm obliged to be polite to him. Too many people about who'd make a point of protecting his dignity."

"There's a very practical interpretation of 'better manners'." As they rounded Westgard's curve and rejoined the Milk, Thornaster frowned and shifted in his saddle. "Is Arun well-regarded by those in the Commons? By those less, ah, full of manners than you?"

"Right now people are impatient for him to marry. But there's a lot of talk about his review of the laws, and all the Aremish ways he's picked up. A few say that you and the other foreign Luinsel have some sort of power over the Rhoi, that it's your will that's law in the land, not his."

Thornaster sighed. "Unsurprising, I suppose. He is not certain of his ground, yet, and that might seem to people to be weakness. And it's true enough that he wishes to follow Aremal's lead, not least because he, too, feels Montmoth is out of Balance in some way."

"Does he plan to make a lot of changes?"

"From what I've seen, Montmoth's laws aren't precisely the problem, though he will do what he can to strengthen them. It's like that teaching text you had – the interpretation is the problem. For instance, that house you and your guardian lived in – the land there isn't bonded. It's only covered by the Rhoi's wider protections."

"Landhold Dunn hasn't enough property yet to become a Visel."

"But that's no reason to leave the land unbound. Luin spoke a great deal on the responsibility of Visel, Setsel and Decsel because large tracts of land require more management, but Montmoth ignores the clear implication in Luin's words that all land should be bound and kept so far as possible in Balance. It's so bad here that an entire district of the city is clearly direly under managed." He nodded in the direction of Mockhold Valley and the Shambles. "It's all smallholdings, without a single Luinsel bound over even the public paths and roads. That needs to be corrected as soon as possible."

"The Rhoi's going to make all the Smallholders be judged?" The idea of Charity Dunn being tested by Luin made Ash giddy. "What if they all fail?"

"Luin rarely judges Smallholders harshly, especially since the holding is often only house, without garden or well. The important step is the binding, in giving them an awareness of the state of the land they occupy."

"Still going to cause an almighty flap," Ash said appreciatively.

"Another glaring issue is Luinhall's Mern," Thornaster continued. "Luin requires that an understanding of the Balance is taught. Montmoth has piecemeal teaching in all quarters, but the Mern is the only place that undertakes formal, in-depth instruction. No promising students from outside the Kinsel attend, and even among the Kinsel there's an obvious and complete absence of half of those with heir's right to be first judged."

"Girls?"

"A situation certainly not as Luin intended. And again there is no express law which requires or forbids, just an interpretation which no other Rhoimarch has taken. And the reasoning is so..." He shook his head. "The question Arun is debating there is whether to merely permit girls to attend the Mern, or if he needs to require them to, given the limited number whose parents will voluntarily send them."

"Because they'd be shamed by their daughters acting manly?"

"Exactly the problem. What is 'manly' about the Balance? Even Arun, who wants very much to improve the situation, keeps finding himself using words like 'unseemly' and 'indelicate'. I can't say whether this strange...binding with impropriety is part of the reason Montmoth is out of Balance, but it's certainly unlikely to help."

"You sound like Genevieve," Ash said, hoping strongly that the Rhoi introduced girls to the Mern while she was there to watch. And help. "My aunt was always scathing about what she called Montmoth's culture of incompetence. Though it's not nearly so bad outside the Kinsel. Is this something that really matters to the Rhoi? Because the fuss over binding Smallholders will be minor in comparison, and it wouldn't be fair to try half-heartedly."

Thornaster nodded. "It has become a matter of pride for him. The first thing Arun did on arriving at Crown of Stars was get himself rescued from a would-be robber by the Rhoi's daughter. She is, ah, everything Montmoth teaches its women they are incapable of being, and he fell into a heap at her feet. She liked him well enough, for a short while, but not enough to come to a Rhoimarch which would treat her as so much less than herself."

"That's why he's so anxious to bring reform? Will she accept him if he makes progress?"

"No and no. Her refusal is final and he knows that. That is not where Arun's determination came from. Arun's wish is to be a truly great Rhoi, worthy of Luin and Astenar's trust, and he has become convinced that to do so he must overcome...even himself." Thornaster tilted his head to one side, as if evaluating his own words, then nodded.

Ash had heard no gossip about the Rhoi's failed romance, let alone any hint that he intended to open the Mern to girls. But plenty of talk all the same, and as they headed into the Deirhoi Valley she thought through where this might lead them.

"Does anyone else know he plans this?"

"He's made no secret of the review of Montmoth's current laws. There's a handful with which he's discussed specific changes. The Master of the Mern. Setsel Enoren, Decsel Enderhay, Decsel Carlyon. I would say that only Setsel Hawkmarten and myself have seen the whole of his plans. He hasn't even taken his brother into his confidence, though that is out of some ingrained belief that the boy is delicate."

Four people. Who could well have told anyone. But they would make useful first suspects, and Ash promised herself that this designation had nothing to do with the name 'Carlyon'.

ooOoo

Ash had an opportunity to observe Lauren Carlyon for signs of guilt that night, when Thornaster decided it was time she took on another duty of seruilisi.

"Now the idea here," Thornaster said, as she trailed him into the Rhoi's own quarters, "is for you to stand around doing very little unless I should indicate some need. Don't join in the conversation or even seem to listen to it, but don't look bored either. You'll probably be asleep on your feet by the end of it, but bear up. I expect you'll find it instructive."

Standing around doing little was far from Ash's idea of a useful occupation, particularly when she wanted to keep her mind from tomorrow's funeral, but she did want to get a look at both the Rhoi and the other foreigner said to have influence over him. In theory, standing attendance on a Luinsel was an opportunity to learn how they conducted their duties, but since Thornaster led their way into a room dominated by a trigle table, Ash doubted any serious business was on the schedule.

Two men were already seated at the three-sided table. One, short and wiry, with a close-trimmed beard and skin a touch darker than Thornaster's, was obviously Hawkmarten, the Setsel from Nyreem. The other, gold-haired and blue-eyed, smiled at the Visel before turning to study Ash.

"So I'm finally allowed to meet your latest acquisition, Thorn!" he said, amusement competing with curiosity. "Well, lad, what do you think of being a seruilis?"

Ash hesitated, suspecting Thornaster of having described her in highly coloured terms, and intensely aware of two gold and black-clad figures standing attendance behind the Rhoi. One had a face blank of any expression, the other, Veirhoi Heran, glanced briefly at Carlyon, and then frowned at Ash. If she was going to get anywhere with her fellow seruilisi, she needed to keep hold of her tongue.

"It's very different from anything I have ever done, Ser Rhoi," she replied, sticking to quiet obedience. She was a little disappointed that the Rhoi's eyes, while a nice shade of blue, were neither glowing nor mesmerically compelling.

"And what's Thorn like as a master?" Hawkmarten asked, his voice deep, mouth curling with mischief. "Not too strict, I should hope?"

That was more difficult to answer and she glanced at Thornaster's faintly smiling profile before responding. "I have never had better, Ser," she said solemnly.

Thornaster laughed. "So I'm the best of a group of one? Fulsome compliment indeed. Leave be, Hawk. Ash has a decided tendency to answer honestly when asked for his opinion and I doubt he will be able to continually produce non-answers if you press him. I came here to play trigle, not have my character dissected."

"We can do both," Hawkmarten replied, equably. But he turned his attention to the three-sided gaming table, asking what layout they should use that night, and Ash was relieved to be able to fade into the background and only have to deal with the two pairs of eyes facing her over the Rhoï's shoulders. There was no third pair, so it seemed that Hawkmarten did not keep a seruilis.

Carlyon looked away, focusing his gaze on nothing, but Veirhoi Heran continued frowning at Ash. To match his stare would probably be construed as a challenge when the serious young Veirhoi obviously already considered her an intruder, so Ash copied Carlyon, gazing at nothing and listening attentively to talk of a hunt arranged to rid the Rhoï's Preserve of a stag which had taken to savaging does. The Rhoï's Preserve was unfamiliar territory for Ash, who had had no right to ride there, but the Rhoi helpfully described much of its terrain over the course of a half-dozen games.

Her own hunt was less simply arranged, and could progress only fitfully unless her quarry was flushed from cover by the Guard's surveillance. She was unlikely to be taken into the confidence of anyone in the Mern, even if she undid her misstep with Lauren Carlyon, and she was too rarely in the Veirhoi's presence to be an effective guard for him.

But as she listened to the men's light-hearted conversation, other possibilities opened up to her.

"What did you think of Arun?" Thornaster asked, when they were back in the privacy of his room.

"He doesn't like being Rhoi."

"True." Thornaster kicked his short boots off, then quirked an eyebrow at her. "Is that the extent of your observations? I was expecting an unsparing dissection."

Ash shrugged, more interested in other matters. "Do you three talk like that all the time? In front of those two?"

"We don't generally discuss the changes to the laws while they're in attendance, if that's what you mean."

"Is Pembury extremely important politically? Or made up completely of diamond mines?" she asked.

"No." Startled blankness in the man's voice. "Why?"

"Did you once save Rhoi Arun's life? Or were you rescuing him constantly from unfortunate situations?"

"Once again I have an unaccountable feeling that I've missed a large part of our conversation," Thornaster murmured. "No, stripling."

"Oh." Ash pondered, aware of the man's gaze on her frowning profile. "Are you sure you're the Visel of Pembury, then? You're not someone else?"

"Are you accusing me of lying again?" The voice wasn't quite chilly, but the man wasn't amused any more.

Ash sighed, and sat cross-legged on her sleeping pad, eyeing her so-called master with faint exasperation.

"I'll tell you what I saw tonight. Three friends. One, Hawkmarten, is full of jokes, irreverent, with an ache in his eyes when he looks at the friend he followed to Montmoth. And that friend is, well, earnest and serious, not too different from the Veirhoi. Whether or not he succeeds in being a great Rhoi, he's obviously weighed down by his duty, and finds relief in the time he spends on lighter matters. And then there's you." She paused. "Are you older than them?"

Frowning now, Thornaster shook his head. "Hawk and Arun both have a couple of years on me."

"And yet, every time there was some question or dispute, they looked to you to settle it. Deferred to your opinion. Over and over." She shook her head. "I have no idea whether Lauren Carlyon or the Veirhoi have ambitions on the Rhoimarch, but tonight showed me they would both be overjoyed to see the last of you. And if you three behave like that in front of anyone else, I've found not a possible suspect, but a likely target for this maybe-assassination."

Thornaster sat down on the end of his bed, clearly startled. "I'm not driving these changes, stripling. Killing me wouldn't make any difference."

"And how many people know that? Your opinion of the Rhoi hasn't stopped everyone from worrying that you've influenced him into Aremish ways. Why wouldn't they think that if they got rid of you, the Rhoi could be made to see sense?"

"I–" Thornaster blinked, tilted his head to one side, and gazed at the ceiling for a while, finally straightening when Ash shifted restlessly. "Perhaps they do defer to me," the man admitted. "Though when it's a question of trigle rules, that's only natural, since we're playing the Aremish version of the game. And the Estarrel blood often gains me some not necessarily warranted respect. But most of it comes from me shepherding them around the Collegium and Crown of Stars when they were new to Aremal."

"It doesn't matter if their attitude is misplaced. Just that people see it."

He'd recovered his smile. "With you around, I can at least be assured that I won't suffer from any overweening pride. And I don't see any need for these preliminary deaths if I'm the target. But you make a fair point. Be careful with any food intended for me: you don't have my constitution."

As if she wasn't already watching what she put in her mouth.

During preparation for bed, Ash considered Thornaster's likely ability to survive any serious poison. It was possible, she supposed – the descendents of the gods were supposed to be hard to kill.

But she would watch his back, all the same.

CHAPTER ELEVEN

A particularly cruel visitation from Comfort left Ash with less grit than she needed to face Genevieve's funeral. Even Thornaster's morning display failed to distract her from the possibility of damnation, and she was filled with a strong desire to find a way to knock herself out until evening. Things she couldn't change were always the hardest for Ash to deal with. If only she could simply run away, as she had from Eward Carlyon.

Focusing on small tasks, she fetched fresh water, then washed herself in the sluicing room. On her return she discovered Thornaster dressed in the most formal of his robes, eyeing himself in his small shaving glass.

"Want me to see about finding you a proper preening mirror? We could fit one on the wall."

Her over-bright tone prompted the Aremish man to look her up and down. "If you're going to be ill, perhaps we should skip breakfast."

"I'm not going to be ill. And why would that make you skip breakfast?"

"The green colour of your face would likely put me off. Never mind, lad. It's not a bad idea to fast before a funeral."

She appreciated that he led the way to the stables without prying questions. Sympathetic silence, and the increasing tightening of her stomach as they rode through the palace grounds, pushed her to talk despite previous intentions.

"Have you ever killed anyone?"

Comprehension lit his eyes. "Yes. Two Beldranian border raiders."

"Do you worry that Astenar will not accept your soul back? Or does your bloodline help?"

"If anything, Astenar judges direct descendents against a higher standard. But I don't believe my actions were unjustified, or without cause."

Ash studied Cloud Cat's dark mane, knowing there were no solutions to be found in this discussion. The gods did not forbid killing in defence of self or Rhoimarch, but after a person's death the Sun weighed their whole life's actions. Damage to Luin and unwarranted deaths counted as the strongest negatives, a taint which might lead Astenar to send the soul to Luin to be washed – scoured – clean. In the worst cases, both gods might refuse the soul, leaving it damned, trapped in a rotting body. When that body decayed to bone or was burned, the soul was left adrift, until time shredded it to nothing.

It was said to be agony: voiceless, unrelenting.

"Who did your aunt kill?" Thornaster asked. And when Ash didn't respond, added: "Astenar is not unreasonable. And from everything I've heard of her, your aunt gave deeply of herself. If she genuinely strove to balance any wrong she had committed, you should not fear the Sun's regard."

You couldn't buy Astenar's mercy, but you could try to balance wrongs. Save lives, help others, offer genuine regret and changed action.

"I don't think Genevieve ever thought that would be possible," Ash said, wearily. "She helped people because she liked it. She didn't believe anything would spare her from damnation."

The Aremish man's usual light good humour dropped away entirely, but though startled he didn't speak, waiting until Ash was ready to go on.

"After she left Cadoken, Genevieve...I don't know where she lived, or what exactly she did. She said she worked for someone who abused her trust. A situation she barely escaped from. Montmoth's so out of the way that she could start again here, be herself." Ash took a deep breath, trying to ease the heavy ache in her chest. "Genevieve – Genevieve knew a great deal about killing people."

How many, Ash didn't know. Too many had been all Genevieve would say, and the only life Ash could put with any certainty to her account was Eward Carlyon's. Who had been the last person in Luinhall whose soul the gods had refused.

To have Genevieve placed in the same category as Eward Carlyon! Whatever Genevieve had done, it could not be comparable, and it was the worst kind of injustice to have people think of Genevieve the way they did the Black Carlyon. But there was no way to stop Astenar's judgment.

"Is there any chance that your aunt's employer traced her here?" Thornaster asked. "Could she have been the target of this series of deaths?"

"What reason would they have to hide that she was the target? The only person who obviously benefits from Genevieve's death is..." Acid rose to sear her throat, and Cloud Cat stuttered to a halt as Ash sat back in the saddle, hands clenching to fists. "She couldn't have. She – I'll –"

Thornaster nudged Arth forward and gripped Cloud Cat's bridle, discouraging the mare from responding to Ash's mistreatment of the reins. "Verel's been investigating that angle," he said. "She's found no connection thus far."

"When did you–?"

"Who benefits is the first rule of crime investigation," Thornaster said. "According to Verel, at any rate. While early possession of a house doesn't seem like stake enough for so many deaths, the idea is being given due regard, so you will allow the Investigator to exercise her competence. Is that clear?"

There was a note of pain beneath the stern command, surprising Ash into taking a temper-controlling breath.

"Genevieve couldn't change that she was damned," she said, gesturing for him to let go of Cloud Cat's bridle. "But she would have had years, decades. Shouldn't whoever took them from her pay?" But even as she asked the question, she shook her head. "I know. No good killing someone without being absolutely certain they're the right person. Genevieve would tell me to remember the difference between justice and self-indulgence. It's just...people will think such horrible things of her, and want to know why Astenar refused her, and she'll be in such pain, and there's no way to *fix* it."

"I know, lad. But what we can't change, we face. I'll stand with you through this."

They followed the curving road into one of the deepest folds of Westgard's foothills, and Ash saw that it would be worse than she'd anticipated. The last stretch into the Blue Valley was made narrow by carts and horses, and dozens of late coming walkers were straggling up the final rise. Genevieve had touched many lives in the handful of years she'd lived in Luinhall, and people had turned out in droves to pay their respects.

Even with the crowd just past the entrance, the first impression of Blue Valley was that of an immensity of blossom. The sloping curve, narrowing and rising toward the far end, was a thick mass of flower-festooned greenery. The garlands of the dead, a remembrance planted for every person who had been buried: the only markers for the bodies.

Somewhere among all that riot of colour would be a freshly dug scar, waiting. But the body of one Astenar had damned would be taken far from the city and burned.

Leaving Arth and Cloud Cat to the care of a cluster of obliging children, Ash and Thornaster followed the slow flow of the crowd to a stepped cup of worn granite paving, a Sun Circle, where Astenar's judgment would be made. Toward the rear of the small amphitheatre was a table of stone, roughly oval and broad enough to hold more than the single, linen-wrapped figure that waited.

Eyes flinching from the muffled shape, Ash looked at her feet, and the skirt of Thornaster's embroidered robe, then the gold and brown gown of one of the waiting Godskeeps as he struck a deep, imperative note on a large gong. The crowd quieted, last handfuls slipping into the Circle. Ash grit her teeth, lifted her chin and took her position as chief mourner at the forefront of the steps.

The gong sounded again, and the senior Godskeep, a woman with faded blond hair, signalled two others to begin pouring honeyed water from the urns they carried. This ran into a narrow channel around the rim of the stone on which Genevieve's wrapped body lay. The urn bearers then began to sound two smaller gongs, barely tapping them so that their resonance was little more than a hum.

"The soul is present," announced the senior Godskeep, as a faint golden shimmer touched the creamy linen. "Speak."

The Godskeeps claimed the Speaking made no difference to Astenar's judgment; that the words were for the living. Ash, as first speaker, was supposed to tell of her sharpest memory of her guardian, but that would always and ever belong to a smoke-scented girl, sitting beside the Milk in the dark.

Under a pale sky and a false name, that girl looked around at people who thought they knew whom they mourned, and said: "I made a promise to Genevieve, the day I came to her in Luinhall. And I made another, the morning I found what had been done to her. I haven't kept either of them. But I will. And I'll remember every day I had with her as a gift."

Not a traditional speech, and she saw Captain Garton frowning, but there were nods from the large cluster of blond heads that marked out Larkin's family. Others stepped to the front row to speak, story after story of pain eased, lives saved, gestures of kindness. So many. Surely, whatever Genevieve had done in the past, surely...

The Godskeeps gently tapped the gongs, producing little more than a suggestion of vibration. Warning that the time for Speaking was coming to an end. Ash remained chin up, looking at the wrapped body. She could not change what was going to happen, but she would not turn from it.

As the last speaker stepped back, the four Godskeeps began sounding the gongs in earnest. Funerals weren't strictly necessary. Astenar sometimes took the dead before any ceremony, and would find them all eventually. But the ritual drew the busy Sun's attention.

Ash had stood in this same circle with Genevieve, watching as Astenar had taken the souls of the Kinriddy twins. The response had been swift, the first gleam of gold appearing almost as soon as the Speaking had ended. Minute golden wings rose from the linen wrappings, joined by dozens of others, a lifting mass as the gongs thrummed, and the air filled with butterflies: a tiny, fluttering pyre rising into the sky.

With little hope of gold, Ash looked instead for grey, for the moths that Luin would send if Astenar judged a soul needed cleansing. But there was nothing, not one single flutter, and Ash could feel the shift in those around her as the Godskeeps struck a little harder, as their practiced rhythm took on a moment's discord, as realisation began to filter through.

As dismay grew obvious around them, Thornaster lifted one hand to rest on Ash's shoulder. Never before had she stood so determinedly upright, so unwavering. How long before the Godskeeps gave up, before they accepted what was already clear? Before all hope died and Genevieve officially became one of the damned.

A burning feather drifted from the sky.

Stiffened to tight rigidity, Ash could not even look up, could only stare at the feather as it came to rest by Genevieve's wrapped foot. It was soft, curling, and shimmering white, with flames lifting from but not charring its delicate strands. The Godskeeps' steady gonging missed a beat in earnest, then thrummed to dying echoes as people gasped, shouted, ducked.

White so pure it burned afterimages into the eye. A golden throat, red-tipped wings. The tail, a trailing fall of blazing motes. Heat beat at Ash's face, dried her throat, as the stone table filled with a bird of fire.

"Yurefaen!"

The cries as all around her mourners retreated several steps confirmed what Ash's mind could barely accept. This was not a creature of Luin, but belonged to the shattered moon, Yurefaer. When the old sun, Karaelsur, had struck Yurefaer a near-fatal blow, most of the burning birds that were Yurefaer's children had been killed. Those few survivors, Astenar had taken as messengers. They lived in the hot places of Luin, and appeared outside them only when...

Ash's legs gave beneath her, and she sat heavily. The Yurefaen, turning on the now-blazing table, cocked its vivid head in her direction, then the round, black eye seemed to stare at Thornaster. It spread red-tipped wings, sending a wave of heat beating out, then lifted back into the air, leaving behind a stone table completely bare of anything but that single feather, drifting languorously off the edge onto the ground.

Reborn.

The word rode the crest of the growing outcry. Genevieve's soul had been taken by Astenar, and would be gifted to a new-formed child. In years to come that child would begin to remember a past once lived, and would be set to complete some task that Genevieve had left unfinished. To be reborn was considered a sign of greatness.

The crowd gasped out the implications while Ash sat numb. Then, when Thornaster moved to speak to the Godskeeps, friends and strangers came and shouted into her face, hugged or shook her, wept. Never in Montmoth's history had anyone been taken to be reborn. The few tales that seared the histories of other lands were of heroes taken too soon, giants of the past.

"Ready to go? Or have you decided to become an ornamental fixture?"

Despite the light words, Thornaster's eyes were reserved, solemn. He glanced at one of Larkin's sisters, holding the burning feather gleefully aloft and racing about trailing lines of fire, then back at Ash when she spoke.

"Did you do that? Intervene somehow with Astenar?" If he had then Ash scarcely knew how to feel. But she would cleave a few mountains for him, to even begin to repay such munificence.

"No. I have nothing like that kind of power. To my regret, since I doubt I will ever again win such a starry-eyed glow of approval."

"Probably not." Despite his denial, Ash couldn't help but suspect a connection. "It looked like it was talking to you."

"Did it?" Thornaster held a hand down to pull her to her feet. "I wish I'd had a chance to meet your aunt. I'd guessed she was out of the ordinary, but for a Yurefaen to come for her, she must have been remarkable."

"I thought so."

Ash glanced around, catching the eye of a few of her particular friends now she had the heart to do so. With a promise to meet him at the horses, she left Thornaster to grab a few words with one of her Huntsmen, Melar, and then Captain Garton. Though light-headed, dizzy with delight, she kept herself to brief exchanges, and had calmed down enough to think by the time she reached the horses.

"So, what did it tell you?" she asked, as soon as they were riding back down into the city. And when he lifted his eyebrows at her, added: "Don't give me that look. You're acting like you've gone to the granary and found only mice. Genevieve being reborn wouldn't make you *worried*."

"No." Thornaster studied her, mouth stern. Weighing, once again, a question of trust. "It said the city smelled of Karaelsur."

The old Sun? "What's that supposed to mean? Karaelsur is–" Ash paused. The stories only spoke of Karaelsur's Sunhood being taken away. "Don't gods die? The far gods stripped Karaelsur of power, but Karaelsur didn't die?"

"Think what it means to die, and the magnitude of Karaelsur's crime. Most gods do not carry smaller lives. They burn or they freeze, and...well, my father calls it 'dancing'. An existence very different from ours, beautiful but arid. For a Sun and a World to start life is considered a special achievement, a matter of pride, but the Yurefaen were Yurefaer's alone, born from fire held in Yurefaer's heart. Their existence was a thorn in Karaelsur's conceit, and so Karaelsur committed treachery of a magnitude to damn a god."

"In the same way as–?"

"Substantially. The body, the ability to act is taken away, and because there is no greater whole to return to, what remains faces a gradual dissolution. With a god, that takes a great deal longer." The Aremish man gazed down over the city, face grim. "With a god, there is a way back."

Ash stared. "Are you sure? How do you know? Does everyone know this?"

Thornaster's quick glance warned Ash she was close to babbling, so she pressed her lips together and waited.

"I know because there have been incidents in the past, attempts by Karaelsur to regain strength. You've probably heard of them, even if you don't have the full story. One, in Firuvar, ended the Imperator line. Halide's death – that explosion in Diadem – was another."

"...that means Karaelsur's return can be stopped," Ash said, only a little breathless, for all that the Imperators had been god-descended, and Halide a hero without peer. "So what do we do?"

The Aremish man was frowning down at his hands, and Ash realised that he, too, was feeling overwhelmed. Daunted. But no more ready to back away than she.

"In part, the first step is already underway. Land which is not bound to a Landhold, whether a Smallholder or Luinsel, is...not hidden entirely, but obscured from Luin's regard. Arun's change to the laws regarding the binding of Smallholdings needs to be made as soon as possible. And I need to talk to Verel about some disappearances she mentioned."

"Why disappearances?"

"For every birth, the Sun gives a tiny spark of life. Soul stuff. As the child grows, that spark grows with it, and the soul the Sun takes back after death is more than was given. In the past incidents, Karaelsur found accomplices to...procure souls in such a way that Astenar would not be aware of their passing." He stared at the line of houses they were approaching. "If that's happening here, then it's no wonder Rhoi Malaster felt Montmoth was out of balance."

"Does this mean – are the murders related? Or just coincidence?"

"I don't know. A Rhoimarch without a Rhoi is vulnerable, and removing both Nemators would produce a delay while the Landsmeet decided on first candidate, just as the timing of Rhoi Malaster's death during Arun's absence meant weeks where the Rhoimarch was unbound. If the deaths thus far have been a precursor to Arun's, then it's probable Karaelsur's accomplice can be found among the likely candidates, and that the ceremony itself would bind Montmoth through Karaelsur rather than Astenar. And yet, I would know if I met someone who had been tainted by the old Sun. The corruption caused by the use of those stolen souls would be marked."

"So, the Rhoi hurries his law through. You try to meet all the potential candidates for Rhoi. I'll ask the – some friends of mine to scratch about for any details about the people who have gone missing."

"That would be best left to Verel." Thornaster was frowning at her. "Don't put your friends in way of danger."

"Given that most of the disappearances I've heard of have been people their age, I think my friends are already in danger." Ash weighed tactics to keep the Huntsmen from racing into trouble. "Don't worry, I won't say anything about the old Sun. Not sure they'd believe me on that one, anyway. Do seruilisi get days off?"

Thornaster didn't respond, attention on a fast carriage as he guided Arth into the flow of the Great River Road. Ash didn't push, mentally composing a note to send to Lark. It would be best for the Huntsmen to get about in pairs when they went into the Shambles, but even in their home territory of the Commons there needed to be a better watch kept. The disappearances she'd heard about had been put down to family squabbles, or the usual departures from Montmoth after winter, when all of the rest of the world seemed so much better an option.

They climbed to the Deirhoi District, but instead of following the road through grassy estates to the palace, Thornaster drew Arth to a halt on the first flat verge.

"Ash, this situation is more hazardous than I anticipated. You were right in suspecting I could be a target and, particularly once Arun starts passing the Smallholdings law, there may come some form of direct attack. I'm going to be sending word to my Rhoi, and having you take the message will give him a direct witness to add detail, and see you safely disposed of. And...you are pulling the most remarkable face."

"It's not often I hear such idiocy," she said, not hiding her scorn. "You think I should run away because it might get dangerous? When I know dozens of people who will pass on to me city gossip they'd never give you or Investigator Verel? When I'm the one with the background in herbalism, and can keep an eye out in the Mern? You think I have less reason to risk myself than you? Show some sense."

The Aremish man looked stymied, searching for a counterargument. But then dancing good humour returned to his eyes, bringing with it a provoking grin.

"And you thought you didn't want to be a seruilis. Not a week's gone by and already you're refusing to leave my service."

"The way I see it," Ash said bluntly, "you're the one serving my purposes."

She shook her head at his laughter and touched her heels to Cloud Cat's sides, but didn't resist her own smile. All this talk of Karaelsur did not change the day's glorious reprieve. Genevieve reborn, not damned. Even stopping a god seemed a little thing beside that.

CHAPTER TWELVE

Two days later, at the edge of a swirl of horses and riders, Ash turned over the problem of getting closer to the Veirhoi. Carlyon kept her to separate lessons in the Mern, and even on occasions such as this, amidst the confusion of half the Landsmeet turned out for a hunt, she had little chance of breaching the wall of seruilisi who surrounded the boy.

Still, there were advantages to standing back. Already she had gained a better sense of the Mern's undercurrents, watching her new peers clumped to one side of the gathering. Among the older seruilisi she'd already noted Marriston, Lirindar and Kittihar as a clear sub-group. Carlyon and Vendarri were friends. Gibrace seemed to be the one the uncertain Veirhoi consulted most frequently, while Pelandis jittered unhappily around the edges. Could he form an opening?

Cloud Cat snorted tremendously in the crisp dawn air, and then pretended to be startled by the clouds of steam. Stroking the mare's neck, Ash shifted her attention to the general crowd, searching for faces from her own past. Kiri. Where was her old friend? Had the Arpesials not returned to the city in spring?

"Ready to face the chaos?"

"Frog!" Ash turned as the boy led up a raw-boned bay. "I was starting to wonder if you'd left the Mern for good."

"It's not that easy to get rid of me," Frog said, grinning lopsidedly before adding: "My father's been ill, so I was roped in to help until he was back on his feet." He darted a conspiratorial glance at Ash. "And probably learned more in the last week than all my time following Setsel Crimmorne about."

"You're not convinced of the benefits of standing at a Luinsel's elbow while they eat or play board games?"

"I can live without dubious lessons in humility, and standing attendance rarely comes close to the detailed instruction of the Mern. Who would be fool enough to do any real business in front of a seruilis?" Frog shrugged. "But enough about me; I'm all over with curiosity. A Yurefaen? Really? Who in the world was your aunt? What was so important for her to do she warranted being reborn?"

"I wish I knew." Ash sighed with genuine frustration. "I guess it's something in Khantar, but unless years from now she chooses to contact me, I don't see any way to find out. Maddening. And everyone keeps asking and acting like I'm hiding something. Except the other seruilisi, who for some reason are even less inclined to talk to me than ever."

"That's because you've made it worse."

"What? How?"

"Well, while it's not easy to be close to a fellow like Lauren Carlyon – teeth-grindingly virtuous as he is – it's also hard not to respect him. And you – you not only acted like damnation was hereditary, but you end up with the very opposite of his situation. It's a salt in the wound thing." Frog surveyed the other seruilisi critically. "Don't worry about it too much – Carlyon's too just to keep you entirely on the outer, and they'll inevitably fall in line just because he wants them to. It's only a matter of time."

"You don't like him."

"Why do you say that?" Frog flicked a hand in light dismissal, but then shifted uncomfortably. "Or, well, no and yes. Did I mention the teeth grinding? All that talent in one person is the kind of insufferable thing you can only endure. Have you seen him at sword practice yet? There's none in the Mern to match him. Let's not even get into how hard it is to keep a girl's attention when he's in the room."

"He sits a horse well, too," Ash said mildly. "But Lauren Carlyon's not my current concern. What are we supposed to do on this hunt?"

"Well, *you* just ride along in back and try to keep up." Frog eyed Cloud Cat. "Though it looks like that won't be a problem. Thornaster hasn't stinted with your mount, has he? Don't fall off, because we likely won't even notice, let alone stop to point and laugh."

"Why is everyone so convinced I can't ride? I used to work in a stable!"

"And that prepares you for fast work over rough ground? I suppose you've never hunted before?"

"Not on a horse."

"What? Don't tell me you're a poacher? Anyway, after Turing Dell the seruilisi let the main body of the hunt go ahead, but that doesn't necessarily mean we'll miss the action since the stag could break back past the leading edge." Frog nodded at an unstrung short bow strapped to his saddle. "It's not easy to shoot from horseback, and given what I've heard of your archery skills it should be no surprise you're just along for the ride. I, on the other hand, am aiming for the prestige of first blood. Carlyon might look good on a horse, but I'll make up for it with luck and charm." Running a hand over his hair, Frog puffed up his chest and paraded a few steps.

A short horn blast sounded, warning that the hunt was soon to leave, and Ash hoisted herself into the saddle. "Good luck. While you're decorating yourself with glory, I'll just enjoy the ride."

She glanced around for Thornaster, who she'd left trying not to laugh at sidesaddles, and spotted him now talking to a bluff, ruddy-skinned woman. They seemed to be discussing Arth, whose pricked ears and pluming tail announced the stallion's opinion of the morning.

The woman was Setsel Ormsley, one of Montmoth's two female Luinsel, and the owner of the horse stud they'd visited. Not on the long list Thornaster had written up of Luinsel he needed to meet personally to check for taint, but perhaps a good person to ask about likely candidates for Rhoi.

"...go all day. No problems," Vendarri was saying as Ash worked her way into earshot of the seruilisi.

"I don't see why half these people start out," the Veirhoi said. "This is a serious hunt, not a picnic, and even if it weren't, half of them won't get past the first ridge. Look at Bardolphin there. His horse is almost as round as he is, and breathes as easily. He'll turn back within a quarter-measure. Why does he bother?"

"Their participation hurts no-one," said Carlyon. "So long as they take care and don't hinder the other riders."

The first seruilis stood in his stirrups, taking a quick count of those around him. The red highlights in his dark hair only gleamed a little in the cool light of morning, but the muted colour did little to diminish his good looks. Ash pushed queasy reaction aside, and focused on favourably comparing Cloud Cat to the other seruilisi's horses. The Veirhoi's honey-gold palomino and Carlyon's blood bay were both nice pieces, but Ash's mare, jittering in anticipation of the run, would still be her choice.

"Keep your mounts in hand," the first seruilis added, with a possibly coincidental glance in Ash's direction. "Those who have been permitted to carry weapons, use them only when your line is clear."

"Thornaster's not carrying anything?" Frog asked Ash. "Whyever not?"

"I don't know," Ash replied. "Maybe he shoots as well as me?"

Thornaster, egotistical creature, had actually been confident of his chances, but had laughed and said that Arth would much prefer not to be distracted from the run by petty concerns such as making concessions for his rider's aim.

"Most likely considers himself above proceedings," said Marriston.

Ash returned wide-eyed incomprehension to this abandonment of the policy of ignoring her. She was willing to bet she wasn't the only one who'd been comparing horseflesh.

"Really, Carlyon, it's too bad," Marriston went on. "I guarantee you our day will be spoiled because this gutter trash is over mounted."

The boy was as subtle as a baited bull. No longer weighed down by thoughts of Genevieve's impending damnation, Ash decided to change tactics as well. "I'll outride the lot of you," she advised them cheerfully.

Frog's snort of laughter was the only positive reaction, but not all of the rest looked at her with anger. Carlyon, however, took back control of the scene before it could escalate.

"Marriston," he said, hazel eyes flat as a cat's, "if you do not wish to participate, you need only say so. Don't put me to the trouble of punishing you for your behaviour."

The blond seruilis checked a hasty reply, and cast a fulminating glare at Ash, but nodded. "I apologise. You will have no trouble from me this day, Carlyon."

"Good," the first seruilis said. "I expect the same from everyone here," he added, raising his voice so that it could be clearly heard by the entire group of tabard-clad youths. "We are seruilisi of the Mern and will conduct ourselves accordingly." Then his stern face softened. "That, of course, should still permit you to enjoy yourself thoroughly."

And a well-timed speech, as a second signal sounded on the horn, and riders and horses began to shift, to form a stream following a leader Ash couldn't see. Carlyon held his group back, then set them off at a slow trot, behind a mass of movement and colour, with the dim yelping of dogs to the fore.

The sky clearing to a thin blue above, it was a fine day for a hunt.

CHAPTER THIRTEEN

Ash found herself quivering almost as much as Cloud Cat, and controlled herself before the mare took her excitement as a signal to surge ahead. This was not the time to race, but simply to travel in a mass out of the Deirhoi Valley, around the northern face of Eastwall to the flat-topped hills of the Rhoi's Preserve.

More used to the fields and lanes of the Southern Valleys, Ash kept to the back of the pack and concentrated on her surroundings, matching them to the Rhoi's description of the ground they would cover. It was primarily wooded on the slopes and flat hilltops, with wide grassy stretches over low-lying areas. The valleys were higher than Luinhall's, and the streams not glacial like the Milk, but still swift and chill with late snowmelt from deeper in the mountains.

One stream drained into a small valley thick with knee-high grass: Turing Dell. Here, servants waited beneath the scattered trees with food spread on groundsheets. Carlyon sent the seruilisi to tend their various masters, so Ash waited at the edge of the swirl of confusion until she spotted Arth's proud head near one of the central trees.

"Enjoying yourself, stripling?" Thornaster asked, handing her Arth's reins as she led Cloud Cat up. The stallion greeted her also, a rough buffet which he usually reserved for the Visel. She found this delightful, though it nearly robbed her of her footing.

"I'd like to ride here without the hunt," she said, smiling. "It's nice."

"Nice!" cried Hawkmarten, on Thornaster's far side. "One of the least-spoilt hunting grounds I've ever covered deserves a less feeble term than *nice!*"

"Well, I own I think it nice too," Thornaster said, eyes dancing.

"Not too backward for you, *Visel?*" asked a new voice. "I hear hunts are out of fashion in Aremal."

Arn Marriston, Setsel of Strathaden, whose son obviously took after him in temperament as well as looks. Picking pointless fights for the sake of it. Unimpressed, Ash didn't wait to hear Thornaster's response, leading Arth and Cloud Cat to the stream. Testing the water, she decided it was too cool, and followed the lead of another rider a short way downstream, where the water widened and became shallower, trapping itself in eddies by the shore for the high sun to warm. After drinking herself, she moved well to one side of the clearing.

With Arth trying to eat her hair, and Cloud Cat pulling to the length of her reins in an attempt to explore, Ash pondered the advisability of adding the pair to the general picket so she could grab breakfast, but was spared the decision by Kittihar, who ungraciously thrust a meat-stuffed roll at her and quickly made off. Should she thank Carlyon's determination to be correct?

Using her kerchief to wrap half for later, Ash munched while she watched Rhoi Arun trying to enjoy his own hunt. Thornaster had told the Rhoi of Karaelsur's possible presence, and recommended investigation behind a guise of business as usual, but while Thornaster chatted and mingled the Rhoi a little too obviously looked around him for a monster.

Ash looked herself, but saw only people. Marriston running attendance on thin, scholarly Decsel Enderhay. Lauren Carlyon with a man who could only be his older brother, Eman. Vendarri talking earnestly with a girl who looked away from him, while Frog watched and smiled. Which of them? None? More than one? It could be an alliance of Kinsel, or someone completely unconnected with the Luinsel. Or Enderhay, the obvious suspect, though if his reputation was to be believed, the most unlikely.

When the hunt split, a full third returning to the Deirhoi District, it was a subdued but still excited group that headed into the tablelands to the northeast, where the stag had already been tracked to harbour. Ash, again keeping to the rear, shivered as the scent-hounds' cry was followed by the mournful call of a horn. Somewhere ahead, the stag was hearing that noise. Alerted to dogs and men, it would begin its run.

This was sport? A day of pleasure, something to boast of after?

Ash had only once allowed her own Huntsmen to chase down their prey. One of the skarl – the shadow wolves of Naggol – had strayed into the Shambles, providing a problem that couldn't simply be trussed and delivered to the Watch. That had been a hunt to the death, too dangerous and too wild, and the exultation and shame of the kill had stayed with Ash for months afterwards. Only an animal, but it had fought to live. Had Genevieve remembered every one of her kills? Would Ash feel pleasure, or only sick, when she flushed her guardian's murderer from cover, and the chase began in earnest?

The stream of horses curved up into woods on top of one of the flat hills, and the riders separated into clusters of two and three, following multiple paths. Ash found herself suddenly alone. The trees were not close-set, mostly evergreens surrounded by blankets of needles, and she slowed to a walk to cross one of Montmoth's inevitable small streams, looking for movement, her eyes tricking her into seeing hunters in every direction.

The horn sounded again, and Ash oriented on it, breaking out of the trees above a dry, grassy valley. The main body of the hunt was well ahead, but immediately below was a loose cluster of tabard-clad riders, picking up speed.

"That's more my kind of chase," she murmured. "Let's show them what you can do, Cloud Cat."

Cloud Cat needed little encouragement, bounding down the gentle slope. Kittahar was the laggard of the group, and Ash and Cloud Cat passed his grey as if he were standing still. Then came a clump: Marriston, Gibrace, Pelandis and, surging ahead, Lirindar. They were more of a challenge, but it was the three frontrunners who were her real difficulty. Carlyon and Vendarri's mounts, and even Frog's raw-boned bay, all had a fine turn of speed, enough that Cloud Cat couldn't simply prance past them. It would be a matter of taking advantage of the terrain, choosing the best path among the tussocks.

Ash grinned when Vendarri responded to a glimpse of her by urging his roan to greater efforts. Frog didn't glance her way, all his attention focused on Carlyon, and Carlyon...was alight. Low to the withers, eyes bright, lips parted: for once first seruilis abandoned. Ash laughed at him as she came abreast, and liked the nod he gave in return even as he urged his blood bay to greater efforts.

But even in that brief instant, Ash's eyes had gone beyond Carlyon to a laggard animal well behind, just faltering down the slope. A palomino, riderless.

In her shock she reined in, scattering the riders in her wake into confusion as they struggled to avoid her. An angry, exasperated shout rose, but she'd already turned, urging Cloud back the way they'd come.

"*Lenthard!*" Vendarri's voice, and Marriston's, unified in fury.

"Keep them going, Vendarri!" Carlyon's shout was cold. "I'll fetch him."

Ash rode, ignoring for the moment the hoof beats behind her that told her that Carlyon was in pursuit, searching instead for the riderless horse. And there he was, limping through a scatter of saplings. She dropped down a pace so that Carlyon could draw up to her, and reflected that anger improved him more than was fair.

Before he was close enough to speak, she pointed to the palomino. "It's the Veirhoi's horse, isn't it? Heran's horse?"

Her expression probably got through to him more than her words. He followed the line of her finger, then slewed in his saddle and stared back at the seruilisi, who lingered in a disordered mass. The Veirhoi was noticeably absent.

Grey-faced, Carlyon gestured to Vendarri, a 'follow' signal, then urged his blood bay forward. They intercepted the palomino, bracketing him between them to bring him to a stop. Foam-flecked, covered in scratches, and clearly lamed.

Ash dismounted as Carlyon snatched the trailing reins, but before she could speak a thicker line marring the fine gold coat caught her eye.

"Carlyon." She pressed fingers high on the palomino's left hind leg and lifted them away red.

"What?"

"I think he's been shot."

CHAPTER FOURTEEN

Carlyon dropped the foreleg he had been examining, ducked under the palomino's head and stopped short, staring at the telltale line.

"A score mark," he breathed. "A graze, but the shock must have driven him beyond Heran's control. If he hadn't an arrow in him as well. How could I not have *noticed?*"

"It must have been when we all split up," Ash said, glancing towards the rapidly closing cluster of seruilisi. "There were a few slow riders behind us, weren't there? It wasn't just the seruilisi?"

He stared at her, then abruptly took command of himself. "Only a few." He frowned at the slowly oozing wound and at the rapidly approaching seruilisi. "There's no way to hide this from them. Blast. *Blast* it all."

Not sure why they wanted to hide it, Ash turned to Cloud Cat, stroking her neck to soothe the mare before extracting her kerchief from the remainder of her lunch and wadding the cloth against the palomino's side. The gelding flinched, but had spent himself and only hung his head again, sides heaving.

"He's got plenty of other scratches," she told Carlyon, as the rest of the seruilisi reached them. "This is just a big one. He must have run madly."

Carlyon's hazel eyes met hers, measuring and judging, then he handed her the palomino's reins.

"Vendarri!" he said, as the dark-haired youth practically leapt from the saddle. "Per's thrown the Veirhoi." He gazed up the pines at the top of the slope. "We'll have to set up a full-scale search. How winded is Nerance? Do you think you can intercept the main body of the hunt?"

Vendarri nodded and was back on his horse in an instant. "I heard the horn sound for the kill, so they'll have stopped," he said, breathlessly. "I'll be as quick as I can."

Carlyon turned from his retreating figure immediately, studying the rest of his shocked audience. "Lirindar," he said, decisively. "Can you locate the point where we emerged?"

The boy nodded, face grim.

"Good. There's no guarantee that Per didn't career off in some other direction, but we can use it as a starting-point. We have to do this systematically or we could miss him. Gibrace, you stay here with Lenthard, see if there's anything you can do for Per. He's badly lame and completely cut-up." A glance at Ash told her that Gibrace was allowed to see the wound.

"We're wasting time here talking, Carlyon," fretted Frog, no cheer at all on his worried face.

"Then we won't waste any more," Carlyon replied, mounting and gesturing to Lirindar, who apparently had a keen sense of place, leading them directly to the spot they had emerged.

Ash watched them go in silence. She had failed the task Thornaster had set her. Now it was a matter of learning how badly.

ooOoo

Gibrace muttered darkly when he saw the arrow wound, but didn't speak to Ash, turning instead to carefully examine the hoof the palomino was favouring. He found and removed a stone, then turned his attention to the swelling bruise that decorated the front of the other foreleg. Ash handed him some salve from her saddlebags, which he took automatically and, after smelling it, began to apply to the leg. Obviously someone who knew horses.

They moved to the long, still-bleeding score next. Ash washed it clean with water from her canteen. "D'you have a needle?" she asked.

The other seruilis shook his head. "Keeper will. Leave it to them."

She nodded. "It'll scar," she said, sparing a moment's regret for the palomino's fine coat, then gazing along the valley. Had Vendarri reached the hunt? All she could see was distant trees.

"He loves this horse," Gibrace said. They glanced at each other and away. Loves or loved?

"When did you last see him?" she asked.

"Before we went into the trees up there."

"Same here." Ash distinctly remembered seeing two black tabards, but had been so caught up in the chase she hadn't even noticed the absence when she reached the valley. She stared up to where Carlyon stood marking the entry point, obviously foregoing his own desire to search in order to coordinate, and tried to estimate the area they had to cover. The hill formed a long rectangle, and they had crossed the breadth. She had moved over it at a slow trot. How far could Per make at a gallop?

"Here they come," Gibrace said, as a small clump of riders emerged in the distance, tardily followed by the larger assembly. The advance group was moving fast, the Rhoi in lead. His palomino was a match for Heran's.

Carlyon rode down to meet them and, after the briefest of explanations, the small group broke into two. Ash nodded in approval. Time for more questions later, once the search was underway. The hunt caught up, swirled for a time around the little knot of lead riders, and was swiftly broken into search parties. Soon only five riders remained. The Rhoi, Thornaster, one of the Guard, Hawkmarten and Carlyon. They turned and headed for where Ash and Gibrace waited with Heran's palomino, Carlyon in the lead.

She studied their faces as they neared. Grim, grim and grim. But not angry. They didn't know, yet.

"What is it you need to show me, Lauren?" the Rhoi asked as they dismounted. "Ah, Per, you've lamed yourself have you? Damn, I'd never have thought he'd throw Heran. He has the gentlest temperament."

"It's...his leg, Ser Rhoi," Carlyon said and the three seruilisi waited as the older riders circled the palomino. Ash removed the bloodstained cloth from the animal's side and heard the Guardsman's breath hiss through his teeth.

"Arrow shot?" the Rhoi said, in complete disbelief. "*Arrow shot?!* Someone *shot* Heran?"

"We're the only ones who've seen that," Carlyon said. He had almost managed to revert to the perfect first seruilis, but there was a blackness to his eyes. "I told them Per had bolted, lamed and scratched himself up, but nothing else."

"That was well done," Thornaster said, while the Rhoi spent a moment longer staring at the red line on the palomino's coat.

Carlyon shook his head. "I hadn't even noticed his *absence*."

There was anger in the Rhoi's eyes now, but not directed at his seruilis. "Lauren, this falls at the feet of the one who loosed that arrow, not you," he said. "I will not hear you blaming yourself again. Do you understand me?"

Carlyon nodded.

"Gibrace, isn't it?" the Rhoi said, looking at the green and russet-clad youth. "I commend Per into your care. Dashelk, go with him back to the palace. See that that wound remains hidden."

"Yes, Ser Rhoi."

"Who, other than the seruilisi, was in the tail of the hunt, Lauren?" the Rhoi asked.

The black-clad youth replied with a half-dozen names.

"And who among the seruilisi was carrying a bow?"

Gently said, but Carlyon's face still pinched. "Myself," he replied, quietly. "Lirindar, Marriston, Vicardie, Gibrace, Vendarri."

"I see. Well, for now the best thing we can do is join the search. Farpatten will assign us a section."

Ash was assigned a sweep along the southern half of the search area, and rode in as nearly straight a line as possible through the loosely placed trees. The long, flat top of the hill rose toward this southern end, and there was more undergrowth: mostly morrion bushes thick with dagger-like thorns. No wonder Per had been so scratched up.

Carlyon rode parallel, some fifteen feet to her left, with Hawkmarten the same distance to her right. Ash glanced at them only occasionally, her attention for every shadow and hollow. No sign of a black-clad boy. At last they reached the southern border of the hill. Before her was a vista of green land, dark trees and Montmoth's numerous mountains, but most immediately an unpleasantly long drop. This was no negotiable slope. Falling water muffled the sound of the other riders in the line emerging.

"At last!" Hawkmarten said, as a shout rose above the noise. "That's not far from us."

A short enough distance that Ash didn't bother to remount, following Carlyon through the trees to a split in the southern edge of the hill which provided a deep-cut channel for a waterfall.

The tumble of water to her left descended to a rocky stream at least eighty feet below. The gap wasn't more than ten or fifteen feet across at top. Three men on the opposite side were staring at a ledge nearly thirty feet down an otherwise sheer drop.

The Veirhoi lay tangled in a largish tree branch, as much off the ledge as on it. As they watched, the breeze blowing along the split gusted a little harder, whipping through the leaves of the fallen branch, and sending it rocking back and forth, perceptibly moving the otherwise motionless boy.

The Rhoi, emerging from the trees in time to see this, said: "Oh, Astenar, you mock me," in a horrified undertone, just as one of the men on the far side yelled something that sounded like 'hope'.

"The lad must have come off as his animal avoided plunging into the gap," Hawkmarten said. "He would have grabbed at the branch on the way down and it broke his fall, swung him in to the side."

"I can't tell if he's breathing," was the Rhoi's distracted reply. "Does anyone have any rope?"

On a hunting trip? The keepers had less than fifteen feet between them, brought along to tie the carcass. More people arrived, someone suggested vines. The edges of the split became crowded. Heran swayed again.

Ash studied the crevice wall directly below her. Unlike its fellow opposite, it was rough and had plenty of footholds, though it wasn't the driest prospect she'd ever seen. Her gaze went from a projecting spur of rock to her left, to the kyola tree growing directly out of the rocky side about ten feet down. Source of the Veirhoi's leafy tangle, it looked firmly rooted, and there were other, thicker branches.

Quietly she removed her tabard, slung it across Cloud Cat's neck, and handed the nearest person the mare's reins. Working through the gathering crowd to the best starting place, she knelt and slipped over the edge before anyone could notice and waste precious time arguing. The Veirhoi had spent...how long on the ledge already? It was obviously not so unstable a position as it looked, but waiting was too much risk.

Ignoring the exclamations above her, Ash did not allow herself to rush. This was difficult. There should be nothing in her mind, just now, but the slow progress of handhold, foothold, handhold, foothold. Her fingers chilled immediately, and her boots felt huge, even though this would be an easy enough climb in other circumstances. But it was slippery and windy and high. Why did that height make so much difference?

She reached the spur of rock, maybe twenty feet down, a little above the branch of the tree she had thought most suitable, pointing along the chasm as it did. With unhurried care she reversed herself, facing out over the drop, feet on two different angles, bracing against the surface behind her for a brief rest. Not a good place to jump, but she could hardly do it from the top – that would only break the branch, as had happened with the Veirhoi.

"Ash!"

It was Thornaster's voice, so she cautiously tilted her head back, and saw a great many faces peering down at her. Finding the Visel, she gave him an enquiring look. They looked a long way up, distances magnified by a bright sky over the shadow of rock.

"Can you swim?" the man called, dimly audible.

"No!" Ash felt her face split into an involuntary grin. "But the fall would kill me, don't you think?" Then she banished him as distracting, studying the branch, which was not as close as she had thought.

"Ash Cat," she said, softly. "Why are you doing this?"

If Ash Cat answered, the words were lost in the falls, so she took a deep breath, and leapt.

ooOoo

Grabbing the branch wasn't difficult. Ash hadn't expected it to bend so dramatically, though, and, for a terrifying moment, she was convinced the wretched thing was going to break. Then it steadied and she was dangling in the middle of the chasm, breathing the watery mist rising off the falls.

"You're doing this because you like to show off, aren't you?" she said, waiting for her pulse to steady. "He's not going anywhere. He's been there for a decem. You just had to be the centre of attention."

To give lie to her words, the wind gusted hard, and the Veirhoi came within a whisker of rolling off the ledge. Ash swayed in the wind, wincing as the branch made a nerve-raking noise. Then, not wasting any more time, she began to swing back and forth, fixing her attention on the ledge. The problem here was judging a feet-first leap exactly. Too short and she would have an opportunity to learn to swim, too long and she'd bounce off the cliff-face and be in the same situation, but with a broken nose.

She swung once more, released her hands, and arced neatly to the ledge, took a tiny, gasping breath, then curled sideways so that she was almost laying on the foot and a half wide shelf.

Solid. Safe.

She lifted her head, and for a horrified moment couldn't see the Veirhoi at all, then realised that his black clothing was blending in with the growing afternoon shadow and his blond head was out of sight, hanging over the edge. At least he was on a wider part of the ledge. Quickly she moved forward, pulled him in, and tossed the branch into the darkness below. At first she thought she'd rescued a corpse, his skin was so cold and clammy. But he stirred, and groaned faintly in pain.

Pulling the boy securely against the cliff-face, she looked up, blinking at the blue, blue sky. It was dark down in this rip in Luin's skin. "He's alive!" she yelled, as loudly as she could manage.

Ignoring the resulting babble of voices, transmuted by the roar of the falls into something completely incomprehensible, she knelt beside the Veirhoi, testing his body for injury. Lots of scratches, but no arrows, thank Luin and Astenar both, and no wound to the skull, as she'd thought possible. He flinched when she pressed his left side, just about where he'd been hanging over the ledge, but there was little she could do than shift him to a better position for breathing, and check his lips for blood.

"Broken ribs!" she yelled.

Several people answered, to her exasperation. She made out a few words, but figured they couldn't be telling her anything interesting. "Anyone got a cloak?" she called, her throat protesting the yelling as she did so. "He's cold as..." She decided not to say 'death'.

There was a pause, then someone, Vendarri she thought from this difficult angle, pointed to a spot just above her. She cautiously looked directly upwards. A dark shape dropped down, wafting away from the wall, and she had to lean precariously out over nothing to catch it. Not the thickest cloth, but it would have to do. She wrapped it around Heran's upper body, then sat down, holding the boy's head on her lap.

Feet dangling over the edge, Ash settled in for a wait.

CHAPTER FIFTEEN

"Am I dead?" asked a faint voice, just as the sky was fading into a strip of grey above them. Sunsets came early in Montmoth's mountains.

"Would you be in this much pain if you were dead?" Ash asked. "Speaking of which, what, other than that broken rib, hurts most?"

"Broken rib? Where *are* we?"

"Well, if you'd woken earlier, you'd have seen the loud but unimpressive waterfall just behind us. It's really in a bad position for viewing, tucked in a crevice on the flat hill we were crossing. You remember the hill?"

"Yes. Oh, Luin's Heart, that's right. Per threw me and there was a branch. It must have broken."

"Well, you landed on a ledge and now we're waiting for someone to show up with some rope." She looked upwards. "I think most of the hunt's been sent home. Either that or they've found something more interesting to stare at. I felt like we were the main exhibit in a menagerie for a while."

The Veirhoi moved, struggled to sit upright, gasped in pain and subsided.

"Hurts, doesn't it?" Ash said. "I had cracked ribs once and it was like knives, but with a constant ache thrown in. You wouldn't think cracks would hurt so much, would you?"

"Is Per all right?" said the Veirhoi, after a moment. "I couldn't stop him, he was going like a bull."

"He'll recover. Bruised hoof, scratches, no real damage. Do you remember what set him off?" She aimed for a casual tone, but, really, subtleties were lost in the roar of the falls.

"No. He just ran mad, took off. I was trying to catch up with Lauren, then Per leapt sideways on me and went headlong." The boy sighed. "I thought maybe he'd been bitten by a snake. You're sure he's not badly injured?"

"Better than you, I think," Ash replied, electing not to worry Heran with talk of arrows. "Can you remember who you were with at the time? Who was behind you?"

"Behind me? I wasn't looking behind me. Why?" Suspicion in his voice now. "What aren't you telling me?"

Ash was silent, looking up at the sky, and he shifted irritably on her legs. "Damn it, Lenthard. I'll order you to tell me if I must."

She laughed. "I'm not all that good at obeying orders, you know," she said. "But, yes, I'll tell you after all. I don't think I'd like to have it kept from me and you'll need to know to be quiet about it." She stroked his brow absently, then recalled herself. The Veirhoi would probably resent such familiarities. "Um. We think Per was shot, that an arrow set him off. So, can you remember who was behind you?"

"*Shot*?!" Incredulity, much like his brother's. "He's...!"

"He'll survive. It was just a graze, though it'll scar. You going to answer my question now?"

"I don't think there *was* anyone behind me," Heran said, after a pause. "Not directly. I was following Lauren, but I went around the wrong side of a rock."

"Can you remember the noise of a follower? The sound of an arrow, maybe?"

"No." The Veirhoi shivered. "How long have I been down here?"

"A couple of decems."

He tried to sit up again, lapsed back with a groan, and passed out. Ash frowned down at him, and explored his skull minutely, wondering if that was a slight swelling behind his left ear. Her mouth was dry and she thought about yelling up for some water or hot food or something. A flask of brandy if they had it: the damp and chill were making her ache. But that would mean standing up and disturbing the unconscious Veirhoi.

"How did you get down here, Lenthard?"

"Awake again, are you? I climbed."

"Truly?"

"Riding and climbing – it's what I do. My friends call me Ash Cat."

"You–" The Veirhoi fell silent, perhaps pondering the idea of the gutter seruilis having friends.

Something fell on her head, and Ash gasped and flinched as it piled on one shoulder then snaked down her back.

"They finally found some rope," she said, when her heart had started once more. Another fell to her left and this one began to jerk and wriggle. "Someone's coming down."

"Good. I'm starving."

She laughed. "Now that's a sign of a healthy constitution. I've been thinking I can smell something cooking, but that could be wishful thinking. Or they might have roasted us some venison. A little food and a good long drink and I think I might enjoy a moonlight ride back. I don't often get to ride under the stars."

"Oh, Astenar, it's forever back to the palace."

"About three decems of travel, since we won't be going at a pace worth mentioning, not at night with you in a stretcher."

Someone reached the ledge. "Hello," Ash said. "He's got one broken rib and a couple cracked, I think. Dark down here, isn't it?"

There was a pause, then light flared, rather to Ash's surprise. The Rhoi's man, Farpatten, stood looking down at them, an eerie blue glow outlining one hand. Were all Montmoth's mages in the Rhoi's Guard?

"Now for the fun bit," Ash said. "Being hauled up a cliff-side with broken ribs. I'd pass out now, if I were you."

The Guardsman knelt awkwardly and checked the Veirhoi over, then produced a small flask.

"Drink this, Ser Veirhoi."

The Veirhoi hesitated, then sighed and accepted the liquid poured into his mouth. "I want to talk to you again, Lenthard," he said. "Don't forget."

"I won't."

Ash watched as his lids lowered and lifted, lowered and stayed shut. She looked suspiciously at Farpatten: nothing ordinary would have acted so immediately after being swallowed. It must have had some sort of magic-touched ingredient.

"Hold him upright," the Guardsman said, lifting Heran into a sitting position. Ash steadied him there as the Guardsman looped and knotted a sturdy-looking harness about the boy's upper body, working to create something that would distress the ribs as little as possible.

The harness completed, the Guardsman tugged on the first rope three times and steadied the boy's unconscious form as he was pulled upwards, climbing along the other rope as the Veirhoi rose into the air. Ash watched them go, lit only by that bluely glowing hand. She wished she had mage ability. It would be handy to be able to conjure light like that.

As they rose, Ash began rubbing her calves, then levered herself into a standing position. She was stiff from staying in the same position for so long, but feeling soon returned and she shook off the chill as she waited for the Guardsman's rope to stop moving about. When it did, she started up herself. It was an easy enough climb, since the rope was nice and thick, but she was grateful all the same for Thornaster's hand as she reached the lip.

Pulled up into a world of light and people and the mouth-watering smell of venison roasting, she was a little inclined to go weak at the knees, but resisted the impulse.

"Remind me to take something with me to eat next time I decide to show off."

"If you'd given me a chance to plan your activities," the Visel replied, with a lamentable attempt at sounding stern, "I doubt you would have been allowed to indulge in your craving to be the centre of attention."

"Oh well," she began, pleased, and was nearly sent back over the cliff when Hawkmarten came up and gave her a congratulatory buffet.

"Well done, boy. A rare display throughout. If you ever grow tired of Thorn here, there'll always be a place for you at Tye's Haven."

"Thank you, Ser Setsel," she managed, trying to get her breath back. Then she was surrounded by people congratulating her, until these stepped back for the Rhoi.

"Young man," he said, beaming. "I owe you a great debt. Name your reward."

Now why did he have to ask her in front of an audience? She sorted rapidly through her options, contriving to present a little modest confusion to interested eyes.

"Bigger quarters would be nice, Ser Rhoi," she said, and gave Thornaster an apologetic glance. "I really don't much like sleeping on the floor. If it's not too much trouble, Ser Rhoi."

Rhoi Arun shook his head. "None at all! I've been trying to get Thorn to move out of that cupboard since autumn. Now he can't refuse. But that's hardly enough. Something for yourself, boy. Is there not something you particularly desire, something you would be pleased to own?"

Would he insist she put a value on Heran's life? "If..." She paused, looked doubtful. "If you would allow me, Ser Rhoi, I would like to read the books in the Rhoi's Library. Or, at least, the interesting ones."

"Only the interesting ones? Well, that shouldn't take you more than a decade." The Rhoi embraced her formally, much to Ash's discomfort. "With my blessing, Ash Lenthard. You will always have use of the Rhoi's Library." He looked over at Thornaster as he released her. "Take care of this one, Thorn. I predict he'll make you proud."

Thornaster took Ash by the elbow, leading her across to the fire and providing her with some steaming cuts from the remains of a haunch that had been roasted there.

"I predict you'll make me burst a blood vessel with that so-innocent expression of yours," he told her cordially.

She grinned greasily, looking around. "Where's Cloud Cat?"

"Not far away. Don't worry yourself; I haven't let her walk off a cliff while you were admiring the waterfall. Did it occur to you that you could have asked Arun to give you that mare?"

"Yes. But she's not his to give is she? And you're not the one sleeping on the floor, so don't complain about my priorities."

Thornaster made a strangled noise, and then lifted his hands. "Well, I inflicted you on myself. I suppose I shouldn't protest while you change my living arrangements. Is there anything else you'd like, while we're on the subject? Your own suite? A carpet of rose petals scattered before you whenever you make your progress?"

"A booking for one of the private bathing rooms? I'm a little too betwixt and between to use the group ones without someone telling me I'm in the wrong place." Her attention was on the arrangements for carrying the Veirhoi home. "He said he thought a snake had bitten his horse. He didn't know who was near him at the time, only that he was trying to catch up to the first seruilis." She gratefully accepted the skin of watered wine Thornaster handed her. "I told him about the arrow wound because it wasn't fair not to. He'll need to know why he's got more security. I think I'm going to tell him more about what's really going on – it's stupid that his brother's keeping it from him."

"You must have been a most horrific infant."

"I climbed up my bedroom chimney when I was four," she said, reminiscently. "My parents only realised when the fires were lit and I started howling."

Thornaster shook his head. "Most definitely a creature of nightmare. Cloud Cat and Arth are just beyond that whitebark. I'll catch you up."

Ash went quietly. She was tired, happy to lean against Arth's warm flank and play with Cloud Cat's whiskers until Thornaster came back. And her abandoned tabard cut the night chill just a fraction. Why had she taken it off?

When the Visel returned she climbed into the saddle and didn't say a word for the entire, dreamlike ride back.

Chapter Sixteen

A hand, shaking her. "Wake up."

Ash sighed gustily, and blinked at the shadowy outline of Thornaster. "What's wrong?" If he wanted her to fetch things for him, she swore she'd hit him. She hadn't had enough sleep for a sense of humour.

"There's been another murder."

"Oh." She sat up. "Who?"

"A woman by name of Prentice. Ran a store on Broad Street."

"Arianne." Ash shut her eyes.

"You don't have to come if you can't face it, stripling."

"Just give me a moment to get dressed," she said, shaking off the comforting hand.

Thornaster withdrew, letting the curtain fall back over her alcove, and Ash bit into her own hand in frustration, wanting to hurt someone. Arianne, who sold as many vegetables as herbs? Ash had barely considered her a probable target. And Sonia? She ached to get hold of the killer, all her fury over Genevieve returning triple-fold.

Running her fingers through her hair, Ash found Thornaster scraping his face clean, and left their rooms to make her own morning toilet. Investigator Verel was waiting for them at the stables, and led them grimly through the early-morning bustle of the city to the southern sprawl of the Commons: Soward. Ash chewed her lip until she saw the little storefront Arianne had put such effort into making bright and friendly. A Watchman was standing before it, big and bluff and out of place. He looked like he'd rather be anywhere else.

"Who found her?" the Investigator asked tersely, cutting through the Guardsman's awkward attempt at greeting them.

"Holder opposite," the man said, nodding to a chandler's store. "Friends of a sort. When the lass didn't answer a morning call, Holder had her husband to break the door down. They've been keeping an eye on her ever since the killing started up. We made sure t'herblist was past help and sent right for you. Haven't touched a thing."

"Gerint, who was it set to watch this one?" the Investigator asked, turning to one of her men.

"Vaisy, Sera Verel."

"Find out where he is."

"Yes, Sera." The Guardsman hurried away.

"Captain, make sure that crowd doesn't get any closer."

Having divested herself of the Watchman, Verel led the way into the tiny store, took a brief look around, and then went on through to the even smaller room beyond. Arianne had not been wealthy. Her entire world was crammed into the storefront and one other room, plus the garden out back. Her body lay in a tangle of blood-spattered bedclothes. Like Genevieve, death had come to her during sleep.

Ash bit her lip, searching the room for the other body, seeing only the frugal possessions that Arianne had gathered through hard work and determination. A bed, a table and single chair, a brazier and cooking utensils. The tools and wares of a herbalist. A small, discarded shoe.

Shivering just a little, Ash slipped past the other occupants of the room, and stared down at Arianne's pale face, a strand of black hair draggling across the brow. She dropped to one knee and looked under the bed, then, finding nothing, twitched back the covers a little from the body, just to be sure.

"Boy! You're not to touch anything!" Annoyance and admonition in the Investigator's voice, but Ash ignored it, turning wide, distressed eyes on her.

"Where's Sonia?" she asked, then thought of the garden and twisted past them to unlock the back door and step out into row upon row of carefully-tended plants. But then, if the door was locked, Sonia couldn't have come out there. Trying to control herself, she turned back to the Investigator. "Arianne had a three year-old daughter. She's not here."

The Investigator exchanged a startled glance with her Guardsman, then gestured him to the front of the building. "Go get that Captain."

The shutter above Arianne's bed was resting closed, but wasn't fastened. Gingerly, Ash tried to look out of it, but found only an alleyway beyond. She was prevented from going out to inspect the alleyway by Thornaster, who took her by the arm and made her go into the garden and sit down on an overturned bucket until she could control some of her horror and fury. She tolerated this because she noticed she was shaking.

"I'm sorry," she said, eventually, watching through the open back door as the Guard moved about the house. "It's just that I was there when Sonia was born. She's so..."

"There's no need to explain, Ash," Thornaster said. "I quite understand." He stood, dusting damp leaves and dirt from his knees as the Investigator came out the back door.

"Not in the house, not with the neighbours," Verel said, in her brief way. "Not a trace. The chandler woman confirms that she was with the mother yesterday, so she hasn't been sent off to relatives."

"Arianne doesn't have any relatives who'll acknowledge her existence," Ash said, unhappily. "They threw her out when she got pregnant."

The Investigator nodded. "Vaisy, the man I had stationed on the neighbouring roof, is dead. Throat slit in the usual way, no sign of struggle. We'll just go up to see if she's left any traces here."

There was more of the grey dust. Ash watched in silence while the Investigator sat with closed eyes in a ring of chalked symbols.

"I'd say the woman's a hired professional," Verel said, eventually. "There's no sense of any personal involvement, no anger or strong ambition. Light-colour hair. Probably foreign, since we don't get much in the way of assassin-mages here. Imported for the job."

Verel and Thornaster talked about mage craft for a little while, and the possibilities of checking any border movements of known assassins. Thornaster was apparently able to get information on any who might have departed Aremal in recent months, though it would take weeks for the answer to come. Ash watched a body being removed from the roof of the building next door – only a short hop away across a narrow alley. If she'd posted the Huntsmen to watch Genevieve's roof, would one of them be dead now, as well? Should she come out at night, and cover one of the last few remaining roofs herself?

"Is there anywhere you know of where this child might go?" the Investigator asked her, breaking into her reverie. "Friends? Favoured places?"

Ash shook her head. "She clung to her mother's side like a limpet, and Arianne rarely went out. A stick-thin rag doll of a child who looks too small to even be walking. Huge black eyes. Hardly ever talks. The killer couldn't have taken her, could she? This spell she uses, would it let her take Sonia to the roof?"

"No. And she definitely used the return capability. So we've got a terrified three year-old running the streets who might be the only person to have seen our assassin and survived. I'll have her name added to the missing children's list and the Watch can come hard on the places runaways usually end up in, though she's young for that line. She can't have gone far. Do you require anything else, Visel Thornaster?"

He shook his head and they headed back to their horses.

"Can I have the rest of the morning?" Ash asked, as soon as they were out of the street. Seruilisi had an afternoon free from the demands of the Mern once a week, but that had been taken up by the hunt yesterday and what they did with the time depended on their masters anyway.

Thornaster gave her a Look. "Do you know of a place this child might have gone?"

"No, I want to set more people to looking for her."

"Indeed. I think I shall need to ask you about your street gang, some day soon. No, I hadn't forgotten Captain Garton mentioning them. Yes, you may have the rest of the morning free. And I suppose the afternoon will be devoted to transferring to a different part of the palace, so I will send your apologies to the Mern."

Ash nodded and turned the mare away without another word, heading deeper into the Commons, running through strategies until the twining stalks of the Three Vines Bakery's sign came into sight.

She looped Cloud Cat's reins around a post, positioning her so that she would be able to see the mare even within the shop. Heading inside, she had to struggle with the odour of fresh baking, which combined very badly with her empty, sick stomach.

"Ash!" Lark's mother, Tanar Rogadney, folded her into a floury embrace. "You look dreadful! What have you been doing? Is it true, you saved the Veirhoi's life? Have you had breakfast? Here, sit down. Lincy! Lincy! Go out front and take care of Ash's horse. Mind you don't get yourself stood on."

"Ash!" Larkin appeared, dusting his hands. "Have you stopped being a seruilis already? Ma, you'll let Ash stay if he's nowhere to go, won't you?"

"If that's what's needed," Landhold Rogadney said. "Here, child, drink this while I spread some butter on a roll for you. I swear you've lost weight. Doesn't he look like he hasn't eaten for days, Larkin? You'd think in a great huge palace like that they'd manage to feed growing boys properly. What can Mirramar be thinking?"

"I'm still a seruilis, Lark," Ash said, being used to Landhold Rogadney's verbal barrage. She took a sip of sweet, thick Firuvari chocolate, savouring the rare treat. "I need to talk to you for a measure or so. Can you come?"

"Of course. Just let me get cleaned up." Lark disappeared through the inner door and was replaced by a row of blue-eyed, blonde-haired girls of varying heights.

"You look...different," sixteen year-old Arras told her, blushing.

Linnet, eight and a good deal more forthright, climbed onto Ash's lap and examined the tabard briefly. "Did you really jump off a cliff and catch the Veirhoi before he plungered to his death?"

"I think the word you're looking for is plunged, Linnet," Ash said, setting her back on the ground. The girl immediately dashed into the back of the shop.

"What's he look like? The Veirhoi? I've never seen him. Is it true that he's more beautiful than any of the women at Landsmeet? And his hair is more golden than wheat in the sunlight? And his eyes are violet? What's his voice like? Did he thank you for saving his life?" Thirteen year-old Asaen had her mother's way with words.

"We didn't talk about it," Ash said.

"Look, Ash," said Lincy, returning. "Still burning!" She held up a lantern using a feather instead of a candle.

Bitty, third-eldest of the Rogadneys, and one of the newer members of the Huntsmen – much to Lark's dismay – gave Ash a brief nod as she took her mother's place at the serving counter, while Tanar Rogadney returned almost immediately, handing Ash two buttered rolls.

"Put that back where people can't see it, Lincy. Do you want it stolen? And didn't I tell you to go look after Ash's horse? Leave the boy be while he's eating. Do you need anything, lad?" But then Landhold Rogadney inhaled sharply, and darted into the bakery's depths. "Who's looking after the oven? If you children have let a batch burn...!"

"Why didn't you talk about it?" Asaen continued. "How did you get to be a seruilis anyway? Are these that foreign Holder's colours? What's he like?"

"Leave him be, Asa!" Larkin said, pushing her away unceremoniously as he returned. "You finished with that?"

Ash nodded and hastily put the cup down, escaping the room before Asaen could begin another volley. Linnet was standing out the front of the store, a good five feet away from Cloud Cat. "This is a big horse," she announced.

"Too true!" Larkin said, mussing her blonde curls. "You can go back in now, Lincy. I hope you don't expect me to get up on that, Ash. I'm not nutty about horses at the best of times, let alone ones twice the size they should be."

"No, we'll walk," Ash said. "It's not far."

She unwound the reins and led Cloud and Larkin away from the bakery. Linnet stayed where she was, gravely watching them till they were out of sight.

"What's wrong?" Larkin asked, as they turned the corner.

"Another murder. Arianne, the herbalist over in the Soward. Her daughter, Sonia, do you remember me telling you about her? She's missing. Out the window, probably. The killer mightn't even know she exists, or might be hunting for her. I don't know."

"You want us to look for her?"

"Yes. But the Soward's not our territory, so it'll need to be more than that." She led Cloud down the alley beside Genevieve's still empty house. "Landhold Dunn must be fuming to have the house shut up like this," she remarked.

"Can't say she's been in the best mood lately. But she gets it in two more days, apparently."

"Just in time, then," Ash said, using Cloud Cat to boost herself over the fence. "I'll be a little while, sorry," she said.

Fetching the spare key from under a handy stone, Ash went into the house. The bed had been stripped of even its mattress, but she could still smell the blood. This would always be the place Genevieve had died.

A visit to the stillroom later, she returned outside and, businesslike, began harvesting.

Back over the fence, she handed Lark two stuffed bags. "The left can go to Ketter's Tavern. And the right to Tye Varden. He's the only reputable herbalist left in the city – I hear he's hired bodyguards. Both of them will give a fair price for this if you say it's from me. Use what it brings to offer a reward for Sonia."

Larkin hefted the bags, and grunted. "Right now, half the city would look for free. But this'll help with the rest of them."

Ash leaned wearily against Cloud Cat's neck and described Sonia carefully. The child had one distinguishing mark – a semi-circular scar on one knee where she'd fallen on a shovel in the garden. It would do to prevent mistakes.

"Ash, you're strung out," Lark said. "If half of what I've heard you did yesterday is true, I'm surprised you're standing. Let's go somewhere and sit down for a while."

"Where do you want to go?"

Larkin eyed Cloud Cat doubtfully. "Well, we can't go the skyways with this lummox in tow and we'd be begging for it if we went into the Shambles afoot. We're keeping out of there at the moment anyway – there's another skarl been sighted. Lammer's Field?"

Ash shrugged and suggested collecting Melar, the third of the Huntsmen's unofficial leaders, for the quick walk to a patch of common ground on the slope of the nearest foothill. Nothing but grass, rocks and stray children.

Melar, nondescript and whip-smart, narrowed his eyes after she'd caught them up on the investigation, and asked: "Do you believe this Thornaster? About Karaelsur?"

"At this stage, I've no reason to doubt him. I asked, if the old Sun really does keep coming back, why it's not common knowledge, why the Aremish Rhoi doesn't warn everyone–"

"Bad idea," Melar said. "You'd have folk saying Karaelsur is the true Sun and that Astenar is an usurper. Which is technically true, forgetting the whole nearly-destroyed-Luin thing, and ignoring the soul collecting, if that's really what's happening. Still, not in the Estarrels' interest to admit to any remnant of Karaelsur still existing. Besides, Karaelsur must offer these accomplices some particularly tempting advantage." He stretched, and then began ticking off points on his fingers.

"So, we have a probably foreign mage killing herbalists, possibly as clumsy prelude to poisoning the Rhoi. But there's been no move against the Rhoi. There've been two not-quite-accidental attempts on the Veirhoi. The former Rhoi told the Aremish Rhoi that Montmoth was out of Balance and asked for help. A Yurefaen told your Visel Thornaster that it could 'smell' Karaelsur here. Karaelsur is damned, and in the past has tried to use human souls to gain strength. People have been going missing – more than usually go missing in spring. You want us to find out more about foreigners who arrived this spring, particularly women. Find the missing child. Don't go missing ourselves, or get our throats cut. Anything else?"

"The only recent disappearance in Mids was Nate Trevel," Lark put in. "And you know he's argued with his father and sworn he was heading south at least a thousand times."

"And not followed through a thousand times, 'til now. Send me a note if he shows up. And Lark, don't try to keep Bitty out of things. You know she'd follow along behind – I certainly would if I was her – and that'd be ten times more dangerous than including her."

Larkin sighed, but had long ago lost the argument about whether Bitty – a better roof-runner than he – should or should not be included. "What bothers me is this Guardsman killed along with last night's herbalist. One of the Rhoi's wouldn't be an easy target."

"Yes, we daren't underestimate how dangerous these people are. No need to sit at home hiding, but make absolutely sure the Huntsmen travel in pairs and threes."

"That's easy to do at night, if we go out of home territory," Lark said. "What with these new skarl sightings, the murders, and your note about the disappearances, we've hardly poked our noses out of Mids the last few days anyway. But during the day there's no way to watch each other's backs."

Most of the Huntsmen were 'prentices in the section of the Commons called Mids – not at all the 'street gang' Captain Garton liked to talk about – and they spent a good portion of their day playing fetch and carry. Any errand could put them in harm's way.

"Heightened alertness and common sense." Ash eyed Cloud Cat sampling tussocks of grass at the limit of her reins. "And I'll go back to learning about sewers, and cleaning Thornaster's boots."

"Right after you tell us in complete detail how you rescued the Veirhoi. My sisters will torture me to reveal all and I need something to say to them."

"You're not just curious yourself?" Ash asked, and he grinned, shrugging.

"That's not like you, Ash," Larkin said, when she finished a run-down of the previous day. "I'd have thought you'd ask for a horse, not books! That's a punishment, not a reward!"

"I want to research a few things."

"I know that look," Melar said. "What are you up to, Ash Cat? Decided to set yourself up as Rhoi instead?"

"Sun spare me. No, this is just a bit of digging about for my own satisfaction. Nothing interesting."

"Last time you told me 'nothing interesting' a mysterious someone tied ribbons around the throats of all the statues on the Grand Walk. Pink ribbons. Marshall Vikence had a frilly bonnet on."

"You know, I remember that happening. Some people have no respect."

"Now you can't come over all innocent, Ash! You admitted to it, remember!"

"Stupid of me," Ash grinned, but absently. She was watching a child in a tattered shift standing behind a tree. A girl of an age difficult to determine, whose eyes did not waver from Cloud Cat for a moment. "I'm sorry to disappoint you, but nothing spectacular this time."

Twisting the reins in her hand, she thought of her task, then raised her voice. "You may pet her if you wish."

Larkin looked about in surprise, and then scowled. "Ash! That grubby thing has no business in this park, let alone near us."

"You sound like half the Kinsel in the Mern," Ash said, watching as the girl, who had retreated behind the tree, poked a nose into view, obviously caught between distrust and desire. "Don't you ever look at street children, dirty and hollow-cheeked and so full of want, and think that all that separates you from them is who your parents are? And sometimes not even that?"

"No. Not people whole enough to get themselves jobs and clean themselves up. It's not as if the Godskeeps won't feed them in return for a little hard work."

Melar laughed. "So ruthless, Lark."

"She's decided Cloud Cat is worth the risk of a beating," Ash murmured.

The girl, whose dark curling hair and brown skin declared Firuvari ancestry, would have an interesting, maybe beautiful face if she were not so bone-hollow and dirty. She came closer with a show of confidence, though her eyes were always on the three seated boys, even when her fingers encountered a silken coat. Cloud Cat turned her head curiously, and blew on the girl, lipping at tangled hair. Not really a child, Ash decided, a little surprised. Terribly underfed, sunken-cheeked and all angles, but there were breasts beneath that shift. Hard to say how old exactly. Over thirteen.

"Climb up if you can," invited Ash, with a smile that was all challenge. "If you dare."

There was a flash of anger in dark brown eyes and the girl scrambled up into the saddle, then sat there, staring at the world from Cloud Cat's height.

"C'mon Lark," Ash said, grinning at her friend's disgust. "Your mother'll have the search parties out if I keep you too long." She stood and started walking, leading Cloud Cat. She did not glance back. The girl would stay or go. If she were anything like Ash had been, she would stay, for Cloud Cat was a fine, fine thing to ride. To sit a horse was to suddenly feel like a Rhoi. From Melar's chuckle, and the expression on Larkin's face as he matched her step, the girl had likely stayed.

When they reached the bakery, Ash looked back, and found those suspicious dark eyes fixed on her. "Each morning and evening," she said, "you need only come to this bakery and you will be given a meal. Only you, mind. I trust you have more sense than to spread the word around, for you'll only be bullied. Good luck." She turned to wind the reins around the hitching post, and when she looked back, the girl was gone.

"*Ash!*" Lark exploded. "You..."

"...will pay for the food, of course. Split off a little of the take from those herbs to start, and I'll bring you more."

"But why? You do the most unaccountable things, Ash."

She sighed, looking down at her grey and blue colours. "Partly for Sonia. In a few years, if she survives on the streets without rescue, she'll be that girl, or something worse. And, partly, that was for Genevieve. Genevieve was always...kind to children she found alone on the streets. Besides, it made me feel good. I hope she decides to find out if I was telling the truth."

"I don't," Larkin said, disgustedly. "But whatever you like. Play the bountiful Luinsel, if that's what takes your fancy."

"I've yet to meet a Luinsel who would think to do that," Ash replied. "Too little a problem for them."

"What? Not even your oh-so-wonderful Visel Thornaster?"

Ash blinked, because she hadn't thought her description of Thornaster had been effusive. "Well, I haven't seen Thornaster do that, either. Though – while he had ulterior motives, I guess that's what he thought he was doing with me. Orphan boy being thrown out on the street and all that. It just happened that I didn't need the help." In a number of ways they were very alike, this foreign Visel and the 'boy' he had adopted. She frowned. Was that a good thing?

"I'd better go. Take care, Lark. Melar."

"You're not coming back, are you?" Melar said, unexpectedly. "To pass through, maybe, but you've moved on here." He touched his chest.

Knowing she owed them honesty, Ash asked herself if that was true. "I think you're right. I've no real reason to stay in Montmoth, now Genevieve's dead. I've often thought about going to – going back to Khantar. Once this mess is tidied up, I'll be the one disappearing south."

CHAPTER SEVENTEEN

The new quarters were more than generous: seven rooms to spread Thornaster's possessions among. The Visel quickly pointed out that Ash had more than tripled the amount of space she had to keep clean.

"If you think I'm cleaning all these, you're..." Ash stopped, and then sat down on the trunk she'd just finished packing. "I expect, so long as you leave occasionally, I can arrange for you to never be sure whether it's me cleaning them or not."

That eased the frown he'd been wearing all afternoon, and he laughed. "You undo me, stripling," he said. "I'm already too inclined to levity to withstand you."

"Who told you you were too inclined to levity?" she asked, catching a note of quotation.

"Oh, any of a thousand people," Thornaster said, flicking his hand to indicate an invisible horde. "My father for one. My sister, when she's annoyed with me. My brother, who has always been more serious than I. My mother tells me it's my best quality and indulges my whims. Much of the Landsmeet – Aremal's that is. I've been restraining myself here, so only Arun and Hawk have of late."

"Which one are you always writing to?" Ash asked, thinking of the amount of time Thornaster spent at his desk, covering thick paper in minute script.

"My sister. My mother also, and various friends and other relations occasionally, but my sister and I have always been close."

"What's her name?"

"Aria. You will like her, I think. She has a soft spot for levity."

"You miss her," Ash observed, deciding to let Thornaster's assumption that she would one day be meeting his sister pass without comment. She was beginning to see that she would have to disappear one afternoon when he wasn't looking, to counter his persistent belief that she was a seruilis for real.

"Yes. Very much." His eyes went distant, then focused back on Ash. "You may have the rest of the day free, stripling. Tomorrow I think I shall see about beginning your lessons in swordplay."

"Do you think I can learn, then?" she asked, wondering if she wanted to bother, since she'd never have the time to learn properly.

"I don't know yet. We'll find out tomorrow."

Ash bowed with a fanciful flourish and wandered off to the room that was now hers. She had an actual four-poster bed, which she hadn't had since she'd become Ash Lenthard. Not to mention a desk, bookshelves and a divan. Four chests, which completely overwhelmed her clothing. And there was plenty of floor space left spare, covered with heavy, soft matting. She wondered what hand the Seneschal had had in room allocation this time.

Deciding to get some business done, Ash picked up her book of tales, and then wandered through the palace until she reached the Rhoi's quarters, where she stopped and regarded the two Guardsmen outside the door with grave interest.

"I'm supposed to give this to the Veirhoi."

There was the briefest hesitation, but, as she had suspected, the clothing marking her as Thornaster's seruilis had transformed into a powerful pass. She wondered how long and how much she could trade on that notoriety. The two men opened the door and directed a wide-eyed page to lead her to the Veirhoi's room.

In a drowsy-warm room, propped on a huge number of pillows, the Veirhoi looked weary, listening to a plump man lecturing him. Whatever conversation they were holding broke off mid-word as Ash entered, and the man harrumphed.

"I will return when you are less troubled, Ser Veirhoi," he said, and brushed past Ash out of the room. Ash closed the door behind him and turned to consider the blond boy, who seemed caught between relief and apprehension.

"Lenthard." The Veirhoi's quiet voice was a study of mixed emotions. "A book?"

"An excuse." Ash walked to his bedside, sparing a glance around the over-heated room. She dropped the book of tales by his right hand. "It's rather old and very precious to me, so be careful with it. If you're feeling enthusiastic, it's a great way to start learning Khanteck. Give it back when you've read it."

While he examined the book, Ash crossed to the windows and pulled curtains and then shutters open. "How you can sit closed in here on a day like this I don't know."

"Master Tsimon says the cool air is bad for my lungs."

"So it may be. But this isn't cool right now, is it? Just remember to get someone to shut them when the sun falls." Ash considered the exceptionally good view, then knelt on the low sill and leaned out to check the distance to the nearest windows. "It's not as if you have a cold anyway, Heran."

Sitting on the sill, she looked back at the Veirhoi. His eyes *were* almost violet – very blue, at least.

"You're supposed to address me as 'Ser Veirhoi'," he said finally, watching for her reaction.

"Of course, Ser Veirhoi," Ash said, immediately. She smiled faintly and stood up. "I hope you have a speedy recovery, Ser Veirhoi. I'd better be getting back now."

Ash headed for the door and had it halfway open when he said "Lenthard!" Pure exasperation.

She looked back at him, still holding on to the door.

"You saved my life. Risked your own. Why?"

"Would you rather I'd let you fall?" she asked, still holding on to the door.

"Of course not!" He sighed. "Come back here, will you?"

Obediently she closed the door and went to stand by the bed. "Yes, Ser Veirhoi?" she asked, the picture of willing servitude.

"Oh, sit down and call me Heran," the Veirhoi said, crossly. "And stop making a game of this. Why can't you be serious?"

"I guess I'm just a little too inclined to levity," she said wryly, sitting down on a chair by the bed. "I can think of worse faults to have."

"It's not very helpful," Heran groused. "I've got to think of a way to thank you for saving my life. It's an important matter. Having you going all blankly uncomprehending and saying things to provoke me isn't helping."

"You don't have to thank me," she said. "You didn't ask me to do it. And your brother already rewarded me."

"Oh, yes, access to the Rhoi's Library. Arun would probably have given you a Decselry if you'd asked for it!"

"I doubt it. Not only aren't there any up for grabs, but I'd make a particularly awful Luinsel. Just think of me in the Council of Luinsels – everyone trying to figure out how to get rid of me, and refusing to talk to me."

"We..." The Veirhoi shook his head, grimacing. "Point taken. We haven't been treating you too kindly. But that makes the way you risked your life for me all the more incomprehensible."

"I can think of a half-dozen motives for saving your life. After all, I've won the gratitude of a Rhoi and a Veirhoi, haven't I? It's too awkward for you to ignore me any more. Even Thornaster's decided to reward me, though if I'd known I was going to let myself in for swordcraft lessons I might have hesitated longer."

"Is that why you did it then?" The Veirhoi was staring at her. "People don't usually outright admit to cultivating me."

Ash shrugged. "Well, to be boringly honest, I didn't really consider the advantages at the time. I do a lot of climbing and I saw a way to get to you, so that's what I did. There's no point letting the Veirhoi fall off the cliff while you're working out what you'll get out of it."

"You're saying that jumping over a ravine is a minor thing to you?"

"The branch worried me. But I've hit worse situations, roof running. I did have a life before Thornaster dumped me into the Mern, you know."

"Roof running? You're a burglar? That's why 'Ash Cat'?"

"No! Though I'll keep the suggestion in mind. I simply meant running around on roofs. Great fun."

"It is?" The youth's expression was dubious.

"Yep. There are a few parts of the city where you can spend most of your time off the ground. Especially in the Shambles, where the buildings lean together over the streets and you can pole straight across."

"And this is fun?"

"Definitely."

"I don't think I'd enjoy it. Luin's Heart, I don't think I'll even be able to stand by my own window any more."

She shook her head. "That's the wrong attitude altogether. If you tell yourself you won't be able to cope with heights any more, you will have a problem."

"Lenthard, you are such a..."

"...know-it-all? Yes, I guess I am."

"Chatterbox," the Veirhoi finished. "It's a complete contrast to the way you've been behaving, sitting quietly in corners. You talk more than Frog does."

Ash grinned. "Sometimes. I have talkative periods and then I go quiet. It depends on whether people ask me questions I feel like offering opinions on. And I love telling people what to do."

Heran looked down, and then back at her. "I don't know what I would have done if I'd woken up on that ledge alone."

"Fallen off, I expect," she said, cheerfully.

"Maybe. It didn't even occur to me to wonder what you were doing down there, at the beginning. I was too busy trying to deal with being down there at all. Someone's trying to kill me."

"I know."

"Arun says there's a high probability that it was one of the seruilisi. That Marriston or Lirindar or Vendarri or Frog or Gibrace or even Lauren had the best chance of shooting Per." He shook his head, violet eyes wide and distressed. "I told him it couldn't have been Lauren, that there was no way he could have gotten behind me. And that none of the seruilisi had any *reason* to hurt me. Why would they?"

"Why would anyone want to kill you?"

"Because I'm Arun's brother. Because I'm a Nemator." A fisted hand thumped once on the coverlet of the bed. "That's always the reason for anything that happens in my life! I can't do this or that or the other because I'm a Nemator. I must always conduct myself in a certain way because I'm a Nemator. People like or hate me not for who I am, but because of who fathered me. Girls chase me because I'm the Veirhoi. Someone is trying to kill me because of my parentage, not for any insult I've offered them. If I'm going to be murdered, I'd at least like to deserve it!"

"You're wrong about one thing," Ash said, watching this minor tantrum unconcernedly. "Girls don't chase you just because you're the Veirhoi. They chase you because you're an extremely pretty Veirhoi. If you weren't the Veirhoi, women would still toss themselves at you because you've plenty of looks."

Heran dismissed his features with a brusque gesture. "That just makes it worse – two reasons that have nothing to do with who I am at all."

"So you wouldn't romance a girl you liked if you knew that the only reason she was doing so was your face and fortune?"

"No! Yes. I don't know." The Veirhoi sighed. "Why am I talking about this with you?"

"Who knows? There's no point you looking to me for sympathy over being born with position and good looks. You could try Carlyon, but he's so proper that the conversation would be horribly one-sided."

The Veirhoi smile faded.

"Are you going to get upset every time I mention Lauren Carlyon?"

Shifting fretfully, the Veirhoi winced, then took a cautious breath and met her eyes: "Why did you act like that?"

He put enough emphasis on the question to make clear he wouldn't accept a glib answer. Lauren Carlyon mattered to him. Ash considered her answer equally carefully.

"I saw Eward Carlyon the day before he died," she said slowly. "He was especially notorious in the months before his death because he treated the world like a joke he'd orchestrated. Like he could do anything. He was riding a monster of a horse, a vicious-tempered creature which was nipping at other mounts it passed."

She had been trying out her brand-new boyish disguise, and the Black Carlyon had been like a bogeyman, inescapable in his determination to find her.

"There was a boy, eighteen or so. He was a natural, and most ways deaf. He didn't get out the way of the horse, which nipped him, and he swung at it instinctively, didn't even connect. And Eward Carlyon laid his face open with his riding crop. He did it with such open enjoyment that the entire market just stopped and stared at him. Stared and didn't dare do a single thing. Not because he was Luinsel – though his position protected him from too many consequences in life – but because he was waiting, hoping for it. By that stage he must have known his damnation was a certainty, and yet he took such delight in himself. It was a...disgusting display."

"What did you do?" Heran asked in a small voice.

"Nothing," Ash replied, closing her eyes and remembering the way her hand had closed around the hilt of her knife.

She opened her eyes to find Heran staring at her worriedly, so she smiled lop-sidedly. "What could I do? Kill him and be jailed for it? No. The Black Carlyon sat there, enjoying our fear and our hatred until we all looked away and then he enjoyed our cowardice as well. Then he left, the personification of everything that is hateful."

And Genevieve had gone out that night, even though no one had called for her. In the morning, Ash had heard that Eward Carlyon had died, cause unknown.

"I had nightmares for months about that. About the price others might pay for my own inaction. About whether I was running away, or being sensible, or a true coward. I'm someone who – I'm forever getting involved, trying to fix things. I have to make myself *not* step in at times, when it isn't my business. But the Black Carlyon – in truth, there were things I could have done. Spooked his horse, for a start. But I was just plain scared of him.

"When I first encountered Lauren Carlyon I didn't, as was obvious, know who he was. I was impressed by his air of command, thought that at least the first seruilis was someone I wouldn't mind taking orders from, and so there I was, trying to impress in return, wondering vaguely who he reminded me of."

"Then he told you."

Ash inspected faint abrasions on the palms of her hands, remnant of the previous day's exertions. "I think that Lauren Carlyon is as far removed from his father in personality as anyone I have ever encountered. I have no problem, no difficulty with him at all; can only feel sorry for him. You're not the only person in the world who suffers because of his parentage. Yours is too high, and Carlyon's..."

"Yes. I never speak to him of it. No-one does."

"What could you say? But enough of this. It's depressing." Seeing that he was sagging into the pillows, Ash stood up, postponing part of her planned conversation until later. "Make a quick recovery, Ser Veirhoi." She made her way to the door.

"Ash. Come and talk to me again, will you?"

She smiled, flipped him a vague salute, and left, turning over ways to keep him alive.

CHAPTER EIGHTEEN

"Do you think there are two killers?" she asked, not long before she was due to go to the Mern the next day.

Thornaster looked up from the sword he was oiling, and raised his brows. "Do you?"

"I don't know." She sat down on the long lounging chair that was a central feature of the Visel's new receiving room, where Thornaster had been teaching her to maintain his weaponry. "It doesn't make sense that someone should hire a foreign assassin to kill all the herbalists unless they were planning to use some sort of herb for something important and poisoning people is the logical conclusion there. But if the Rhoi or Heran is the target, why the obvious attempts to finish off Heran? And why him? There still haven't been any attempts on the Rhoi's life, have there?"

"Not that we know of. One occurrence that could easily have been an accident. But he is a little more difficult to come near."

"If they could block Heran's chimney, why not the Rhoi's? They live in the same apartments. And, if there's a woman out there who can appear in people's bedrooms, why doesn't she just appear in the Rhoi's? Or Heran's?"

"There are wards on many of the palace rooms. There are wards in these rooms. Old ones, very faded, but still operating."

"Really?" She glanced around in automatic futility. "How long does it take to put a ward on a room?"

"Months. For a permanent one."

"Oh." She lifted the sword from her lap, correcting her grip the way Thornaster had shown her, and moved it thoughtfully back and forth. "I don't think this is my weapon," she told him, considering the weight of the blade. "It feels very wrong."

"Does it?" He was being amused again, but she ignored that.

"Yes. But I suppose you could teach me the best ways to get past a swordsman's guard. Where did you put my knife?"

The Visel, eyes dancing, produced the thin, precisely balanced throwing blade he'd confiscated as soon as he'd discovered her carrying it. "You consider this the better weapon, then?"

"It doesn't have some of the advantages of a sword, of course. I expect there are good and bad points to both, but I've carried a knife for years and I can't see myself becoming more adept at a longer blade at this late date."

"You're past learning at sixteen? But what if you find yourself with only a sword as a weapon?"

"Facing someone who's been learning since he was knee-high? I'd have a better chance throwing the thing at him as a distraction and legging it. Why are you finding this so funny?"

The man brushed his hair back out of his eyes, smiling down at his sword. "I have had two seruilisi before you," he explained. "I was just considering their reactions if they heard you glibly producing reasons why I should not spend too much effort instructing you in the sword."

"Did you teach them?"

"On occasion. If they had done something particularly deserving, I would reward them with a few lessons."

"Wasn't there anyone else to teach them?"

"Of course there was, stripling," Thornaster replied, lips quirking. "And don't point that wide-eyed expression in my direction. If you ever had an ounce of naiveté in you, it's long since moved on to more convivial surroundings."

"I take it you are accounted particularly good? And my predecessors would consider it nigh-on blasphemy for me not to fawn at your feet in gratitude at the mere idea of you attempting to pass this skill on?"

"Exactly."

She pretended to give this due consideration. "I suppose it would be impolite of me to suggest that they were probably trying to keep on your good side?"

That opened the man's eyes wide. "Why cultivate politeness now?" he asked. "I wouldn't want you to abandon the habit of a lifetime out of any desire to please me."

"Oh, good. I thought for a moment I'd have to pretend I was enjoying myself."

Smiling, the Visel shook his head. "Having established your unwillingness, shall we go on to the Mern? I'll speak to Master Humboldt first, and take you for the second session."

With exaggerated reluctance, Ash rose and followed him down to the Mern, leaving him to make her way to the Common Room to face her fellow seruilisi.

They were, she sensed immediately, now split into two distinct camps. Those who had grown more hostile towards her and those who were unsure how to react. She suspected Gibrace had thawed towards her the most, and perhaps Vendarri. Only two people hadn't changed, one being Frog, who greeted her enthusiastically, plumped himself down beside her and talked non-stop until Carlyon arrived. Carlyon, as before, gave her no more attention than any other seruilis. Ash kept her own reactions to modest shrugs and a few 'yes-no' answers as Frog plied her with questions.

The first session was another lecture on sewers. Keeping the Milk uncontaminated was a major concern, though it sounded like the Luinsel in charge of the city districts did little more than retain experts. Ash wasn't the only one struggling to keep her attention focused, and was relieved when Carlyon returned and told Vendarri that he could instruct the group in archery before indicating that Ash should follow him.

"I owe you my thanks, Lenthard," he said, pausing at the entrance to the main practice ground.

She met his eyes, abandoning the meek obedience that she'd been using in the Mern. This wasn't something she could answer flippantly, not with this so-honourable youth she had insulted. But it would be easiest to keep absolutely to business. "You were ahead of him. Was there anyone with or ahead of you? Who can be ruled out?"

He didn't shut down the discussion, had likely been given some intimation that Ash's role was in part to protect the Veirhoi. "Vendarri. He's always break-neck in the rough."

Ash nodded. "It must have been spur of the moment. Too difficult to arrange on purpose – suddenly finding oneself alone behind one's target. If he was alone."

"You're suggesting a conspiracy? False alibis?"

"Can't rule out the possibility. Even the ones supposedly unarmed. I could have concealed a crossbow in my saddlebag and fired when the opportunity arose. Thornaster has one of astonishingly small proportions."

Carlyon just shook his head, but, as they came up to the two older men, he added in an undertone: "Not if you shoot as wildly as Vendarri claims."

Ash's opinion of swords did not improve, despite Thornaster's patience. She felt awkward with them, and it didn't help that not only Carlyon, but Master Humboldt as well, were apparently to share her lessons. They handled their blades as if they were goose down and, while they were apparently learning a new style, they were quick to adapt. Ash, seeing no immediate escape from these lessons, boredly copied the moves Thornaster demonstrated, her mind on more important matters.

Thornaster's eyes rested on her thoughtfully while they made their way back to his rooms, but he didn't chastise her for her probably too-open dislike of her 'reward'. He understood, at least, where her priorities lay.

CHAPTER NINETEEN

Two days later a note was delivered via Mirramar, and taken by Thornaster to Investigator Verel.

"Wagoner found her hiding in a barrel behind Varitty's. She's cold and scratched up, but no serious injuries. The only thing she'll say is that a Sera turned into a black dog and chased her. Ma and Da say you can find her here if you want to talk to her – from the sound of it, we won't get any argument about who keeps her from her so-called grandparents."

"Shapeshifter?" Lips pursed, the Guard Investigator handed the note back. "Shapeshifting is rare – few mages can achieve it. Though it would explain why we're having so much trouble finding a foreign female mage."

Thornaster turned the note over before handing it back to Ash. "A clever tactic for an assassin. How many dogs, black or not, are there in any city? Who would pay attention to one roaming at night? Accessing the palace grounds wouldn't be difficult either, though she'd stand out inside the buildings. And she would have traces of power about her while transformed, so I would know her if I saw her."

"Well, if we manage to line up all the dogs in the city for inspection, I'll be sure to call you," Verel said sourly, and left.

"I wonder how she'll go about arranging that search?" Thornaster said, entertained.

"Can I go down into the Commons?" Ash asked. "I can get there and back before I'm due at the Mern."

"Of course." He dropped a hand briefly onto her head. "Take Arth, if you like."

Ash blinked up at him, then realised he was still trying to reward her. "A *much* better idea than waving swords about," she said, and left to the sound of his laughter.

After a detour by the kitchens for an offering to appease Cloud Cat, Ash almost skipped to the stable, and had to rein herself in before approaching the stalls. After lavishing suitable attention on Cloud Cat, she took immense pleasure on saddling the Aremish stallion. Arth turned his head to look at her as she set her foot to the stirrup, but made no objection to her mounting, and took mincing little steps until they were out of the stable.

"Don't you laugh at me, too," she told the stallion, and wished she had an excuse to let him have his head. As it was, she reached the Rogadney bakery in record time, and sent Bitty out to watch over such valuable horseflesh.

Merit Rogadney, Lark's towering father, came out to shake his head admiringly, then made a number of genial remarks on Ash's determination to increase the size of his family. Her street waif had been appearing morning and evening for the promised meals, but had so far resisted Sera Rogadney's dismayed attempts to clean her up and extract a name from her.

"Can I see Sonia?"

"She's asleep right now," Larkin said, emerging from the bakery in his usual dusting of powder. "Take a walk with me, and maybe she'll be up when we get back."

"I can't stop," Ash said regretfully, inviting him to admire Arth, which he did from a safe distance. And once they were safely out of earshot of Larkin's extensive family, she added: "Tonight, take Melar and Bitty to the Shambles. See if you can spot the skarl. Don't do more than observe it: confirm its existence. And its colour."

There was a long, slow intake of breath, then a frown. "The first skarl was grey."

"That's why I want you to look. It's logical to connect shapeshifting mage with magical wolf, but the last one didn't show any hint of being originally human. Look for any differences, any sign of increased intelligence. For Astenar's sake, don't engage it."

"Considering how close I came to buying it with the first skarl, I'm not overwhelmingly eager to tangle with this one. But...do you want me to test to see if the rowan works on it?"

"If it's our killer, we don't want to make her think we've spotted her disguise. Look and leave."

"And then what? You thinking of calling in your new friends to clear up?"

She shook her head. "The Guard and the Watch would be hopeless trying to deal with the Shambles. They don't know it; don't know the short cuts, the boltholes. All they'd succeed in doing is putting her in more intensive hiding. If it's her, we're dealing with a skarl-mage-assassin-shapeshifter which we have to capture alive, to find out who hired her."

"Alive?! Well, I hope you've got a solid plan, Ash, because even if it is just a skarl, no shapeshifting involved, I don't know if we could manage that."

"I'll think on it," Ash promised.

She failed to even appreciate the ride back to the palace, and paid no attention to the afternoon of dancing lessons, completely forgetting that Montmothian formal dancing was something an ex-Khanteck stable hand was unlikely to know. Fortunately she also kept forgetting that she was supposed to take the male role, and flubbed often enough to seem unlearned. Her session with Thornaster would certainly not make him believe she had a future with the sword, her mind fully occupied while her body swung the practice rapier back and forth.

Thornaster noticed but didn't bother her with questions, and she made no attempt to explain, though her preoccupied air lasted through the evening. She stood behind him in the Rhoi's study and failed to track the conversation at all, beyond recognising a level of constraint in the previously light-hearted chatter. How to capture a skarl, who was a mage, alive?

ooOoo

"It's there. It's her."

Ash shut the door of the storage room, closing any eavesdroppers from the kitchen away. "Tell me."

"I took Sho along as well as Bitty and Melar – this 'no-one in the Shambles alone' thing makes for complications." Larkin shrugged. "We figured on either the Wet Yard or The Pile being the best place for a skarl to hide out, and split into pairs to sit watching the easiest roads in and out. Wasn't much past sundown when we saw her, coming out of The Pile. Skinny black thing, a little smaller than the last skarl, but that same weird effect of almost seeming to bring shadows along.

Damn hard to see. Me and Sho waited till she was long gone, then whistled for Melar and Bitty. Melar nixed the idea of backtracking into The Pile, and instead took all the food we had along, tied in a kerchief with a couple of coins and a comb Bitty had with her. He bounced along the street like he was running from something, fell flat on his face – still not sure if he did that deliberately – and left the kerchief behind, rolled into a tangle of old boards. He and Bitty headed home, and Sho and I sat it out till midnight."

"I suppose 'just confirm there's a skarl' was too much to ask from you lot."

"Like you'd do any different, Ash Cat. I suppose any dog, skarl or not, would have smelled that kerchief. Nice bit of bacon and cheese, which Melar pointed out was silly for me to bring along in the first place. And he'd dropped it in a good spot, not just laying out in the open. Instead of trying to nudge the boards away, or stick her head into them, the skarl looks around and then..." Larkin pulled a face, waving his hands as if trying to outline something intangible. "Sho kept calling it 'vomiting' and I guess that'll do. Except all over. It was quick, thank Luin, and then there was this woman. Gaunt, pale, with close-cropped hair. She even had clothes on, though it looked as if she'd put a hole in a sheet, and then sewn pockets on it. She grabs the kerchief, quick and easy, tucks it in a pocket, and two breaths later there's just the skarl again, trotting off into The Pile through a hole she'd have to crawl to get through in human form. So, do you have a plan?"

Ash made a face. "Tell the Huntsmen to be ready for something tonight. I'll get word to you before the sun sets, after I've found out more about shapeshifters. She mightn't be as difficult to kill as a real skarl."

"She might be harder. And wasn't the point to *not* kill her?"

"That's the hurdle."

Ash took advantage of the Rhoi's reward for the first time, and ventured into the largest collection of books she'd ever seen. The librarian was happy to point her toward works that dealt with skarl and shifters, but Ash didn't learn much of use, other than there was no reason to presume that the shapeshifter wouldn't be as difficult to deal with as a real skarl. The skarl of Naggol, 'cursed' like most of that large island's fauna with strange mutations and powers, could not be damaged – or even touched – by ordinary weapons. They were part shadow, insubstantial at will.

Accepting that the books were not going to provide an easy solution, Ash decided she might as well take the opportunity to start her original library project. First, she unrolled a detailed map of Aremal. It was a huge Rhoimarch, more than four times Montmoth's size, and she almost decided that Pembury didn't exist, but eventually located a tiny notation southwest of the capital.

She tapped the map thoughtfully, and then turned to genealogies and histories. Thornaster's mother was a cousin of Aremal's Rhoi, or so he'd claimed. That was probably true, since he had the abilities of Luin and Astenar's bloodline.

The Estarrels were of such importance that even Montmoth kept a detailed family tree. The current Aremish Rhoi, Vorlan Estarrel, and his wife Kintairy, were listed at the bottom of the enormous sheet of heavy paper, their three children – Romar, Cenaria and Morrion – mere notations below. Above, hundreds upon hundreds of names in minute script. The Rhoi had two first cousins, both male, three second cousins and a number of more distant connections, then a host who could claim extremely tenuous relations. None of the women were named Thornaster, or had married a man named Thornaster. Ash skimmed through the entire genealogy and could not find the name Thornaster anywhere.

Had he lied? He had sounded sincere when he'd assured her that he was the Visel of Pembury. Staring at the closely written sheet, Ash suddenly laughed, spotting an obvious subterfuge. But surely someone had worked this out before her? The rolled sheet had been suspiciously clean of dust.

The discovery made her decision more difficult. He had lied to her, told her he was Rion Thornaster, Visel of Pembury, and she had not been able to spot the lie. Dare she trust him? More to the point, did he trust her? Playing an impish teen had its disadvantages, and the response to the plan she'd spent the last day considering was too likely to be "the Guard will take over." Ash could not gamble this chance to capture Genevieve's killer on Thornaster's opinion of her.

He had allowed her to ride Arth.

This was probably not a solid basis for an important decision, but it settled Ash's mind, at least enough to postpone the question and engage properly in the afternoon's session at the Mern. After a discussion on why Luinsels should not excessively purify water, she even found positive aspects to swordplay.

"Lauren didn't come at me immediately, just because I was holding a sword," she told Thornaster as they walked back to his apartment. "It would give me time to put a knife in him."

"You could just use the sword, stripling. Though a knife in reserve is not a bad idea. So you've decided that I'm not totally wasting your time with my lessons, have you?"

"I never thought they were a *total* waste of time."

"You have some talent for the sword, you know."

She looked at him with patent disbelief, and he laughed.

"I have never met anyone so inclined to doubt my word, Ash. With a little, no, to be honest, several years of instruction, you would be a competent enough swordsman. You have the reflexes and the coordination for it. If, perhaps, not the eager attitude I am used to."

"Would you like me to fawn a little?"

"You mean you know how?"

"I expect I could pick it up after a demonstration or two." She grinned at the thought, but, as he opened the door to his rooms, added: "I need to talk to you seriously."

A quick glance, then he led her into his new study and sat down. "Very well."

"The mage is in the Shambles. There's been word of a skarl in there, so I had it checked out last night. It's her all right. They saw her change."

Thornaster straightened, but she couldn't follow the expressions that flickered across his face. "Can you lead us to where she was sighted?"

"No."

Black eyes narrowed, studying her. "Why not?"

"The Guard doesn't know the Shambles. It's a maze, too ruined for them to risk. We only get by because we use the roofs. There's no way the Guard could catch her. But we could. We've done it before."

"'We' being your street gang?" There was a silky edge to Thornaster's voice that she hadn't encountered before, and didn't particularly like.

"The Shambles is one of our...haunts. We hunted out a skarl a couple of years ago. Killed it. Rowan is their bane, and we had staves of it made up specially. But it was a difficult kill. Most weapons can't touch one at all."

"You've been deciding whether or not to tell me this, haven't you?" A cross between disbelief and chagrin.

Ash nodded.

"What did you imagine you would do with a group of untrained boys against this killer?" He was not quite angry: more outraged.

"That's what I've been working over. If it was just a skarl – well, we've done that. It's dangerous, but possible. But a skarl which is really a mage-assassin? Maybe if I was just out to kill her, yes. But capturing...that's something else altogether." An admission of defeat. Ash didn't like not being able to do things.

"It is indeed. This is far enough, Ash. If you think Verel or I will place a group of children at risk, you are sadly mistaken. You will tell me the location of this skarl, now." All the haughty arrogance of which his face was capable came to the fore. It was a very stern, commanding man who gave her that order.

"I thought you had more sense," she said, caught between anger and sorrow.

She had misjudged him. Or was just impossibly trapped by her own disguise, the badinage and impish mien hardly the thing to inspire confidence in her leadership. This was the price she paid for running away from herself.

"There's no way the Guard can capture the skarl when it's in the Shambles. If you go in there on foot, she will escape. Easily. And I'll wager you anything you please Investigator Verel couldn't raise a force who not only knows the Shambles of old, but has driven a skarl through it."

They stared at each other. Ash, pulse pounding, hated herself for the misstep, and struggled to set her mind to finding a solution that did not include Thornaster.

But then Thornaster flicked back the shining dark wings of his hair, and the moment passed. "Stripling, you are an implacable force. And I would do well to remember how close this is to your heart. We will see what Verel says to your plans – if you can convince her, I have no grounds for objection."

She let out a relieved breath, and a wry smile touched his lips.

"Though in future, Ash Lenthard, I would appreciate it if you'd tell me what you learn as you learn it. Not after you've decided whether I would be useful."

"I'll think about it," she promised, and he shook his head.

"I shall be interested to see if and how you convince Investigator Verel."

But the Investigator was surprisingly reasonable, especially after Ash had laid out the method they had used previously to corner and kill a skarl, and what she thought necessary to capture this one.

And so Ash went to call her Huntsmen to the chase.

CHAPTER TWENTY

Three rooms, once an attic. A portion of the long roof had collapsed, blocking the stairs to the building below, but the remainder was intact and seemed solid, for all it was only accessible from the roofs. That made it an ideal meeting spot for the Huntsmen, a dry and completely private place to gather.

Ash, having finished laying out the plan, stressed the dangers involved, and watched her friends' excited, determined faces. She always gave them an opportunity to refuse, though she knew none would this time. Too many people owed Genevieve. She could have asked them to brave all the Beasts of Naggol for Genevieve. And for Ash.

The loyalty, trust and friendship that surrounded her here was a complete contrast to the wary tolerance she'd now achieved at the Mern. But then, Larkin's group of friends had been anything but accepting of "that little pest" when she'd first arrived in their neighbourhood. She had proved herself to them, as she still might do to the Kinsel. And she knew the Huntsmen would not follow her half so readily if they knew who she really was – she had faced and settled that question years ago, when they were arguing over whether Bitty and Kate would be allowed to join. She led them thanks to a limit on her trust.

But tonight she didn't care. These were her Huntsmen, her sky-runners. This would be their last hunt together.

"It's time," Melar said, as the valley passed from the long halflight when the Sun was blocked by the mountains into true night.

Ash nodded and gave them one last survey. It was obvious that Sim and Carl were barely restraining exuberance, that few of them were as daunted as they should be.

"This one isn't a game," she said, quiet because that would make them listen. "This isn't an animal. Nor is it one of the idiots we bag and deliver to the nearest Watch House. This is the woman who killed

Genevieve. Stop having fun, and start thinking of all the years stolen from her, and how you absolutely can't be the scut who lets her killer get away. The first one of you who breaks from the plan, I'll stuff down a chimney."

She nodded at Lark to take his group out first, then followed with the other half into a night where both Cuinefaer and slumbering, broken Yurefaer coloured the shadows. Dressed dark, each holding a distinct, light-coloured staff of stripped rowan longer than they were tall, the Huntsmen aimed for speed and quiet. Many of them wore boots purchased specifically for their thin, supple soles, and claimed they could feel the buildings breathe beneath them as they ran between sagging slopes of tiles, following safe routes discovered through years of testing. Run soft and avoid unshuttered windows, and the ever-present danger of a loose tile, a weak support, a slippery patch of wet or grease.

Despite the circumstances, Ash could not help but enjoy herself. Sky-running – the air cool and crisp, the high moons, the sheer challenge of moving over a house full of people who had no notion that their roof had become a highway. She set her staff and arced across a blackly cavernous street, hearing only the faintest audible echoes. It was a different world up here, away from the dark, torturous and frankly smelly lower reaches of the Shambles. Where a ground traveller would be led astray by back-winding streets and gates rusted shut, their way obstructed by abandoned temporary dwellings, and the occasional deliberate barricade, sky-runners soared unhindered.

Mockhold Valley had once been the best address in Luinhall, when the area immediately around the Milk had begun to fill and the attractively broad western valley had offered a perfect location for spacious houses. It had prospered in the centuries after the Breaking, but then the southern passes had been reopened, making travel into Montmoth easy during the warm months. With the travellers came stories of Montmoth's waters, and both the glacial Milk and Luinhall's hot springs acquired fame as waters of youth, blessed by Luin. For a brief time, Luinhall faced summer crowds greater than the city could handle, and responded with cheap, dangerous, firetrap construction to accommodate them. By the time the stories were finally deemed exaggeration, and the crowds died away, Mockhold had tipped well over the edge of a long slide to the blot it was today: an eyesore, a fire waiting to happen.

At night, moonlit, its crazed architecture became the city's jewel.

Ash slowed her progress to a crawl as they neared the centre of the Shambles. These tight-packed roofs were less than stable, and ahead was The Pile, a cluster of buildings that had leaned together into total collapse a decade ago.

They prowled closer, poling only rarely out above the streets now that they were in their prey's territory. Ash broke her group into two sets of three, and took one set ahead to settle at the location where Larkin had originally sighted the skarl. Larkin's group were south of her, staking the other street a creature like a skarl was likely to use to exit the tangle of fallen houses.

Sim, least able to keep quiet for extended periods of time, had been sent to the peak of a roof between the two ambush sites. He would relay any signal from Larkin with gestures, so there was no possibility of the skarl detecting their usual whistle-talk. Scent should not be a major issue, with so many in the buildings beneath them, but without calm there was too much chance of detection.

Seating herself against the canted wall of a second story, Ash looked over her group, and then nodded. No one in a position that would cramp them or be visible from the ground. She leaned back, wrinkling her nose as the breeze wafted fetid stench out of the tangle of tumbled buildings, then fixed her gaze on the street.

Ever active, her mind immediately wandered to that day's lecture on water purification. She'd noticed a distinct change in Marriston's attitude. Not the "he saved the Veirhoi but I don't know how to apologise" hesitancy of most of the seruilisi, but...anticipation. Marriston would be the type who responded with petty vengeance to being proved wrong. She wondered what it would be. A quick scuffle in a deserted part of the palace? No, too open to consequences. If she were out for revenge, she'd work out a way to make Marriston make a fool of himself with the maximum audience. There was a garden party and a banquet coming up, where the seruilisi would stand about in the full scrutiny of half the Landsmeet. Did Marriston have the skill – the subtlety – to bring off anything worth caring about?

Irritably she rubbed the hilt of her knife, which Thornaster had returned without comment. The Mern still felt like a distraction, especially while the Veirhoi kept to his sickbed. Carlyon was better positioned to play investigator among the Kinsel. But, after tonight, her role as gutter seruilis may no longer be an issue. If they uncovered the identity of the assassin's employer.

A flicker of movement caught her eye.

With effort Ash kept her breathing even, letting out no telltale gasp. Time to loose the hounds.

Lifting a hand, Ash watched for Sim's reaction. She could see him only as a silhouette, one that turned and crossed its arms over its head. Once she was sure he had seen, Ash turned her head and met the eyes of each of her group of Huntsmen as the skarl padded into sight. Her hand signal was now a command to hold. It would not do to give themselves away and send the beast skittering back to her lair.

Not that the skarl seemed at all inclined to skitter. Trotting confidently down the centre of the little street, a lean animal made large by coarse, shaggy black hair, bringing shadow in its wake. A cursed wolf of Naggol. Ash trembled as her target passed beneath her – the creature that had come into her home, and cut the throat of the person Ash loved most.

She waited until the shapeshifter reached the end of the street, and then closed her hand into a fist, rising silently to her feet as she did so. Gesturing to Carl and Bitty to indicate that they were to move ahead, Ash ran with swift, light steps along the roof's edge. As she came within range, she chose a strong-looking gutter and dropped, clutching the rim and hanging down to swing her long, rowan staff, striking the animal hard across the rump.

The skarl screamed.

Ash bared her teeth. Rowan was the bane of many magical animals, and had been the key to the first skarl hunt. It could not only touch the shadow-cursed, it caused pain. Excruciating pain.

Swinging back to solid footing, Ash hurried after her Huntsmen as the skarl headed toward the first junction. It turned the wrong way at the corner, but half of Lark's group were waiting, and a second keening yelp rose over triumphant human voices. Bitty struck as the four-footed assassin went past, and the hunt was engaged in full.

The plan was the same as their previous hunt in the Shambles. To drive the animal into a prepared trap, directing her with goads of rowan, never letting her have a chance to stop or turn or think. Racing in frantic leapfrog moves to block street after street with crossed staves, to strike again and again, to keep the pain and confusion and noise at maximum pitch, so that a human woman in the form of a skarl would not have time enough for any thought beyond RUN.

"Get off the street!"

Startled by Bitty's yell, Ash almost lost her footing, dropping a pace behind. Someone had strayed onto the carefully chosen route, and Ash cursed them, trying to judge the distance. Would they be able to get whoever it was out of the way in time?

"Mad dog!" Melar yelled, not too far away, his voice cracking. "*Mad dog!*"

The cry was taken up by other Huntsmen, and must have been effective because Ash, panting as the pace began to tax her, passed a wholly confused and frightened man, who almost took a nose-dive back into the street when she leapt around him.

The skarl tried to turn and Dest caught her across the lower jaw with an upswing. Ash joined him and a hail of blows of varying strength beat the shapeshifter into continuing on her way. The creature tried a different tactic, putting on a stunning burst of speed which no human could keep pace with, but she was defeated by the Shambles. Although Ash had chosen a relatively clear path, it was still incredibly twisted, and the Huntsmen only managed to keep pace through a combination of knowledge and practiced skill. A stitch in her side impeding her almost as much as her burning lungs, Ash thanked Astenar that she had not placed the trap too far away.

The skarl burst into what had once been a market square and immediately a jury-rigged gate fell into place behind her, leaving the shapeshifter trapped in a hastily fashioned but solid cage. Ash, driven by her momentum, almost fell into the enclosure with the skarl, which would have been as embarrassing as it was fatal. Gasping for breath, she dropped to her knees on the corner of the building as Investigator Verel, standing on the far side of the makeshift cage, said something loud and incomprehensible which made the hotchpotch collection of doors, broken wagons, gates and rubble shimmer with an only partially visible blue light.

Howling, the skarl slammed into the gate that had fallen behind her. A flash of light threw her violently backwards, but this only enraged the creature and she threw herself at the barrier again and again. Watching the scene scarce feet below her, Ash wondered if the cry of "mad dog" had not been correct after all. But then, quite abruptly, the shapeshifter ended her frantic attempts to escape, and turned to study her prison with burning eyes, circling the cage once then pacing into the middle of the enclosure and stopping, facing Verel.

As the creature transformed, a murmur ran through the gathered audience – from the panting Huntsmen on the rooftops to the emerging collection of Guard and Watch. 'Vomiting'. Ash could not help but bring Sho's description to mind as thick fur regurgitated pale flesh and faded cloth.

The bruised, crop-haired woman which took the animal's place, with her odd, many-pocketed gown and her cloth-bound feet, seemed to have no relation to the animal she had been. Nothing but those burning, red-rimmed eyes.

"Why?"

Ash had meant to keep quiet. Her voice seemed to echo, though she had barely raised it above a whisper.

The woman turned to stare up at Ash. They searched each other's faces, Ash seeking reasons or reasoning, the shapeshifter looking for Astenar knew what.

Something grabbed Ash's shirt from behind, yanking her backwards just as the woman's arm blurred upwards. The staff Ash had been holding clattered noisily to the ground as she landed on her back, eyes wide open when the flash of steel passed overhead.

There was shouting from below, and chanting. Hastily Ash sat up, gripping Melar's arm tightly as the shapeshifter tore away at the barrier, a stream of incomprehensible words accompanying her movements as she tried to combat the spell and climb at the same time. Almost, it seemed that she would escape, because the faint limning of blue light flickered out of existence, but then it returned in a skull-piercing flash and the killer was thrown backwards, as far as the opposite side of the enclosure, falling into a twisted heap of wrong angles.

"Oh, damn," Melar whispered.

Ash, though momentarily paralysed by a variety of pure fury she rarely experienced, was able to release his arm, aware that he would have bruises where her fingers had sunk into his flesh. She took a deep breath.

"You saved my life, Melar," she said, evenly. "Thank you."

He was still staring down at the body.

"And that 'mad dog' thing was quick thinking," Ash continued. "You probably saved that man's life as well."

Melar looked at her then. "But it's all wasted!" he blurted, his usual calm lost to the night's failure. "She's dead! We'll never find out who hired her now!"

Ash shook her head, watching as Verel disbanded her spell and the Guard efficiently began to dismantle the physical cage. The death touched her less than she had expected. For all she had driven the woman into this trap, it had been the assassin who had chosen to fight rather than be captured.

"Wasted? Genevieve's killer has died as she should – surrounded by her enemies, scrabbling for her freedom. As for her employer...well, perhaps we will discover something of that one when we track back to wherever in The Pile she was sleeping."

"Never give up, hey, Ash Cat?" Larkin asked, coming up behind them.

She looked up at him and watched him react to her expression. Then she shrugged and rose to her feet, became all business again, sending her Huntsmen on their way, all but Larkin and Melar, who were less easily ordered and who knew the heart of the Shambles best. The three of them dropped lightly to the ground, where Thornaster and Verel waited. The Aremian handed her her staff, his eyes flicking over her in a quick, precise search for injury. Then he nodded.

"Formidable," he said, the words both congratulation and comment.

"Anything useful on the body?" she asked.

The Investigator shook her head. "Food. Weapons. Trinkets. Nothing."

"You want to track back to her nest tonight, or wait till daylight?"

"How long before the scavengers move in?"

Ash shrugged. "It would have to be a brave scrabbler."

Thornaster and Verel exchanged a look. "Tonight," Verel said, decisively. "Tracking is very limited, and best not delayed. Can you lead us to the point you first sighted her? I'll cast from there."

After a pause, while Verel removed one of the bindings from the dead shapeshifter's foot, presumably to be used in her casting, Ash and her friends resumed the skyways and returned to the start of their hunt at a much slower pace, guiding Thornaster, Verel and two of the more hulking Guards.

The trail led directly to the narrow entrance of The Pile, and Thornaster had to remain behind with Larkin and the guards, while Ash and Melar crawled with Verel to the place the shapeshifter had spent her days. There, among the mouldering blankets and scraps of a life lived rough, they found buried three purses heavy with gold. Nothing else.

It was not until Ash and Thornaster had returned with Verel to her office in the palace that they thought to empty the purses, and found two signet rings. Thornaster scooped them up, studying them with disbelieving eyes. In response to the Investigator's anxious question, he displayed one next to the ring he wore on the smallest finger of his right hand.

The other was Hawkmarten's.

CHAPTER TWENTY-ONE

"Hello, Heran."

"Ash. You came."

"Why wouldn't I?" The window was once again curtained and shuttered, and Ash busied herself in opening it, then sat down on the sill. "Still bedridden? I would have thought you'd have recovered enough to get around by now."

"Master Tsimon says I have to stay here for another week."

"Whatever for? Come over here," she ordered. "I like your view."

She smiled vaguely into the distance while Heran decided to do as she said. He came to a stop by the sill and looked resolutely out.

"You're doing this deliberately, aren't you Lenthard?"

"You'd find being afraid of heights terribly inconvenient, Heran. Don't convince yourself that you are." She dangled her legs out the window, drumming the heels of her boots against weathered stone.

"Brilliant advice. How do you suppose I go about it?"

"Sit down." Ash gestured at the remainder of the sill.

Heran looked at it, then at Ash, then gingerly lowered himself to sit legs inside, keeping a white-knuckled grip on the stone. Leaning against the folded shutter, he closed his eyes, and then cracked the lids enough to see her and her alone.

"The way Arun was acting last night, I know your Visel Thornaster was out doing something interesting. What was it?"

"Ha, so that's the reason for your invitation. Doesn't that fall under the heading of gossip about my Luinsel?"

"I don't give a damn if it's gossip or not."

She cocked an eyebrow at him, not surprised by the frustration. And then, after glancing at the nearest windows to reassure herself that they were firmly closed, she told him, not quite everything, but more than enough.

"Thornaster and Verel's faces were a picture when they found those rings. Total shock from him, and Verel like a shutter had slammed down. Then they lined up the possibilities, all neat together. That Thornaster and Hawkmarten were behind the murders. That someone intended to make it seem that way. That either Hawkmarten or Thornaster had hired the assassin with the intention of implicating his fellow. That both of them were the assassin's next targets, after she'd run out of herbalists. That last is the one Thornaster *wants* it to be. I haven't seen much of Hawkmarten outside these trigle games, but Thornaster considers him a friend, and he really didn't like when Investigator Verel pointed out the man could be preparing the ground for Nyreem to invade."

Heran scrubbed his hands through his golden curls. "Why doesn't Arun tell me these things? I knew there were murders, and the rumours about poisoning. But for Father to ask Aremal for help! For – for *Karaelsur* to somehow be a threat?"

"You'd certainly be left floundering if someone does succeed in killing Rhoi Arun. Do you think he doesn't trust you?"

"No." The dismissal was immediate, total. "It's just I'm his baby brother, always getting chills, not ready for responsibility. Prone to falling off cliffs."

"And busy suspecting Thornaster of everything under the sun, because the Rhoi hasn't told you why he's here. Does knowing more about what's going on help you at all guessing who shot you?"

Heran shook his head, staring out the window. "None of them seem like killers to me. Lirindar? Vendarri? Marriston? Frog? I'm so glad Lauren was ahead of me – no matter how well he behaves, always there's this expectation he'll follow his father's path."

Hiding a wince, because she was guilty of that herself, Ash said: "Don't forget Gibrace."

"Gibrace is too well-mannered to shoot me," Heran protested. "Frog too much a joker. Marriston would gain nothing from it. None of them would benefit. If both Arun and I were dead, Decsel Enderhay is by far the most likely to be put forward as candidate for Rhoi, and I can't imagine Astenar rejecting him – or any of the seruilisi being so attached to him they'd be willing to kill. And his sons aren't even old enough to be in the Mern yet."

"Have any of the seruilisi been behaving strangely, lately? Differently?"

"Different from what? Most of the differences started because of you. Marriston's been acting right in character there, I assure you. Vendarri's annoyed about having to teach you archery. Lirindar's been given a couple of demerits for lateness, but everyone thinks that's because he's in the middle of a love affair. It's all just–" He lifted his hands.

"A mystery. Problem is, I'm not sure we're clearing the thing up, or making it murkier."

Ash left him sitting on the windowsill, lost in thought. And, she barely resisted pointing out, entirely unconcerned about the drop.

ooOoo

An afternoon in the Mern learning a tactical game called skarrance brought Ash no closer to answers, try as she might to guess the thoughts of those around her. Frog invested the pieces he moved around the map with names and characters. Pelandis blossomed, abandoning jitters for an absorbed progress to victory. Lirindar was subdued, and Marriston annoyed with him. Vendarri kept frowning at Carlyon – perhaps in concern, because the first seruilis barely seemed to pay attention to those around him, his eyes shadowed.

Gibrace had been given the task of explaining the game to Ash, and she made quiet progress toward being able to chat with him, all the while trying to see behind the surface. Mild, observant and intelligent, he rarely offered his own opinions, but listened keenly as the other boys discussed the lack of support for the Rhoi's new law regarding smallholdings, which had yet to be passed by the Landsmeet. The Rhoi's laws could be overturned if two-thirds of the Rhoimarch's Luinsel objected, and the senior seruilisi were totting up numbers.

"I don't really understand the objections to it," Ash confessed to Gibrace as the seruilisi, with a great amount of clatter, packed away the dozens of intricately carved skarrance pieces. "Maybe there will be a tiny number of people who don't pass, but they'd have to be truly failing to maintain the Balance to do so. Where's the harm?"

"Administration costs and favours," Gibrace said with a shrug. "There's a significant expense in not only arranging for every smallholder to be judged, but also to maintain that process into the future. And unbound smallholdings are a useful place to drop problems you want cleared out of your own lands." He gave Ash a hint of a smile. "Of course, there's also the matter of making Montmoth over in Aremal's image. You won't find many who support that."

A word from Carlyon sent the seruilisi clattering out the door, a process that involved a few too many elbows for Ash's tastes. She ducked her head, slipping out of the crowd, then paused on the threshold. Something had been out of place.

Stepping mentally back through the tangle of movement, from the elbow to the skull, to the shoulder banging against hers, there had been the tiniest tug.

Sliding hands into trouser pockets, she brought out the day's accumulation. A fresh kerchief. One of Larkin's notes. Two walnuts. And a General. Creamy, gold-shot quartz carved in the shape of a bearded man, and mounted on a silver base.

Her breath hissing out between her teeth, Ash turned on her heels, marched over to Carlyon, and dropped the skarrance piece into his hand. Then she stalked off to her swordcraft lesson, cursing annoying pests and the necessity of spending any longer in their company.

But with the assassin dead, there was little choice. Investigator Verel was attempting to track the mage, the money, and the origin of the two signet rings – and no doubt thoroughly looking into the backgrounds of Setsel Hawkmarten, and Visel Thornaster. Ash wondered whether Thornaster had fed Verel the same half-truth about his mother being a cousin of the Aremish Rhoi, and if the woman would find any other connections between the two foreign Luinsels and the spate of deaths.

Ash refused to rule it out. Like the man as she might, partiality was not the same as real certainty that Thornaster was innocent of involvement. She could not trust her instincts on someone who amused her, and so would continue to afford him the limited trust common sense prescribed, while keeping an eye out for developments.

Her activities in the Mern followed the same approach. Some of the seruilisi were starting to warm to her, and she was slowly gaining a better sense of their personalities, but showing off and chat would not get her inside their heads. Instead she watched them for suspicious activity, hoped to overhear careless conversation, and held herself ready to follow any lead that came her way.

While not being so thick-witted as to have one of them set her up as a thief.

Chapter Twenty-Two

Heran made his official return appearance at the Rhoi's Spring Celebration, which was a garden party held in the last month of spring each year. It was, the boy said, a perfect opportunity for everyone to gawk at the 'poor little injured Veirhoiling', and his expression of endurance was clearly mistaken for suppressed pain by the Landsmeet host wandering through the extensive palace gardens.

"We're here as seruilisi," Heran said, following Ash behind the spiral of topiaried greenery she'd sought for respite. "They're supposed to treat us like furniture while we're in uniform, not make conversation."

"Furniture? As in sit on us, or put their little plates of cakes on our heads?"

"Statues, then."

"That would involve them standing around discussing what we looked like. Though I admit that would be better than having the same conversation over and over and over. Describing what it was like to rescue you and talking about how wonderfully heroic I am was only fun the first dozen times."

"What do you say when people ask you what it was like to rescue me?"

"That depends on who's asking. I told Lark and Cassia it was cold and boring. Anybody important, I say that I was very relieved to find that you were alive. And all the rest I just say 'nerve-wracking' and they seem to like that as an answer."

"Lark is one of your Huntsmen, yes? Is Cassia as well? You have girls who run around on roofs?"

"Lark is more or less the leader of the Huntsmen, and we include two girls among our number. Cassia's one of the palace laundry maids, though, oh Veirhoi of the ivory tower. She's about the only person of my acquaintance who hasn't asked me what it was like to rescue you as if it were all a great adventure."

"You're romancing a laundry maid? Be careful, or you'll find yourself tripping over the Mern's code of conduct."

"She's just a friend – she keeps me up to date on the gossip." Though Ash suspected Cassia had begun to consider a flirtation with the gutter seruilis. Romance was a complication that Ash had had to learn to sidestep the last couple of years, and it always left her feeling guilty for the deception which bought her so much freedom.

Through the gaps in the topiary spiral, she spotted Carlyon against the hedge opposite. With his upright stance and blank expression he appeared entirely oblivious to the mix of admiring glances and speculative whispers directed his way. The shadow of Eward Carlyon made it unlikely any Carlyon would be a contender for the Rhoi's position, but that had not prevented Lauren Carlyon from becoming a prime suspect in the attempt on Heran's life – for all that the official position was that no such attempt had occurred. Rumour had triumphed over all their precautions.

Frog strolled into view and took up a position at Carlyon's side, clearly trying to tease him into a smile. But then his broad grin faded, his attention fixing on something in the centre of the square of hedges. Curious as to the cause of his almost reverential expression, Ash stepped out from behind the topiaried tree to see the Rhoi, nodding polite greeting to...Kiri Arpesial.

Tall, elegant, her early promise of beauty fulfilled and surpassed. Masses of soft black hair reached her waist, bound loosely by a long rope of beads and framing skin of cream and roses, with no flaw or blemish to distract from feathery lashes, clear grey eyes and a high brow. The curves Ash lacked were set off wonderfully by a dress of muted simplicity, the lack of ornamentation somehow making every other female seem garish or fussy.

Most of all, she was 'wearing her reserve'.

Kiri had been practicing her reserve for as long as Ash had known her, ever since they were neighbours in stiff little dresses, allowed to visit each other so long as they were on their best behaviour. Ash had taught Kiri how to climb from her bedroom window into the Arpesial's attic, where they played dress up among Kiri's great-grandmother's expensive gowns. In return Kiri had tried to teach Ash her reserve. The ability to be attentive and remote, lips never quite curving to a smile, but with no air of hauteur — as if she existed on a slightly different plane, untouchable — was something Ash had never really needed or mastered. For Kiri it was the core of her daily defence.

"Don't go falling for The Incomparable." Heran peered around the edge of the tree. "Not that there's usually any choice about it, I admit. But look at Frog."

Glancing back at the two seruilisi, she found Carlyon practicing his own reserve, and Frog stilled. Without his usual animation he seemed older, and there was deep pain in his stance, a weary ache lacking all hope of ease. As she watched, his eyes widened, and a complicated tangle of emotion made him briefly ugly. Ash found her own face stiffening, and the breath she took was a cold knife, her entire body tensing around sudden, unexpected hurt.

The Rhoi had moved on, and another stood before Kiri. And she smiled. Only a slight shift of expression, but with a genuine warmth that made her transcendent. If the attention of the garden had not already been fixed upon her, now it was entirely riveted as Thornaster, the shining wings of his hair gleaming in the sunlight, bowed over her hand. Together they were magnificent.

Years of daily comparisons to Kiri had long ago prepared Ash for a moment such as this. While they'd been neighbours it hadn't bothered her at all, because Ash liked climbing and horses, and did not care that her braids were inadequate rat-tails, her skin sallow, her figure sturdy. Only in the last year of their friendship had Ash begun to recognise that there might be a day when Kiri's beauty would cost Ash dearly, and back then she had thought she could philosophically accept inevitable defeat.

Today that comparison brought to her the discovery that Thornaster mattered. Mattered completely, so much more than Ash could ever have imagined. Inevitable defeat became a bitter dose to swallow. Caught in a trap built by lies, she looked down, seeking the very techniques Kiri had once tried to teach her, to relax knotted muscles, to smooth the betrayals of the heart from her face.

The fact that Thornaster looked at Kiri with open admiration cost Ash Lenthard nothing. That Kiri broke her own rules to smile back at the Aremish Visel would only be useful ammunition for a gutter seruilis keen to tease his so-called master. Ash put pained discovery away behind a wall, and then eased her breath out, remembering that she was Ash Cat, and what mattered to her was finding Genevieve's killer.

Straightening, she found Thornaster was glancing around, and, catching her eye, he gestured her closer.

"There you are," the Visel said as Ash obediently presented herself. "Your exploits have become famous, stripling. Sera Arpesial has been cultivating me merely to gain an introduction to you."

For a moment Ash thought Thornaster spoke truer words than he realised, but then Kiri's lips parted, just a fraction, and her grey eyes widened.

"Sera Arpesial," Ash said, bowing hastily. When she lifted her head, all evidence of surprise was gone and Kiri nodded at her with bland courtesy.

"I have been hearing reports of your valour from all sides," Kiri said, her voice a note deeper than Ash remembered. "You are fortunate in your friends, Ser Veirhoi."

"I know that, Sera," Heran replied, halting by Ash's elbow.

"Perhaps, if you permit, Ser Visel, your seruilis could take me about the further reaches of the garden? The chatter here is a little overwhelming."

"Of course, Sera." Thornaster shifted so Kiri could transfer her hand from his arm to Ash's.

How should Ash Lenthard, gutter seruilis, react to this? With a delighted grin, and a hint of a strut? No, with an echo of Carlyon's extreme correctness, supplemented by the focused care of someone carrying an overloaded tray: afraid of the slightest misstep.

Kiri said vague and appropriate things until they finally reached a deserted pathway, then she fell silent, her step quickening as she led them to a small sunken garden, a secluded little nook. Here she stopped, spun Ash to face her, and raised a wondering hand.

"It *is* you! Oh, Daere, I knew you weren't dead!"

Pulled into sudden embrace, Ash's mixed emotions were swept aside by fond memory. "I should hope so," she said. "Given I've been tying ribbons all over this city every year so you'd know I was still around."

"I'm so glad you did. That first night, with the fire, I thought – thought – Luin's Heart, Daere, what happened?"

"Ash," Ash said, firmly. "Daere is dead, Kiri. I'm Ash. You must remember not to call me anything but Ash. Never Daere."

Kiri searched her face, then nodded, and drew Ash down on the small stone bench that served as the focal point of the garden. "Very well then. Ash Lenthard. Tell me what happened, in detail: everything. Right now."

Ash smiled, because Kiri had not changed in the slightest. But the answer was not easy to tell.

"You remember the day we went to the Gods' Hall?"

"I'm not likely to forget. The only time I saw That Man."

"After that – well, we were never a wealthy family, and of a sudden there was a run of delays, thievery, breakages. Minor things, but all at once, until they added up to loans, and defaults, and Mother and Father shouting at each other behind closed doors. They were going to have to give up a lot of land. And then both of them one day wouldn't look me in the eye. Told me we had a guest for dinner, and to make sure I didn't go out.

"Mother...Mother had never quite forgiven me for being a girl. And, if I had to be a girl, for not being you. She knew what Eward Carlyon was, had heard those rumours about his second wife's death, but I'd swear she genuinely thought I should in some part be pleased that Eward Carlyon had bought up all their debts and offered to exchange them for me. One of the richest Decsels in Montmoth, after all! And if I didn't go through with it, they would lose too much land to still qualify for a Viselry, would just be common smallholders."

"My parents guessed some part of that. But I could hardly believe you'd go through with it."

"I didn't." Ash shook her head in remembered disgust. "I told them in no uncertain term what they could do with the Viselry. And tried to leave. But Carlyon had brought two servants with him, men he owned body and soul, and... It must have looked ridiculous, that ceremony. Carlyon holding my hand, and his two men holding the rest of me, like a rolled-up carpet that kicked and writhed. I shouted 'no' whenever I was supposed to say 'yes', and swore and tried to bite them as my father bound my hand to Carlyon's..."

She stopped, and let Kiri hold her, just for two deep breaths, then pushed it all away and managed a self-deprecating shrug. "I dream about that a lot. Fighting to get free. The whole of that farce. They were going to call that a marriage, and the problem was that Astenar didn't reject it. The marriage cord didn't turn black, despite the bond being made in the Sun's name. I–" Ash paused. "I wonder if that might be related to some of the things happening now? Father only invoked 'the Sun'. I've been resenting Astenar for years, because the truly wrong marriages are supposed to be rejected. I just assumed that Astenar wasn't paying attention, but maybe it was more complicated than that."

"What do you mean?"

"The recent deaths in Luinhall: there's a chance they're related to the old Sun. I've been thinking of this as a problem which only rose in the last year, but–"

Ash tried to run through the implications of Eward Carlyon having some involvement with Karaelsur, but now was not the time to go into it.

"Anyway," she said, focusing. "Carlyon and my father had papers to sign, so my mother had his men lock me in my room, which had the advantage of bars on the windows. I definitely regretted all the night excursions that led my parents to put them up, but I still had the chimney, and wasted no time hauling myself up to the old nursery. Thankfully the kitchen was on a separate stack. After that it was short work to climb down through the pantry window, sneak a leg of pork, and make a pyre for it out of my bed. I waited the fuss out on the roof – worried spitless that even a stone house might burn down if no one caught the fire in time. When it was quiet, I walked to the Commons and became Ash Lenthard."

"But why didn't you come to me?" No reproach, but a shadow of old pain in Kiri's even voice. "You must have known my family would shelter you."

"Would they? Your parents adore you, but they never really approved of me. And I was his wife, Kiri. So young that there'd be questions and scandal, yes, but with parental consent, no objection from Astenar, and witnesses who'd swear I'd agreed. Bought and paid for."

"I could have hidden you in my room."

"They would have found me within the day, especially when they discovered no human body in that bed. Father would have immediately thought of you and come looking."

"But they didn't realise! No one searched. I went to your *funeral*, Dae– Ash."

Ash shrugged. "Maybe it was for the sake of appearances. One leg of pork couldn't possibly be mistaken for a girl of nearly thirteen, so staying anywhere near was too much risk. And...to be honest, I wouldn't have come back even if I thought it safe. I wanted things people kept telling me I shouldn't be interested in." She reached for her friend's hands, and examined their manicured softness, her own blunt and rough by contrast. "I'm sorry I left you behind, Kiri."

"I'm not." Kiri laced her fingers through Ash's, and gave her the full force of her smile. "You were happy, and you made sure I knew you were alive. Though if we should part in future, I demand letters, not ribbons."

"It's a promise."

"Len*thard!*"

Carlyon. Ash jerked around in dismay, then gasped and hastily dropped Kiri's hands, bolting to her feet. At least ten people were crowded in the entrance to their hideaway, a group featuring the Rhoi, Heran, Thornaster and Carlyon. The first seruilis was the only one who wasn't gaping in disbelief and that because he was too busy frowning.

"Yes, Ser?" Ash said, after a moment.

"You are–!" Carlyon began, but Kiri interrupted, effortlessly resuming all her cool and gracious poise as she rose.

"A wonderful storyteller," she said, firmly. "Ash has been telling me some tales of Jacian I had not heard before. I must compliment you on him, Visel Thornaster. He has a great skill with words."

Thornaster, for once without a ready response, did not recover until Kiri reached the entryway. It was patently obvious that no one believed her explanation, though they were clearly having considerable difficulty with the alternative. Heran's expression was the best – he was staring from Ash to Kiri and back again with something akin to awe.

Ash watched in silence as Kiri took Thornaster's arm and walked away, trailed by an incredulous crowd. Heran and Carlyon remained but Carlyon only said, "I will speak of this to you later, Lenthard," before leaving. Ash, lips twitching, cocked an eyebrow at the Veirhoi.

"How?" Heran breathed.

"I really was just telling her stories."

"I don't believe you. You don't have to hold hands to tell stories. And the way she was looking at you!"

"Mmm, yes. I get the feeling I'm about to develop a reputation for more than saving your life. This could be tiresome."

"Tiresome? *Tiresome*?! You have Kiri Arpesial looking at you like that and you call it *tiresome*?!"

"Definitely," Ash said, and amused herself by not giving Heran another word on the subject.

Thornaster was a different matter. The Visel maintained a decidedly solemn expression for what little remained of the garden party, and didn't speak as they walked back to his apartment. Still raw from the discovery of unexpected feeling, Ash could not find the funny side of this. Surely he couldn't be genuinely annoyed by whatever he thought he'd seen? Was his admiration for Kiri that deep-seated?

As Ash closed the main door behind her, Thornaster strode to one of the study windows and stood looking out. Ash stared at his back, unsure whether to shrug and head to her room, or to try to reassure him she was no rival.

Then she caught the faint quiver of his shoulders.

"Are – are you *laughing*?"

Thornaster turned around, sat unsteadily on the corner of his desk, and let his silent amusement overtake him, covering his face with one hand and laughing in painful-looking spasms until what sounded suspiciously like a hiccup interrupted him. Dropping his hand, he took several gasping breaths.

"Stripling," he managed at last, "the *look* on your face! Oh, and you put your hands behind your back! Like a child caught stealing sweets." He began to laugh again, until another hiccup brought him up short.

Ash shook her head in amazement. "I thought you were annoyed."

"Annoyed? When you so handily accomplished what I had been trying to do all afternoon?"

This was beyond comprehension. At least, it was until Ash started thinking again. "Oh," she said. "The Rhoi."

"The Rhoi," Thornaster repeated, inclining his head.

"The only man there who wasn't making up to her. You were trying to make him jealous."

"Well, at least make him react. Please, you incredible youth, tell me how you accomplished what I had begun to believe impossible? Does Sera Arpesial perhaps have a weakness for heroics?"

"Don't you like her?" Ash asked, heading down the path more interesting to her. "How could you not like her?"

Thornaster's brows lifted. "Ah, have you lost your heart then, lad?" he asked kindly. "I mean no insult to the Sera. Indeed, I find her quite breathtaking, and extremely perceptive. It's merely that I marked early on that there was something between her and Arun. He behaved nothing like himself, every time he encountered her, while she never met his eyes."

"I thought you said Rhoi Arun had been romancing your Rhoi's daughter."

"Ye-es. I don't pretend to know what's going on. And should probably not meddle." He swallowed another hiccup, and then looked her up and down. "However, no matter your heroics, I find it very hard to credit the idea that Sera Arpesial would conduct a liaison with you, stripling. What promise were you talking of?"

"How much did you all hear?"

"Just that."

"Good. Obviously I was simply promising to tell Kiri more about my adventures." Ash shrugged. "Truth is I knew her when she was little, but don't go telling people that. How many did you get today for your meet-all-the-Luinsel project?"

He started to say something, hiccupped again, and tched. "Pest. I haven't done this to myself for years. Where's the list?"

Heading into his bedroom, she extracted a thin roll of papers concealed in his gear, and watched as he marked off another dozen names.

"What do we do if you meet every Luinsel in Montmoth and still can't find someone with this taint?"

"Then I'll visit every piece of unbound land in the city. And the law about smallholdings may pressure whoever is behind this into a response, so hold yourself alert for developments." He hiccupped, gave her a Look, and then sighed. "Not that I'm happy to be making such poor progress. Go entertain yourself, stripling, while I stand on my head or something to get this to stop."

"Watching that would *be* entertainment," Ash said, but left him to it.

Thornaster never mentioned Hawkmarten when considering plans of action. He was leaving that investigation strictly to Verel, and the trigle games continued as usual. If Hawkmarten had noticed any faint thread of constraint, he gave no sign.

Lying down on her bed, Ash tried to think of a positive plan of action. She would wait a few days, then find a way to talk to Kiri uninterrupted. Both to recruit a useful ally in her hunt, and to ask about the Rhoi. To offer help, if it was wanted, though at this stage it was difficult to tell if that would be for reconciliation or a proper scorning of the unfaithful.

Grimacing, Ash put aside the question of Kiri's heart, and closed her eyes to better contemplate a man who called himself Rion Thornaster. A descendent of Astenar and Luin, able to sense magic and heat things with a glance. And laugh himself into hiccups. 'Cousin' to the Rhoi of Aremal.

Tentatively she began to turn over plans and schemes to convince this man that she was the only one for him. As an exercise it was highly amusing, but for now her hunt for Genevieve's killer took precedence.

Besides, she was not quite certain she was brave enough to try.

CHAPTER TWENTY-THREE

Crisp and upright, her boots polished, her hair brushed to an orderly gloss, Ash stood against a wall, gazing at another wall. Carlyon was on her right with Heran beyond him, while Marriston was on her left: four of a long row of seruilisi uselessly standing about. In front of her was Thornaster, sitting at the Rhoi's left hand at the Rhoi's Banquet.

Seruilisi at these occasions did much the same thing as she, Lauren and Heran did during the trigle games: very little. There were real servants to fill glasses and carry the food. Occasionally a seruilis was sent off to fetch something from their master's rooms, but otherwise they stood there lending their Luinsel prestige, and proving that they were able to act like seruilisi should. Ash thought it immensely tedious.

Thornaster hadn't required Ash to stand attendance on meals before, so she couldn't be sure how many courses were usual, and whether there were always acrobats. How cruel to have acrobats, but expect her to pretend she wasn't watching them. Every time she leaned to better see through the gap left by the empty seat in front of Marriston, Lauren Carlyon's disapproval became almost tangible. She was already in his bad books for failing to behave with proper restraint at the garden party.

This was an informal banquet, which meant the Rhoi could seat his friends on either side of him. Lauren Carlyon's older brother, Eman, was on Hawkmarten's right. Ash tried not to look at him too often, because at fifty-odd years and greying, he resembled his father more distinctly than Lauren. Especially in the firm, almost harsh set of his mouth. There were rumours that Eman took after his father in more than looks, but then there were rumours that Lauren had shot the Veirhoi.

To her left Marriston shuffled in place, and Ash almost felt sorry for him, standing behind an empty chair. He had been sent ahead of his master, Decsel Enderhay, and half the meal had already gone by.

Enderhay was said to be strongly opposed to the smallholdings law, and his absence began to amount to a deliberate insult to the Rhoi. There were other empty seats, even on the horseshoe of the high table, and Ash had noticed more than one less than friendly glance thrown in Thornaster's direction.

Would the poison, if and when it came, be for her Aremish Visel?

Since she could not think of any food-related precautions more effective than those the Rhoi's Guard had already put in place, Ash instead took advantage of a pause between performances to scan for Kiri among the throng. A mere Visel's daughter would be seated among the rows of tables on the far side of the room. Ash tried to see without obviously craning her head.

"The passes are open until the beginning of winter, yes?" Hawkmarten said.

"Technically," the Rhoi replied. "But early autumn is safer, and a good deal less uncomfortable. I'll be sorry to see you go, Hawk."

"Can't winter here again without our bonds as Luinsel lapsing. Still, we've all of summer ahead of us."

Quiet dignity lay beneath the easy good humour. Had Hawkmarten noticed the Rhoi's change in attitude toward him? If so, there was no return reaction, for the Rhoi's attention was on the diners, gaze shifting restlessly from person to person. Weary, the strained undercurrent in the room reflected on his face, the Rhoi showed little interest in his own banquet's entertainments as a trio of men flipped their way to the centre of the performance area.

The larger two joined arms and tossed the third into the air, and then seemed to hurl themselves after him as two women ran in from the right, adroitly avoiding Decsel Enderhay hesitating in the doorway. Ash watched, transfixed, as the new arrivals spun with a seeming lack of control, then bounced to a landing on the shoulders of the men. She had thought herself agile, but she was nothing compared to these performers.

A girl of fourteen entered, leading a spangled tot only a little older than Sonia. Even the Rhoi began to pay attention as the elder girl climbed onto the shoulders of the women, and acted out broad gestures of encouragement while the child ran in a circle around the partly formed pyramid.

"Clap for her!" one of the women cried, and the crowd obliged, cheering and calling until the little girl began to climb. It was a scene after Ash's own heart, as the child made it to the summit of the human mountain and threw her hands into the air in triumph.

"NO!"

Location was everything, for Decsel Enderhay had been crossing directly in front of Ash when he'd fumbled with his jacket and turned. She didn't even really see the knife, just a glint of light, and hurled herself forward, catching the Decsel's upraised arm.

There followed a frozen moment, all of Ash's focus on his hand, the gleam of the blade, and his nails blue and white with the intensity of his grip. She thought he sobbed, breath sharp with aniseed, then with his free hand he grabbed her right wrist, and the knife came down.

Dragged so that she faced away from him, Ash tried desperately to bend out of reach as metal parted cloth and flesh, the blade skipping across her back. He let go and she tumbled forward, slamming into Marriston as he rushed at them. They both fell to the floor amidst shouting, and a scrape of wood, harsh over the ringing in her ears.

Ash looked up from her tangle with Marriston to see that Thornaster, trapped against the table, had thrust his chair back, knocking Enderhay off-balance as the Decsel turned again to the Rhoi. And then Hawkmarten, surging to his feet on the Rhoi's other side, ended matters through the simple expedient of clouting Enderhay with a heavy silver tankard. The older man dropped like a log.

Marriston grabbed Ash by the upper arm, and she gasped at sudden fire, spots dancing before her eyes. There was blood on his face, but she could see no weapon.

"Hold him here," Marriston ordered, as Heran dropped to his knees beside them, transferring Heran's hands to her upper arm. "I think it's the deepest." Then he stopped still, staring from the wash of red covering his hands to the Luinsel he had served, lying not a foot away.

Thornaster, on his feet at last, lifted Marriston's tabard over the boy's head and pressed it firmly against Ash's back. She shuddered.

"Heran, keep hold of his upper arm and try to put pressure on his forearm as well. And keep up." Thornaster lifted Ash to her feet and tilted her partway over his shoulder, an arm wrapped across her upper legs as if she was a toddler, the other holding the makeshift pad in place.

"I'll fetch Master Tsimon," Lauren Carlyon said, as Thornaster moved quickly toward the door.

Stairs followed, Thornaster taking great strides and Heran struggling to keep pace. Ash began to fade, and fought to clear her head, divided between outraged flesh, the realisation of inevitable exposure, and another point of primary importance that hovered just out of reach.

"Key's in my right pocket," Thornaster said, and Hawkmarten loomed into Ash's view, opening the way to a receiving room lit only by Yurefaer's dull purple glow. "Grab one of the lamps from the hall, and then my travel kit out of the big chest in my bedroom," Thornaster ordered, depositing Ash on the lounging chair. "Heran, keep the pressure up on his arm. Stay upright, Ash."

He lifted Marriston's tabard away, then swiftly stripped Ash of her tabard before pressing the pad back into place.

"How is he?" the Rhoi asked, following a lantern-laden Hawkmarten back into the room.

"Thoroughly filleted." There was no humour in Thornaster's voice. "It's the length that's the problem. He's already lost more blood than I'd care for. We'll bind the arm tight, then work on the back. What about Enderhay?"

"Dead."

"What?" Hawkmarten stopped halfway to the bedroom door. "What of?"

"Tankard to the temple," said the Rhoi's senior guardsman, Farpatten, surveying the scene from the door. "My men are trying to revive him."

Hawkmarten made a low noise, and then disappeared into the bedroom. Returning with the leather satchel Thornaster used to store medicking supplies, he dug out rolled strips of cloth and had Heran hold Ash's arm up.

Carlyon arrived as they finished a hasty job of wrapping. "Master Tsimon's on his way."

"Good, we'll need more bandages," Thornaster said, cutting off Ash's shirt. "Keep the pressure on that shoulder, Hawk and hopefully the bleeding will have stopped by the time we've—"

Lifting the remnants of her shirt away, he paused. Enderhay had slashed a long twisting line down her arm, deepest and bleeding ferociously where the knife had come up against the thicker material of her tabard. There was a short expanse of skin left unscathed across the top of her shoulder, then another line starting a diagonal across her back, deepening where it had dug under her breast bindings before cutting through them half-way and skipping to below her shoulder blades, the wound thinning then becoming abruptly deeper as it reached the band of her trousers and the slight cushion of fat which marked her hips.

"When did you hurt your ribs?" Heran asked.

She looked at him helplessly, and then glanced up at Thornaster, whose face had gone still, wiped of expression. He slid the knife through the already half-cut binding, and she lifted her uninjured arm to hold it in place against her chest.

"Ash?" Heran's voice dropped to a whisper. "You've got–?"

"Yes, thank you, Heran. I had noticed."

"Thorn, I cannot begin to imagine what you find funny in this situation," the Rhoi said.

Thornaster was indeed laughing silently, still holding the knife he'd use to reveal her. He smiled at her expression, put the knife down and flipped open a leather wallet, revealing a practical array of tools, including needles and the sort of thread suitable for mending wounds.

"To think I once prided myself on my powers of observation," he said. "But I must truly have been blinkered not to notice that my seruilis was a valarn."

A valarn was an Aremish term for female warrior. Ash knew that much. So did the Rhoi, who stopped abruptly and stared down at her concealing arm.

"Heran, fetch the jug from my room," Thornaster said, his voice going mild and measured. "And Carlyon, I would appreciate you closing that door. When Master Tsimon arrives, accept any bandages he has, and send him on his way. Guardsman, could I perhaps borrow Investigator Verel?"

Heran moved to obey first, the motion smacking of retreat as he collected the jug of water from Thornaster's bedroom. He handed it to the Visel and stood back. Thornaster began using torn-off squares of Ash's tabard to clean blood from her back. The water was warm.

"Lean forward Ash. Arun, keep pressure on the upper section." He waited until the Rhoi had collected himself enough to take over the job of preventing Ash from draining to nothing, and then plied his needle.

Gritting her teeth, Ash shut her eyes as the Visel stitched together the hip wound. She needed to think, to fight off distractions and keep herself awake and put together the pieces that nudged at the edge of her thoughts.

"This is beyond anything," the Rhoi muttered, as they switched to the cut on her upper back. "That a girl should be struck down in defence of me. It shames me."

"You're fortunate Aria isn't here to hear you say that, Arun."

"Dammit Thorn, you know what I mean!" The Rhoi took a deep breath. "Perhaps you should think of what your mother would say."

"She's certainly going to call me careless." Thornaster sounded irritatingly cheerful. "I suspect that my mother's reaction to Ash would be to try and add her to her collection. She does love to play mentor to talented valarns."

"But *you* can't – it's not appropriate–" the Rhoi began, then fell abruptly silent, and Thornaster focused on his stitching until Farpatten returned with Verel.

"What of Marriston?" the Rhoi asked.

"His father quickly realised the boy might be compromised by his association with Enderhay, Ser Rhoi," Verel replied, smoothly replacing Rhoi Arun at Ash's back. "Whether he has any idea what the extent of his son's involvement might be, I don't know. The boy certainly had the means and opportunity to be the Veirhoi's assailant."

"Heran," Ash said, and watched hard angles change the boy's face. He was not happy. "There's a thick book in Khanteck somewhere in my room. Pictures of plants inside. Would you please fetch it?"

"Are you thinking the knife was poisoned?" Thornaster asked, hands stilling.

"Just sharp." She waited until Heran returned, and rested the Herbal on the curving arm of the lounging chair. "Open it for me. Further on. About two pages more. There." She paused to read.

"Kismollen?" Thornaster and Verel were both peering over her shoulder.

"Blue fingernails, and breath that smells like liquorice. I didn't see his eyes – were the pupils dilated?"

"I've heard of Kismollen." Farpatten abandoned his guarding-the-door position. "The puppet drug."

"A small dose upsets the balance of the mind, makes the subject vulnerable to suggestion." She touched the flowing Khanteck script. "Regular doses – dull you, makes you obedient, unquestioning. If that's it, his lips will turn blue after death, and the skin around his eyes. Not every herbalist would recognise it, but Genevieve most certainly. They must have been killed against the possibility that a description of his body would be circulated. On a *possibility!*"

Ash shuddered, and found herself tilting forward, vision hazing. Verel lifted the Herbal away, and they lowered her so she was propped against the raised end of the lounging chair.

"If Enderhay was a cats paw, there must be a second stage to tonight's attack," the Investigator said. "Something that could be blamed on Enderhay. A trap, a poisoned drink."

"It would be best if you and Veirhoi Heran do not return to your apartments tonight, Ser Rhoi," Farpatten said. "We will undertake a thorough search."

"Very well," the Rhoi said. He sounded sick.

"How difficult would it be to obtain kismollen?" Thornaster asked.

Ash sighed, and struggled to put words together. "No respectable herbalist would supply it, because it doesn't have any legitimate use. It's native to Naggol, and has...liquorice taste. Long exposure...builds up to fatal dose. Genevieve didn't have any. Not likely to grow well in...don't know – don't know anyone who..."

"That's enough, Ash." Thornaster paused in his stitching to press fingers to her throat. "Let's lie her down fully. Heran, grab a cushion to raise her feet."

Ash briefly tried to remain awake, then wondered why she was bothering. The important point had been made, and the Guard would not treat Enderhay's attack as the conclusion of their investigation. Everything else – she'd rather think about when not being sewn together.

CHAPTER TWENTY-FOUR

Wiping grit from her eyes, Ash levered herself stiffly upright, her arm and back burning in protest. No one in the room. Verel had been there during two previous wakings, matter-of-factly changing Ash's bandages, salving, feeding her and helping her with a chamber pot before mercilessly dosing her with something syrupy and bitter.

Taking it slowly, Ash managed to dress herself, finding movement easier the more she tried. Once tidied, she sat on the bed and thought through her next step.

Enough with playing seruilis, surely. The reason behind Genevieve's murder had been uncovered, if not the culprits, and Ash's herbal knowledge was no longer a critical hidden card. Nor, she suspected, would Heran make it easy for her to act as unofficial bodyguard after the revelation of breasts. Her time would be better spent looking into the disappearances.

This settled, she went to face Thornaster, but the apartment was empty. Caught between relief and disappointment, Ash headed to the kitchens instead, and was disturbed by the number of people who outright stared at her, even though she'd left her spare tabard behind.

"Mirramar," she said, spotting the cook conveniently close to the kitchen's inner entrance. "Could I bother you for some food?"

Mirramar nearly dropped her mixing bowl. "Ash!" She hastily put the bowl down and took Ash by her uninjured arm. "What are you doing up and about?"

"Dying of hunger."

"Star's Grace, you little idiot, sit down before you fall down," Mirramar said, whisking a chair from nowhere and manoeuvring Ash into it.

"I'm fine, Mirramar. Don't fuss."

"Fine? You look like death warmed over. Don't you move from this spot."

The whole kitchen was staring, and the loaded tray Mirramar brought back came accompanied by the head cook, congratulations and compliments. Ash dealt with this by assuming mortified shyness until the man went away.

"How you can put on that butter-wouldn't-melt face without a blush is beyond me," Mirramar said, once the head cook was out of earshot. "And why you must go jumping onto knives, I don't know. I've had Larkin in here two days running asking after you."

"You know I love being the centre of attention."

"Truer words have never been spoken."

"What have they been saying, Mirramar? Not about me – about Decsel Enderhay."

The junior assistant cook gave her a dubious look, and then a more serious one. "Of course, everyone knows that Decsel Enderhay tried to kill the Rhoi and you stopped him. I've heard a thousand stories as to why Enderhay would act that way. He was such an upright man, generous to a fault, and..."

"And some people are saying he had to have had a good reason," Ash guessed. "That the Rhoi is weak, that Thornaster controls the Rhoi, and all sorts of outlandish claims as to what the real story might be." She sighed when Mirramar nodded. "Anything else being talked about?"

"The Rhoi moved out of his apartments," Mirramar said. "A spider infestation. Another lad's gone missing out of the Commons. The high snows are lingering late this year, and the Milk's sluggish."

"Who are they saying would have been put forward for judgment, if the Rhoi had been killed?"

"Why, Veirhoi Heran, of course," Mirramar said, with a sharp glance.

"But a wide open field after him."

"Don't go borrowing trouble, Ash Lenthard. The Veirhoi's fine."

Wishing she could be sure he would stay that way, Ash left a message for Larkin and started toward the stables. It was most important to reassure Cloud Cat that any neglect wasn't intentional. But she was hardly out of the kitchen before she discovered an urgent need to sit down. A nearby barrel spared her from ignominious collapse, and the fortunate advent of Cassia turned the situation into an opportunity to collect further rumours. Nothing new, and obviously plenty Cassia wasn't quite ready to mention.

"I was going to the stable," Ash said finally, "but I think maybe I should put that off 'til tomorrow. Would you mind very much giving me a hand back to Thornaster's apartment?"

"Happy to. Especially if we can go via the Water Court because then I won't even have to say anything to be the envy of the entire laundry."

"Sounds like a fair bargain."

An easy favour, but as Cassia escorted her past the stares of the Water Court, Ash began to wonder if she could escape the notoriety of the gutter seruilis without abandoning Ash Lenthard altogether. Being the centre of attention was only fun when it was on her own terms.

ooOoo

Thornaster was at his desk, writing. Pausing in the doorway, Ash struggled again with the question of playing gutter seruilis. Did her role in the palace hold any further value? Should she walk away from the official investigation to start out on her own? And could she even make it to the Commons without collapsing?

But staying meant enduring this unexpected ache, as large as the sun and as dangerous. Thornaster had enjoyed partnering with an imp, and was not going to object to that imp being a girl, but would most certainly have some qualms if that girl revealed her overwhelming desire to slide her arms around his neck. It did not matter whether or not that was incredible, impossible: what mattered was that the question could not be raised. Genevieve was more important.

She had to remember her anger and step back, not to the precocious brat, but the girl she had been a few days ago – amused by Thornaster and not yet lost. That version of herself had one purpose, and no qualms about allying with this man to achieve it.

The glossy black hair was as usual trying to fall into his eyes, and he swept it back with an absent hand. Unnecessarily tall, but finely built, possessing a grace born of strength and restraint, he was infinitely desirable.

"I'm guessing you won't be requiring me to dress you any more."

Her Aremish Visel started, then fulfilled her expectations by laughing, and shaking his head ruefully.

"You guess correctly." He rose, indicating that she precede him back into the receiving room. "I doubt I'll be calling you stripling any longer, either. Now my turn to guess – you've been out hunting up information about the disappearances?"

"Asked for an update on them." She checked the lounging chair for stains, then sat down heavily, and waited until he took the opposite chair.

Thornaster surveyed her, mouth ominously flat. "Sera Arpesial has been visiting. Most insistent that I don't mention her presence to anyone else, though. I imagine she'll return later this afternoon. How old are you, Ash?"

"Twenty-one in about a month." She met his eyes, unwavering. "Too old to be a seruilis."

She couldn't read his immediate reaction, but then he sat back, becoming brisk. "Well, technically, too old in a month, if there's some reason to strictly enforce such rules. It's certainly my preference to resolve this mystery before then."

It was an offer to continue their partnership, and Ash hid a sigh of relief, and then let herself focus on the problem at hand.

"What's the story with the Rhoi's apartments?"

"Nests of thar-spiders. Tucked down beneath the coverings of the Rhoi and Veirhoi's beds. Our opponent wasn't counting on Enderhay succeeding with the kill – only to take the blame. Farpatten has a team going over Arun's apartments in case there's anything further, but given how tightly those rooms have been guarded these past few weeks, the question of spiders is exercising his security detail considerably."

More suspicion for Carlyon, living temporarily under the Rhoi's supervision. He had remained carefully in the background during last night's drama, and Ash couldn't hope to guess if that suspicion was misplaced.

"Did his lips turn blue?"

"Yes. Your diagnosis shows no flaws as yet."

"What chance that they might just stop? They can't blame further attacks on Enderhay."

"Limited, I should think, given Karaelsur's possible involvement."

Ash realised that she'd started to tilt, and straightened, a recovery that Thornaster didn't comment on. But a corner of his mouth turned up.

"It's going to be another couple of days before I can really get about," she said, giving him an admonitory frown. "I just wanted to work out what's happening next. Does this clear Hawkmarten?"

"Not unequivocally, but it has reassured Arun that Hawk doesn't want him dead, which I never did find easy to believe. It doesn't explain the rings. Verel will continue to take both of us with a few precautionary grains of salt, I suspect, but is now favouring the idea that we were to be the next targets. As for what now, Arun has arranged for a detailed map of ownership of smallholdings in the city to be prepared. We'll see what information your sources bring, put it together, and hope for inspiration."

CHAPTER TWENTY-FIVE

"I've never known anyone so determined to convince me of her death."

"Kiri." Ash shifted slowly upright, and then held her arms out to her friend. "I am being more than ordinarily dramatic lately, I must admit."

"You are ridiculous," Kiri said, squeezing her gingerly. "And impossible. And if you ever do that to me again, I swear I'll strangle you myself."

"I can only promise to try."

Even the most cautious embrace was not yet possible without winces, but Kiri's arrival at least solved the problem of how to change her bandages. While Kiri unwrapped and salved and wrapped again, Ash caught her up with the long tale of murder and poison and their diminishing number of leads, and Kiri listened with the same grave air of appraisal she had given to the not-always-truthful stories with which a younger girl had entertained her.

"Decsel Donderry," Kiri said, when Ash was done. "Setsel Gibrace, Setsel Vicardie and Visel Itratan. Those four are the most likely to be put forward now that Decsel Enderhay is dead."

"Itratan? I haven't heard his name suggested before."

"He's a favour collector." There was a flat note to Kiri's voice. "Of the others, Setsel Gibrace is by far the most capable. Vicardie is considered reasonable, and is well liked. Donderry has greater resources, but is so full of enthusiasm that many believe he would gallop Montmoth into disaster. Still, he has a core of supporters and, if the Landsmeet vote is split among too many, he might unexpectedly find himself in the lead."

Ash watched Kiri's face as she fastened the last bandage. How little had changed. This was still the Kiri she had once seen only when they were alone, her reserve receding as she switched between amusement and an almost severe intelligence, analytical and detached.

"You've kept to your goal?"

Heavy lashes swept up. "Why would I give it up?"

"'*My father is Visel*'," Ash quoted. "'*I am his only child. So I will study the Balance, and the duties of the Landsmeet, and stand before Astenar and Luin. No matter what my parents plan for me.*'"

"That at least has improved. They still want me to marry well, but Father is so pleased to be sure that Ariancy will be properly managed when he's gone he verified my first heir's right as soon as I was sixteen. Of course, it helped that cousin Ryovar grew up to be a tremendous idiot."

"Always was," Ash muttered, having clashed more than once with Ryovar. She flexed her newly bound arm carefully. "Thanks for this. I didn't want to bother Investigator Verel again."

"Given how peculiarly unconcerned Visel Thornaster appears to be, I'm almost surprised he hasn't taken care of this himself."

"He's just acting." Ash glanced at the door. "He wouldn't have made me his seruilis if he'd known I was a girl. Aremal might have 'valarns', but just by having a particular word for 'female warrior' they underline there's a difference. Maybe not a negative one, but enough that the Rhoi's not wrong to worry about whether it's appropriate." She clicked her tongue in exasperation. "He relaxed when I told him how old I was. That let him decide he could in conscience keep up the pretence."

"Should I ask if you care for him?"

Ash shrugged, winced as the stitches pulled, and wished she could simply be entertained by the prospect of Thornaster.

"Kiri, he was made for me. And once this is over I will do something about that, because never asking is the type of thing I'd regret." Even though she'd yet to discover any signs of concealed attraction. "But he is..."

"Accustomed to being pursued," Kiri said, speaking as one recognising her own situation. "If he finds it amusing when he's insulted and slighted here, it most likely is because in Aremal he is competed over."

"Egotistical wretch. He also seems to think everyone should really love sword fighting. Let's hope that isn't an absolute requirement." Ash blew her breath out, and then met Kiri's eyes. "Are you going to tell me what's going on with the Rhoi, or would you rather not talk about it?"

In the years that a younger Ash had known Kiri she had never seen her blush. But as quickly as the deep colour rose beneath clear skin, it receded, and her friend summoned a faint smile instead.

"Nothing to my credit."

"Did your parents–?" The Arpesials had always had very high expectations.

"No, I am the one at fault." Kiri minutely rearranged her long skirt, and sat tall and proud, an image of perfection. Ash had just decided that was all she meant to say when her friend went on.

"My parents had already had in you an example of how terribly wrong an advantageous marriage could be. They chose not to push me. It was the entire Landsmeet – people who looked at me and said, 'Yes, that is worthy of Veirhoi Arun' – who brought a weight of expectation to our every interaction. And I was, oh, ready to mark any fault. He was too small-minded, impossibly earnest, never questioning what he was saying when he told me he intended to live up to the role he'd been born to. That he hoped for my support."

"To be a truly great Rhoi?"

"Like his father, who I could barely look at because Rhoi Malaster had never stopped Eward Carlyon. Disapproved of him, lectured him perhaps, but done nothing of substance. Irrhoi Lasantra did not help – to her it was a foregone conclusion that I would accept her son's interest and be grateful."

"I'm still not seeing where you're at fault in this."

"When the Irrhoi died, Arun told me that he had always looked to his mother for advice. And, for a time, I decided to see whether that would be enough." Kiri's gaze was fixed on a wall, unseeing. "It was slow work. His views were conventional, and if I spoke directly he would correct me. He'd had so little practical experience, yet thought to teach *me*. And would break into what I was saying to recite poetry. Bad poetry."

Ash burst into laughter and then stopped as her stitches warned her this was too soon. "Oh, Kiri."

"It was Rhoi Malaster who changed that. The Rhoi was – now that you've told me of Karaelsur, I suspect that even then the Rhoi was uneasy, had sensed something was wrong with Montmoth's Balance. I learned that he held a deep regret over his handling of Decsel Carlyon – that he'd hesitated to overstep the process of law. He brought many new books in from Aremal and Firuvar, trying to widen his outlook. Sometimes they were books I had studied, and he would talk to me as Arun would not. With that example, Arun began to *listen*."

"Less poetry?"

"Thankfully. And – it was a heady wine, that attention. I began to see Arun anew. The genuine desire to do his best, the willingness to learn, and the struggle against the way he had been shaped. The walls put about him were not so obvious as mine, but they were there. When Rhoi Malaster began to speak of sending him to Aremal's Collegium, I encouraged the idea. I saw it as a final step toward Arun and I sharing our lives."

"Did you have a formal understanding?"

"Oh, yes. He had the leave of his father, and my consent. It wasn't until the day before he left that I learned that I had led myself astray."

"Then?" Ash was startled. She'd assumed matters had gone awry when Veirhoi Arun had fallen at the feet of the Aremish Rhoi's daughter.

"You understand, all that time I had been this." Kiri gestured down at herself, the motion the epitome of restraint and grace. "A very decorous courtship, with barely a held hand between us. But I had grown to appreciate him, and he was leaving for years, so I kissed him: a farewell so he would know I truly loved him. If he had walked out of the room, I could not more clearly have felt his withdrawal. I received a letter a few days after his departure, breaking our understanding. He had mistaken his feelings."

Kiri's lips parted, then curved. "It was a game to me once, my Reserve. When I first noticed that I could change how people behaved toward me simply by controlling my reactions, it felt like magic. But practice became second nature, and I knew part of Arun's attraction for me was because I matched the Montmothian ideal. I'm not certain it had ever occurred to him that I might want him physically, or could collapse into laughter, or climb through an attic window. That I wanted someone who I could be Kiri with. And I did not see until it was too late that Arun was in love with this...this idea of a woman. I have not spoken to him since."

"Shall we run away together then, Kiri?"

This time Kiri's smile was real, a wry curl. "No. I will not give up Ariancy for something so trivial as a broken heart. And I have been teaching myself to be Kiri again, at least there. Among the Landsmeet it is difficult not to wear my Reserve, because it spares me so much, but there's no need to spend my time in the city."

"Then would you mind very much if I hit him a little? I think I've done enough Rhoi-rescuing to get away with it."

"If it relieves your feelings."

"It would at least be entertaining watching him trying to explain away a black eye." Ash laughed, but then more soberly considered her friend. "I know enough not to try to fix this for you, and it sounds like he's behaved idiotically. But I think you may have succeeded better than you realise, having Rhoi Malaster send him to Aremal. You wouldn't know this, but he plans a law to require Kinsel girls to attend the Mern."

Kiri's chin went down. "Your Thornaster's influence?"

"He says not."

"How...unexpected."

"Of course, none of that will matter if the scut behind these murders succeeds. We've made it impossible to blame the Rhoi's death on Enderhay, but that doesn't mean they'll stop trying."

And Ash was running short of ideas.

CHAPTER TWENTY-SIX

"What do you expect it to tell you?"

Thornaster weighted the corners of his newly delivered map. "If nothing else, it will help me keep track of a foot tour of every unbound piece of land in this city. For the sake of my sanity, I hope you bring back something to narrow this down before it comes to that."

"For the sake of your feet at least," Ash said, and headed for the door.

"Arun wants to talk to you," he called after her. "You're excused the second session of Mern. Think up a suitable reward."

Ash waved in acknowledgement and headed for the stable. Four days after Enderhay's death, she was finally feeling up to more than fetching dinner, though her need for rest had at least postponed some of the consequences of the revelation of breasts. Heran was the current sticking point. While Thornaster wobbled between giving her orders and treating her as a free agent, and the Rhoi's gratitude meant that those who followed his command were not going to get in the way of her hunt, a Veirhoi who had discovered his new friend was not at all what he'd thought him was a chancy keeper of important secrets.

Debating her approach, Ash took her time cosseting Cloud Cat and then made no bones about finding a hay bale to help herself into the saddle. Her stitches were healing well enough, but she'd already torn a couple just trying to find a way to sleep comfortably, and the whole of her back and arm tended to throb relentlessly when she moved about too much.

She'd arranged for the Huntsmen to gather as much gossip and talk about the disappeared as they could, hoping to come across information people were unwilling to pass to the Guard or the Watch. Melar had compiled it all into an impressive collection of notes for Larkin to pass on.

"And much good it'll do you," Larkin told her, once she'd been properly exclaimed over and they'd escaped into the bakery's storeroom for serious discussion. "Different parts of the city. Different times of day. No way to tell if the handful who are older and younger are coincidence, or if it's all connected."

"So many," Ash murmured, turning pages. "I hadn't realised."

"Well, it *is* spring. Season of starting over. Or at least of having had enough of the damn cold. So, what comes next?"

"How well are they holding?"

Larkin grimaced. "The problem with you off playing hero is everyone else wants to as well. Collecting gossip's not exactly our strength."

"Start patrolling again. Groups of four. Concentrate on the Commons. If you spot anyone at all suspect, follow if you're four together and it's possible to stay quiet and in each other's sight. If not, then get a good look at whoever it is, so we can at least start collecting descriptions."

"And if we spot someone mid-kidnapping?"

"Make a lot of noise. Play drunkards. The one thing Thornaster's been clear on is that this agent of Karaelsur is incredibly dangerous. I don't want anyone thinking our usual tricks are an option."

"Options would be–" Larkin paused as Linnet poked her head through the door. "Go away Lincy."

"Go away yourself," Linnet said, poking out her tongue. "I'm looking for Sonia. We're playing hide and seek."

Larkin started to his feet, glancing quickly around at the neatly stacked sacks and boxes of stores. "I told you to stop that, Lincy."

"She *likes* it."

"And *I'd* like it if for once you did what you were told."

Larkin began a systematic search of the storeroom, which Ash decided to forego, since it involved a lot of bending.

"Sonia?" Larkin's voice was as soft as he could manage. "Could you come out of there please?"

Stifled movement behind a stacked shelf, but nothing more.

Ash realised that the girl might not remember her from her visits with Arianne, and didn't want to come out while she was there. "I'd better get going," she said, and philosophically took herself off.

But as Ash headed out, Bitty, minding the shopfront, held a finger to her lips and nodded out the door. Ash paused, and discovered her horse-mad street girl in the process of offering a fragment of bun for equine consideration.

"Her name's Cloud Cat," Ash said, after the mare had accepted the morsel.

The girl immediately retreated, so that all Ash could see of her was a pair of brown legs beneath the curve of Cloud Cat's belly.

"Do you have a name?"

Cloud Cat tossed her head, and the girl moved, a proud, angry profile emerging around the mare's neck. Dark, searching eyes, full of distrust, met Ash's in challenge.

Holding out a hand, palm up, Ash took a step forward. "Talk to me."

Something hit her, a wind that buffeted Ash against the bakery doorway. Twisting as best she could to avoid disaster for her stitches, she staggered and almost fell.

"What happened?"

Bitty, abruptly at Ash's side, hefted the stout cudgel the Rogadneys kept behind the serving counter.

"Not sure." Ash looked for the street girl, but she was already out of sight. "Have you had any trouble with her?"

"If you can call being treated like we're infectious trouble. She's no plans to trust us any time soon. Don't say as I blame her – she didn't get those bruises tripping over her own feet."

"But no mysterious winds?"

"Nope." Bitty, far from easily impressed, returned to the counter. "Doesn't stick around any longer than she has to."

"Let me know if that changes."

Taking it slow because her wounds had started to complain, Ash snagged a bun of her own and headed back, trying to make sense of this new bit of information. Could the girl be a mage? Was mage-craft something which could be done on the spur of the moment? Was that wind something inborn, like Thornaster's powers? Or something more sinister?

ooOoo

Ash's plans to tackle Heran were foiled by his absence from the Mern, but she enjoyed herself otherwise by describing her numerous stitches in great detail to an interested crowd, and then by solemnly thanking Marriston for trying to quell the bleeding. He could not quite stop himself from preening.

Being slit open would not have been Ash's chosen method for winning over the senior seruilisi, but they were at least no longer intent on ostracising her. Ash only wished she could be sure one among them wouldn't turn around and try to kill her, if the opportunity presented.

Arriving on time and almost tidy for her appointment, she found herself kicking her heels outside the Rhoi's meeting room with Investigator Verel. She immediately asked the Guardswoman whether mage-craft always required preparation.

"Yes and no. Any significant casting requires three steps: draw, shape, and release. Although most mages carry at least a small reservoir of power, significant casting usually involves coiling any available environmental power, then using it to cast. It is possible to hold off the release, so I could cast a spell in another room, come in here and release it and to you it would appear immediate. But hold a spell too long and it will warp. There's very little which can be done absolutely immediately – crude force responses, usually."

Crude force sounded about right. "How do you go about training as a mage?"

"In Montmoth? The only options are to be 'prenticed to a mage...or work from written instruction and try not to kill yourself. We're the only Rhoimarch that doesn't have a formal school of some description. I trained in Praxas." The Guardswoman looked Ash up and down, clear grey eyes assessing. "You've no mage talent – who are you asking for?"

"You can tell if a person has mage talent?"

"I tested you."

Ash blinked, then laughed. "We're all suspects, I suppose." She studied the utterly controlled woman sitting upright and at attention beside her, and asked impulsively: "Why did you come back? To Montmoth?"

"My family is here," Verel said, shortly, but then unbent enough to add: "I'm also considerably better paid in Montmoth than I would be in a Rhoimarch where mages are more common. Neither Farpatten nor I are more than the most minor of mages, and we command enviable salaries for interesting work. Whether I will continue to raise my daughters here...we will see."

"You have daughters?"

"Three year-old twins."

Ash didn't know why the idea of the stern Investigator having twin daughters should be so surprising, but before she could indulge in prying questions, the door opposite opened and a grim-faced Farpatten came out.

"Go in," he told Ash, and held the door until she'd obeyed.

The Rhoi, sitting at a round table next to a wide window, was bathed in streaming sunlight that picked out the gold in his hair. It wasn't until Ash followed his gesture to sit down opposite him that she saw the pallid skin and shadowed eyes. He looked like he hadn't slept at all in the four days since his banquet.

"Ash Lenthard." The Rhoi's voice was hoarse. "My debt to you grows ever larger. I trust you are able to think of a reward which is suitable to that debt."

Ash, who had been determined to resent him on Kiri's behalf, was distracted into concern. "Are – I didn't realise you were ill, Ser Rhoi."

He waved a dismissive hand. "A cold. Given recent events, I'm avoiding creating any new rumours."

"Is Heran ill as well? He wasn't at Mern."

"No. Regrettable as it is, until this is over it seems advisable to limit his exposure to the other seruilisi." The Rhoi coughed, then added: "Though I've no doubt Heran's failure to object to this course hinges on a hope of avoiding you."

"Most likely," Ash agreed, working not to look entertained. "I'll fix that if I can. As for rewards, I'd like permission to carry my knives. And to have arranged some kind of recompense for Arianne Waylan's daughter Sonia, and the other dependents of the murdered herbalists."

"Granted," the Rhoi said immediately. "You are, of course, a dependent who will be included in that outlay." Rhoi Arun produced a charming smile, but as quickly as it appeared it faded and he looked her up and down. "Ash Lenthard. You arrived in Luinhall in the spring, nearly nine years ago?"

Blue eyes searched hers, and Ash realised that she was about to have a very different conversation to the one she'd anticipated.

"You really did have the Guard investigate me."

"I had Farpatten arrange for protection of Thorn's quarters, against the possibility of reprisals. And learned that Kiri Arpesial has been visiting daily." He paused, and just the faintest colour touched his cheeks, as if he guessed that Kiri would have told Ash their history together. "While it's possible Ki–...Sera Arpesial immediately discerned what so many did not, and quickly befriended a most inspiring girl, nine years is a highly significant number."

"Impossible to overlook?"

The Rhoi passed a hand over his face, perhaps because she had not denied his suspicions. "How glad my father would have been to know you survived. I can scarcely begin to–"

"Don't." An absolute command. "It was a disgusting situation, but I got myself out of it, and found a life which suits me extremely."

His eyes dropped, but then he raised them and met hers steadily. "Still, on behalf of my father, I give you my deepest apologies. More should have been done." He straightened in his chair, continuing briskly. "Both Thorn and Hawk have taken the time to point out to me that you would provide an excellent example when we begin to introduce girls to the Mern. Am I right to suspect that would be the last thing you want?"

"People would stop seeing Ash Lenthard and start putting two and two together, and I have no intention of dealing with that unless I absolutely must. Why do I have the impression that you want my past brought up even less than I do?"

"My concern is for Lauren," the Rhoi told her. "He has spent years caught in the shadow of his father, unable to allow himself the slightest weakness. And now, because he had access to my apartments, the full weight of suspicion has been added to that burden. To learn your identity at this juncture – I think it would take him past a tipping point."

Carlyon had been crisply professional during the little Ash had seen of him at the Mern, but she had expected nothing else of him. Perfect First Seruilis made a more than useful mask.

"You don't suspect him?"

"No. In terms of motive, of personality – none of this makes any sense where Lauren is concerned. The whole Carlyon family spends much of their energy proving they are nothing like the former Decsel, and I can't believe they would ever involve themselves in this conspiracy." He laughed sourly. "But then, I never imagined I would spend days wondering if Hawk was preparing ground for an invasion. I'm reaching the point where the only people I trust not to be trying to take my life are those who have actively preserved it."

The Rhoi stopped abruptly, and poured himself a glass of water, perhaps having spoken more openly than he'd planned.

"Have you discussed the Black Carlyon with Thornaster?"

"Not in detail. Why?"

Frowning, because she hadn't wanted to discuss it, Ash explained the circumstances of her 'wedding'.

"I thought it a failure on Astenar's part. But if Karaelsur was active in Montmoth even then, if there was some tie to the Black Carlyon..."

"So long ago?"

"I don't know if investigating Eward Carlyon's activities at the time will help at all, but...I always wondered how anyone could dare to behave as he did. He might be able to manipulate Montmoth's laws, but eventually we all have to face Astenar's judgment. And yet, he relished the way he was, almost flouted it, as if the Sun's judgment meant nothing to him. As if he thought himself immune."

"That – you make a solid point." The Rhoi looked far from happy. "I will sound Thorn out, and ask Investigator Verel to look into the question discreetly."

Duly dismissed, Ash took polite departure, and wondered if Thornaster would be astonished that she could summon proper manners when she chose. But Ash had been more impressed by Arun Nemator than she'd expected, enough to not even twit him about Kiri, let alone take him to task. Perhaps he'd be good for Montmoth, after all.

Behind her, just before Verel closed the door, the Rhoi coughed.

CHAPTER TWENTY-SEVEN

In the week that followed, the most Ash learned was that she'd successfully spooked her street girl away from the Rogadney's bakery. For whatever reason, the child hadn't returned for a meal since Ash had spoken to her.

Ash's long cut healed without infection, so Investigator Verel removed the stitches, passing her as 'fit enough'. That had led directly to Ash standing irritably on the Mern's sandy practice ground, facing Carlyon over a sparring rapier.

"Don't drop the point of your weapon," Thornaster advised. "And remember your feet."

"I think my new mission in life will have to be getting you to stop trying to teach me swordplay."

"But consider the fields of heroics opening up to you." Her Aremish Visel was in a fine mood, despite a fruitless morning touring the city. "There's nothing like a really rousing piece of blade work to win over a crowd."

"A better understanding of the sword will increase your advantage in the weapons you're more comfortable with," Hawkmarten put in, with unexpected gravity. "The exercise here is to familiarise yourself with your opponent's strengths and weaknesses."

"No need to aim so low." Thornaster leaned forward on the shaded bench he and Hawkmarten had parked themselves upon. "Just think of Lauren here's expression if you manage to disarm him."

Ash doubted that it would change. She wasn't even certain she'd seen Lauren Carlyon do more than blink since the banquet, even after new rumours of the Guard investigating the Carlyons had begun to circulate. Still, it would tell her something if she pushed him to a reaction, and her goal today was as much to learn about her opponent as the weapon.

Spotting a fractional tightening of Carlyon's stance, Ash blocked just in time, then took a step to the right, looking for some advantage in the sun's direction. The first seruilis completely outmatched her, but still held himself contained, alert and ready, not taking her lightly. Following a shift of her own weight, with a quick movement to suggest that had only been a feint, she attempted to reach him.

Carlyon met her effortlessly, and Ash responded with several quick jabs in succession, earning herself a rap on the arm for her haste. She pressed on, trying to find a way past his guard until Thornaster finally called a halt.

"Hawk will give you a match, Lauren. Just till first touch."

Ash handed her weapon over to the Nyreemian Setsel, and sat down. This was the first time Hawkmarten had come to a practice session, and she was mildly interested to see how the Nyreemian, who was closer to her own build and height than Carlyon or Thornaster, managed the first seruilis' superior reach. Rubbing her arm, she watched the pair dance around each other, moving far more freely across the practice area than Ash had managed. But there were more important issues on her mind.

"Is the Rhoi still sick?"

"Unchanged." Thornaster didn't take his eyes off the pair before them, but his mouth set. "A minor persistent cold; certainly not the rapid decline rumour would suggest."

"I suppose the Guard aren't letting him eat anything someone else doesn't sample first."

"Eat, touch, breathe. He says he's begun to believe he's simply having a reaction to an excess of cotton wool."

"But you're worried?"

"This – it may be a symptom of the state of Montmoth's Balance." Thornaster scuffed a toe through the sand at his feet. "This morning, these past few days, I more than once felt suddenly certain I was near a source of corruption, that I was in the right area, but just as quickly it was gone. And I have this increasing, ever-present sense of...wrong. Arun's not the only one who is ill, you know – there's a spate of minor chills and fevers. As Rhoi, Arun will both be strengthened by Astenar, and more vulnerable to illness due to the link to Luin. The Balance is more complicated than keeping your waste out of your water, or basic crop rotation. Is it even possible to Balance stolen souls?"

"How much time? Before it's more than minor ills?"

"I think we're reaching a tipping point," Thornaster said, unconsciously echoing the Rhoi. "That we – nice touch, Lauren!"

"Bah! I'm out of practice," Hawkmarten said, though he smiled and clapped Carlyon on the back. "Keep it up, lad, and you might get Thorn up off his rear to truly test your mettle."

"Isn't he out of practice as well?" Ash asked, since she'd yet to see Thornaster do more than demonstrate drills.

"I'm certainly not at competition level at the moment," Thornaster said easily. "Whipping Ash into shape gives me an excellent excuse not to shift myself. Up you get, Ash. Drills for the rest of the afternoon."

Ash rose obediently to her feet, but gave him a weary look once there. "Seriously, if someone came at me with a sword, I'd just throw a knife at them."

"So you've said before. And then?"

She looked at him warily, spotting mischief in dark eyes. "Do you mean if I miss? My aim's not that shabby. And I carry a spare."

"So you throw your spare. And then?"

"Are you trying to make some kind of point?"

"Here, Hawk, give me that." Taking Hawkmarten's sword, he moved out to the centre of the training ground. "Go on, then. Throw."

"You haven't given me a reason to put a knife in you," Ash protested. "Though the urge is rising."

"Throw."

The insufferably smug expression decided her, though she aimed carefully for his shoulder. Given the build-up, she wasn't particularly surprised when a deceptively lazy movement of the rapier sent her knife spinning to the sand.

"Now knife number two."

More than insufferable.

Ash drew her second knife, then held out an imperative hand. "Borrow your weapon, Carlyon?"

"Being bigger won't make it impossible to parry," Thornaster said.

Carlyon won many points by simply handing over his rapier. Ash took it with her left hand and swung it to gauge its throwing capacity, then flung the sword at Thornaster's face and her knife fast and hard for his knee. The smile dropped off her Aremish Visel's face most wonderfully, and she almost regretted the speed with which he dived to one side.

"What would happen if I was behind you?" she asked, watching dispassionately as he picked himself off the sand.

"It would depend on if he knew you were there," Hawkmarten said, face merry with suppressed laughter. "Oh, Thorn, I wish Aria had been here to see that! I really need to find myself a Montmothian seruilis as well. The sheer entertainment value is incalculable."

"I'm not sure you'd survive the experience," Thornaster said, brushing himself off. But he smiled at Ash and said: "Very well, no drills this afternoon. Hawk and Lauren can give me a match instead, if you'll bring us another two weapons."

Ash lifted her brows, but obediently fetched the rapiers after retrieving her knives. Master Humboldt, who had been caught up with Mern business, appeared as if summoned as Thornaster folded his coat onto the bench and began some loosening-up exercises, and Carlyon warily collected the weapon Ash had thrown, while Hawkmarten took the last with a wry smile.

"Got your blood up, Thorn?" he said, then added to Lauren: "Don't hold back."

It wasn't just speed. Ash had assumed that Thornaster's Estarrel heritage was going to give him some unnatural advantage, but while she thought he was moving slightly faster then either of his opponents, she'd learned just enough to recognise some of the technical skill involved. Precise, controlled movements, considerable strength and flexibility of wrist, and an unerring ability to anticipate attacks.

The bout brought Carlyon out from behind his mask, a fierce competitiveness lighting him up and making him human. Having discovered her feelings for Thornaster, Ash was able to appreciate Lauren Carlyon without being distracted by any irritating skipping of her heart. Though she spent little enough time looking anywhere but at the laughing eyes and seemingly lazy movements of her Aremish Visel.

"Touch, Lauren!" the Master of the Mern called, but Carlyon had already stepped away, acknowledging a neatly placed blow.

Thornaster discarded his second weapon, and he and Hawkmarten fought on, the pace increasing, both men smiling and trading gibes on their lack of condition. Ash saw why Thornaster kept trying to coax her into appreciating the art of the sword. It was a sport to him, a game with a deadly context, just as roof running to her was a matter of exultation and delight, even when she was hunting down thieves, or skarl.

He would have to be content with their shared enthusiasm for horse riding, because the main thing this display of swordsmanship inspired her to was the removal of his clothing. Since this was not practicable at the moment – particularly since he had given her no sign he wanted such an event – Ash instead busied herself with collecting together the swords and returning them to the weapons room.

"You have most curious boots, Ash."

"You have a most curious master, too."

"I can't argue with that second one," Ash said, turning to consider Frog and Gibrace, together blocking the doorway. "My boots are quite ordinary, however."

"I beg to differ." Frog bent, and drew out one of her knives. "You really threw that at him. Luin, just think if you'd actually hit him!"

"I wasn't aiming anywhere fatal."

"I'm guessing, since the Master didn't immediately toss you out on your ear, that you've permission to carry these?" Frog, holding the knife by the wrong end, made several mock-throws at the opposite wall. "Seruilisi are hardly ever given permission to carry weapons outside hunts."

Gibrace, however, was not interested in knives. "Your Visel spoke of not currently being at competition level. He'll be talking about Aremal's midsummer festival, the competitions of sword matches and horse riding. Do you know how good you have to be to even qualify for some of those events? I wonder if the rumours about him being–"

"Horse riding?" Ash asked. "Do you mean races? Or jumping?"

"We've already seen enough of Thornaster to know never to fight him, Gibbers," Frog said. "This, however–" He waggled the knife. "This is something else – not exactly a sporting weapon. Don't tell me we have a real, stone-cold killer in our midst? How many should we mark on your tally, Ash?"

"None," Ash said, forthrightly. "Not directly, at least. I..." She decided on the truth. "It gives me the horrors, actually, the thought of killing someone. Taking away all that they could become. A knife in the thigh stops anyone coming at me handily enough."

"Didn't Thornaster just demonstrate that you can't rely on that?" Gibrace pointed out. "Sometimes you don't have a choice."

"Bah, we can't all be as cold-blooded as you, Gibbers. Stick to your principles, Ash." Frog returned the knife. "But be careful."

"Advice for us all," Ash said neutrally, hating her inability to be sure, even with these two very likeable boys, whether she was among friends or enemies.

She returned to Thornaster, who promptly told her she could have the rest of the day free and headed off with Hawkmarten to enjoy the palace bathhouse. Ash frowned at his retreating back, wondering what he was thinking. It had seemed to her that Thornaster, as much as possible, had hidden his strengths since arriving in Montmoth. He'd taken no weapon on the hunt, kept his Estarrel heritage to a trusted few, and chosen not to display his skill with the sword. With so few leads, had he decided to set himself up as a target? Would that really make any difference to their opponents?

Puzzled and worried, Ash visited Arth and Cloud Cat, and took her mind off conspiracy with a currycomb and plenty of elbow grease. Arth particularly loved being groomed, and fussed in his stall while she worked on Cloud Cat, until a hovering stable hand bribed him with molasses and oats. Heading back, Ash amused herself unjustly comparing master and horse. Really, Thornaster had been behaving a little like Arth today, not quite prancing about with an arched neck, but–

Ash stopped. Stopped right where she was, staring at nothing, the whole of her body jolted as if with lightning.

"He was showing off. *Showing off.*"

"Ash? Why are you standing here grinning?" Cassia, resting an inevitable basket on her hip, nudged her with a foot. "Ash?"

"Because I think I just received the biggest compliment anyone's ever offered me," Ash replied. "Only took me a decem to notice."

"Not from Sera Arpesial, I hope," Cassia teased. "Or is this the start of a new and even more exciting rumour?"

"Who knows?"

About to change the topic, Ash caught a glimpse of black and gold out of the corner of her eye. Lauren Carlyon, pausing casually by the corner of the Mern, fiddling with his cuff, then moving on. It was out of character for Carlyon to hesitate or fidget so and, intrigued, Ash bid Cassia a good evening and set off to follow Carlyon, wandering along as if she were out for a meander, keeping her stops and starts as inconspicuous as possible.

Caught between suspecting Lauren Carlyon and feeling thoroughly sorry for him, Ash had made little progress in discovering the truth behind the perfect first seruilis mask. The Rhoi trusted him, and it was true enough that any Carlyon was exceedingly unlikely to be put forward as a candidate for Rhoi, but Ash still struggled to produce any kind of impartial judgment. Eward Carlyon's son. Part of the conspiracy, or victim of it?

Carlyon hesitated at the entrance of the Gods' Hall, and Ash ducked back, out of sight. What was he doing? Why this of all places? Coincidence? Or had that chance meeting with Eward Carlyon been more significant than she'd ever realised?

Impossible at this angle to see whether Carlyon had stayed among the glass and metal gods, or gone through the intersecting walls to whatever lay beyond. If this was finally the chance she'd been waiting for, the opportunity to catch a conspirator in a moment of betrayal, Ash needed to get closer without being spotted.

Unable to approach the building's entrance without crossing the empty space before it, Ash chose to move directly, and then stood with her back to the wall beside the open doors, listening.

Nothing.

In such a large room anyone speaking wouldn't necessarily be audible, so all Ash could do was risk a glance inside. And then, seeing no one, she stole across the circular room and repeated her performance at the outer of the two criss-crossing rear walls.

All seemed quiet, so Ash rounded the wall and discovered a stair to follow down. She descended, quickly at first, and then slowing as she rounded a full curve and reached a lantern fixed to the wall of the stair.

Dimly, she could hear a noise. Someone shouting. And...splashing? Ash grimaced at the gloom below. If she went further her shadow would be cast down the stair by the light, putting her at a distinct disadvantage. Drawing one of her knives, she used it to snuff the lantern's candle, and then sat on the stair until her eyes had adjusted.

It was not completely dark ahead, so it was now a question of whether the dousing of the lantern had revealed her presence even as it hid it. And how much the delay had cost. The shouting had stopped. It had only seemed to be one voice, probably Carlyon's, and there was that splashing again, far distant. How deep did the stair descend?

Pausing on every step, Ash moved forward, and after another almost complete circle a partial explanation came into view. A well. A single circular room, poorly lit by a lantern on the far wall, with a well in the centre, two ornate semi-circular covers opened out like wings, and a pivoting bucket suspender drawn to one side.

Carlyon could not have come down here and simply fallen in. That didn't make sense. But if he'd been pushed, where was the second person? Hiding flat against the wall to one side of the bottom of the stair? Or on the far side of the well?

Working for absolute silence, Ash eased herself the last few steps downward, craning her neck to see the blind spots to either side. No-one. The far side of the well, then?

Shouting again and it was definitely Carlyon's voice, though she couldn't make out much of what he was saying. Ash stepped carefully into the room and, keeping her back to the wall, circled until she could see behind the well's stone casing. No one. There was no one in the room.

Torn between suspecting there was some kind of ladder down the well, and fantastic possibilities of ghosts or invisible people, Ash hesitated, then approached the wellhead.

"Carlyon?" she asked, in a too-soft voice, taking a firm grip on the well's rim and looking down. Black. Peering into Luin's depths would tell her nothing, but if he really was down there, she needed to lower the bucket to give him something to hold on to, then go for help.

Too late. Too slow to react to the flurry of movement behind her. Strong hands grabbed her firmly by the ankles and upended her. Straight down the well.

CHAPTER TWENTY-EIGHT

Few Luinhallers had any use for swimming. The public bathhouses were no more than waist deep, and the Milk was too fast and far too cold. Outside the city there were streams and pools that were more inviting, at least in the middle of summer, but Ash, in both her lives, had had little chance to enjoy them.

She'd even obligingly announced to half the Landsmeet that she couldn't swim.

Falling, at least, she'd had plenty of experience with, and she kept herself from flailing, only brushing a flank against stone as she dropped. Then the water, a chill slap, and she gasped and choked as liquid rushed into her mouth. She tried to find some footing, but couldn't even discover which way was up. Black! and cold! and–!

A hand closed on her collar and hauled. Ash gasped as she found her head out of the water, but could not keep herself from struggling anyway, choking and sputtering, and then trying to keep her mouth above the surface as she coughed.

"Stop fighting, blast it."

With an arm beneath her chin, and one around her waist, it took sheer force of will for Ash to obey, and then she found herself crowded into the curving wall, which was a thing she knew how to deal with, immediately searching out the ridges in the stonework, her boots scraping beneath the water, offering a tiny bit of extra support as she clung and shuddered. The hold on her changed to a supporting hand against her back.

"Carlyon," she said, when she could.

"Lenthard." He sounded exasperated.

Less disoriented now she had a wall, Ash managed to look up. The only source of illumination was a grey circle some measureless distance above them. The shadow of a head projected from one side of the circle.

"Who is it?" she whispered, the sound reflecting from the walls oddly.

"Frog."

The shadow disappeared. Then, with a subdued clang, half of the grey circle did as well. Then the other. Frog had closed the well's cover, leaving them in total blackness.

"It's like being damned," she whispered. "Trapped and helpless as they throw dirt on top of you."

Long pause. "Thank you, Lenthard," Carlyon said, eventually. "I couldn't have put it better myself."

Foot in mouth. Ash hid a mad impulse to make it worse, to correct her statement and point out that, of course, the damned were burned. She dug into the wall, scraping her boots for purchase, and already her fingers were dagger-cold, aching. The well's water didn't seem as icy as the Milk, but that didn't make it comfortable.

"Are you sure?" she asked, choosing the marginally less awful subject. "That it was Frog, I mean? I didn't see who it was."

"Quite sure. Unlike you, I didn't lean so handily over the edge of the well for him."

"How then?" Carlyon was as tall and much better built than Frog.

"A rock, I think. More fool me to walk into a trap."

"He hit you?" Ash couldn't quite bring herself to alter her fingertip grip of the wall to try to check on him. "Did you pass out completely?"

"I woke when I hit the water. I don't think he was counting on that, or you appearing. Were you following me, Lenthard?"

"You looked so suspicious. Can you show me how to float?"

Carlyon's voice, after a very long pause, held a note of laughter with the disbelief. "You want me to teach you to swim?"

"If you pass out again, I'll have to keep you above water."

"I won't pass out."

She made an exasperated noise. "You lost consciousness once. Don't be stupid."

"Did you tell anyone you were coming here?"

"How could I? I was following you. And you were following Frog, and it's my strong intuition that he won't be mentioning this. How soon before you're missed?"

"After sunset."

"And I've the rest of the day free. The Godskeeps come to adjust the position of the gods with every bell, though. We could listen for it, and yell, and..."

"Could you hear me? Yelling?"

"Not till I was halfway down the stair," Ash admitted. "And that with the well's cover open. Still, the Godskeeps might use the well for something, and at any rate my fingers are starting to cramp, so let's start with lessons and then try to work something out."

"Does nothing daunt you, Lenthard?"

"Yes. This. But I'd rather learn how to swim than cling here terrified 'til my fingers give out. I–" Her voice had gone ragged, and she stopped and made herself breathe, then forced herself back to business. "Just show me."

It helped a great deal to listen to Carlyon's explanation of how she should move, and to practice while he supported her. After a few false starts, she was able to paddle tentatively about, exploring the narrow circumference of the well, the stones very smooth and cool, with few finger holds worth the name.

"What are you doing?" she asked Carlyon, who was making the oddest splashing noises.

"Take off your boots," he said. "And your tabard. You'll find it easier with them gone."

The tabard was simple enough, but she hesitated over the boots. Retrieving her remaining knife – and wondering what had happened to the one she'd been holding – Ash handed it over to Carlyon, then searched out a narrow handhold in the stonework to clutch while she fiddled with swollen laces.

She'd just kicked off the second boot when the level of the water in the well surged, and she lost her handhold, bobbing on an unexpected tide of warmth.

"What–?" As quickly as it had risen, the water dropped, though it was impossible for Ash to tell if the level was now higher, lower or the same. "What was that?!"

"The outflow from the bathhouse," Carlyon replied. "This is Montmoth's original Well of the Heart. It draws on an offshoot of the

Milk, but during the Breaking the rock separating the offshoot from the bathhouse outflow ruptured. Rather than attempt repairs, they consecrated a new Well of the Heart, and built the Gods' Hall here."

"That's–" Ash fumbled through the implications. "So, this is where Karaelsur's judgments were made, where the old Sun declared Luinsel and Rhoi." And Eward Carlyon had been down here. "No chance of swimming out that way, I suppose. Let me get a better measure of this wall."

"You're not seriously going to try to climb out?"

"Try, yes." The well's stonework was tightly constructed, offering only fingertip holds. "Succeeding's another matter. Stay as much as possible to my right – oh, and try to use my knife to prise loose a stone."

"You don't want it with you?"

"I'd push myself off the wall trying to use it."

Ash's skin was already waterlogged, and the lower few feet of stonework slick and slippery, causing two early falls in quick succession. Her third attempt took her to drier stone, and then Ash's true climb began.

With no certainty of how far she had to go, and no possibility of looking ahead for the best handholds, the ascent had to be a matter of touch and caution. But the cold, while nothing compared to the Milk's, still dulled sensation, competing with the pain of bearing her whole weight on little more than the tips of fingers and toes. Each handhold and foothold, every shift of weight, had to be deliberate, measured, controlled.

Twin lines of pain opened across her back. The muscle burn she could deal with, at least for a limited period. The other concerned Ash far more. Her wound had progressed satisfactorily, enough to remove the stitches, but it was far from completely healed, and she could only guess how much strain the climb placed on it. Was it only sweat trickling down her back? The ache in her upper arms grew intolerable, while her toes and fingers were passing through fire, and the climb had become an eternity. Ash paused at a larger-than-ordinary toehold, where she could wedge one side of her forefoot in place and lean into the wall to take most of her weight. How much further? Had she made it halfway? More? It had not seemed like a long fall, but not being able to see made everything unreal, and her head was in danger of spinning.

Below her, Carlyon was completely silent, no longer scraping her knife at one of the stones. For all she knew, he could have passed out, and silently drowned while she inched her way upward. What would she do if she called out, and he didn't answer? What–?

Ash closed her eyes. She could not fail. To die here, without even beginning a quarter of the things she wanted to do? Without seeing more than Montmoth? To be disposed of by Genevieve's killers, her hunt an abject failure?

Before finding out whether Thornaster had been showing off just for her?

Stone by stone. If the climb as a whole had become too overwhelming, then she would step back from that and concentrate only on the next handhold, the next foothold. Other matters she could worry about when there were no more stones.

Wincing as her fingers protested their return to torture, Ash shifted slowly back into position, and slid her hand up – and over.

The surprise almost cost her everything. She inhaled sharply, and one foot slipped, but the hand she'd curled between the lip of the well and its cover held firm. Gripping hard, she repositioned her feet, and then used her free hand to explore the metal above her. Two half-circles of what had looked like beaten copper, it would be a solid weight to lift. Wedging herself firmly into place, she heaved. Metal clanged.

"Lenthard?!" Carlyon's voice, rising to a high point of hope and incredulity. "You made it?!"

Throat tight, Ash couldn't summon the words. She hung from her one solid handhold, blinking in the dark, until Carlyon shouted again.

"There's a bolt." Her throat still tried to shut the words away, and Ash forced them out. "He bolted it."

Utter silence. Ash wouldn't have had a response either. Unwilling to admit defeat, she beat on the metal until her strength finally gave way, and then, calling a warning, fell once again into the dark.

ooOoo

"Why were you following Frog?"

It was the first either of them had spoken since Ash's failure. Initially, all she'd been able to do was float, her hands and feet stinging relentlessly, using one of the handholds Carlyon had prised loose to take some of her weight. But the silence began to press unbearably, and it was never in Ash's nature to do nothing at all.

"Did you have some idea that he was responsible for Heran's accident?" When only a stirring of water followed, she added irritably: "We're not dead yet. Talk."

There was a marked difference to Carlyon's voice when he finally responded, the words dragging.

"I checked all the seruilisi's quivers, to see if they were short any arrows. Frog had one extra. It was hardly conclusive, and, well, it was Frog."

Ash understood that. Of all the seruilisi, Frog had been the most reasonable. She wanted to track him down and shake him for making her like him.

"So you didn't tell anyone?"

"No."

"Didn't want to smear his good name if you were wrong?"

"That's correct."

"Great. Was there anything else to make you suspicious? Why were you following him tonight?"

"A note. It said 'Meet after Mern: the usual place.' Only Frog could have dropped it, and all I had time to do was follow him to find out what was going on. Straight into this trap."

"I can hardly believe it of Frog. Does he want to be Veirhoi so much? What can be worth all this death?"

"Kiri Arpesial."

Ash held back an indignant little gasp. "If you're expecting me to believe Kiri a scheming murderess...!"

"No. What Frog wants. So very much."

"Oh." Becoming Veirhoi would not automatically gain Frog Kiri, but a Montmoth under the influence of Karaelsur was unlikely to increase Kiri's protections. And Ash had no way to warn her.

Not finding it in themselves to say anything more, Ash and Carlyon floated in the dark. Ash's various hurts faded thanks to the cold, and were replaced by a bone-deep ache. While not inflicting the icy shock of Luinhall's glacial main river, the well was still too cold for health, and the infrequent surge of warmth from the bathhouse became a necessity, a brief revitalisation that Ash began to look forward to with an edge of desperation. She tried to think of Thornaster, displaying himself in the sunlight, but the memory didn't seem real any more. There was only water, and darkness.

"Lenthard?"

"Mmm?"

"I think you may, perhaps, be correct about my losing consciousness."

"You feel faint?" She grasped his arm.

"I can barely keep my eyes open." He said this evenly enough, but his voice was hollow.

"This cold isn't helping any."

"No." His voice was breathy. "Lenthard?"

"Yes?"

"I don't want to die."

"No." Ash faltered, unable to find something more substantial to say on the subject. She didn't want to die. She'd never felt less inclined to die in her life. "I can't think of anything else to try."

"I can try following the feeding stream out – should have tried that sooner."

"If you can fit through whatever opening there is at the bottom of this shaft. If it stays wide enough for you. If it doesn't take you directly into the Milk." She shivered, and shifted her grip on him, taking his hand. "It would be even worse, trapped down there, beneath all that weight of rock, unable to go any further, unable to turn back. Horrible."

"Quicker."

"Quicker doesn't fit with not wanting to die, does it? It must be long past sunset by now. They'll be searching for both of us."

"They'll think I killed you and fled."

The weary matter-of-factness of his words made her wince. And it was true. Lauren Carlyon, perfect first seruilis, son of a monster. No matter what he did, no matter how many hard-earned honours he won, suspicion would fall on him at the first opportunity.

"Only people who don't know you," Ash offered, which was a very feeble response indeed. "I, uh–"

"You flinched the moment you heard my name," he pointed out. "Was that simply at the Rhoimarch's bogeyman, or had my father directly harmed you?"

Strongly suspecting that the last thing Carlyon needed right now was an announcement that she was his nearly-stepmother, Ash briefly repeated the same half-truth she'd told Heran. Carlyon listened without comment, then said:

"I loved my father."

A black, bitter announcement, filling Ash with dismay. She could hear in the words Carlyon's need to speak, but this was not a conversation she wanted to have.

"He was everything that a father should be. Strong and wise and accomplished. Never, not once, did he raise his voice to me. His punishments were always fair, designed to make me understand the error of my ways. He spent time with me, taught me to understand the Balance, to defend myself, to believe in honour. I worshipped him."

"You don't have to tell me this."

"*Don't I?*" he asked, then added, just audibly: "Who else can I tell it to?"

"I – you–" Ash grimaced. She'd known that she didn't really want to see behind the perfect first seruilis mask. Holding hands with Lauren Carlyon in the dark, waiting for death or rescue, and talking about the man who frightened her most. But she didn't let go, and eventually the words began again.

"I spent most of my early life out at Morncriffe, was due to start attending the Mern after my thirteenth birthday. It had been a strange few weeks leading up to that, because Father had abruptly married a girl my own age, who had immediately been killed in a fire. I couldn't understand it, and Eman, the only person who I could bring myself to ask, would only say that it was better not to talk about it. And then word arrived that Father had died.

"We went into Luinhall immediately. The day I arrived one of the servants, a woman who had never even spoken to me before, took great pleasure in destroying my father's memory for me. She said, oh, the most monstrous things about him and called me a fool when I didn't believe her. She told me he'd beaten my mother to death."

"Lauren..."

"I–" His hand tightened on hers. "I still didn't believe it of him. Wouldn't. Shut my eyes to the strange expressions, refused to hear the whispers. Then, his funeral."

Ash grit her teeth with the effort of not pulling her hand away, her abused fingers firing back to agony. But now would be a terrible moment to flinch from him again.

"After that, when it was impossible not to face, Eman confirmed every story, and added...too many of his own. He'd gone through the same childhood, but Eman had been privileged to discover the truth through observation of the man himself, and cannot bear to have him mentioned. Our father, who I'd longed to emulate, and who I now spend all my energy trying not to become."

"Why would you–?"

The faint metallic scraping that interrupted might as well be the explosion of one of the chancy new flintlocks. Ash certainly jerked as if shot. She stared upward, gasping as a grey half-circle appeared.

"*Hallo!*" She screamed it, even as it occurred to her that it might be Frog, come back to check. "*DOWN HERE!*"

"Ash?"

Barely audible, but Ash still managed to recognise the voice.

"*Cassia?!* Cassia! Thank Luin! Lower the bucket! Oh, Sun." She was going to cry, at the stupidest moment.

"...all right?"

"Yes! The bucket! THE BUCKET!"

"...moment."

The head disappeared, and the circle opened up fully.

"Cassia?" Lauren's voice was hoarse, choked by shock and emotion.

"Laundry maid. Astenar incarnate. I'm going to have to think up something really nice to do for her."

A little cough of laughter, and then Lauren took a deep breath and seemed to forcibly summon back his usual first seruilis self. "But how did she find us?"

"Who cares? I'll ask when we get out of this pit. Oh, Luin's Heart, I didn't really believe we would."

"I don't think I shall until I'm standing on something solid."

A squeaking noise was all the warning they had before the bucket free fell toward them. It struck Ash painfully on her shoulder, enough to bruise, but not to make her sorry.

"...get help..." drifted down.

Ash called an encouraging response, but it looked like Cassia had already departed, so Ash pulled out some slack, and looped the rope, bucket and all, under Lauren's arms.

"I was thinking I'd just climb right out," she said. "But my hands and feet feel like soggy dough. Could you manage?"

"Possibly," Lauren replied, but didn't need to test his ability as rescue came with rope ladders, and extra lines to twist into harnesses, taking their weight as they climbed. Ash sent Lauren first, but quickly followed, and found herself hauled up the last few rungs by Investigator Verel.

"Investigator," she said. "You are beautifully warm."

Her legs trying to give out beneath her, Ash gave a moment's attention to the inordinately large number of people in the room. Guards mainly, and a couple of Godskeeps. She found Carlyon sitting on the floor, leaning against the well, a Guardsman examining a bruised and swollen lump decorating one temple.

Business first, Ash hung a moment on Investigator Verel's arm. "It was Frog," she said, in a terse undertone. "Athan Vicardie. Laid a trap for Lauren and tossed me in after."

The Investigator responded with a blanket and a nod, handing Ash off to another Guard. Ash was finding it difficult to stand, her bare feet swollen and painful, but that did not stop her from searching out Cassia and soaking her with a well-earned hug.

"How did you find us, you wonderful creature?"

"I followed you," Cassia admitted, a blush competing with a beaming smile. "At least to the Gods' Hall. You were acting so oddly.

When I heard the Guard were searching for you, I came to check." She produced a shining slip of metal. "Is this yours?"

Ash laughed in pure delight, picturing Cassia following her as she followed Carlyon as he followed Frog. Then she had to sit down.

After inspecting her tender feet, she smiled at Cassia. "I don't suppose I could impose on you for a pair of soft shoes?"

"I'll fetch some," Cassia promised, and dashed off as Ash's trailing Guard minder produced a jar of what smelled like semaileon, and set fire to Ash's fingers and toes by rubbing it into the skin.

"That's one way to wake me up," Ash gasped, trying not to writhe away. Strangely, being out of the water seemed to be robbing her of her remaining warmth. She used the blanket to dry herself as much as possible, then frowned around at the crowded room.

"I still don't see how he managed to get behind me," she said, as the Master of the Mern arrived, with Thornaster at his elbow. "I made certain there was no-one else in the room before I went anywhere near."

Thornaster smiled with relief at the sight of her, then checked, his attention shifting to the well.

"What is this place?"

"Former Well of the Heart," Ash said through chattering teeth. "Not used for that since the Breaking."

Her Visel's openly shocked expression, hastily suppressed, told Ash that fact was no small matter, and she decided not to make several pointed remarks she'd saved up on the sheer pointlessness of putting bolts on wells, and whether the Godskeeps had thought something was going to come climbing out.

Perhaps they had.

CHAPTER TWENTY-NINE

One advantage of having few answers was that detailed discussion could be put off in favour of getting warm and dry. Two Guards linked arms and carried Ash off in style, only pausing to accept some slippers from Cassia. Thornaster caught them up just before they reached his quarters, and Ash suspected at least one of them would be spending the night uselessly guarding the corridor outside, even though she'd only wandered into the mess by accident.

"Can you manage your clothes?" Thornaster asked, pulling her nightshirt and her thickest socks from a chest.

Ash murmured vague assent, and fumbled her way through the change, listening to voices in the receiving room. Thornaster returned briefly with a glass and a plate. The plate held pastries stuffed with fruit and goat's cheese, which Ash inhaled, but she hesitated over the glass. Brandy. Another bout of shivering decided her, and she gulped it down. Liquid heat.

"Frog will run," she said when Thornaster appeared again. "With Lauren still alive, he can't do anything else."

"He won't get far." Thornaster sat beside her on the end of the bed and dropped a drying sheet over her head. "Here – a family party trick." The sheet grew abruptly warmer, and Thornaster made quick work of drying her hair.

"Was the well...wrong?" Ash asked, through the muffling cloth. "What would have happened if we'd died there?"

"Montmoth would have been pulled further out of Balance. That place – it's not the centre of corruption, but I suspect it was the weakness which allowed Karaelsur entry here in the first place. *Two* Wells of the Heart! And Arun didn't even think to mention it!"

"How long were we down there?"

"It's around a decem from midnight."

"Really? It felt longer." She sighed. "Well, at least I learned how to swim. I'll have to try that again, somewhere brighter and warmer."

He laughed, a helpless sputter. "You *would* transform this into a positive experience, stripling."

Ash glanced at him over her shoulder. "I thought you weren't going to call me that any more."

"I was going to do a great many things. Take my share of the heroics so this hunt took less of a toll on you. Not declare myself until you were safely in the charge of my mother."

What happened next hardly felt real. Two warm arms, sliding around her as her Aremish Visel drew her against his chest. Breath tickling her ear when he curled down to press his cheek to hers. He couldn't be doing exactly what she wanted him to do. But the sensation of being held didn't go away. It was not a hallucination.

Disbelief turning to delight, Ash promptly leaned back and started enjoying herself.

"I don't know that I'd call being tipped down a well heroic."

"Yes, truly careless." His arms tightened. "Ash, I – oh, Sun, this is the worst time to have this conversation."

"Not from where I'm sitting."

"Perhaps, but proposing to exhausted girls I've just dosed with brandy is not precisely the kind of behaviour I'd care to boast of. We'll finish this in the morning."

He pressed his lips to the top of her head, then let her go and stood, moving to pull down the bed's coverlet.

"No arguments."

"Very optimistic of you," Ash said, but clambered beneath the sheets and let him tuck her in before adding: "You thought you'd manage to get me all the way to Aremal without *me* declaring myself?"

This produced an expression that stole Ash's breath and left them staring at each other. Thornaster managed a shaky smile, and said: "Ambitious of me, admittedly. Goodnight, stripling."

The last thing Ash wanted to do after that was sleep, but there was little choice. She dreamed, inevitably, of falling, and then of trying to hold the lid of a well shut, as something tried to push its way out, and she thought she could hear her own voice crying out through the metal.

ooOoo

Waking to sunlight, Ash found Thornaster asleep in a chair beside the bed. He was freshly dressed and shaved, and a breakfast tray sat on the table by the window, so she guessed he'd been up all night and had not quite managed to push on through the morning.

How long had it been since she'd last thought herself in love? Seventeen and fascinated by Melar, working herself up to tell him her secrets until she'd realised the depth of his interest in Larkin. Brief spurts of attraction over the years, never solid enough for her to chafe more than a little at the confines of her deception. And then this man, with his inclination to levity, quick intelligence, and that shining dark hair that had once again fallen over his eyes. The idea that she could be free to smooth it back filled her with wonder.

He'd tired himself enough to not wake when she slid out of the bed, or even when she collected clean clothes and took herself off to another room to dress. Refreshed, she returned and sat on the bed to eat breakfast and contemplate a hasty marriage.

Beneath her fizzing delight Ash discovered a strange reluctance. It was not that she didn't want him. But there was a league or two of difference between pretending to be Thornaster's seruilis, and tying their lives together. He might start believing she should do what he said, or smother her with unnecessary caution. But, no – even when he'd thought her nearly a child, he'd accepted sense. A more significant factor would be his family – and all Aremal – which would likely have opinions about sudden marriages. That was daunting on one level, but not something she could treat as a real hurdle without admitting to a shameful level of cowardice.

Ash looked down at her hand, remembering a night too many years ago: how she'd tried to break free, had fought and struggled with all her strength. There was no similarity in the situation at all, but she realised the source of her hesitation. Fear.

Hateful how nightmares of Eward Carlyon still had the power to bind her. If she could set them aside, was there any doubt that Thornaster suited her, that all she needed was for him to wake up and ask his question? Though it seemed to her that a proposal was unnecessary. He'd made his intentions clear.

Sliding from the bed, she padded slowly up to him. For all her confidence, her heart started pounding, and her hand shook as she lifted it, but still she smoothed back his hair, and waited for the moment of sleep-born surprise to pass, and his eyes to focus on her. And then she said: "Yes."

Perhaps Thornaster's best feature – besides the horses – was his ready comprehension, which meant that he dispensed with unnecessary questions, any tiresome delays, and simply swept her into his lap and kissed her.

Perhaps he'd been drinking mead, for the taste of him was sweet fire, and Ash burned up, intent on nothing else but making him hers. Any lingering qualms could be brushed aside, and even the reason she was so successfully 'Ash Lenthard' cast no shadows. While taking off her clothes certainly didn't make her face or figure less boyish, the intensity of Thornaster's reaction made clear that he found no deficit.

They didn't waste breath on words until long after, when Thornaster sighed breathily, linked fingers with hers, and murmured: "Home."

"What do you mean?"

"Something my father would say. He and my mother were pushed toward each other by a great many people who thought they were an appropriate match, so of course they resisted. But my father realised that whenever he was with my mother, he felt like he could most truly be himself." He lifted her hand, examining the scrapes left by her attempts to escape the well. "I don't think I'll ever again feel at home, unless you're there."

This effectively ended the conversation as soon as they'd started it, but the ninth ardeca bell reminded them of the world outside.

"Arun is expecting us at midday."

"They didn't catch Frog, did they?" He would have told her if there'd been news.

"No. The Setsel's entire immediate family was gone by the time the Guard arrived. The servants and remaining relatives have admitted no knowledge. Someone is likely sheltering them, but that investigation is only beginning."

"I'm so angry with him," Ash said. "Which is a stupid thing to say about someone who just tried to kill you, but I never imagined him to be the sort of person who would sacrifice people's *souls* for his ambitions."

Thornaster touched the long line of scar tissue down her arm. "I've met the whole of the Vicardie family – none of them bore the corruption I've been sensing. The capture of the Vicardies is unlikely to end this."

"So you'll keep up your walking tour of the city?"

"Possibly. I first need to do what I can about this second Well of the Heart." A slow smile lightened his expression. "If, that is, I can bring myself to get out of bed. Arun suggested that if I was going to try to marry you out of hand, we should start by telling each other our real names. I'm most curious as to why he knows yours."

"Kiri. I guess she talked about me, back when they were engaged."

Thornaster's eyebrows lifted, but then he frowned. "Was Arun engaged when he came to Aremal?"

"He – well, Kiri thinks he broke it off with her for the way she kissed him goodbye. Which is...I presume Aremal improved our Rhoi *enormously*, but I'm still inclined to black his eye for the line of reasoning which must have led to that."

"Sun." Reverent disbelief.

"Exactly." Ash let out her breath, then settled herself on the comfortable cushion of his shoulder and slid her hand across his stomach, contrasting her pink and tan skin against his brown and bronze. "My name was Daere Ridenalt," she said, very cool and clear. "My father was Visel of Sirule, but he died a few years ago, and my mother's since remarried. She stays away from the Landsmeet, having never quite recovered her social credit after selling her twelve year-old daughter to the former Decsel Carlyon."

The muscles she rested against turned to stone, but all Thornaster did was cover her hand with his and say: "Tell me."

She did, unsparingly, including the fact that she thought Genevieve had killed Eward Carlyon in order to protect Ash, which was something she was unlikely to ever admit to anyone else.

"It's not that I can't return to being Daere Ridenalt," she said, coming to the end of it. "But, putting aside how it will impact other people, I don't want that. I think because people will start treating me first and foremost as the girl forced to marry Eward Carlyon, a little like Lauren can't escape being the Black Carlyon's son. Sometimes I wonder if that's running away from myself, but–"

"No, it makes sense. Though I have to say 'Daere' suits you immensely. And 'Ash' becomes a very macabre choice for a replacement." The calm of the words didn't match the reactions his body had transmitted, and he sat up so he could squeeze her tightly. "I hate that there's nothing I can do to help the girl you once were, but I can at least offer the simple solution of giving you my family's name. Ah, my name being–"

"Morrion Estarrel," Ash said.

A morrion was a thorn bush. Aster and Estarrel both meant star. And he'd said his first name was Rion. Combined with a sister called Aria, an older brother, and the Estarrel bloodline, it had seemed inescapable. Still, Ash hadn't been absolutely sure until he squeezed her tighter.

"Yes – I've been entertaining myself thoroughly not being treated first and foremost as the Aremish Rhoi's younger son."

"And making such a big deal about not being called a liar."

"Oh, I expect I could make an argument for having done no more than shaded the truth," he said easily. "I am most certainly the Visel of Pembury – it was my mother's property. And mother is my father's second cousin. Even the name is almost true."

"What rot."

They laughed, and pushed away thoughts of the past, hurrying to dress in time to meet the Rhoi in a spacious, sunny receiving room, which seemed to Ash to be full of different places to sit, and a suspiciously large number of flowers.

Rhoi Arun took one look at them and said: "So I'm to congratulate you?"

"I'd say shout it from the rooftops, if not for the multiple complications of identity," Thornaster said. "As it is, we'll remain our current selves in Montmoth, and Ash will become Daere on the journey home. Perhaps we'll officially meet in Nyreem, since Hawk at least knows most of the story. He can usefully serve as our witness as well."

Ash hesitated, then added: "I'd like Kiri to be here, if that's possible."

Rhoi Arun nodded without any change of expression, and left the room to make arrangements. Ash took the opportunity to give Thornaster a dismayed glance because the Rhoi looked worn to a nub: the bones of his skull standing out, and his skin papery. Thornaster grimaced in response, then made a delaying gesture, so when the Rhoi returned Ash was occupied teasing Thornaster about her unfortunate lack of tabards in which to get married. Hawkmarten and Kiri arrived in short order, both not quite able to hide the same momentary shock when they saw the Rhoi, though they just as quickly suppressed it.

"You could at least have the decency to look nervous, Thorn," Hawkmarten complained. "If not at the prospect of an eventful married life, then at the thought of Aria's reaction to being left out of your wedding."

"Aria will get over it," Thornaster said cheerfully, then held out a hand. "Ready?"

Ash gave Kiri a quick squeeze, then pushed several hateful memories aside and firmly returned his clasp. It took more effort than she would care to admit, but Thornaster's surface good humour was accompanied by a quiet comprehension. Seeing that, Ash was able to smile when the Rhoi produced a silver marriage cord and bound their hands together. Keeping her gaze on Thornaster-who-was-Morrion allowed Ash-who-was-Daere to say her name and simply be glad.

Then Thornaster's smile faded, eyes widening, and Ash looked down to discover that the silver cord knotted around their joined hands had begun to glow with a pale, white light.

"What–?"

The light increased in intensity, until Ash had to shield her eyes with her free hand, but there was no pain. Instead she felt only a pleasant warmth as the glare faded, along with the cord, disappearing as if it had never been there, though a ghost of sensation remained. She lifted her eyes to Thornaster's and found an expression of such intense, incredulous joy that she smiled at him in wonder.

"Astenar has joined our souls," he explained, voice wobbling. "It happens very rarely, even among the Estarrels. We were meant, Daere."

Someone made an incoherent noise and she turned to find Heran and Lauren both standing in the furthest doorway, their faces mirrors of horrified disbelief.

And then, beside her, the Rhoi quietly collapsed.

CHAPTER THIRTY

"Dramatic, but actually a positive development," Thornaster said. "The power of the binding pushed back some of the imbalance Arun's been suffering. He's resting comfortably for the first time in days."

"But he's still ill, yes?" Heran looked from Thornaster to Guardsman Farpatten for confirmation. "He kept saying it was just a cold, nothing serious, but he's not getting better is he?"

"He won't, no, not until this is over."

Thornaster surveyed the informal Council of War that had assembled in the receiving room following the Rhoi's collapse – Ash, Kiri and Hawkmarten, Lauren and Heran, Farpatten and Investigator Verel. The sumptuous arrangement of spring flowers that filled the centre of the main table made an incongruous focal point for the discussion.

"If Montmoth's Balance remains as it currently stands, Arun faces a continual decline, probably over several years. It's very unlikely, however, that those involved in Karaelsur's rise will give up simply because the Vicardies have been exposed.

"I think the initial plan must have been to replace the Rhoi with Setsel Vicardie, who would be bound to Karaelsur instead of Astenar. Karaelsur then could use the bond as a conduit to Luin's own strength. After that Karaelsur would most likely try to move against Astenar. I–" Thornaster grimaced. "I have no idea what the attitude of the further gods would be to such an event. But even if they returned to again cast Karaelsur out, the effect on Luin – and us – would not likely be minor."

"So what's their next move?" Hawkmarten asked. "Direct attack?"

"It's likely there will be more disappearances, a sudden increase." Thornaster glanced at Captain Farpatten and Investigator Verel. "A human life is a candle compared to the strength they would have gained from Luin, but I don't believe they're simply...feeding lives to Karaelsur. That would not explain the level of imbalance Arun is experiencing.

They have some secondary plan, based upon that imbalance, and will work to increase it. The two obvious ways to do that are to take more lives for whatever purpose they are being used, and to kill Arun. Even if they can no longer replace him with their own tool, it may be sufficient for their purposes to ensure Montmoth does not have the protections of a Rhoi."

"Heran will also be in immediate danger."

It was the first time Lauren had spoken since he'd walked in on a wedding. Although he'd managed to resurrect his first seruilis' mask, giving his complete focus to the danger Montmoth faced, his eyes were unreadably dark and the livid bruise on his temple seemed to Ash to be a proclamation of damage she'd inadvertently inflicted. He was doing a better job than Heran at pretending Ash didn't exist.

"A quick transition to a new Rhoi would not be in their interests," Thornaster agreed. "And on that point, Ash, I heard you say yesterday that you didn't see Vicardie. Yet there's only one way in and out of that well room, and no obstructions beside the well."

"I still don't see how he managed it – I kept my back to the wall until I was sure the room was empty."

"This relates to the still-unanswered question of how those thar-spiders were brought into Arun's heavily-guarded quarters," Thornaster said. "Something that has sewn a great deal of distrust and concern among his household."

"You're suggesting a mage at work?" Farpatten said.

"If they imported one foreign mage, why not two? Or simply some invested enchantment? Those don't last long, but would be more than useful for specific tasks. Montmoth has so few mages that the usual negatives to using magic would hardly apply."

"Mages can 'hear' magic," Verel explained. "And secure rooms can be warded to sound an alarm if magic is used within them. Something that is beyond my abilities, unfortunately, though there are a few exising wards in the palace."

Thornaster nodded. "It would be best if you were detailed to the Rhoi's immediate Guard for the moment, Investigator," he said. "And for Veirhoi Heran to be kept elsewhere in the city – close enough to produce at short notice, but somewhere not easily found by our opponents."

"I'll arrange that," Farpatten said, carefully not noticing the Veirhoi in question's expression.

Thornaster then suggested Lauren go with Heran, and Hawkmarten stay watching over the Rhoi, which Ash thought a neat demonstration that Montmoth's deep-held fears had been realised, and an Aremish Visel had taken control of the Rhoimarch. But none of those present seemed inclined to object, and Thornaster moved on to Kiri, asking for her assistance in reviewing the maps of the city and the locations of the disappearances in hopes that she might make some connection that they had not.

"Will every death in this city feed Karaelsur?" Kiri asked. "Or do they need to perform some form of ritual?"

"If we reach the point where every death is going to Karaelsur, Montmoth will have been lost."

On that note, Lauren and Heran were sent to collect their belongings, and the Guards' conversation turned to a discussion of precautions. Kiri extracted Ash to the far end of the room, sitting them at a smaller table frothing with cornflowers and laceweed.

Kiri touched a delicate white floret. "There's a remarkable dissonance between the discussion and the occasion... I haven't even congratulated you yet, Daere."

"Ash," Ash said. "I'll never be Daere again in Montmoth. Besides, after so long I tend to think of myself as Ash. I'm trying not to let myself call Thornaster 'Morrion', either – or even 'Rion'. At least not 'til it doesn't matter if I'm overheard. I'm glad you could be here, Kiri. I hope it wasn't too awkward."

"Old insults aren't a high concern just now." Kiri glanced in the direction Rhoi Arun had been taken, then said: "May I?" and examined Ash's hand.

"I can sort of see it," Ash said. "When I'm not looking directly at it."

"And you're not happy about it."

Kiri had always been able to read her.

"No. Well, yes, on one level. Who doesn't like the idea of their marriage being affirmed in such a way? But I've read the stories. Jacian and Halide were bound this way – and when Halide died, so did Jacian. The next time I get tipped down a well, it's Thornaster I'll be killing."

"You weren't planning to avoid that anyway?"

"I *always* plan to avoid being tipped down wells. But I – you know what I'm like, Kiri. I climb and I ride straight at fences and I hardly ever stay back and keep out of things. How do I be me if every time I do that, it's not just my life I'm risking?"

"You were always too devoted to Rommy to set him at fences beyond what he could jump. Has that changed?"

"Of course not. Have you seen my grey? I'm not going to...stop laughing, Kiri."

Kiri, eyes brimming with amusement, said: "Somehow I don't think you'll treat your husband much worse than your horse, Daere – Ash." She smiled at Thornaster as he came to join them. "My congratulations to you both."

"I'm glad Daere could have a friend here." He pulled up a third chair, and took Ash's hand, putting business aside to briefly exchange pleasantries, but then said: "Sera Arpesial–"

"Kiri."

"Kiri. It seemed to me that when you asked about the need for a ritual that you had some other question in mind."

"In a way. It was what you said about a human life being little more than a candle." Kiri's heavy lashes swept down. "If you light enough candles at once, they'll still make a bonfire."

ooOoo

It said something for Ash's wedding day that while her new husband spent his afternoon trying to boil a well, she found herself stuck in a lumbering coach opposite a young man who might as well have edited her out of existence, and a boy who had given up on a similar attempt to instead outright glare at her.

Heran, having stewed over the revelation of breasts ever since the banquet, was overdue an opportunity to shout at her, but Ash merely smiled at him vaguely and sat apparently lost in thought. Alone, she could probably have made some progress with an affronted Veirhoi, but she was reluctant to have that conversation in front of Lauren. His wounds were too deep, and freshly exposed.

Her presence in the coach at all was due to Farpatten. When she'd mentioned an intention to check in with her Huntsmen, the Guard Captain had suggested she travel down with the Veirhoi, putting the coach at her disposal for the return journey. For a moment Ash had suspected Thornaster of becoming immediately and excessively protective, but then realised this was a different impact of her marriage. Farpatten had reclassified her.

The unhappy prospect of being a matter of consideration for a Rhoimarch's security detail kept Ash occupied during the short trip to the Lower Commons. And in Montmoth she was merely married to a foreign personage. What would it be like in Aremal? Ash knew she loved Thornaster, and would be spending a great deal of her time happily thinking back to what they had done together that morning. But she hadn't been able to predict all the consequences of marrying him, and was finding them increasingly difficult to swallow.

The coach rumbled to a stop as Ash told herself for the tenth time that Thornaster and the possibility of horse races would likely make up for a reasonable amount of being guarded. She rubbed her left hand, which was tingling uncomfortably, then shivered as a chill ran down her spine.

"Did it just get colder?"

Heran's startled words were followed by an exclamation from Lauren, and the first seruilis drew his feet up and snatched at Heran as patterns of frost raced across the coach's floor. Ash hastily followed suit, the soles of her second-best pair of boots making a cracking noise. Balancing on the coach's seat, she reached for the nearest door, but pulled her hand back at the last moment as a filigree of ice and a strong desire to keep her fingers warned her off.

"Kick it out!" Lauren ordered, and shifted to make good his own words, only to hastily grab for a firmer hold of the seat as the coach lurched into motion. The driver was shouting, urging the horses to greater speed.

"He's sprung 'em!" Ash gasped, her breath misting.

Everything bounced, and Heran and Lauren both tumbled to the floor, Lauren's rapier whipping against Ash's legs as he tried to avoid the frost. But already the unnatural cold had faded, breath no longer marking itself with mist, and the pair merely slid on melting ice.

Being away from the cold did not necessarily mean they were out of danger, particularly if the driver continued to corner at a speed to make the coach slew and skip. Ash clung to her seat, trying to make sense of the noise outside, and hoping the coach wouldn't overturn. Was that pursuit, or simply Farpatten and the other Guard who'd been accompanying the coach on horseback?

"Stay down, Heran," Lauren said, as the Veirhoi tried to haul himself upright. "Brace yourself, but try to be ready to move."

They rounded another corner, and then raced breakneck along a downward slope, a circumstance that had Ash certain they were going to crack up at any moment. But as they bounded onto flatter ground the pace dropped, and the driver began to haul up.

Ash slid open the nearest screened window and made a cautious survey, then relaxed when she saw Farpatten still mounted. He caught her eye and made a belaying gesture, so she simply double-checked her knives were in easy reach, and waited till the coach came to a stop. Lauren and Heran picked themselves up, and Lauren drew the rapier that had added to their tangle.

"I'm going to put 'inconvenient in bouncing coaches' down on the negative side of learning swordplay," Ash said, and was not in the least surprised when he ignored her.

The glossy flank of Farpatten's bay blocked the window, and the Guardsman leaned down to glance inside. "Any injuries?"

"No. What happened?"

"You know almost as much as we, Ser Carlyon. We arrived at the safe house and the coach started to freeze. If Vishen had hesitated at all before driving on, I don't doubt we'd still be there." Farpatten glanced in the direction they'd come, and then restively at a dung-gather and a pair of riders who'd paused to stare. "There's been no sign of pursuit, but then we didn't see the attacker in the first place. Hold fast – we'll head to the nearest Watch House."

"They knew where we were going," Heran said, as the coach began to move again. "We only decided on this less than two decems ago and they had time to set up an ambush with a mage powerful enough to kill the lot of us. What's to stop them from coming to this Watch House and doing exactly the same thing?"

"Nothing," Lauren said crisply. "But I doubt we'll stay there long. It may be that we'll head out of the city altogether."

"If they're moving this openly against me, what are they doing to Arun?" Heran asked, but then closed his mouth on any further questions and said instead: "Can I have one of those knives of yours, *Lenthard?*"

"No."

Heran might possibly have anticipated a refusal, but nothing so tersely flat. Momentarily stymied, he wavered, then snapped: "Just sit here and be protected, is that it?"

Unable to resist a smile, Ash shook her head. "Borrow a sword off one of the Watch, if you want one. But there's no sense me giving you a weapon you've never used while leaving myself half-armed."

At this point Heran remembered he wasn't talking to her, and firmed his mouth, but since they'd reached the Watch House Ash was already halfway out the door. That would be the last time she'd agree to ride in a coach when a horse was available.

The Lower Commons was not home, but she'd ridden through it often enough exercising mounts for Reeders Stables. The day had already shifted to halflight – the period when the sun had passed into the shadow of Westgard, but had not yet set – and most folk would be returning home, or preparing dinner. It was also shift change for the Watch and, barring a flop-eared dog, the yard of the Watch House was empty.

"Captain." Ash joined Farpatten in checking again for any sign of pursuit. "Send them with me."

Farpatten gave her a brief glance. "We're not yet at so desperate a pass."

"I can put them somewhere reached by a rooftop path known only to friends who have no Luinsel connections," Ash said.

The Guardsman simply shook his head, and Ash made no attempt to push the point further, following him into the Watch House. But she could see the idea take hold as Farpatten tried to organise sufficient Watchmen to send back to the safe house to investigate. The attempt on the Veirhoi could only have been arranged by someone deep in the confidence of the Rhoi's Guard. Until Farpatten had discovered the traitor, any arrangement he made was at risk. And all this while he had no idea whether his primary charge, the Rhoi, was facing a similar attack.

"What guarantee?" he asked, turning on Ash almost mid-sentence.

"None. But I'd give odds he'd be safer with me than back at the palace."

Farpatten was a decisive man, quickly making arrangements for contact. Ash then had a helpful discussion with the Watch Sergeant, borrowing a few stray items of clothing, which she handed to Lauren and Heran.

"The rapier will make you stand out a little, but I guess it's safer to keep you armed. Luckily it's getting on for dark."

Heran looked at the oversized cap she'd given him, sighed, and pulled it on. Then he glowered at her reaction, even though all she'd done was widen her eyes and keep her mouth firmly closed.

"You're truly obnoxious, you know that?"

She grinned. "You're not the first to mention it."

"Can't you take this seriously? Someone just tried to kill us!"

"This is me taking this seriously, Heran," Ash said, surveying Lauren doubtfully. A worn coat was not going to make him look less upright, and the bruised temple stood out like a brand. "Let's get moving in case they did try to follow us. We'll go over the back wall, Captain."

Farpatten nodded, and came to offer them a leg up. "Don't make me regret this."

Ash nodded. "Tell Thornaster–" She hesitated, then said, "Tell him I'll see him soon."

CHAPTER THIRTY-ONE

"Wait, we're going into Mockhold Valley? That's your idea of a safe place?"

"It's my idea of a place that people who usually ride around the Deirhoi District would be more likely to get lost than to find us."

"And what do we do about the locals? How do we avoid getting mugged – or worse – while we're hiding from assassins?"

"I told you, remember? Roof running. This way."

There were hundreds of routes to the roofs of the Shambles, but with two beginners, one of them tall and reasonably solid, she'd be using the safest. First an easy climb up an old wrought iron fence onto a stone wall that had once circled one of the original large estates. The wall had been used as a support for dozens of less solid buildings, but still provided a safe crossing to a tight row of three-story houses which were better quality than most, and from there to the estate's manor house, a solid core in a sea of lesser structures.

Ash took them up on the wall, pausing to survey the terrain and play lecturer.

"Three rules. First, walk light and keep your mouth shut. These are people's homes, and we don't want to damage them any more than we want them to know we're running around on them. Second, walk where I walk. I'll be going slow, giving you time to watch my feet and my hands. Third, if I yell 'jump', leap in whatever direction I'm heading and grab for anything that looks solid. That shouldn't happen on this route, but it's still the Shambles, after all. Any questions?"

"If we are separated?" Lauren asked, voice lowered but as crisply correct as ever.

"Get up as high as you can and wave at anyone around my age who happens by. There are a few who do use the roofs outside the Huntsmen, but most of them will head the other way if they spot you. Just tell them Ash wants you stashed, and they'll look after you."

Without further ado she led them up and along a far more convoluted route than she'd usually bother with. But Ash was glad of the need, aware – though Thornaster had no plans to leave for months yet – that this was the start of a long goodbye to a life she'd loved. The beginning of the end of Ash Lenthard.

During the late afternoon and early evening the Shambles was at its liveliest. Cats that had dozed during the day stirred, eyeing off the flights of birds choosing their roosts. Voices rose in chatter or shouts, dogs barked for table scraps. The deep streets were already disappearing into shadows, but the halflight made for easy navigation of the roofs. Ash walked the sky as the broken moon rose, and thought the world glorious.

Heran and Lauren kept to her rules, and just past sunset she had brought them to the building opposite the Huntsmen's headquarters. A trio of spare staves were tucked against the base of the chimney.

Ash collected one and murmured: "I'll go across and swing over a walkway for you two," and immediately put words into action.

The walkway – two boards lashed together – had been useful for outfitting the attic with a few larger items. Ash set it carefully in place, and then stilled, staring along the street below. Then she snatched up her staff and said tersely, "Go inside and wait. There are candles and a tinderbox on the table immediately to your right. I'll be – I'll try not to be long."

Before either of her charges could respond, Ash left them, hurrying toward the crossroads at the end of the block of buildings. Lit by an open taphouse door, it had offered her a brief tableau of three figures – two male, and one much smaller, kicking at the legs of the tallest of the three as he carried her.

Five winding streets connected at the crossroads, all alley-narrow. Two were possibilities, and with no means of choosing between them Ash had to rely on speed, racing quickly along one, and then finding an easy roof and attempting a light-footed sprint to the ridge. A dangerous risk – new routes did not mix with speed – and a tile slid down behind her as she balanced on the roof's apex.

It shattered in the first street as she crouched gingerly above a none-too-stable piece of guttering, but the noise usefully drew the attention of someone well ahead of her in the street below. She couldn't make out more than a suggestion of a shape, but it was a shape that made a noise – a question – and was briefly answered.

Toning down speed in favour of care, Ash prowled closer, and reached the corner of this new clump of buildings in time to see her targets vanish into a particularly decrepit two-story building. All the windows were boarded up and the place looked a few nails short of collapse. The roof was the kind she would avoid unless suicidal, so she found a way down to the packed dirt of the street.

There was no front door, only a piece of wood hanging from a twisted hinge. The entryway was musky with old urine, and a gaping hole in the floor could be seen through another door to her right.

Dim light and voices led her up a stair to her right. Ash tested each step, straining her eyes in the dark and trying to hold her weight from creaking boards. At the head of the stairs the ceiling had fallen to the left, thick timbers riddled with mites and worm. To the right was a door, half-open, and she slid towards it across a sagging landing which had long since lost its balcony railings.

The captive was Ash's horse-mad charity case. Even skinnier than the first time Ash had seen her, if that was possible, glowering defiance as she tried to kick the one who held her, despite a jagged and clearly infected cut on one leg.

"...that it's worth it?" the other boy was saying.

The first laughed. "She aint dumb enough. Are you Tongueless?"

Ash swapped her staff to her left hand and slid a knife out of her boot. She took two steps forward, flung the knife into the thigh of the shorter boy and, covering the remaining ground in a rush, drove the staff at the other's knee.

Too slow.

Letting go of the girl and stumbling back before the blow had quite landed, the taller boy stared at Ash incredulously, and then grabbed her staff with both hands. Ash, at a strength disadvantage, lost the staff and moved backwards, hampered by the rubbish in the room. He swung at her wildly, and then tossed the staff as she reached for her second knife.

"I'll teach you, you damn rat!"

He leapt at her, connecting as she straightened, and they crashed to the floor in a billow of dust. Her knife gone, Ash brought knee and elbow into play immediately, and did her best to avoid a couple of flailing blows. But then he got hold of her throat, and shook her like the rat he'd named her.

As he began to squeeze in earnest, Ash raked for his eyes while scrabbling for her dropped knife with her other hand. She had to get him off – had to – !

The boy bellowed, jerking back and trying to reach over his shoulder for the knife, which had been buried in his shoulder by his former captive. Ash used the opportunity to squirm away, scrambling for her staff.

They both made it to their feet at the same time, but now the boy had her knife, and his friend had stopped yelling and was struggling upright. Breath tearing her throat, Ash struck hard at the larger boy's chest, thrusting with all her might so that he staggered backwards, then fell onto the sagging balcony, and through it.

The entire building shook with a second crash, and creaked dismayingly. The floor shifted, the walls leaned, and the entire building considered tumbling into a graceless pile. Then it settled.

"Damn," Ash croaked, and then switched her attention to the second boy, who took the better part of valour, backing away.

"Get away from me, scut!"

Fright turning to annoyance, Ash rubbed her throat, then said: "Stay there, we'll leave, then you can check on your...friend."

His friend wasn't making any noise, but that was fine with Ash right at that moment. Keeping a wary eye on the remaining boy, Ash ushered the former captive toward the door, tested and then walked with swift surety across the landing's exposed support beam to the top of the stairs.

They protested her weight and she frowned again, glancing back at the girl, who was watching from the doorway. "Can you cross it?" she asked, and the girl considered for a long moment, then set a bare, scabbed foot onto the rotting wood and started across. Daere nodded and went ahead down the stairs. She doubted it would hold both of them. Below, the fallen boy started swearing, flinging words out of the dark as if he could knock the escapees down with them.

Ash didn't waste any time, getting outside and scanning the nearest buildings for a good route up and then herding the girl toward it. Her new charge was slow to move, and favoured one leg, but at least accepted Ash's help with the climb.

"We'll rest here a while," Ash said, once they'd reached the relative safety of the roof. She guided the girl so she could sit against a chimney, and tried not to be too obvious about how badly she needed to sit down herself. "My name's Ash. What should I call you?"

Still no response. The boys had called the girl 'Tongueless', so perhaps she couldn't speak at all. But why hadn't the girl at least tried to scare that pair off with the gale she was able to summon? And why was she here? Ash hadn't thought her a Shambles dweller, despite obviously living rough.

With her throat so sore, Ash wasn't inclined to try to coax answers, and concentrated on gripping her hands together to quell a growing tremor. What had happened in there? She'd been so slow, had had all the weapons and still she'd nearly – nearly killed Thornaster, had hesitated because the stakes were higher than she could accept. Marriage to Thornaster was something she could embrace, but this soul bond...

"Telat."

Ash blinked, and then studied the girl in the rising light of Cuinefaer. A single word, but it made Ash realise she'd overlooked an obvious possibility for why this girl wouldn't talk to her.

But with Lauren and Heran waiting, now was not the time to experiment. "Nice to meet you, Telat," Ash said. She pointed at the infected gash on the girl's leg. "Come with me, and I'll give you medicine for that."

Thankfully, there were no problems getting back – a fortunate circumstance since Ash was far from at her best, and Telat seemed to be staying upright out of sheer grit and determination. Ash had never been gladder to see the Huntsmen's headquarters, gently lit and inviting.

Also more crowded than it had been when she'd left it, with Lauren and Heran at the far end of the long attic, facing three of her Huntsmen. Lauren had his hand on the hilt of his rapier, but the atmosphere was of wary discussion, not confrontation.

"Lark, Melar, Bitty – how handy."

Her friends turned, and then paused to take in her appearance.

"You sound like you have a severe case of someone tried to strangle you," Melar said appreciatively.

"I have a severe case of need to sit down, anyway. This is Telat, and it looks like you've already introduced yourself to Lauren and Heran. Melar, can you clean out that cut on Telat's leg? And if any of you speak Firuven, that would be handy, because I think I overlooked an obvious–"

Her voice had faded to a scratchy whisper, so Ash gave up, made a general 'get on with it' gesture, then dipped herself a drink out of the rain barrel.

"Something tells me that even before you ran off this was more than an exciting excursion to show the Veirhoi the seamier side of the city," Melar said, turning to hunt out their collection of medicking supplies.

"Making it harder to assassinate him," Ash said, plopping herself down on one of the piles of mats they used for seats, and trying to coax Telat to join her instead of backing toward the entry bridge. "Matters are coming to a head."

"Ash!" Larkin exploded. "You're running from assassins and you just left them here? Fine! You abandoned the Veirhoi in the Shambles and then nearly got yourself killed, but who cares? We all know you're completely indestructible, so let's have an explanation instead of an argument."

"Hiding, not running." Ash sipped her water and sighed.

"*Do you speak Firuven?*" asked Lauren.

Telat froze, then seemed to become visibly taller, the whole of her attention fixing on Lauren. Then she crossed the attic in one concerted rush to stand, almost vibrating, before him.

"*Say that again,*" she demanded, in almost the same language Lauren had used. Formal Firuven rather than Trade Firuven.

Lauren, after only a momentary hesitation, switched to Formal Firuven: "*Forgive my mistakes: I am conversant but not expert in your language. This one wishes to tend the injury on your leg.*" He nodded toward Melar.

Telat didn't so much as glance in Melar's direction, the whole of her focus still on Lauren. "*Again,*" she breathed, as if she thought her ears were playing her false.

Eyebrows drawing together, Lauren tried: "*How did you come to be in Montmoth, Sera?*"

And the storm broke.

The whole of the attic stilled in respectful awe, the girl's tirade no less powerful for being incomprehensible to most of her audience. Eyes fixed on Lauren's face, Telat worked her way from indignation through fury to a kind of exulting glee, and finally stopped not because she had run out of things she wanted to say, but because she was sick and starved and exhausted.

Lauren, too startled to maintain his first seruilis mask, caught Telat's arm as she swayed, panting, and he and Melar helped the girl to one of the piles of mats.

Larkin gaped at the scene. "What was all that?"

When Ash didn't respond, Heran said: "She is — I think she said that she belongs to a Firuvari crafter house. That when her grandfather died, those appointed her guardians announced they were taking her to be trained. And brought her to Montmoth and just...left. Most of what she said is what she wants to do to them."

"She is House Docenti," Lauren said, glancing up from an examination of the swollen, seeping gash on Telat's leg.

This produced another respectful silence. Firuvar was too far away to be more than stories to most of Montmoth, but among those stories House Docenti featured not infrequently as the source of fabulous extravagance. And should you have no use for staircases of frozen flame, or fountains that sang, they offered more practical items, such as goblets that nullified poisons. In Montmoth, where even the glowing stone used in the Gods' Hall was an expensive rarity, House Docenti was almost literally a name to conjure with.

Even Bitty blinked a few times, but then pragmatically unpacked a bag of stale bread she'd brought along from the bakery and offered it around while Melar and Lauren worked to clean, salve and bind Telat's leg. Ash tore a bun to tiny fragments and washed it down, and when Sim arrived with Carl and Dest in the middle of this she drew a rough map and sent them off to check on a house where a piece of trash might still be in the cellar, one of her knives in his back. If he was, they'd deliver him to the Watch.

"But she must understand Old Tongue," Larkin said, after this interruption had been dealt with. "When you told her to come each day to the bakery, she did!"

"I understand Firuven much better than I speak it," Ash said, struggling to make herself audible. "I wonder how well I'd do if I'd tried to learn just by listening?"

Melar looked over at her. "Ash, do you want to have a voice tomorrow?"

"Bah."

"Why didn't they just kill her?" Heran asked, and then haltingly repeated the question in Firuven.

"*You speak as if your tongue is stuck to the roof of your mouth,*" Telat observed, obliging Ash to gulp rather. "*They are all cowards. They think I am – they think that if they kill me, they will be cursed. So they put me here, in this frozen place.*"

It was not a full explanation – Lauren certainly wasn't the only person in Montmoth able to make himself understood in Firuven – but Ash could readily picture this extremely proud girl caught between need and distrust, struggling to find answers in a completely strange place.

Telat had had no Genevieve. Would Ash, who had thought Genevieve's intervention a great blessing, but not critical, have really done so well without her? Tonight she was finding doubt in every corner, and the more she second-guessed herself, the less able she felt.

"Why did you stop coming to the bakery?" Bitty asked.

"*Because of the Cold Man,*" Telat said, after Lauren had translated, and then frowned mightily because Lauren, Heran and Ash all reacted as if stuck with a pin.

"Coincidence?" Lauren wondered, then asked Telat: "*What do you mean by 'Cold Man'?*"

Made suspicious by their reactions, Telat searched his expression, then gestured at Larkin and Bitty: "*I go to a place of theirs for food, but the last time a man, all ice, came to me after I left and looked at me and...spelled me in some way. There was no understanding it. He looked at me and I followed him, though I did not want to, and he put me in the room of a house even colder than him. There were bars on the window. But I came back to myself and opened a way out, and slipped free. That is where I did this.*" She gestured at her leg.

"*After that, twice I came to their place for food, but I could feel the cold man near, waiting. And later I could feel him where I usually sleep, so I came away.*"

Astonished, Ash took a quick sip of water, then said: "Lark, have you noticed anyone watching the bakery lately?"

"Why?"

Lauren answered. "We believe – it's possible the man who attacked our coach this afternoon has been lying in wait for Sera Telat there. She must be a particularly desirable target. *Sera, what did he look like?*"

A moment's quiet consideration. "*Shorter than him.*" She indicated Larkin with a faint motion of her chin. "*Pale. White hair. White eyes.*"

Lauren translated crisply. "Have you seen anyone like that?"

"No," Larkin said, as Bitty said: "Yes."

"A rich man," Bitty continued. "Came in a few days ago. Didn't seem interested in what he bought. Did seem interested in the back of the shop. I thought he might have been one of Sonia's relatives."

Larkin was on his feet. "We've got to—"

"Wait," Ash whispered, then added to Telat: "*Can you—*"

"*Sera Telat, can you lead us to where he took you?*" Lauren put in quietly.

Telat wavered, caught between self-preservation and the important discovery of people who could speak her language.

"We'll be going in numbers," Ash managed to say, then gave up on talking in favour of finding bits of paper she could write on. Lauren was more than capable, anyway, and soon had established that the house was in the Rockways – a part of the Commons northwest of Mids – and that Telat could definitely remember the rough location, and probably identify the exact house if she went there.

Even narrowing the search down to the Rockways was more than enough information to warrant a response in force, and by the time Ash had finished writing, Lauren had succeeded in ensuring Telat would not bolt off into the night. Probably.

It helped Ash enormously to have a definite goal, to set out a plan of action and make arrangements. It helped even more when Melar opted to stay, so she could allow herself to be shooed off to sleep rather than be concerned with keeping watch or herding Luinsel.

Curled on one of the mat piles, she studied her hand, turning it so that she could glimpse the lines of light below the skin. Ash still did not in any way regret marrying Thornaster, but it had taken her less than half a day to nearly kill him.

Had it been knowledge of the consequences that had slowed her blow that evening? How could she prevent herself from hesitating in future? She had as usual used disabling rather than killing blows and, low as those two scuts had been, she was still glad not to have their deaths weighing on her.

Genevieve hadn't hesitated. She had killed Eward Carlyon, and given Ash years of happiness free from the threat he posed. Ash knew part of her reluctance to kill had come from the ease with which Genevieve had done so – and much of the rest from the horror of damnation, hanging for so many years over her guardian's head.

Sighing, Ash tried to dismiss thoughts of death altogether, and think back instead to taking Thornaster's clothes off, and the heady sensation that had come from kissing him. But her throat was in no condition to be easily forgotten.

So much for her wedding day.

CHAPTER THIRTY-TWO

"Any better?"

Ash, sitting on the broad stone wall surrounding the Mids Watch House, turned in slight surprise to Lauren. It was the first non-essential word he'd offered her since the well.

"Better in that I'm at least half audible. It was hard to sleep. You seem...more centred today."

"I suppose you could say events have overtaken my self-pity."

"Ha." Ash shifted on the wall, checking that none of the rest of her group had strayed from the shelter of a nearby roof during the wait for the Guard. "For what it's worth, I'm sorry I didn't tell you who I was when we were talking."

"Sun, I'm not. I don't think I could have–" Lauren took a slow breath. "I'm taking a lesson from that Firuvari child. Wearing rags, starving, and yet still the heir to one of Firuvar's great houses. She knows who she is, unequivocally, despite all evidence to the contrary. Surely I can still be Lauren, no matter who my father might be."

He didn't quite sound like he believed it, but Ash let that pass. "It's a lot easier to be positive when you're not stuck down a well in the dark."

"How is it you are still alive?" he asked, the words careful. "There was a body in that fire."

"Yes, and I'd love to know how anyone could believe a leg of pork was me, once they'd put the fire out."

"What?!"

"I thought it a delaying tactic at the time. It occurs to me that someone might have intervened for me – saw that it wasn't a human body but told my father it was me because they disapproved of what had happened. Or maybe they were just really stupid. Who knows?"

His mouth worked, but he couldn't quite find the situation funny. Ash looked him over, knowing she couldn't just fix him, but always ready with helpful suggestions.

"The other day I asked Investigator Verel why she stayed in Montmoth, despite having to work twice as hard for half the respect. She told me it was for the money, which is reason enough I guess. But why do you stay around being the Black Carlyon's son?"

"I don't know that hiding from myself is a better solution."

"Who said anything about hiding? 'Carlyon' is just a name anywhere but Montmoth. Go to this Collegium place in Aremal – I'm sure they can produce endless lectures on sewers too."

This produced a small cough of laughter, but then a thoughtful pause. "It would be something to see your – your husband compete seriously. If, that is, I can ever adjust to the idea of him being your husband."

"You and me both." She slid off the wall. "They're nearly here."

"I don't see them."

"No." Ash lifted her hand, considering the gleam of criss-crossing lines. "I think I can tell where he is, now that he's closer."

She turned and gestured to Sim and Melar to bring Telat down. Being 'prentices, most of the Huntsmen had a great deal of difficulty taking unexpected days off, and she had refused to allow the bulk of them to risk their positions, knowing she could divide her reduced numbers between guarding Heran back at headquarters and providing an escort for Telat because the Guard would supply the lack.

Farpatten had delivered beyond anticipation, supplementing his Guardsmen with troops from Montmoth's small army. After the previous day's ambush, he had clearly decided there was little advantage in trying to get about quietly. They were all mounted, and the noise of so many horses drew the residents from their breakfasts to stare, and Captain Garton out of the Watch House for a brief reunion. But then Thornaster was there, riding double with Bitty and leading an out-of-temper Cloud Cat, highly unimpressed by Larkin's efforts to stay on her back.

Because this was not an occasion to hug her new husband, Ash wrapped her arms briefly around the mare's neck instead. Thornaster's gaze fixed inevitably on her livid throat, but all he said was: "The rest of your knives are in her saddlebags."

"The Veirhoi?" Farpatten asked.

"Safe. Guarded." Lauren accepted the reins of his blood bay from the Guardsman. "This is Sera Telat deas Docent. *Will you take us there now, Sera?*"

Telat nodded once, firming her jaw, but then eagerly scrambled onto the blood bay's back. Horses made up for a great many trials.

Farpatten wasted no time – perhaps hoping to regain through speed what they lost to noise. With a grand clatter of hoofs, they headed to the Rockways at a brisk trot, Ash's Huntsmen doubling with several of the Guard, and Captain Garton hurrying to collect and meet them with a Watchman from the Rockways District.

There was no difficulty at all in locating the place. Thornaster reacted before they even reached the street, and Ash – another side effect of the soul bond? – was shivering by the time their target came into sight.

An unremarkable house. It even reminded Daere a little of Genevieve's – a single-level construction of wood with a fenced-off garden. There were peach trees. Windows shuttered, no smoke rising from the chimney, nor any hint of activity.

They paused several houses away to dismount and break into groups. A half-dozen quickly circled to the back to watch for anyone trying to flee, and a handful more spread among the neighbouring buildings, knocking on doors. While Farpatten and Thornaster conferred, Ash gestured to her Huntsmen, and gathered them well back with those assigned to looking after the horses, seeing no advantage in tangling with the initial rush. Lauren brought Telat to join them.

"Odd."

Ash, retrieving her spare knives, glanced up at Melar. "What?"

"If this circus turned up in Mids, there'd be doors wide, heads out every window, curtains twitching. This place has only a few passers-by. It's like all the houses are abandoned."

"No, there's someone," Larkin said, as one of the doors a Guard was knocking on was opened by a frazzled man in a nightrobe.

Frowning, Ash passed Cloud Cat's reins to Melar, and crossed to stand at Thornaster's elbow as the Guardsman returned to Farpatten.

"It's been empty this past year, Captain, after the merchant who owned it died. The Landhold there thinks there's been someone coming and going since last autumn, tidying the garden and keeping the building maintained, but not daily. We're sending for details of the new owner."

"Take care – if the description matches our 'Cold Man', do not approach."

"They're sick," Ash said, peering about at the slow responses to other knocking Guards. "Everyone in these houses – they're all sick."

Farpatten looked at her, then Thornaster. "Odds are good this isn't where the Vicardies are hiding, that there mightn't be anyone here at all. Any objections to going in?"

It was rare to see Thornaster hesitate. Ash couldn't be certain what the building felt like to him, but the closer she came to it, the more she became aware of an icy pulse, like a deep-set toothache. Farpatten seemed to feel it too, but most of those around them were merely wary, not oppressed by that relentless throbbing.

"I'll take point," Thornaster said at last. "I don't think there's anyone in there, but the place itself is inimical. Bring a small group." He glanced at Ash. "Stay close behind me."

As they broke down the door, Ash wondered at herself, because even though she'd replaced her knives she hadn't been planning to go inside, and that again was unlike her. Though perhaps a natural reaction to the place, where even the most stolid of the Guards flinched as they crossed the threshold. Breath misting, they crowded into a bare kitchen, seeing nothing but empty rooms and gloom.

"Take down the shutters. Don't touch anything else." Thornaster, hand on the hilt of his rapier, padded forward, and Ash followed, ready to protect his back, keeping the possibility of invisible people firmly in mind.

"Frost on this door," one of the Guard said.

Thornaster drew his rapier and used the tip to prod the door open, revealing stairs descending into blackness. The Guard was sent for a lantern, Farpatten began a soft murmur intended to make his hand glow blue, and Ash, shivering, stood a little closer to Thornaster, who was by far the warmest thing in the building.

"You're going to be useful in winter," she murmured.

His frown eased, and he ruffled her hair, and then grinned when she pulled a face. "Was it your unique diplomacy which led to the strangulation?"

Ash blinked. "Talking may have been the better option," she said. "Need to act outran me, I think."

She slid her hand into his, which brought an entirely different expression to his face and she smiled, feeling much warmer, and then let go as the Guardsman returned.

They moved in a tight cluster down to a large, square cellar. The walls were crusted with flowers of frost, and icicles speared from the ceiling. At first Ash thought it otherwise completely empty, but then she realised Thornaster had stopped several stairs from the bottom, and that the lower steps were covered by what she had thought to be the floor. Deep blue and viscous, it...rippled.

"There's another well under that," Farpatten said, through chattering teeth. "See — you can just make out the circle of the well cover."

Behind him, the lantern swayed.

"Back up," Thornaster said sharply, and more or less hauled the Guardsman away from the cellar. He didn't stop at the top of the stair, but looked around and led them through the now-open back door into the walled rear garden, ordering the other Guards out as he did so.

It was still unnaturally cold there, but nowhere near as bad as indoors. The Guardsman dropped his lantern and collapsed to his knees, shuddering, while Ash found the warmest spot of sunlight she could and stood with hands in armpits near some rows of chest-high plants. Even Farpatten sat down, stone face cracking in favour of open shock. But only for a few deep breaths, and then he climbed back to his feet.

"If you have recommendations I'd be glad to hear them. I've not seen anything remotely like that before."

"Nor I," Thornaster replied, less than happily. "Though I can guess at what it is, since it began to function on your man here, drawing his life out. It's the soul-stuff of sacrifices, shaped to become the vehicle of sacrifice. The souls it draws will be delivered up to Karaelsur. And it's sitting over a *well*."

"What can we do?"

"Take the roof off and rip up the main level's floor, to begin with. Expose it to sunlight. After that–" Thornaster looked back into the now-empty building. "It's vastly more powerful than I am," he said, bluntly. "And I doubt setting a bonfire on top of it will do more than risk damaging the well cover. Finding the instigator, whoever created this, may be the way forward."

"We're having the owner of record traced. And there's this Firuvari witness – if I could have your assistance interviewing her, Ser Visel? We may get a better description."

"Of course. Ash–"

Ash was walking along the nearest row of plants. The leaf form and structure was much like a poppy, but the petals were fleshier, more like a rose. White, with blue stamens.

"Kismollen," she said, glancing back at the men. "So much of it."

It had been planted in such a strange way. Widely-space, the far rows the tallest, and the nearest decreasing in size from right to left, with the left most little more than a seedling. She bent to examine it, and then shifted uncomfortably, a chill rising through the leather of her boot. Stepping back, she glanced down.

"Captain."

Ash tried to be calm, but could not stop herself from backing away, staring in nauseated horror. It was as if someone was standing right below her, on the wrong side of Luin. Through the dirt she could see the heel, the unmistakable curve of the arch, and each pale toe outlined separately.

The underside of a foot.

Farpatten strode over, bending to scrape dirt away. "Fresh-turned," he murmured. "Sun, why upside-down?"

"There'll be others," Thornaster said, and surveyed the long rows of plants, then looked sharply at Ash as she exclaimed, leaned forward, then backed away further. "What is it?"

"Frog-shaped birthmark," she whispered. "That's Frog."

CHAPTER THIRTY-THREE

No neighbourhood would overlook dozens of men working to tear down a house as swiftly as possible, even without the frozen corpses being unearthed in its garden. Soon Farpatten had to put some of his resources to crowd control, keeping back a growing stream of gawpers. There was no way to prevent word from spreading, but no one could anticipate whether the 'Cold Man' would flee or attack.

A Smallholder at the top of the street opened his house to the Guard, providing a base of operations, a steady supply of food, and a place to retreat to when the chill set too deep. Farpatten settled Telat in a second story room overlooking the street, asking her to alert them if the Cold Man should appear.

Unable to face the increasing collection of corpses any longer, Ash soon joined her Huntsmen there, and found Lauren assisting in an impromptu lesson in Firuven. Telat, in a dress Bitty had brought down from the palace, seemed to be thoroughly enjoying pointing out objects in the street below and naming them.

"Have they established how many?" Melar asked, turning to Ash.

"One under every plant," she replied wearily. "Tied with their hands beneath their knees and buried upside-down, all looking like they were just buried. Frozen solid, and showing no signs of thawing out."

The whole of the Vicardie family had been there, but the Guard had chosen not to share that information, and Ash was glad of their reticence because she could hardly bear to think about them. Just tools, used and discarded, and she would never be able to ask Frog why.

"You're losing your voice again," Bitty observed.

"I think it's the cold air. Though I'm glad for the excuse to not stand grimly watching any more." She summoned a smile, apologised to Lauren and Telat for interrupting the lesson, and then led her Huntsmen to a small bedroom at the back of the house.

Once the door was firmly closed she began with: "There's something I've been meaning to let you three know," but then she trailed off. Last night, and most especially that morning, had left Ash keenly aware of important things which needed doing, but it was harder to make this particular shift than she'd anticipated.

"Are you going to finally tell us you're really a girl?" Bitty asked, interestedly.

"What?" Larkin sputtered.

"And that you're having some kind of thing with this Thornaster person?" Melar added.

"*What?!*" Larkin gaped around at them all, and then threw up his hands. "Why am I always the last to know?"

"I had no idea you two had guessed," Ash said, immensely cheered.

"Ash, if you were really a boy, I'd have made a play for you years ago," Melar said.

"Same," Bitty added. "Don't tell Arras, though. She wouldn't take it well."

"I won't! I'm staying Ash Lenthard while I'm in Montmoth – I just wanted to square this with you three. Though I'm obviously going to have to control my expressions if it took you less than a morning to spot the thing with Thornaster, Melar."

She explained her future, though not her past, and accepted congratulations, then sat on the bed smiling as Melar and Bitty teased Larkin for failing to be observant. Her friends. She had underestimated them: after so many years they would never fail to support or cheer her. Nor were they afraid to boss her around, ordering her to get some rest, and threatening to tuck her in when she protested.

And then she was being strangled. Frog knelt over her, his hands around her throat, and she struggled for breath enough to ask him why, how, and then, inevitably, he turned into Eward Carlyon, and she was trying to pull her hand away from him, desperately, but the marriage cord glowed icy black and sank beneath the skin of her hand.

"Ash. Beloved. Wake up."

The hand she was trying to pull away was simply tangled in the blanket. Thornaster, sitting on the side of the bed, gently smoothed the hair back from her forehead, and smiled when she finally focused on him.

"You're very prone to nightmares, stripling."

"I know. Look forward to years of being kicked to death."

He seemed to find this an immensely romantic thing for her to say, but eventually drew back from kisses. "The timing involved in this is excessively frustrating. I came up to tell you they've finished with the roof, and are starting on the floor – using hooks and chains pulled by horses because it's not safe to work any closer to it."

"What happens if the Cold Man escapes, or finding him doesn't change anything? A stalemate, with Karaelsur unable to gain more souls, but us not able to get rid of that thing?"

"No." Thornaster curled his fingers through hers, and then held up their joined hands, staring at the glowing lines beneath the skin. "The people all around here are sick because it's feeding on them. It's growing stronger, and I have no idea how to stop it, and, Sun!, I wish I could run to my father."

"So your father could stop it?"

"I think so. The combination of Astenar's blood and the Rhoi's bond gives him a great deal of strength. And this is most certainly a matter of such importance that it would warrant him going outside Aremal's borders. But by the time he arrived it would most likely be beyond him, and all Montmoth frozen corpses."

Ash shuddered because she kept seeing Frog, freshly taken out of the ground. Dirt griming all the small crevices of his face, and his mouth turned down.

"I'm not liking myself because part of why I'm upset is I feel cheated," she said. "I suppose he would have been executed if we'd captured him, but at least we could have found out if there were mitigating circumstances. Could kismollen be involved? With the bodies frozen I couldn't check for any telltale blue. Or perhaps he was led by his father's ambition. I hate the idea that Frog might have done this because he thought Kiri was some sort of prize which came with the Rhoimarch."

Thornaster squeezed her hand. "Arun asked your Kiri if she would be willing to spend the next few months acting as Setsel Ormsley's seruilis."

"Truly? She agreed?"

"She did. I promptly offered her sword lessons, for most obscure motives."

Ash gasped, and tried to swallow laughter, which made her throat hurt rather more.

"You don't give up, do you? I'd far rather watch you fight than learn a new weapon. They're not a sport to me, and anyway, right now I think I'd end up second-guessing myself more." She gestured at her throat. "I took Telat away from two boys, and I don't know if I was slower than usual, or one of the boys unusually fast, but there was a bad moment. Would having a sword instead of a staff have made a difference? Or would I have hesitated either way, because of this?"

Ash held up their joined hands, turning it so that she could better see the knotted marriage cord, and decided that, again, this was not a conversation to put off.

"Telat saved *your* life last night. And I'm...hanging back. I'm not used to that. Healthy caution, yes, but – I'm sorry, I know you feel this is a great blessing, but I can't help but wish Astenar hadn't done it. It's pulling me off-balance. Usually the only life I risk is my own."

He had listened wordlessly, brows lifted in surprise. "You've never worried about leading your Huntsmen to their deaths?"

"Of course. But I don't let them take undue risks. While I sometimes – when it's necessary – push further than I'd let them go. But it's not even that, it's ordinary things, things I shouldn't hesitate from. Knowing I could kill you is paralysing."

"You're looking at it backward." He lifted their joined hands a little higher. "This isn't a sword at my throat, it's a safety rope. If I'm mortally injured, your life force will sustain me, giving me a much greater chance to recover. We'll both be less likely get ill – you'll benefit from my bloodline there, since Estarrels rarely sicken. The bond won't do much for a beheading, though, so try to avoid that."

"Are you sure?"

"About the beheading? Absolutely. The rest – it's been decades since the last known bonding, but the records are fairly clear on the subject. It's a little like a Rhoi's bond to the land, but the benefit is to each other."

"Is that why I felt warmer when I held your hand back in that cellar?"

"Possibly. I –" He stopped, staring at nothing, then said: "I'm an idiot."

"Are you expecting me to agree with you? We've only been married a day. My opinion of you hasn't had a chance to drop that low."

"Gratifying as the bond might be, Astenar doesn't do this as an affirmation of our choice. It's usually been in response to some larger danger. I thought it a means to keep those doing Astenar's will alive long enough to carry it out. But this is a bond like a Rhoi's. In its way, it's a conduit to Astenar. And Astenar's strength."

Remembering the light that had accompanied the bonding, Ash looked at him unenthusiastically. "You're suggesting we should, what, try putting our hands in the soul-stealing goo?"

He grimaced, then shrugged, and kissed her forehead lightly. "It's something we'll need to think about. But not yet – they must have found something about that building by now."

CHAPTER THIRTY-FOUR

Downstairs they found Hawkmarten talking to Farpatten.

"Have you located the owner yet?" Thornaster asked.

"Bringing her in now, Ser Visel." Farpatten replied. "There's been several layers of identity to sift through, but we think this is the last one."

A murmur at the door warned of the arrival and they all turned as several tall Watchmen crowded in, bracketing a woman, holding herself very upright, her hair carefully coiled, but her skin waxen. Charity Dunn.

Without Morton standing at her back she seemed small, and older somehow, and when she looked around the room she passed over Ash without any apparent recognition before she focused on Farpatten.

"Are you in charge?" she asked, with an attempt at her usual honey-sweet condescension. "Truly, the Guard has abandoned courtesy altogether. What do you mean by dragging me here?"

"I've been informed that you are Landhold of the house at sixteen Porter's Way. Is this true?"

"Why, I could not say. I am a very wealthy woman. You cannot expect me to keep track of all my properties."

"You had best remember quickly," Farpatten said. "We have unearthed over a dozen bodies there, and expect more. Do you have any knowledge of this?"

Charity Dunn blinked rapidly, lost what little colour she had, then sagged. The Guardsman nearest her exclaimed and caught at her arm, managing to divert her into one of the sturdy kitchen chairs.

"Landholder." Farpatten was unrelenting. "What do you know of these deaths?"

"Nothing!" Charity Dunn shook her head over and again, as if that would prove her denial. "No. I am...I have...I am merely a name on paper. A favour for another."

"Who?"

"Decsel Pelandis."

Farpatten grunted, then said to Thornaster. "The Firuvari girl's description was of white hair and white eyes. The Decsel, Tranor, is bedridden, but both his brothers and his son share his colouring – glass-pale blue eyes and platinum blonde hair. The lad's unlikely, but either Ryle or Keskedin are possibilities."

"I've met both Ryle and Keskedin Pelandis," Thornaster said. "They showed no hint of the taint this would produce. How certain is it that Tranor Pelandis is as injured as is claimed? I was told he was unable to walk."

"That's so, Ser Visel," Farpatten confirmed. "Though the family arranged for every form of care, including importing a healing mage, he had suffered so many crushing injuries that there was no hope of walking. Even living without constant pain is difficult. He is rarely in the city, but both his brothers are at the family residence in the Deirhoi District."

"We'll start with them, then," Thornaster said.

Ash was trying not to stare at Charity Dunn. This was a woman who had had no hesitation using her position to gain the most she possibly could from those who rented her properties. But the way she sat shrunken into herself felt somehow indecent.

Since Ash lacked any means – or true desire – to ease Landhold Dunn's distress, she did her the simple courtesy of not gawping at her further. That was something Genevieve would have expected: to not gloat, or make a bad situation worse, but to do only the necessary things.

Right now, the necessary thing was Decsel Pelandis. With him, perhaps this long hunt of false trails and innocent blood would come to an end.

ooOoo

Farpatten demonstrated his efficiency, reorganising his forces to leave the deconstruction adequately guarded, and arranging for others to meet him in the Deirhoi District and sweep down on the Pelandis estate. He was taking no chances.

Ash, keyed up for battle, found herself instead standing with Lauren Carlyon, listening to a highly confused family trying to satisfy the small army which had come knocking at their door. No, they knew nothing of any property in the Rockways, or of a Landhold Dunn. The Decsel was at Rimmary, the Pelandis' Decselry, and had been since the previous autumn. No, they had no objection to the Guard questioning other members of the household, if that's what it took to clear them of whatever accusation had been laid.

"If this is just another false trail, I think I might start shouting," Ash murmured, drifting back into the entry hall with Lauren.

"This Dunn woman may have lied. Or been lied to. If Ryle and Keskedin are lying, then questioning the household will expose the truth." He glanced back to where the extensive Pelandis family stood clustered protectively together before the mass of Guard and Watch. "They do appear very convincingly confused."

"Though you notice a lot of them also seem to be ill? And look at Thornaster."

Her Aremish Visel stood to one side, brows drawn together as he listened, as if he were trying to hear something over the conversation before him. While the Guard began rounding up all the occupants of the sprawling manor estate – not a small task given the multiple outbuildings and several towers – he joined Ash and Lauren and said, "Let's look around."

"You can feel him?"

"I feel something. But I've been sporadically feeling taint all over the city. If he's here, getting closer should be enough."

They toured the manor's lowest floor, and then decided on a quick walk among the outbuildings before tackling the convoluted upper floors.

"No, I don't want to go in! I just want to talk to whoever's in charge."

"That's Garet Pelandis," Lauren said, and they crossed quickly to the estate's gate.

"Carlyon! Thank the Sun." The jittery boy in the black and white tabard of Decsel Donderry pulled free of the restraining grip of a Watchman. "Come out here where we can't be seen."

"My orders–" the Watchman began, but accepted a belaying gesture, instead sending his partner off with a message for Farpatten.

Lauren followed the younger boy out onto the street, despite the crowds of highly interested onlookers. "Garet, are you – do you know where your father is?"

"Dead, I think. I can't be sure. I haven't seen him in months." The boy's words were soft and rapid, and he glanced constantly at the estate's gate. "So it wasn't me, after all. I knew it. I knew it."

"Start from the beginning, Garet," Carlyon ordered crisply. "What's been happening here?"

"I can't be sure. They said I was wrong. I've been serving Decsel Donderry as seruilis for two years, and I'd check in on my free days, and for family things, but everything seemed normal. It was only when I was given leave to winter at Rimmary and...I'm sure my father wasn't there. Usually, though it's difficult for him, he will host the midwinter feast. I thought he must be worse, and I wanted to see him, but they'd turn me around every time and it was never 'no', it was always 'not right now' and then winter was over and I still hadn't seen him and they all just go on as if everything's normal, and–"

"Take a breath, Garet." Carlyon rested his hand on the boy's back and waited until he'd obeyed. "Is it simply that you haven't seen your father, or have you noticed anything specific?"

"Count the towers," the boy said. "Then ask one of them how many towers the house has. They locked the door and put a tapestry over it, and act like I'm mad for asking why. The whole lot of them, there's something wrong with them."

The main building sported four towers. Or three, according to every member of the Pelandis household asked, even when brought to a newly-detapestried door and asked for the key.

"There was a lot of kismollen growing in that garden," Ash said, watching Farpatten's face as yet another Pelandis failed to acknowledge the door even when he pointed directly at it. "If someone's been dosing this entire household since before last winter, then I'm not surprised they're sick. I'm more surprised they're alive."

"Can they be treated?" Lauren asked.

"Genevieve's Herbal only mentions a fatal level of toxicity." Ash brushed her hand against Thornaster's. "But it wasn't kismollen he used on Telat, so maybe he's able to control them without it. He's up there, isn't he?"

"Yes." Thornaster stopped staring at the ceiling. "It may be wise to avoid meeting his eyes. Let's do this, Captain."

While the door was broken down, they discussed the ground ahead, and the merits of speed over caution. Garet, though he'd refused to come into the building, had described a wide, square tower topped by a comfortable bedroom. Thornaster, with the partial protection of his blood, would take lead, bracketed by Guardsmen furnished with crossbows and strict orders to fire at the first sign of sudden frosts. And to keep their eyes on the Cold Man's feet. Farpatten, Ash and Lauren would follow the initial rush.

The need to better understand the cellar in the Rockways – and some consideration for the process of law – meant they would try talking first. Remembering all too well the filigree of frost spreading over the coach's interior, Ash shut down how she felt about this confrontation, and concentrated on keeping herself alert for any sign of danger.

No traps, no resistance, just terse words from those ahead of her. The door at the top of the stair was closed but not locked, and Ash was close enough behind to be able to see inside when Thornaster opened it.

Her first impression was of light, pouring through windows formed from many panes of glass. A small bed and a desk were the main items of furniture, and the only occupant of the room sat in a high-backed chair by one of the windows. Unmistakably of the Pelandis family, he looked completely relaxed, one foot neatly crossed over the other, and a glass in his hand.

"No need to stand on ceremony. Come right in."

Something about the amused voice struck Ash in a way she didn't expect, and she had to stop herself from backing a step. Light and pleasant, it wasn't familiar, but it set her heart racing.

"How may I help you Sers?"

"Decsel Pelandis?" Farpatten asked.

"So it would seem. And let me see, you three are obviously part of the Rhoi's collection of babysitters, and the rangy fellow in the dress would be his Aremish nanny. Who's that behind you? Lauren, lad! What are you doing running around with this collection of jackanapes?"

Lauren, rather naturally startled, paused then said firmly: "A young girl asked me to make certain that the one she calls the Cold Man could never capture her again."

"Skirt-chasing, are you? Well, I suppose you're an age for it. So that's what happened to that little piece. A waste. She would have done a great deal for my cause; the power simply roiled off her."

Attempting to regain some control of the conversation, Farpatten said: "You do not deny, then, that you have committed treason against the Rhoi, and heretical acts which have cost the lives of Montmothian citizens?"

"Heretical acts? For that I would need to concede that Astenar has some right to dictate how we live. All life on Luin owes its existence to Karaelsur. I'm not afraid to serve the true Sun."

"You've broken Luin's laws, as well," Thornaster said. "And whatever you thought to gain from Karaelsur, it is Astenar and Luin you will face."

Decsel Pelandis laughed, and Ash shivered all the way from shoulders to gut. She didn't know the voice, but that triumphant, gloating amusement? That was unmistakeable.

"Rest assured, damnation holds no horrors for me! I'm no puling tot, too afraid to sample the pudding for fear of a hiding. I live on my own terms."

"And died on them." Ash, though nearly a decade's worth of nightmares had risen to thicken her words, still managed to say: "This isn't Decsel Pelandis. It's Eward Carlyon."

Lauren flinched, while the seated man stared at her with a kind of delighted surprise. "Who is that back there? Step forward."

Never more inclined to turn tail and run, Ash palmed her knife and moved just enough that Thornaster no longer blocked her.

"What will it take to kill you properly?"

"If it isn't the stalwart defender! Another who got away. How obliging of you to present yourself, my dear."

"Are you sure there's any point trying to question him?" Ash asked flatly.

Again that laughter, grating every nerve. "Is that what you're doing? I thought it was a little light chatter before someone dies. Lauren, lad, you go downstairs now. I'll take care of business here, and then we can talk."

"I..." Lauren sucked in breath like he was leaking.

The depth of his distress helped Ash look at her own. She had not grown up idolising this man. He had intended harm to her – and had succeeded insofar as making absolutely clear how her parents valued her – but Ash had defeated him once already. Strange how she'd always looked at it as running, instead of winning.

Discovering that did not make her hand shake any less.

"You're outnumbered," Thornaster said. "Your plans exposed, your goals no longer possible. What remains is the house in the Rockways, and your death. The question is only with what level of dignity you face your end, and whether you are willing to undo some of the damage."

This produced nothing but an incredulous stare. The man treated the half-dozen people before him as no threat at all.

"You've clearly been keeping bad company, Lauren. Didn't I always tell you to question, not blindly follow idiots? Be assured this is no end. Now, listen to your father and go down."

Lauren straightened, becoming every inch first seruilis once again, this time not as a mask, but a declaration. "I don't know if the father I loved ever existed. But if this has always been you, the truth of you, then I am not your son. I never was."

"Go downstairs. You others, rid us of our Aremish guest."

No change in tone, no visible effort, but Lauren sheathed his sword and turned.

Thornaster knocked up the crossbow of the Guard on his right, and then barrelled into Farpatten. The third Guard released his bolt, which slashed across Farpatten's arm. Ash, uncontrolled and apparently not considered a threat, threw her knife. No hesitation, no qualms about taking this life.

A man should not smile with a sliver of metal projecting from his throat. He certainly should not look elated. The only thing Ash had succeeded in doing was shutting him up. Perhaps not such a small thing, since she guessed that it was his voice, not his gaze, which allowed him to control others. It was surely something he couldn't do to many over an extended period, or he would not need the kismollen.

With no time to be outraged at the failure of the enemy to die, Ash threw herself into the problem of three very competent Guards trying to kill her husband. Leaping on the back of the nearest, Ash locked her elbow around his neck. He turned into the hold, and jabbed fingers toward her eyes, so she tried to haul him off-balance instead, rapidly framing and abandoning half a dozen plans to take down the three Guards without seriously injuring them. The real problem was the frost beginning to decorate the many-paned windows.

Since steel didn't work, she would see how the 'Cold Man' dealt with being thrown off a tower.

More Guards were pounding up the stair, which wouldn't necessarily help the situation. Ash managed to knock hers down, and scrambled to her feet as Thornaster went down under the combined weight of his. It would need to be a straight-out run, no time for the Black Carlyon to react, and hope she had the strength to send him over without going herself.

Everyone knew Estarrels could summon fire. Or heat things until they burst into flame, according to Thornaster, and perhaps he had been trying since Eward Carlyon had sent his son away, fighting the Cold Man's stolen strength. In any case, finally, fire overcame ice and the man in the chair became a torch.

The Black Carlyon plucked the knife from his – Pelandis' – throat, but did not seem able to properly scream and made a thin wailing noise as he staggered to his feet, took one faltering step, and then collapsed.

The Guards came back to themselves at the same time, and Captain Farpatten immediately stopped trying to wrest Thornaster's sword away from him, looked around, then said:

"Someone get some water."

CHAPTER THIRTY-FIVE

"You'd never done that to a living person before, had you?"

"No. Though 'living' may not be the right word." Thornaster opened a door at random and drew her into what proved to be an enormous linen cupboard so he could squeeze her breathless. "If Astenar is kind, I'll never need to again."

"Is he...properly dead now? As dead as damned people usually are?"

"I'm not certain. I suspect that when Eward Carlyon originally died, he had already gained a certain measure of strength through serving Karaelsur, and that allowed him to find and use Tranor Pelandis. There may even have been another cellar, with a life or two he could use for sustenance. The Godskeeps will advise on what to do here. Our problem is the Rockways."

Because the Black Carlyon's second death had not ended anything, just as he'd said. One of the Watch had already delivered the news that the Rockways cellar had, if anything, become noticeably colder. The strange liquid had certainly shown no sign of dissipating, and so Ash and Thornaster would be gambling a great deal on their marriage bond.

Leaving the linen cupboard behind, they found Lauren sitting beside the manor's drive, talking with Garet Pelandis. With Garet's father dead, and his entire family in a state of confusion compounded by kismollen poisoning, the boy was facing as mass of responsibility, not least of which would be standing before Astenar and Luin in hopes of being judged worthy of the Decselry.

"Wouldn't Luin know that one of the Luinsel wasn't Luinsel?" Ash asked, considering the Garet's slumped shoulders.

"Not if 'Pelandis' stayed out of the Decselry. Though the bond would have lapsed if he'd kept away for more than a year."

Thornaster gave the pair a long look – two young men whose fathers he'd just killed – and despite all the circumstances around it, Ash could see that would weigh on him.

Lauren looked up then, and nodded. A "thank you", and an "I'll take care of this", and so they passed on to make a detour to the palace, to report to the Rhoi and recover a little, and fortify themselves with food. Ash visited Kiri, and did not quite let herself sound like she was saying goodbye, while Thornaster wrote a letter that he handed over to Hawkmarten.

Hawkmarten made no attempt to hide his opinion of "if we accidentally feed our souls to Karaelsur". The consequences of that weren't small, and Farpatten was already off arranging an evacuation of the houses nearest to the dismantled building.

"Rapidly followed by the abandonment of the entire city, I presume, if you do fail," Hawkmarten said. "Thorn, write as many messages for your family as you like, but the only result I'm going to accept is you saving me the trouble of delivering them. After all, Astenar has provided."

He formally embraced Thornaster and then Ash, and told them he would ride down with them. Ash thought about his words all during their return to the Rockways, distracted only briefly by the important step of saying goodbye to Cloud Cat and Arth.

"If I followed the idea of 'Astenar has provided' to its logical conclusion, I'm not sure I could face the rest of the afternoon," Ash remarked, as she and Thornaster walked down a rapidly emptying street.

"Sun! What a thought!" Thornaster stared up at the sky, and then shook his head. "If Astenar could manipulate events so exactly, they would never arise in the first place, surely. Though my father's decision to send me in response to Rhoi Malaster's request becomes more explicable. I'd only been Luinsel for a year, and several cousins would have been a better combination of Estarrel senses and experience. I thought my father's choice simply due to the time I'd spent with Arun." He smiled. "I can't say I've previously been first in his thoughts when assigning serious tasks."

"Too inclined to levity?" Ash asked.

"Perhaps. I spent a great deal of my younger days trying to live up to my older brother. And never quite managing to surpass my sister at the sword, or my mother with horses. And demonstrating how little that mattered to me. It's only been the last couple of years that I've gained a better sense of perspective."

A family emerged from a house to their right, assisted by a Watchmen with two children held against his chest. Ash turned to survey other, similar scenes, and shook her head. "So if we fail, and it gets stronger, the best thing to do is deny it food?"

"That's the idea. Though if I thought this wasn't the solution, I wouldn't try it. It makes no sense to give Karaelsur my strength."

"Will the old Sun be actively fighting us?"

"I don't think so. This is a tool, a device. Which is not to say it won't react. I would still rather be anywhere else right now. The fact that Astenar should be able to use us as a conduit doesn't give us any immunity to ill-effects."

Ash blinked, then diverted to a clump of Guards escorting another family, and made several requests. This produced in short order a collection of sturdy coats, gloves, caps and scarfs.

She shared the pile of garments with Thornaster and they fumbled them on as they found their way through the maze of debris into the upturned rear garden. Not wanting to look at the churned earth, or the plants yet to be dug up, she said:

"Not proof against soul-stealing, I know. But a little protection against the cold can't hurt. And...you seriously have to wear that another time."

Thornaster, tugging on a sheepskin cap complete with earflaps, tweaked her nose, and then pulled her against his chest.

"I can't be sorry I married you, stripling, but I could wish it hadn't brought you to such a place."

"I'm here for Genevieve." She said the words tersely, but leaned into his embrace, squeezing tightly. "And Frog, blast him. If I can't be sure why he did it, then I'll choose to believe he was the person I thought him, and had just mislaid himself."

She stood away and finished buttoning her coat, her breath pluming into mist. While she definitely didn't want to be in this place either, she saw it as at least a course of action, and in a way less difficult than the weeks where they'd flailed about failing to make any progress.

"Will the souls of the people who have been fed to it be...are they damned?"

"I don't know. I'm not certain there's anything left of them."

"Let's go find out, then."

The Guard had destroyed most of the building, leaving intact only the area supporting the stair down, and even that creaked ominously as they set their weight on it. The stair itself was lost in a growing mist lifting from the now exposed roil covering the cellar floor.

Ice crunched beneath their boots as they eased their way onto the first step, and they paused to wrap the scarves more firmly across their faces.

"We're going to have to touch it," Thornaster said.

"The way this stair feels, we might end up falling into it."

"If that happens, lead with your fist." Thornaster tightened his grip and raised the joined hands they'd left free of gloves. Silver lines glowed beneath, but her fingers were already numb.

In all her nightmares Ash had never thought to walk into a breathing pit, a spider work of rime reaching out from the stairwell walls, and ice crystal quickly crusting her eyelashes and the knitted wool protecting her face. The air became daggers in her throat.

Drawing his rapier, Thornaster knocked down icicles hanging from the stairwell's partially demolished ceiling, and they used their grip on each other to keep their balance on the cracking layer of ice.

Ash, wobbling, inadvertently put her hand down on the stair's railing and had it stick fast. Immediately she tore free of the glove and left it – and what felt like a large amount of flesh – behind.

"All right?"

"Yes. It's so much colder than before."

"When we reach the bottom, position your feet as best you can, and we'll crouch and touch our hands to it. And..." He laughed briefly, coughed, and slipped a fraction before regaining his balance. "And then Astenar will provide, or I will be a fool, but in either case there is no-one I would rather be doing this with."

Ash didn't reply immediately, because they had reached that unnaturally raised floor, and it was so cold that the already-difficult task of crouching without slipping was made doubly hard by uncontrollable shaking. It did not help that the silvery lines beneath their skin were barely visible through the mist.

Ash had spent long years believing that Astenar had failed her. And even longer trusting those around her only up to a point, and the question of how much she trusted Thornaster-who-was-Morrion was paramount since the lines of her marriage bond were not changing or increasing their glow or doing anything at all to encourage her into thinking this plan was going to work.

They lowered their hands toward dark liquid and still the soul bond showed no sign of reacting, but proximity to the floor was starting to make Ash feel dizzy.

"Right now," she said, looking away from the moment of contact to the misty outline of her husband. "Right now, I'm giving you a starry-eyed look of approval."

Choked laughter accompanied sucking dizziness, while a deep, agonising cold consumed her hand and shot up her arm. She cried out, and fell forward into...gold.

Wings. Hundreds, thousands: a blizzard, a fountain. Sprawled on slick flagstones, Ash let go of Thornaster's hand and rolled on her back, damp and shuddering, too spent to do more than stare up at glimpses of blue sky through the mass of tiny golden butterflies carrying away the souls of the sacrificed.

Astenar had provided.

Trailing the mass, a spiral of grey moths. Luin, taking to be washed those whose sins weighed too heavily. Ash watched them rise until there was more blue than gold above, then turned on her side and looked at her husband as he pulled the scarf away from his face.

"Can – can you tell if they took everyone?"

"There's nothing here but you and I, for what it's worth." He tugged her scarf down around her throat. "We're still here, stripling."

Ash tested her limbs to make sure all of them were present, and then took time to kiss Thornaster properly. He still tasted like mead.

"What now?" she asked, because even kissing Thornaster did not mean she wanted to lie in a puddle indefinitely.

He laughed. "We hope that our second day of marriage is less eventful than the first. And assist your Kiri in being a seruilis, though I suspect she will require very little help. We ensure that the laws regarding smallholdings are passed. Think up a reward for a laundry maid. And perhaps go see the glacier that is the source of the Milk, which Arun tells me shouldn't be approached outside of summer – though I must admit that right now glaciers hold little attraction for me. And I will continue to try to teach you sword-fighting, and we will ride a great deal, and see a thousand new places, and..."

"And just be us," Ash finished, pleased. No matter what names they went by, whatever challenges they faced, or the consequences of the bond that joined them. These things altered the frame, but she always had, and would, remain herself.

EPILOGUE

A sun-browned girl sat far above the River Milk. Early morning light combined with the setting moons to pick out gleams in the turbulent water as it split around Luin's Island, and she was able to look down the length of the enormous statue from her perch on its shoulder.

Moving slowly, she unwound a vividly pink ribbon from around her waist, and knotted it into an elaborate bow in Luin's stone hair. As a message it was redundant, since almost all the people who meant anything to her were on the bank below, watching.

She waved to them. Kiri, proudly wearing a tabard of red and gold, magnificent and assured. Veirhoi Heran, now in Thornaster's colours, trying hard to pretend he was not excited to be sent to Aremal. The Huntsmen, and the Rogadneys, come to see off not only Ash Lenthard, but also Melar, Lark and Bitty, who would travel to Hawkmarten's Tye's Haven, before splitting off to head south, volunteering their support for Telat's attempt to regain her lost birthright. And Lauren Carlyon. It had been inspired of Bitty to suggest he come along – or, as she'd put it – "bring money, keep us out of hedgerows". Lauren was at his best looking after others, and could escape his father's shadow without feeling he was running from his name.

There was even a sizeable contingent of the Guard and the Watch, along with the Rhoi himself, despite it being strictly illegal to climb Luin's statue. He was now a Rhoi she approved of, not for this indulgence, but for a sincere apology made to a good friend. One step among many he was taking toward becoming the sort of Rhoi Montmoth needed.

A crowd of early morning travellers was also gathering to stare and point, so the girl waved at them too, and then climbed down. Directly below, minding the ferry they'd used to reach the island, Morrion Estarrel watched her descent and smiled.

"Ready now?"

"As I'll ever be."

They rode south, but the girl looked back often, and could see it long after they'd left the Commons. A ribbon for Genevieve, in Luin's hair. From Daere.

www.ingramcontent.com/pod-product-compliance
Lightning Source LLC
Chambersburg PA
CBHW070906180626
46817CB00003B/940